Enigma Books

Also published by Enigma Books

Hitler's Table Talk: 1941–1944
In Stalin's Secret Service
Hitler and Mussolini: The Secret Meetings
The Jews in Fascist Italy: A History
The Man Behind the Rosenbergs
Roosevelt and Hopkins: An Intimate History
Secret Affairs: FDR, Cordell Hull, and Sumner Welles
Hitler and His Generals: Military Conferences 1942–1945
Stalin and the Jews: The Red Book
Fighting the Nazis: French Intelligence and Counterintelligence
A Death in Washington: Walter G. Krivitsky and the Stalin Terror
The Battle of the Casbah: Terrorism and Counterterrorism in Algeria 1955–1957
Hitler's Second Book: The Unpublished Sequel to *Mein Kampf*
At Napoleon's Side in Russia: The Classic Eyewitness Account
The Atlantic Wall: Hitler's Defenses for D-Day
France and the Nazi Threat: The Collapse of French Diplomacy 1932–1939
Mussolini: The Secrets of His Death
Mortal Crimes: Soviet Penetration of the Manhattan Project
Top Nazi: Karl Wolff—The Man Between Hitler and Himmler
Empire on the Adriatic: Mussolini's Conquest of Yugoslavia
The Origins of the War of 1914 (3-volume set)
Hitler's Foreign Policy: 1933–1939—The Road to World War II
The Origins of Fascist Ideology 1918–1925
Max Corvo: OSS Italy 1942–1945
Hitler's Contract: The Secret History of the Italian Edition of *Mein Kampf*
Secret Intelligence and the Holocaust
Balkan Inferno: Betrayal, War, and Intervention, 1990–2005
Calculated Risk
The Murder of Maxim Gorky
The Kravchenko Case: One Man's War On Stalin
Operation Neptune
Paris Weekend
Hitler's Gift to France
The Nazi Party: A Complete History
Encyclopedia of Cold War Espionage, Spies, and Secret Operations
The Cicero Spy Affair
NOC
The First Iraq War
Becoming Winston Churchill
Hitler's Intelligence Chief
Salazar: A Political Biography

Michael McMenamin
and
Patrick McMenamin

The De Valera Deception

Enigma Books

ISBN: 978-1-936274-08-6
eISBN: 978-1-936274-09-3

Library of Congress Cataloguing in Publication Available

To Carol and Becca, the loves of our lives.
And to Katie and Kelly, daughters and sisters we love as well.

Publisher's Note to Readers

Some may question casting Winston Churchill as a key character in a series of historical thrillers set during 1929-1939, his "Wilderness Years" when he was out of power, out of favor and a lone voice warning against the rising danger posed by Adolf Hitler and Nazi Germany. They shouldn't. Saving Western Civilization in 1940 when England stood alone as a beacon of liberty in a sea of tyranny tends to overshadow Churchill's earlier accomplishments.

Enigma Books publishes significant works of 20th Century history by scholars and journalists for all readers and now, with this new Churchill series, brings a fresh and exciting approach to the historical thriller centered on one of the last century's greatest movers of history itself. Churchill is, in many ways, the ideal historical figure around which to craft a period thriller. He was an adventure-seeking young man, a fencing champion in prep school, a championship polo player in the army and a seaplane pilot in the early, peril-filled days of aviation in 1910. In between, he was a much-decorated war hero in bloody battles on the Afghan-Indian border, in the Sudan, and in South Africa where his commanding officer nominated him for the Victoria Cross, Britain's highest military honor, and where he escaped from a prisoner of war camp and made his way to freedom over hundreds of miles of enemy territory. In World War I, while other politicians, safely abed, sent millions of young men to their death, Winston was with his troops in the trenches of the bloody Ypres salient daily risking death himself.

More importantly for this new series, Churchill maintained a private intelligence network in Britain and Europe during the 1930s which often left him better informed than his own government. The writing team of the critically acclaimed Churchill biographer Michael McMenamin and his son Patrick McMenamin use this fact as a catalyst for their stories. With Churchill at the center spinning his own web, he lures into many adventures his fictional Scottish goddaughter, the beautiful Hearst photojournalist Mattie McGary and the American law professor Bourke Cockran, Jr., a former U.S. Army counter-intelligence agent. Winston, a romantic at heart, brings the two young people together. Romance blooms but it is not a match made in heaven. Both characters are strong-willed individuals and their Celtic tempers frequently clash. Cockran is the fictional son of Churchill's real life mentor Bourke Cockran, a prominent turn-of-the-century New York lawyer, statesman, orator and presidential adviser whose life is chronicled in *Becoming Winston Churchill, The Untold Story of Young Winston and His American Mentor* by Michael McMenamin and Curt Zoller (Enigma Books, 2009).

The first three novels take place during 1929-1932, before Hitler's ill-fated, but entirely legal, appointment as the German Chancellor. In *The DeValera Deception,* Winston, Mattie, and Bourke tangle with the IRA and a real-life, pre-Hitler, Russo-German conspiracy to dismember Poland. In doing so, they discover a plot in the US to assemble arms for an IRA *coup d'état* in the new Irish Free State and Cockran seeks revenge for his wife's murder by the IRA in the 1922 Irish civil war. In *The Parsifal Pursuit* (Enigma Books, Spring, 2011), Winston sends Mattie on a grail quest in the company of a handsome villain intent on her seduction, a journey shadowed by the Nazis who want the ancient Christian artifact for Hitler. Also at Winston's behest, Cockran travels to Germany to represent a beautiful blonde heiress who is the victim of a Nazi fund-raising tactic—extortion of her business by a protection racket worthy of Al Capone. In *The Gemini Agenda* (Enigma Books, Fall 2011), Winston and his private intelligence network put Mattie and Bourke on the trail of a plot by Nazi scientists to kidnap and conduct lethal eugenic experiments on American twins. Shockingly, they learn the conspiracy is funded by Wall Street financiers and elements of US Army Intelligence who hope to unlock the secret to creating a master race.

I hope you have as much fun reading these stories as I did. A new Winston-Mattie-Bourke trilogy set in 1933-1934 is in the making so stay tuned...

Robert Miller,
Publisher,
Enigma Books

The De Valera Deception

I have long since concluded that revenge is the most expensive luxury known to man. Anyone who pursues vengeance can generally attain it but it is all he is ever likely to accomplish.

Congressman William Bourke Cockran,
27 April 1896 letter to Winston Churchill

Prologue

America and Russia, 1922

After a national struggle sustained through many centuries, we have today in Ireland a native Government deriving its authority solely from the Irish people, and acknowledged by England and the other nations of the world.... and it is the duty of every Irish man and woman to obey it. Anyone who fails to obey it is an enemy of the people and must expect to be treated as such.

Notes by General Michael Collins
August, 1922

It would certainly not be good policy for us to cut Germany off from all trade with the West and leave her no means of development and recovery except in the East. For if Germany turns to Russia, she can find everything in Russia that she requires, not only for recovery of economic strength but for world power... [S]he could develop, free from any treaty stipulation, those great arsenals, ammunition factories, and aviation centres which are forbidden her in her own country.

Winston S. Churchill, "Have We Done With Germany?"
Illustrated Sunday Herald, 23 November, 1919.

Throwing your lot in with Eamon de Valera rather than Michael Collins—the "Big Fella"—during the Irish civil war was not a recipe for a long life. The fact that the Big Fella was in league with Winston Churchill was no excuse. Joseph Murphy was to find that out the hard way.

The evening was cool and the fog had set in as Murphy walked briskly from the Union Pacific Club toward his home. The 45 year old Irish American banker had celebrated the 4th of July there where he drank more than his share of scotch in the cocktail hour, vintage French Bordeaux with the prime rib during dinner, followed by cigars and brandy—much, too much, brandy—in the library later. Still, the plump, prematurely graying man was pleased. Irish Catholics like him were not permitted to be members of the Union Pacific Club and few were ever invited as guests. Perhaps a change in by-laws might even bring him a membership nomination in a few years time.

As he walked, hoping the cool air would clear the haze from his brain, Murphy thought back over the events of the past week after the outbreak of open hostilities in Ireland between the forces of the new Irish Free State and the IRA. The encoded telegram from his control in London. The shipping arrangements made both here and in New York. The rifle orders placed with Colt and Winchester. The new model machine guns ordered from Thompson. All that was necessary, even critical, the telegram had made clear, if Dev and the IRA were to have a chance against a Michael Collins-led Free State Army supplied with all the modern weapons it needed by Winston bloody Churchill, the hated British Empire's Secretary of State for the Colonies. The arms for the IRA were ready to ship and now it was time for Joesph Murphy to do his part.

Tomorrow, when the banks reopened after the holiday, he would arrange the wire transfers from Guaranty Trust in New York. He wished this part of his life were behind him. He didn't relish being the IRA's last remaining paymaster in America—the trustee of three million dollars which Eamon de Valera had raised here to finance the war against the British.

The street lights were glowing in the fog as he walked from one oasis of light in the gloom to another. Murphy honestly had doubts about what he was doing. The Brits had pulled out of everywhere but the North. Ireland had its own government, overwhelmingly elected by the people and led by the legendary Michael Collins, "The Big Fella". The Irish Free State. No different than Canada. The south of Ireland, at least, free from the Brits at last. Was it really necessary for Irish to start killing Irish? To "wade through Irish blood", as Dev had said? Didn't it reinforce the stereotype that his Protestant friends had joked about that evening?

"You're a fine fellow, Joseph," they said, "a credit to your race. But don't you have to admit your civil war proves Irishmen just don't have the necessities for governing themselves?"

No, Murphy didn't think that. But he couldn't shake his misgivings. Still, duty was duty, and the telegram's instructions were unmistakable. The other two trustees were unavailable. One dead, the other missing. Dev was counting on him. Tomorrow would be the day. Then, perhaps, it would at last all be over. Ireland truly free.

Murphy heard footsteps behind him. He wasn't concerned. This was Nob Hill, not the waterfront. He paused at a street light and a tall man with light brown hair walked past, his trench coat collar high and disappeared into fog which was steadily growing thicker.

Murphy was close to home now. He sensed movement toward him from the right, but before he could see anything or react, a gloved hand clamped itself over his mouth, keeping him from crying out. Simultaneously, he felt a revolver pressed into his side as the man spun Murphy around until he was facing him, the revolver now pressed against his heart. Murphy stared into a cold, impassive face whose hazel eyes locked on his own and he felt a shudder convulse his body.

"The Big Fella sends his regards," he heard the man whisper. "You should have listened." Murphy heard the weapon fire, felt the searing pain in his chest and slumped to the damp concrete, the blood pooling beneath him.

Bourke Cockran, Jr. walked away, pushing a large Webley revolver back into the polished leather holster inside his trench coat, the body of Joseph Murphy no longer visible in the fog. He didn't feel better. He had hoped he would. Murphy was the third—and the last—to die. Michael Collins' message—the Big Fella's message—had been delivered. No one would dare lift a finger to help the IRA now. But Nora was still dead and the ache in his heart remained. Even Michael Collins' promise to find those responsible and make them pay wouldn't change that. Nothing would. Not even revenge. But without Nora, he would settle for that.

Moscow
5 July 1922
6:30 a.m.

Madness. Simply madness. There was no other explanation. Oskar Weidenfeld, the German charge' d'affaires to the Soviet Union, resumed pacing in his suite at the Metropol Hotel, his silk dressing gown knotted tightly at his waist, his breakfast still untouched on the silver tray beside his bed, running his hands through his thinning brown hair. His mind worked in a logical, precise way. But his mind would not be still, not after the extraordinary conversation the evening before with Leon Trotsky, the head of the Soviet Union's Ministry of War.

The German General Staff was out of control. *Sondergruppe R!* How high did the conspiracy go? How widespread? The head of the General Staff, General Hans von Seeckt, was certainly involved. And his arrogant aide, Major von Schleicher. Had they really told the Russians that Germany would be ready for a "great war of liberation" in only five years? Had they learned nothing from their mistakes in the Great War? Madness.

Germany and Russia had shocked the world last April at Rapallo, Italy when they signed the treaty he had helped negotiate. Formal relations restored; no war reparations; most-favored nation status in trade. In a single bold diplomatic stroke, Germany had turned east in an effort to rebuild its shattered economy with new materials from Russia. Was all his work for naught? To be destroyed in the fires of a new war? No, he said to himself. He had to act.

At a banquet given by the Russians last night, Weidenfeld had been seated next to Trotsky and, at its conclusion, was invited to Trotsky's private apartments in the Kremlin where they continued, over several bottles of Russian vodka, their dinnertime conversation. A small dark man, like so many of the Bolsheviks, but with incongruously blue eyes, Trotsky talked as if Weidenfeld already knew, had to know. And if Trotsky's story were true—and why tell it if it were not—there were only two conclusions to draw as to why he was not consulted or even kept informed. Either he and the Foreign Office did not have the full confidence of their superior, Chancellor Gustav Stresemann, or, worse still, the General Staff was conducting its own foreign policy.

Trotsky had been drunk, uncharacteristically for him in Weidenfeld's experience, his speech slurred as he recounted the history of the clandestine German military assistance to Russia, a small table lamp and the glowing coals in the hearth providing the room's only illumination. It had started in the spring of 1920 when Poland invaded the Ukraine, their troops quickly capturing Kiev and Vilna. German arms makers had promptly filled the Soviet government's hastily placed orders for 400,000 rifles and 200 million cartridges. Even Zeppelins were used. Zeppelins! On the night of 1 May 1920, six of the giant airships which bombed London and Paris in the Great War had been dispatched to Moscow, carrying arms and ammunition.

The secret alliance had not ended there. Now, seventy five million gold marks a year were to be paid by Germany to Russia. And for what purpose? German rearmament! Junkers and aeroplane factories! Krupp and artillery! I.G. Farben and poison gas! Training stations for tanks and aeroplanes at the German Army's disposal in

Russia. All weapons forbidden by the hated Versailles Treaty. To what end? And what was *Sondergruppe R*? And who were the mysterious men of the Geneva Group, the ones Trotsky said made it all possible?

By the end of the second bottle, Trotsky had dropped all restraint and Weidenfeld learned the secret. "Your generals have too much optimism. Five years is too soon. But ten years is not. Ten years, maybe even eight if Geneva agrees to limit its profits." Trotsky then lurched to his feet to stir the coals in the fireplace. What Trotsky said next, he muttered into the fire: "Poland, economist. Poland. Kill the Poles. Poland must cease to exist. The Chief of your General Staff agrees with us, I think. Germany and Russia will have their revenge. He said so to our General Uborevich. Here, see for yourself."

Trotsky handed him a letter bearing the unmistakable crest of General Hans von Seeckt., the Chief of the German General Staff. Weidenfeld chilled as he read the letter. He wasn't having a nightmare. Worse, Trotsky wasn't lying.

Poland's existence is intolerable, incompatible with the survival of Germany. It must disappear and it will disappear through its own internal weakness and through Russia—with our assistance.

Weidenfeld had looked over at Trotsky who was slumped in his chair, eyes closed, his chin resting on his chest, soft snores coming from his open mouth. He slipped silently out of the room. Chancellor Stresemann had to be told. He would know how to stop this insanity.

Weidenfeld looked at the clock on the mantle over the fireplace. 6:45 a.m. The Chancellor's secretary, Dieter Bernstein, would be here any moment in response to the cryptic note Weidenfeld had sent less than six hours before. "Grave matters discussed with Trotsky last night. Chancellor must be informed. Come to my suite at 6:50 a.m. Tell no one."

There was a knock on the door. Weidenfeld placed his papers on a nearby table and slipped his monocle into his dressing gown's breast pocket as he walked through the sitting room to the foyer. "*Herr* Bernstein, welcome", Weidenfeld said as he opened the door and then blinked in surprise at a tall blond-haired, white-coated waiter.

"There must be some mistake. I have already had my breakfast."

"Excuse me, sir", responded the waiter in flawless German, "but I was instructed to deliver this to *Herr* Bernstein at 6:50 a.m. A double order of sausages and French pastry."

Weidenfeld looked more closely at the waiter. In his experience, the German spoken by Russian hotel staff was rudimentary and heavily accented. He saw that the waiter's handsome face bore a two inch scar on his left temple. But he shrugged it off, smiling at the memory of Dieter's well-known appetite and stood aside. While the waiter prepared the table for breakfast, Oskar returned to his bedroom and again began to review his notes, his back to the door.

Absorbed in his reading, he did not hear the waiter enter the room. The first sound he heard was a pistol being cocked. Turning, the last sound he heard was the weapon's discharge as the bullet entered his right eye and exited the back of his head with a spray of blood.

Kurt von Sturm stepped over the outstretched body and pried loose the blood-spattered papers still clutched in Weidenfeld's left hand. He did not take pleasure in killing but no foreign office bureaucrat could be allowed to stand in the way of Germany's return to greatness and its revenge for the abomination that was the Versailles Treaty. He briefly glanced at the hand-written notes. It wasn't cast in stone but, on the whole, he agreed with Trotsky. Eight years was about right, seven if fortune were with them. But the Geneva Group cutting its profits? He shook his head. No, some things *were* cast in stone. Revenge was a complicated business. And expensive.

Part I

New York and Montreal, 1929

How could Great Britain agree to the setting up of a foreign Republic in Ireland? How could anyone suppose that peace could be found along that road? Not peace, but certain war, *real war, not mere bushranging, would follow from such a course.*

Winston S. Churchill,
24 September, 1921.

From the day that the Versailles Treaty went into effect, it was the Reichswehr's policy to evade and violate the Treaty's disarmament provisions, and to continue to develop and produce the whole range of modern weapons....in Russia, from 1921 to 1933... [T]he Versailles Treaty was an inconvenience—but only that. The German weapons developed in the 1920s were roughly equal to the best weaponry developed in the United States, Britain, and France.

James S. Corum,
*The Roots of Blitzkrieg: Hans Von Seeckt
and German Military Reform*

1.

The Prime Minister

The Canadian Pacific Railway,
Quebec City to Montreal
Friday, 9 August 1929

The morning sun cast a red glow across the train compartment's window and the desk beneath it. A weak scotch and water beside him, Winston Churchill unscrewed the cap of his fountain pen and began to write.

My Darling:

We had a wonderfully good passage with only one day of unpleasant motion. The ship was comfortable and well found, and we had splendid cabins. It was pleasing to see the green shores of Labrador after six days of grey sky and sea. We passed through the great inland sea between Newfoundland and the mouth of the St. Lawrence. It was calm and bright and steadily getting warmer.

I regret your illness did not permit your presence at our departure. We could have had our quiet time together and I could have spoken more freely than by the written word of my meeting with the P.M. the day before. He seems to be settling in to his second time around. With any luck, it will not last longer than the first.

Ramsay was in good spirits and quite pleasant to me on a personal level...

Churchill had not expected to be summoned to a meeting with the new Prime Minister. He and Ramsay MacDonald were poles apart politically but their personal relations had always been warm and cordial. On some matters when Winston had been the Chancellor of the Exchequer, they had even found themselves on the same side of issues.

MacDonald, a tall, gray-haired, sixty-five year old grandfather, whose dark mustache was flecked with white, greeted Churchill warmly. "Winston! So good to see you again. So very kind of you to come at such short notice. I know how busy you must be preparing for your journey. Here, come this way. Let's meet in my study where we won't be disturbed."

MacDonald led Churchill into a small room lined with bookshelves, and containing two comfortable leather chairs with reading lamps behind them. He gestured for Churchill to sit in one of the chairs while he sat in the other, a cup of tea and his reading glasses on the small table beside it. The late morning sun streamed in through several small windows along the top of the bookshelves lining one wall of the room.

Churchill was smiling to himself as MacDonald again thanked him for coming. He had rarely seen the dour Scot so loquacious. "Always happy to oblige, Prime Minister. I am pleased to see the new government has chosen to seek sound fiscal advice at such an early time. Will the Chancellor be joining us?" Churchill asked.

MacDonald ignored Churchill's mild jibe. "No, no, Winston, only you and me. This has nothing to do with the Treasury. Our prosperity is safe for now," MacDonald allowed in what was for him a rare attempt at levity. "Ireland. The Free State. Did you have much opportunity to follow events there during your time at Number 11?" asked MacDonald. 11 Downing Street was the townhouse next to the Prime Minister's own residence, traditionally occupied by the Chancellor of the Exchequer and which Churchill had involuntarily vacated a few months earlier.

"I'm afraid not, Prime Minister," said Churchill who, seizing the opening offered by the questioning, commenced a monologue that lasted for the next ten minutes. Collins' assassination. The bitter civil war successfully prosecuted by Collins' successor, William Cosgrave, and his Attorney General Kevin O'Higgins. De Valera's arrest in August, 1923. His break with Sinn Fein in 1926 and the founding of his own party, *Fianna Fail*. De Valera's election to the Dail in June, 1927. Kevin O'Higgins' assassination in July, 1927. The rapid demobilization of the Free State Army after the civil war. The poor state of their intelligence efforts, hardly up to the standards established by Collins.

"Their economy has not fared so well either," Churchill continued. "Too dependent on agriculture. Just look at the statistics from 1925 through last year."

The Prime Minister hastily interrupted, "I don't think that will be necessary, Winston. You seem to be quite up to speed on matters Irish. It's not the Irish economy which I wish to discuss with you this morning. Something far more serious."

Stopped in mid-sentence, Churchill looked at the tall Scot. "Pray tell me more."

"Our intelligence people have brought us disturbing news. We have advised the Irish government, of course, but there is little they can do. MI-6 thinks we ought to help and I'm inclined to agree. The Irish have been a good member of the Commonwealth. I'd like your opinion as well. You know the Irish. More importantly, you'll soon be in America."

Churchill paused before answering, focusing his entire concentration on the Prime Minister and softly asked, "And what is the disturbing news, Ramsay?"

"MI-6 has hard intelligence from more than one reliable informant that the IRA has mounted a new fund-raising and arms purchase program in America."

"What kind of weapons? What sums are involved?"

"The sums are very large, I am afraid. Close to a million pounds. But that's all we know. MI-6 wants to send a team of their agents to America to find out more."

"Why send our people?" asked Churchill. "Why not ask the Americans to help? Their foreign intelligence is non-existent but I understand their internal security is much improved."

"There's the rub," the Prime Minister said. He didn't want to ask the Americans for their assistance. MI-6 would not reveal its sources and, without knowing that, there would be no place for the Americans to begin their investigation. More importantly, MacDonald explained, relations with the Americans were no better now than they were when the Conservatives were in power. The Americans were still bargaining hard over repayment of British war debts and the Hoover Administration hadn't backed off from its predecessor's position on naval disarmament. The Americans wanted the size of the British Navy reduced while theirs grew larger.

"I will visit America myself in the fall," MacDonald said, "and will personally lead our delegation at the naval negotiations. I do not wish our position at all to be jeopardized by using that occasion to ask the Americans for assistance on an unrelated matter."

Churchill understood the Prime Minister's viewpoint. Bargaining with the Americans over the future of the British Navy was not the time to be asking for a favor, however small, if the price turned out to be the loss of even one British ship of the line.

"Very wise, Ramsay, very wise. I agree completely. How can I be of assistance?"

"By any chance, does your itinerary include a visit to Washington, D.C.?"

"My American itinerary is still unsettled. While I expect to lecture extensively in the United States, nothing yet is firmed up for my trip back east from California," Churchill responded. "What exactly did you have in mind, Ramsay? Because I may well have the opportunity to meet with the President in California. We are both scheduled to be guests of Mr. Hearst at his ranch. He's holding a reception there for that *Graf Zeppelin* crew."

"That would be splendid, Winston," MacDonald said with a smile. "Can you spare the time to lunch with me? I want you to be my personal emissary to the President and a meeting outside of an official setting would be all the better for what I have in mind."

There was a gleam in Churchill's eye as he tucked into his turtle soup and then paused for a sip of champagne. MacDonald was a teetotaler but didn't begrudge his guests their vices.

Churchill listened with growing eagerness as the Prime Minister outlined the plan developed by British intelligence. A team of agents, all with experience in Irish matters, would be sent to the United States. Based on the information they already had from their informants, they believed they could quickly run the plot to ground and prepare a comprehensive dossier with names, dates and places for delivery to the American authorities.

"Your task, Winston, will be to present this dossier to the President and persuade him that continued peace in Ireland is as important to the United States as it is to us."

Churchill had been looking forward to his trip to North America. Three months of rest, relaxation, writing and painting, all in the luxurious comfort of private railway cars and four-star hotels. The newspaper articles he would write along the way would not only pay for the journey but generate a tidy profit. Perfect. And now the Prime Minister had made it even better. All this and an adventure to boot. And with an old nemesis Churchill knew well, the IRA. He could hardly believe his good fortune and casually inquired, "Who'll be leading the team? I doubtless came across them and their work when I was Colonial Secretary."

"I'm afraid I don't know any of the chaps," said the Prime Minister. "But there will be ten men in all and their leader is a David Brooke-Smythe. I met him yesterday. Seems capable."

"I know him," Churchill replied. "He was one of our agents the Irish feared most."

Churchill paused, waiting for the Prime Minister to inquire further. When he did not, Churchill resumed. "So Smythe and his men will be reporting to me?" Churchill probed.

MacDonald dropped his spoon with a clatter. "Oh, dear me, no. Smythe will be in complete control. He is to keep you informed as his investigation proceeds and, of course, he must compile the dossier for you to deliver to the President."

Churchill was visibly deflated. Was he only to be a mere messenger? A protest began to form in his mind but before he could give it voice, the rigid line of MacDonald's jaw persuaded him it would be to no avail. A different tack was in order. "Very well, Prime

Minister. But I wonder if I could not be of more service. You remember that my mother was an American?"

MacDonald nodded and Churchill continued. "I have many acquaintances in America, some of whom may be able to assist us in our inquiries. Surely you would have no objection, Prime Minister, to my calling on these meager resources for whatever benefit they might bring?"

MacDonald looked skeptical but acquiesced. "I suppose it would do no harm. But remember, Winston, this is a holiday for you and you are entitled to a well-deserved rest."

"Not nearly as long a rest, Ramsay, as I am sure you have in mind for me," Churchill said with a chuckle. "Especially if you persist in your policy on India."

"We shall see, Winston," MacDonald replied. "We shall see."

Their luncheon concluded, the Prime Minister and Churchill walked down the stairs. He asked if the Prime Minister could arrange a meeting that evening between Churchill and Smythe to go over the lay of the land together. At the bottom of the stairs, MacDonald reluctantly agreed.

As a servant handed Churchill his walking stick and hat, he turned back to MacDonald and said, "One more favor, Ramsay. You were so kind to allow my bodyguard from Scotland Yard, Inspector Thompson, to accompany me on my holiday. But, given my new assignment, might it not be prudent for me to bring along an additional man from the Yard?"

"I don't see why not," MacDonald replied. "I presume you have someone in mind?"

"Yes," said Churchill as he took his leave, "yes, I do."

I dined with David Smythe that evening after my meeting with Ramsay. He hasn't changed. He is capable enough but all bluff and bluster. The man still hates the Irish. He showed me a list of the agents he's taking with him. All of them served under him in Ireland. I suppose we need men like that in our intelligence services. It's a dirty business. My instinct tells me they aren't the right men for this work. Still, I think I have improvised quite cleverly. With Hazel, Joe, Robert, Martha and young Bourke Cockran as well, we shall make a good accounting of ourselves.

I must close now, my Darling Cat. I have several Marconigrams to send.

Always, your loving husband,

W

Churchill put the pen down, picked up his cigar and looked at his reflection in the window. Imagine that, he thought. The IRA on the prowl. He relished the prospect of taking them on again hopefully in tandem once more with the son of his old mentor Bourke Cockran. He knew what people said about him behind his back. A swashbuckler. An opportunist. A half-breed American. Unsound. Churchill smiled. He didn't care. "We are all worms," he had told a close friend many years ago, "but I do believe I am a glow worm." He took another sip of scotch. He was impatient for the game to begin. The IRA and anyone who secretly supported those terrorists were about to find out just how big a swashbuckler he really was.

2.

Churchill's Cable

New York City
Friday, 9 August 1929
9:00 a.m.

Churchill's cable arrived that morning. The contents were cryptic but to Bourke Cockran, Jr., it meant that the IRA was back. And that was not good for many reasons.

URGENT. IRA 1922 REDUX. MEET ME MONTREAL. SAT. 10 AUG. STOP. MOUNT ROYALE HOTEL. STOP. WIRE IF UNABLE TO COME. STOP.

It was a warm, sunny day and the top was down on his late father's 1921 Packard Touring Car. Its highly polished bright green hood and brass fixtures were gleaming evidence of the care lavished upon it by the garage where Cockran kept it stored. He rarely used it any more but he couldn't bear to part with the Packard. His father had loved it so. His last automobile, he said, and so it was. He had died in early 1923 after being re-elected to Congress.

With young Paddy and his maternal grandmother in the back seat, Cockran turned the big motorcar onto Fifth Avenue and headed toward the lower end of Manhattan. He was taking them to the ship that would carry them to Ireland for a six week holiday. They had left early because Cockran had promised to take Paddy to the downtown skyport at the foot of Wall Street to watch the seaplanes.

The cable was as unexpected as it was inconvenient. Unexpected because Winston was not due in New York until late September after his long rail excursion across Canada and the United States. Inconvenient because Cockran had a firm November deadline from his publisher which meant a rigid writing schedule plotted out through mid-October. Perhaps a cocktail party like the one tonight but no other distractions. The book itself would be distraction enough, a memoir of his experiences as an American journalist in Ireland and the role he played with the Irish and the British as a go-between in the days leading up to the truce in July, 1921 and eventually the Irish Free State. The basic structure of the memoir was already in place. Three long articles in The *Atlantic Monthly* in April, May and June of 1922. All he had to do now was fill in the details. Before she died, his late wife Nora had urged him to sign the contract and start writing. Someday, he promised her. But then she was gone and the newly-widowed Cockran had other plans that summer of 1922 when he returned to America. Writing hadn't been one of them.

But it wasn't the inconvenience of a trip to Montreal that bothered him about the cable. That was the least of his worries. The Packard was approaching the pier for the French Line and Cockran pointed out to his son the *Ile de France* waiting there patiently, small tendrils of steam arising from her forestacks. The young boy was excited. Unlike his father who had crossed the Atlantic four times before he was ten, Paddy had crossed it only once, before he was two.

Five minutes later they pulled up at the sky port and sat on a park bench watching the graceful seaplanes skim across the smooth water, the only sounds coming from an excited "Look at that one, Dad!" from Paddy. Then it was time to head back up to the *Ile de France*.

As they walked to the car, Mary Morrisey said, "Bourke, who was the cable from this morning? You seemed concerned."

"Winston. And no, I'm not concerned. Only more details about

Winston's plans and who he wants to see when he stays with us in October." The lie came easily. Mothers-in-law should be placated, not disturbed.

"Is that Mr. Churchill, Dad?" his son asked.

"Yes, that's right, Paddy, Mr. Churchill."

"He's the one who gave you those toy soldiers you keep in your study. Right?"

"Those are the ones," Cockran said. "He gave them to me as a present when he was visiting your Grandpa. I wasn't much older than you."

"He's really famous as a soldier, isn't he, Dad."

Cockran laughed. "Not any more. He is a member of Parliament now, just like your Grandpa was a member of Congress."

"But he'll still tell me stories about when he was a soldier, won't he? You told me he would even play with me and the toy soldiers. Right, Dad? Will he bring his sword?"

Cockran smiled at Paddy's enthusiasm. "Don't worry, Winston will play soldiers with you. But no swords for you. You'll put your eye out."

Paddy frowned but made no reply to a parent's familiar refrain.

Cockran pulled the Packard into the parking lot in front of the French Line's pier and secured a porter for their bags. After checking them in, they made their way to the first-class gangway and Cockran accompanied them both to their stateroom. Their luggage had arrived before they did and Cockran helped them get settled.

Cockran had sailed once before on the *Isle de France* and took them on a tour of the ship in the sixty minutes remaining before the "all ashore" signal. Paddy's enthusiasm for Churchill's visit was soon replaced by the more immediate prospect of his first sea voyage.

"Time to go, Paddy. Promise you'll watch after your Grandma?"

"I promise," Paddy said.

Cockran turned to Mary Morrisey. "You'll make sure he visits his mother?"

"Of course, Bourke."

"And lays down flowers for her?"

"He will," she said softly.

"And you'll tell Nora I love her."

"She knows that, Bourke. She hears you."

Cockran stood on the pier watching the ship glide slowly down the Hudson until it was almost out of sight. Six weeks of solitude for research and writing. No law school classes. It seemed a good idea when his mother-in-law had tentatively raised the possibility of returning to Ireland for an extended holiday. It didn't feel that way now, Cockran thought, as he stood there, trying to hold on to the sensation of his son's small arms as he gave him a farewell hug.

Cockran drove back uptown, the spidery lacework and gothic arches of the Brooklyn Bridge were off to his right as he passed Pier 21 of the Pennsylvania Railroad and the B&O. He circled around Washington Square, and headed north on Broadway.

Cockran was concerned about Churchill's cable, his assurances to his mother-in-law notwithstanding. It could not be good news. Nothing about the IRA and Ireland in 1922 could be. Now Paddy was on a ship headed back to the land that had stolen Cockran's love and broken his heart. Cockran had never remarried, of course. Never allowed himself to become close enough to a woman to fall in love again. He made sure of that. Paddy and the fading memory of Nora were enough. He no longer believed in happy endings.

Cockran wanted nothing more to do with Ireland or the IRA but Churchill's cable made more ominous than before the two break-ins in the last few days, one at his law school office at Columbia and the other at The Cedars, his country home on Long Island Sound. A coincidence? With the IRA back in the picture, he didn't believe in coincidence. Despite his reluctance, however, he could not lightly turn Winston down. Not someone he had known since he was five years old. Not someone whose letter of condolence on his father's death said that he had been "a great man. I owe the best things in my career to him." Cockran needed more information before he could say no to Winston Churchill. It was time to call John Devoy.

11:00 a.m.

The tall, red-haired woman stood on a diagonal across the street from the townhouse at 991 Fifth Avenue, a canvas bag over her shoulder, a 35mm camera with a telephoto lens in her hand. She was dressed plainly in a blue cashmere sweater over a white silk blouse tucked into form-hugging tan trousers which flattered a figure that needed little flattery. She took several shots of a man in his mid-thirties who stepped out of a large green Packard motorcar and ascended the steps of the townhouse two at a time. He was wearing a battered brown leather jacket and khaki pants, his light brown hair tousled by the wind. He was a big man, several inches over six feet, with broad shoulders and a big chest. He wasn't handsome, his head large and his Irish face long and chiseled. But it was a strong and interesting face, one you would not soon forget or mistake for someone else. She smiled. It would be interesting to know him better. And if things worked out as planned tonight, she'd have that chance.

After the man had unlocked the front door and disappeared inside the house, the woman placed her camera in the canvas bag and walked down the street until she found a phone booth, stepped inside and placed a call. "I have the photos of Cockran. Yes, I'll develop them and deliver them tonight. He'll be easy to spot once the boys see these. Right, before my evening engagement. Don't worry. Of course I can handle him. I'll find out tonight all that we need to know. I do this for a living, my dear. Just make sure the boys are ready. There's a lot at stake."

3.

John Devoy

The sun was streaming in the open window of Cockran's study in his Fifth Avenue townhouse. The hum of an electric fan in the corner unsuccessfully attempted to relieve the humidity of an early August day in New York as he placed the phone back on the hook after talking to John Devoy who agreed to meet him for a late lunch at the Plaza.

Churchill's cable still on the desk in front of him, he glanced at the mantel above the empty fireplace where a set of miniature, hand-painted, cast iron British soldiers were grouped at each end, ready to charge into battle, gifts from Winston to a wide-eyed five year old boy.

Cockran had been looking forward to Churchill's visit. Three books had been published that year recounting the authors' personal experiences with Michael Collins. Winston's was one of them. Cockran's own publisher had been pleasantly surprised to learn that he possessed a resource that was unavailable to the other three authors: six leather-bound volumes of Michael Collins' private journals, recounting the tedium and terror of the day-to-day existence of urban guerillas. To keep them out of unfriendly hands, Mick had made arrangements to have the journals sent to Cockran's father upon his death.

Churchill would have a prominent role in the book, second only to Collins. There were many areas on which Cockran wanted to probe Churchill's memory. Starting with 1920. Cockran and Churchill's friendship had been strained. Churchill imagined dark plots against him around every corner. Scotland Yard bodyguards accompanied him almost everywhere. And he carried a revolver with him, even slept with it, to defend against the perceived threat of Irish assassins. As head of the War Office, Churchill was not pleased with Cockran's articles for *The New York American* which chronicled the savage reprisals on Irish civilians wrought by the "Black and Tans". To Cockran's way of thinking, but not Churchill's, he had evenhandedly covered Michael Collins' campaign of assassination against British intelligence agents and policemen while drawing a vivid contrast between the British indifference to killing innocent civilians and Collins' concentration on informers and military targets. For a time, by tacit agreement, the two friends had simply stopped talking about Ireland.

All that changed early in 1921 after Churchill left the War Office and became Colonial Secretary. For the first time, he had direct responsibility for establishing policy in Ireland rather than being the one who simply supplied the troops. Knowing Cockran had interviewed Collins on several occasions, Churchill had finally asked him over dinner at the Liberal Club in London to tell him about Michael Collins.

"What sort of fellow is he? We know we can't really trust de Valera. Can we do business with this Collins?" Churchill had asked.

Cockran had been the only foreign journalist to whom Michael Collins had given interviews. Churchill had never asked before so Cockran told him then about Michael Collins. Fearless. Honest. Charismatic. Impulsive. A big ego. "In short, Winston, he's a lot like you."

Cockran smiled at the memory but the smile quickly faded. It was shortly after that dinner with Churchill that he returned to his roots as an undercover MID agent and became a player in the bloody politics of Irish freedom. A secret conduit between Mick and Winston.

Had it been worth it? The Big Fella thought so. The last time Cockran ever saw him, Collins said "Tell him for me. I may not have another chance. Tell Winston we could never have done anything without him." Perhaps. But was it worth Nora's death? He didn't think so.

Cockran put the cable on his desk. Churchill was an impulsive man, a romantic even. But a calculating one. What did he want? Cockran hoped John Devoy would have some answers.

1:15 p.m.

The waitress at the Palm Court seated Cockran and John Devoy at a corner table. Cockran had been having dinner with the gray-bearded old man once a month for the past six years, ever since his father died. It was still a shock every time he had seen Devoy in the past nine months to notice how small he had become. He seemed to be shrinking before Cockran's eyes. At five foot eight, Devoy had never been a tall man, but when he stood beside Cockran with his shoulders slumped over, he seemed even shorter, his collar several sizes too large.

When Devoy spoke, the Limerick accent was still there but his voice was only a shadow of its former booming self, the man the *Times* of London had described on his triumphant return to the Irish Free State in 1924 as "the most bitter and persistent, as well as the most dangerous, enemy of this country which Ireland has produced since Wolfe Tone."

John Devoy's real legacy lay in his having molded badly divided Irish Americans into a unified force devoted to attaining freedom for Ireland. Jailed by the British for his revolutionary activities in the wake of the famines, the then-British Prime Minister, Gladstone, had pardoned Devoy on condition that he resettle anywhere in the world except the British Empire. Devoy chose New York and received a hero's welcome when he arrived in 1874. Once there, he conceived and founded the *Clan na Gael*, a secret oath-bound society which functioned as the independent American wing of the Irish Republican Brotherhood eventually headed by Michael Collins. A master strategist and propagandist, Devoy worked tirelessly in America and abroad to raise money so the Irish rebels would be ready to strike whenever the moment of opportunity arose, specifically when Britain's attention was focused elsewhere. Cockran really liked the old man and he had filled a void in Cockran's life when his father had died in 1923.

"You're looking mighty prosperous, you Fifth Avenue lawyer."

"Now John, I'm just a poor professor who works at a law school in your own neighborhood, teaching all those young men who want to become rich lawyers."

Devoy let out a laugh which soon turned into a hacking cough.

"A lawyer's an honest trade, so long as you use your powers for good. And at least you haven't gone off into politics."

They both ordered tea and when it arrived, Devoy raised his cup.

"It's not Jameson's but it will have to do. To hell with the King and de Valera, too!" the old man said, a smile curling the corners of his mouth in that ancient bearded face.

"Amen!" Cockran replied as their delicate cups clinked together.

"So what was so mysterious you couldn't tell me over the telephone," Devoy said.

Cockran handed him Churchill's cable.

"IRA *redux?*" Devoy said. "What's that? Greek? French?"

"You know what it is, John."

The old man coughed. "It's not happening. Trust me."

"The IRA?"

"Them and de Valera. They're finished," Devoy said.

"But why would Winston send this?"

Devoy shook his head. "I don't know. I don't like Churchill and I never trusted him. But Mick respected him; said he was a man you could do business with. So I wouldn't reject it out of hand. But no one in Ireland is going to give the IRA any hard cash. Only in America but I don't see it. If they were raising money here, I'd be the first to know."

"So you don't think I should go to Montreal and see Winston?" Cockran asked.

"I didn't say that." Devoy replied. "Even a blind squirrel like

British intelligence occasionally finds an acorn. Go see Mr. Winston bloody Churchill and hear what he has to say. It can't hurt. Meanwhile, I'll put out a few feelers and see what turns up. Let's meet for dinner after you're back and I'll tell you what I've found."

2:30 p.m.

Tommy McBride watched Cockran and Devoy exit the Palm Court and walk toward the taxi stand in front of the Plaza. He was a large man with close-cropped dark hair, a somewhat bulbous red nose and looked to be in his mid 40s. When Devoy entered the cab and Cockran walked in the direction of Fifth Avenue, the man returned to the hotel lobby, stepped into a phone booth and placed a long-distance call. He spoke with a soft Irish accent.

"Cockran's going back to his house. We took photos earlier and I've got two of the boys following him. I'm certain he's alone. You want us to deliver the message there?"

"No, not there," the voice on the other end of the conversation replied in a Belfast accent, the voice of a man whose code name once had been "Blackthorn" many years ago in Ireland. "Keep following him. He might have servants about. Patience. Exercise patience. There's a good lad. You'll know the right moment when it comes. Seize it. No witnesses, mind."

"What about the cable from Churchill you mentioned earlier?"

Blackthorn laughed. "Churchill? No, don't worry about him. He's well under control. We'll take care of him in due time. You have your men see to Cockran. But, Thomas, I don't want him killed. Times are different. You could have done that during the war. If you had, his wife—may she rest in peace—wouldn't have found her way onto my list. Remember that."

4.

The *Graf Zeppelin*

The Graf Zeppelin
Friday, 9 August 1929
4:30 p.m.

Kurt von Sturm was in his element. Below, the skyscrapers of Manhattan shimmered in the afternoon sun as the great airship slowly turned and headed south toward its destination in Lakehurst, New Jersey, less than an hour away. He sat in the main cabin, the window open, the air stirring his blond hair as it fell casually down over his forehead, briefly obscuring the two inch scar on his left temple. On his lapel was a discreet, rectangular blue and white ribbon, his late father's Blue Max, *Pour Le Merite*, Imperial Germany's highest decoration, a constant reminder of the man who had first introduced him to the magical world of airships.

The airship conveying him, the *Graf Zeppelin*, was a magnificent vessel. Everything he had dreamed about and more. He had not realized, until he heard the command "Up ship" three days ago in Germany, how much and how deeply he had missed the transcendent experience of airship travel. The freedom of floating high above the earth, gliding like a great silver fish through the clouds and riding the currents of air.

Sturm turned to his travel companion, Philip Dru Cromwell, IV, the managing partner of the Wall Street investment banking firm, Wainwright and Cromwell. In his late forties, Cromwell wore a dark gray, English cut business suit, his thinning dark brown hair carefully barbered, his third scotch and water of the afternoon in his hand. He was known as "Manhattan" to the Geneva Group, shorthand for the Geneva Institute for Scientific and Industrial Progress. Sturm was Geneva's Executive Director. Each of the members of the Geneva Group had a code name representing the cities from whence they came, an affectation honoring the group's late 19th century origins. They all were major players in the international arms trade—mining moguls, arms manufacturers, coal and steel industrialists, arms dealers and financiers. In short, the merchants of death.

"You have enjoyed your first airship voyage, *Herr* Cromwell?" Sturm asked.

"Very much, Kurt. Very much. It was all you promised."

Sturm smiled and turned back to the window. The voyage from the *Graf Zeppelin*'s home base in Friedrichschafen had taken only three days but Sturm wished it had lasted longer. These giant ships had once been his life. He could remember and describe in detail every flight he had ever taken. His training flights at Friedrichschafen. The high altitude bombing runs over Paris and London. The more frequent reconnaissance missions for the North Sea fleet.

The last time Sturm had been this close to a zeppelin, let alone inside it, was the night of 23 June 1919. His intentions then were more deadly than his current mission. Only 18 zeppelins had survived the war, standing silently in their sheds at Nordholz and Wittmundhaven, awaiting delivery to the victorious Allies as reparations. Two days earlier, in a daring act of sabotage, the officers of the German High Seas Fleet interned at Scapa Flow in Scotland opened the sea valves on their ships and sank them all. Sturm persuaded his fellow naval airshipmen to emulate the bravery of their seafaring brothers. They plotted their attack in the basement of a beer house in the port of Wilhelmshaven, owned by the family of one of his officers. They split themselves into two teams of ten men each and headed back to the hangars, Sturm taking the group assigned to Wittmundhaven, only a few kilometers from the North Sea and the barrier islands of the East Friesians. Sturm and his team of fellow naval officers, clad in black, had operated with grim, silent efficiency, overpowering six unprepared Allied sentries and slitting the throats of three more. Two sentries attempted to flee in terror and Sturm personally shot them in the back with his silenced Schmeisser machine pistol. These were the first men Sturm had killed at close range. He had felt no remorse. Others had died at his command but those deaths had been accomplished in a more remote fashion when his airship had rained bombs on French and English targets from thousands of feet in the air.

When the sun rose the next morning over Wittmundhaven, all eight of the great zeppelins had been destroyed in vast explosions, leaving them a twisted mass of blackened duralumin, patches of canvas still smoldering in the warm morning light. Sturm's only regret was that the raiders at Nordholz had not been as successful, the result being that six of the ships slated to be given to the Allies had survived. Not that it did them any good, Sturm thought. All the remaining German zeppelins delivered as reparations had either crashed or been retired out of fear. Sturm savored the *schadenfreude*. They can't build their own. They can't fly ours.

Kurt knew his father would be proud if he could see him here now in the salon of this wonder of German engineering, nearly one hundred feet longer than any ship his father had commanded. Sturm's father was Peter Strasser, the legendary head of the Imperial German Naval Airship Service, who had been killed in August, 1918 in a five-ship raid on England. Strasser had been on the maiden voyage of the new L-70, a seven-hundred-foot-long dirigible specifically designed to cross the Atlantic, bomb America and return home. His twenty-four-year-old son Kurt had been a junior officer on one of the other four ships and watched his father die in a blazing hell, shot down by incendiary bullets from a British warplane. Kurt was given his own command a month later and two months after that the war was over.

A warrant was issued for his arrest by the new Socialist government in Germany for his role in destroying the eight zeppelins at Wittmundhaven. Forewarned, Kurt changed his name and, courtesy of an introduction from the Zeppelin Company president,

Hugo Eckener, went to work for the steel tycoon, Fritz von Thyssen, known to the Geneva Group as "Berlin". Germany took care of its heroes, even if its spineless Socialist government did not.

Sturm broke the silence between the two men. "I am pleased you enjoyed yourself."

"The largest airship ever." Cromwell said. "A symbol of Germany's new prosperity."

Sturm nodded in agreement before adding, "But a prosperity without power."

"That will be remedied soon enough. Germany's new beginning is rapidly drawing to a close. In many ways, a new phase commences today when we land. The final piece of the puzzle before implementing our plans for Poland."

"I agree," Sturm said, "but there is much to do. Still, I appreciate your kindness in arranging for this passage. It cost Geneva substantially more than a first-class steamship ticket, but I cannot adequately express how I feel about flying again even if I am not in command."

"The Geneva Group can well afford it and you can put to good use the extra three days in New York. Besides, were it not for my good client, Mr. Hearst, we would not have had the opportunity to return you to the sky in such a satisfying manner."

In fact, the American newspaper empire owned by William Randolph Hearst was one of Cromwell's biggest clients and was sponsoring the forthcoming historic round-the-world flight by the *Graf Zeppelin*, paying $200,000 for exclusive newsreel and newspaper coverage everywhere but Germany, where papers had paid an additional $50,000 for exclusive German coverage. But Hearst had insisted the round-the-world flight begin and end on American soil. Hugo Eckener had no choice but to agree and hence the *Graf Zeppelin* was set to land in Lakehurst, New Jersey where the American—and first—version of the round-the-world flight was to commence. From there, the ship would return to Friedrichschafen where it would refuel and reprovision before it began the long nonstop flight to Tokyo and then on to California for the third and last stop of the trip before returning again to Lakehurst. After a tickertape parade for the crew in New York, the ship would return to Friedrichschafen and complete the anti-climactic German version of the first round-the-world flight by an airship.

"Just one more thing we have Mr. Hearst to thank for," Sturm said. "A three-day voyage to America by air instead of six by sea."

"And nine days, my young friend, is the actual air time Captain Eckener told me it will take the *Graf* to travel from Friedrichschafen to California, even assuming unfavorable weather conditions over the Pacific. By that time, Kurt—only two weeks from now—your mission will be almost over. When you meet the zeppelin in California, Zurich and Berlin will entrust to you the gold bearer bonds that the *Graf* has carried and one more obstacle will be removed from the road to restoring Germany's power."

Sturm took a sip of mineral water. "We still need the Irish to play their part. $3 million is a large amount of money for them to risk."

"Receiving their money back along with a commission of $1 million should provide adequate motivation," Cromwell said. "Still, I wonder. Do you trust this Irishman?"

"De Valera?"

"Yes, that's the one. Not a very Irish name, is it?"

"No, it's not. Born in America, but of an absent Spanish father. Raised by his mother."

"Can you really trust him?" Cromwell asked. "He is a politician, after all."

"That he is," Sturm acknowledged, "and no better than the ones we have in Weimar. Easily bribed. All it took was $10,000 in a numbered Swiss account."

Cromwell smiled. "I don't have to pay much more in America. Will he stay bought?"

"I think so. After the initial numbered account was opened and the $10,000 deposited as a down payment, I insisted de Valera publicly reconcile with the IRA. I told him this would send a signal to the Geneva Group that he was fully behind the plan and it would also help condition the Irish people to the legitimacy of a revolutionary government formed by the IRA."

"And this was done?" Cromwell asked.

"Quite openly, in fact. On the floor of the Irish Parliament," Sturm said. "It was last November. It received no attention outside Ireland, but he made his position clear. He accused the Free State government of having pulled off a 'coup d'etat' in 1922 and claimed the IRA had a right to use force to regain power. We are well satisfied."

"How will the English react when Poland is dismembered next year by the Soviet Union and Germany?" Cromwell asked. "After all, their navy starved your country in the last war."

"It is difficult to say," Sturm replied. "Revenge can be complicated. Over a year ago, we began exploring various alternatives to insure that Great Britain would not involve itself in a Polish conflict. Many prominent members of the Conservative opposition in England have publicly expressed support for restoring Danzig and the Polish Corridor to Germany, along with other German-speaking areas in East Prussia taken from us at Versailles. And that is all we will be taking back. The Russian bear will have a much bigger meal. Besides, Germany is a democracy. Poland is not. Since Pilsudski's advent as dictator three years ago, Poland's friends in the West are few, especially in England. Also, the new Socialist government in England is committed to disarmament and, if it remains in power, the British Navy will not sail."

"Are you certain?"

Sturm shrugged. "Politics are unpredictable. That is why I conceived this mission."

Cromwell nodded his approval.

Sturm smiled, accepting the compliment. "Seven years ago with the creation of the Irish Free State, the thorn of Ireland was removed from the hide of the British lion where it had festered for over two hundred years. The $3 million we are spending here on weapons for the IRA is designed to reinsert that thorn. A *coup d'etat* by the IRA in the Irish Free State. Once that is done, the British will be too preoccupied to care about Germany and Russia once more dividing Poland."

"What about the French?" Cromwell asked.

Sturm laughed. "What about them? They believe in nothing. They are too busy building a wall to keep Germans out. Without the Americans helping them in the last war, victory would have been ours. Without the English at their side, they'll sit on the sidelines and watch while we take our revenge on the Poles."

Revenge on the French will come later, Sturm thought, after Poland. The Rhineland will be re-militarized and the Frogs might even beg us to take Alsace-Lorraine back. Or at least offer a fair election and not a rigged one like the last. Either way, they won't have the stomach for another million casualties. Germany *will* once more be great. Then, and only then, would he be free to fulfill his destiny—to reclaim his father's name and return to the sky in command of a magnificent airship like the *Graf.*

5.

Miss Photo-Journalist

New York
Friday, 9 August 1929
7:00 p,m.

Cockran's taxi pulled up in front of the Beresford Apartments at 211 Central Park West in a driving rainstorm. Designed by Emery Roth, it was New York's newest and grandest apartment building, the largest in the city. The Beresford faced both Central Park and Manhattan Square with towers at each of the three corners facing on the park and the square. It was twenty-two stories high and Cockran's good friends Gregory and Anne Dawson occupied the penthouse on the southeast corner overlooking the park. He came out of the elevator and handed his umbrella to the maid.

"Bourke, how delightful to see you again," his hostess Anne Dawson said. She was a tall, attractive blonde who wore a long, shimmering silver gown. "We don't see nearly enough of you these days. Greg and I are so pleased you could make it."

Cockran took her hand in both of his and kissed her lightly on the check. "I wouldn't think of missing a party of yours, Anne. Your dress is beautiful, as are you," Cockran replied. "How's business, Greg?" he asked, turning to shake the extended hand of Gregory Dawson, a large, red-faced man in his late forties with prematurely white hair. Dawson was a senior vice president in his family's investment banking firm, Dawson & Goodyear.

"Couldn't be better. The Dow dropped ten points last week, but it's temporary. It's only 345 now. We could see 380, maybe 400 by the end of the month. You really ought to let me take some of those bonds your father left you and put them into stocks."

Cockran laughed. "My bonds are fine, Greg. And my needs are simple."

Leaving his hosts, Cockran passed under a glittering chandelier and circulated through the room, pausing at small groups where he knew one or more of the people. The room wasn't as crowded as usual for one of Anne's parties which he attributed to it being August when many people were summering elsewhere. He usually didn't come to affairs like this, even ones given by childhood friends from the Gold Coast like Anne Dawson. He enjoyed small dinner parties more, especially if the guests were interesting. Cocktail parties like this, where there were already thirty people in the room and certainly more to come, all in formal evening attire, were not his cup of tea. Neither was black tie. But Anne had been especially insistent.

Indeed, he had come night only because Anne had promised there was someone she wanted him to meet. "Why else would I throw a party in August", she had joked "except to introduce you to a nice single girl and keep you from the clutches of all those young Gold Coast wives?" A photo-journalist, Anne had told him, and from Scotland no less.

Miss Photo-Journalist wasn't here yet, Anne had informed him at the door, so Cockran continued moving through the room noting familiar faces here and there but not one sufficiently interesting to warrant an extended conversation. He stopped at the windows overlooking Central Park, a crystal tumbler of Johnnie Walker Red Label and water in his hand. It was still raining, but it had lightened considerably from the time he had left his townhouse. He felt the pressure of a hand on his right shoulder and simultaneously a voice was speaking softly into his ear.

"The Dawsons have no taste if they'll invite any mick bastard in off the street."

Cockran turned to look into the broad smiling face of Bill Donovan, his old CO who had led New York's Fighting 69th

Infantry Regiment in action in France. Donovan grabbed him in a bear hug which Cockran returned, slapping him on the back and drawing a few stares of surprise, if not disapproval, from the nearby tuxedoed men and evening-gowned women. Donovan was ten years older than Cockran, a large man, five foot ten, with neatly trimmed, graying brown hair, pushing two hundred pounds, but still almost as fit and trim as he was eleven years earlier when he won the Congressional Medal of Honor and the nickname "Wild Bill". Their Regiment had lost 1,750 of its original 3,000 men in that action and Cockran might well have been one of them that summer of 1918 had he not been wounded five months earlier.

Oblivious to the stares, both men drew back from the hug. "Better than the judgment shown by your Quaker friend in the White House, Bill," Cockran replied. "By shafting you, he made sure his lily-white Protestant cabinet wasn't infected by a rum-loving Papist."

Cockran's comment concerned Herbert Hoover's reneging on his promise to appoint Donovan as Attorney General. As a matter of principle Cockran didn't like most politicians. His father's good friend, Mark Twain, had said it all with his comment that America's only native criminal class were congressmen and, by inference, all politicians. Even presidents. Donovan just laughed. "I'd rather be rich than famous, Bourke. Your father taught me you can do more good that way. Besides, the real reason the Great Engineer stiffed me was because he was afraid I'd find the secret tunnel in the White House you Democrats built during the war for the Pope!"

Cockran smiled. It was a good sign that two good Irish Catholic boys could share jokes over what had been an exceptionally ugly organized campaign of anti-Catholic bigotry in the 1928 presidential election where the very Protestant Hoover had defeated the very Catholic governor of New York, Al Smith. Cockran mentally amended that as he was one not-so-good Irish Catholic boy. Nevertheless, anti-Catholic bigotry bothered him more than it should, having experienced it first hand. He had grown up in the middle of Long Island's Gold Coast amid all the millionaire mansions which had sprung up around the turn of the century,

Prostestants inhabiting them all. Make that almost all. Not the Cedars, Cockran's boyhood home at Sands Point. But it hadn't been a mansion, just a large comfortable old shingle house on 300 acres. Not that different really from the house of their neighbors, the Theodore Roosevelts, in nearby Oyster Bay.

As a boy, he'd never experienced any overt anti-Catholic prejudice. That would not have been well-mannered and Protestants were nothing but well-mannered on the outside, no matter how black their little hearts were on the inside. Besides, with Theodore Roosevelt as his sponsor, his father belonged to as many exclusive clubs as he wished, the token Irish Catholic who had more friends among the British aristocracy than most of the other members. It was not until Cockran discovered girls that he first encountered anti-Catholic bigotry. He had been surprised. His pretty mother who died in childbirth and whom he only knew from photos had been a Protestant. An Episcopalian no less. As a result, Cockran had not become a religious man despite his father's devotion to the church. Once his father had assured the 7 year old Cockran that his mother was indeed in heaven and the good priests and nuns were dead wrong when they said that only members in good standing of the one true church could go to heaven, he had concluded that if the priests and nuns were wrong on something as important as that, what else could they be wrong about?

All the girls he dated were Protestant because there were few Catholic girls to date on the Gold Coast. Unless you considered the servants, but Cockran didn't move in those circles and his father had warned him sternly about that anyway. The good breeding and manners of his father's Protestant neighbors in the Gold Coast, however, had a limit. Don't try to marry their daughters. Well, Cockran hadn't been trying to marry anyone but he certainly had been trying, with considerable success, to get inside Emily Farnsworth's blouse where he had spent a delightful summer. They were in love as only teenagers can be and he was crushed at the end of the summer when she broke off the relationship.

Emily was actually embarrassed to tell him why but he persisted. Which is when he learned that Emily's father had forbade her to see

Cockran any more because he was afraid she was getting too serious. And he didn't want his nearly seventeen year old virginal daughter getting serious about a Catholic because, if the worst happened, she couldn't marry him. Far better—and safer—to become serious about an Episcopalian boy, preferably one whose father was as wealthy as, if not more so than, George Farnsworth.

Cockran had been hurt and confused. After all, he protested, he wasn't even a good Catholic. But soon-to-be debutantes on the Gold Coast did not disobey their fathers, not if they're expected to have the coming out party to which their birthright entitled them.

So he and Emily had reluctantly parted that summer and had in fact remained good friends, indeed more than that, but that was another story. His father told him not to worry about it. Don't give anyone else the power to make you unhappy, he had said. Still, once his father died, he had promptly resigned, without comment, from all the clubs where he and his father had been the only Catholic members. Life was too short to spend it among bigots.

Still, there could be bigots on both sides as he had discovered in Ireland when he met the beautiful, hot-tempered colleen who was Nora Morrisey. After she learned that he had only dated Protestant girls and listened to him complain about their parents' bigotry, she had laughed.

"And wouldn't you be sounding just as bigoted towards the Prods as my parents?"

"What do you mean?" Cockran had asked, confused at the question. *They* were the bigots, not him. And then Nora had explained. She was dating a British officer, much to her parents' chagrin and it was not because he was a Brit with a double-barreled name. No, it was because he was not a member of the one true, Holy, Catholic and Apostolic Church. In short, he was a Protestant, Church of England. It was their first date but Cockran was already in love and she had parried his questions about her British suitor.

"He's nice enough to me, sweet really. But he's such a pompous prig to my friends. You've got a month until I see him again, Mr. American, so if I decide *you're* worth seeing again, it will be in spite of your religious intolerance." Nora had said with that laugh that always melted his heart. Reflexively, Cockran had started to protest and then stopped. He was out to win her love, not an argument. His father hadn't raised a fool.

"I told Al we had to keep quiet about the Pope's tunnel, but he just wouldn't listen," Cockran said, as he and Donovan walked over to a less-populated corner of the room to continue their conversation. "What are your plans now, Bill? Are you back in New York to stay?"

"Frank Raichle and some of our boys from the Antitrust Division have thrown in with me and we've opened law offices in both Washington and New York. We're going to build a top-notch international law firm, Bourke, and we want you with us."

Cockran paused but, before he could respond, he felt pressure on his left arm as Anne Dawson moved in behind him and gave him a quick kiss on the cheek.

"You boys stop talking shop. There will be no business discussed at my party. Colonel Donovan, go find your lovely wife before someone steals her away. Bourke, you come with me," Anne said, as she began to lead him away. Before she could do so, Donovan said "Call me, Bourke. Let's have dinner tomorrow. I'm saving a place for you in my firm."

"I'm in Montreal all day. How about a late supper at the Stork Club?" Cockran replied.

Donovan gave him a thumbs up as Anne Dawson continued whispering in his ear, "She's over there, with that pompous ass, Philip Cromwell. You must go rescue her."

"Rescue whom?" Cockran asked.

"Mattie. Martha McGary. The photo-journalist, silly. Isn't that why you really came?"

7:45 p.m.

It wasn't Mattie McGary who needed rescuing, Cockran thought as he watched Philip Dru Cromwell IV raise his hands as if in defense from the shapely red-haired woman facing him. She was wearing a royal blue silk rep dress with an accented waistline. Her hair was cut fashionably short, in layers, giving her a tousled look similar to the famous aviatrix Amelia Earhart.

As she turned at Anne's request to meet Cockran, he was not prepared for her striking looks. "Bourke Cockran." he said pronouncing his name "Burke" as his father had before him. "Pleased to meet you." Her face was brown with the sun, as if she spent much of her time in the outdoors, a light dusting of freckles across her nose and cheeks which she had made no effort to conceal with makeup. White teeth flashed as she smiled, her large green eyes focused on him as she extended her hand to his. She wasn't a classic beauty but Cockran was mesmerized. He knew he was staring but he must have said something because she laughed and said, "And to think Anne told me that you were a quiet and shy Irish boy, Mr. Cockran. Perhaps you can help resolve a point of dispute between me and Mr. Cromwell," she said, nodding in Cromwell's direction. I told him American money had unnecessarily prolonged the Great War. He didn't agree. What do you think?" Her voice was soft with the barest trace of a Scottish accent.

Mattie paused. "Excuse me. I apologize. Have you two met?"

"We've not met, Professor Cockran," Cromwell said, "but I have enjoyed your articles on war reparations. Can't say I agree with them, but you argue your points well."

Cockran's eyes narrowed slightly. Was it possible Cromwell didn't recognize him? He took Cromwell's proffered hand and answered Mattie's question. "If I were a partner at J.P. Morgan or at Wainwright, I might disagree with you, Miss McGary. But the truth is undeniable. Without their financing the British and Goldman Sachs doing the same for the Germans, the war would have been a lot shorter and we would never have gotten in. It's really that simple."

"Exactly my point, Mr. Cockran. You have been most helpful. Thank you," Mattie said, flashing him a wide smile.

Before Cockran could mumble his thanks, Mattie had already turned back on Cromwell, restarting a discussion from which she obviously needed no rescue.

"But, Miss McGary, everyone financed the munitions industry during the war. While it's true we and a lot of other firms helped Morgan finance British war loans before we got in, it proved to be the right thing to do," Cromwell responded.

"Nonsense!" Mattie snapped. "You Americans made a bloody fortune from us and the only reason you won't support ending German war reparations now is the money you're making off your German investments. The Germans have taken most of their American funds and passed them on to France and Britain, who turn around and give it back to the Americans to pay off your loans to them. So you make a tidy profit coming, going and at all stops in between."

"Well, not exactly..." Cromwell began, but Mattie interrupted before he could finish. Cockran was enjoying this more and more. He knew who Cromwell was even if the older man didn't recognize him. Washington was far in the past but what he knew of Cromwell, he didn't like. Go get him, girl, he thought as he silently cheered Mattie on.

"Exactly what is inaccurate about my observations? Would you like facts and figures?"

"I'm sure you have them my dear but, if I'm not mistaken, you work for the International News Service?"

"Sure, and a lot more besides."

"And INS is owned by Mr. Hearst?"

"You bet. The best boss I ever had."

"Well, Miss McGary, I know Mr. Hearst quite well," he said in a tone which, Cockran thought, invited you to draw the inference that she did not. "I know from several conversations with him on the subject that he does not share your views."

Mattie paused and, uncharacteristically for her it seemed to Cockran in the few minutes he had known her, appeared to carefully choose her next words.

"I am," she said distinctly, "quite familiar with Mr. Hearst's views on America getting involved in the war and on the role of Wall Street financiers in encouraging entry into that war. I can assure you, Mr. Cromwell, that Mr. Hearst shares my views *precisely* on those two subjects. I also know his *present* views on Allied repayments of their war debt. He is peculiarly persuaded by facts. And once I have those facts, Mr. Cromwell, you may be certain Mr. Hearst will print them. And do you know why?" Mattie asked.

"I'm sure you will educate me," Cromwell responded.

"Circulation, Mr. Cromwell. Circulation. Merchants of death, like you and your company, are the only ones who really profit from repayment of Allied war debt. Once I prove that—and I will—our readers will love it, so the Chief will love it, too," said Mattie. "Now, let's talk about all those tombstones. Isn't that what you Yanks call them?"

Cromwell paused and appeared startled, raising a quizzical eyebrow. Mattie filled the void adding, "No, not that kind. I'm talking about all of the secondary positions Wainwright & Cromwell have taken in a wide variety of note, bond and stock offerings in Germany and elsewhere in Europe." She began to recite what had all the appearances of a very long list.

Cromwell visibly stiffened and raised his hand as if to silence her. Mattie ignored the gesture and continued reciting the list until Cromwell interrupted, his voice tightly controlled. "Miss McGary. This is a private gathering and hardly the time or place for me to give an interview to the press. I have an engagement elsewhere at 9:00 p.m. Perhaps some other time."

"How about tomorrow? I'm free if you are."

"I regret, Miss McGary, that my schedule is very busy. Please contact my secretary …."

"I've been trying to do that for the past two weeks, Mr. Cromwell, but your schedule is always busy. That's why I asked Anne to invite you here tonight. I believe her response was 'Whatever for? He's such a bore. I've got someone for you to meet who's so much more.' And I see now that she was right. Thank you, Mr. Cromwell, for talking with me. I have all I need from you for my story. 'When confronted with these facts, Mr. Cromwell declined to comment and once again ducked an interview with this correspondent.'"

Cromwell replied with ill-concealed hostility. "*That* would be a mistake, Miss McGary. I strongly suggest you reconsider," he said, his tone unmistakably conveying the unspoken *if you know what's good for you.* Cockran bristled at this. Not that he needed it but it gave him one more reason to dislike Phillip Dru Cromwell IV.

Mattie said nothing and turned abruptly on her heel, stuck her arm through Cockran's and said, "Come on, Mr. Cockran. Let's see if Anne was right about you."

"Please call me Bourke," Cockran replied as they walked away.

"And I'm Mattie. Anne's a dear, but don't you find parties like this so frightfully tedious? Lawyers. Bankers. The stock market. Is that all you Americans ever talk about?"

"A fair appraisal of most Americans, but not Anne Dawson. The bankers and lawyers she invites to please her husband. The writers and artists she invites to please herself."

"I know, I know. I'm just being wicked. I talked to Georgia O'Keefe earlier, and she's a dear. Hopper was supposed to be here, too, Anne told me, but he is unwell. Have you seen his new piece, *The Lighthouse at Two Lights* at your Museum of Modern Art?"

"Not yet, I'm afraid. Modigliani's show is the only one I have seen this year."

"Really? Too pretentious for me. What else have you been doing this summer?"

"I've spent most of my time working on a book. My publisher wants it by December."

Mattie bored in like the journalist she was and soon had Cockran telling her stories of his secret meetings with Michael Collins during the war, passing on Churchill's messages, Collins' replies, the truce, the treaty negotiations, and the anguish Collins felt at the civil war forced upon Ireland by militants who refused to accept the voice of the people and the English who would not give him the time to work it out peacefully. Cockran even told her what was otherwise a closely guarded confidence known only to his publisher and John Devoy— the secret journals sent posthumously by Collins to Cockran's father and the fire after his father's funeral which destroyed all but six of them. With every word he spoke, he brought the story closer to

Nora's death. He kept trying to change the subject and inquire after Mattie's career as a photo-journalist, but she was too tenacious to let him go. A damn good journalist, he thought.

"Do you ever wish you could do something like that again?" she said, suddenly.

Cockran hadn't anticipated the question. "Do what again?"

"Get involved. Make history. My goodness, you helped create the Irish Free State. What a great story. Don't you want to do something like that again?"

"No," Cockran answered firmly and he wasn't about to tell her why. He actually had once felt that way himself. Not making history exactly, but helping it along, giving it a nudge. Indeed, that was the story he was writing that summer, the story of how he had brought Michael Collins and Winston Churchill together. It hadn't been his idea. His father had instilled in him a healthy mistrust of politics, politicians and governments. No, the person who had persuaded him to get involved and make history was that stunning blue-eyed, red-haired girl from Galway who became his wife and who also was eager to "make history". Cockran had not been persuaded easily. He was a journalist then, having left the law. He didn't want to make history, he wanted to report it and write its first draft, preferably exposing corrupt politicians. But he was in love and Nora was an exceptionally persuasive person. Now she was dead and he could not help thinking that if he had never introduced Winston to Michael Collins, she might still be alive. Yet it had been Nora who eagerly urged him to do so.

Cockran blinked and realized Mattie had been talking to him while he had drifted off. "Excuse me," he said, "my mind was elsewhere. I didn't catch what you said."

Mattie smiled. It was a beautiful smile and Cockran could see he was forgiven.

"Don't worry, I do it all the time. What I asked was why not? Making history is fun."

"Not to me," Cockran said, attempting to close the subject.

"Why not?" Mattie said. "I think it's exciting."

"That's not my idea of excitement...." Cockran trailed off, catching himself before he mentioned Nora. Damn but this woman was aggressive. "Listen, Mattie, you have me talking too much. My throat's dry and my glass is empty. How about another drink?" he said, offering her his arm which she accepted as they moved in the crowded room towards the bar.

In front of the white-coated bartender, Cockran asked Mattie what she wanted. She replied, "scotch and water. Johnnie Walker Red." Cockran placed an order for two.

They made their way back across the room, and Cockran led her down the hallway towards the kitchen in the rear of the apartment, where he stopped, opened a door, and ushered her into a small book-lined room with four leather chairs and a small writing desk. "We'll find some peace in here," Cockran said, closing the door behind them. "Greg is fussy about whom he lets in his library, but I think he'll make an exception for us."

Mattie resumed their conversation where they had left off but, perhaps sensing Cockran's reticence over Ireland, got him talking about his careeer as a journalist before he was posted to Ireland. Twenty minutes later, he raised his hand in a gesture of silence. Any minute now, she could return to the topic of Ireland and he didn't want to go there. He glanced down at his wristwatch, and said, "It's 8:30, Miss McGary, later than I realized. I must leave by 9:00, or 9:30 at the latest. The night train to Montreal leaves at 11:30, and we've not talked at all about you. Aren't a lot of your stories dangerous to cover? And exactly what is the difference between a journalist, a photographer, and a photo-journalist like yourself? You certainly had Cromwell on the defensive, and yet you obviously aren't carrying a camera tonight." Cockran said, as he looked at Mattie's figure which stood silhouetted against the room's lone window.

Cockran was happy when Mattie laughed again. "I like you, Mr. Cockran. You don't miss a thing. Look, I've got an early train myself tomorrow. This party's boring, present company excepted. So why don't you walk me back to my hotel and we'll talk on the way?"

6.

Stay Out of Our Business!

New York
Friday, 9 August, 1929
9:30p.m.

Cockran and Mattie walked out of the Beresford into the cool night air and turned right for the ten-block journey to her hotel, the Essex House. The rain had stopped and he offered her his arm again and she accepted.

"I get questions like yours a lot. Usually in the form of 'what's a pretty little thing like you doing covering all these wars and insurrections, risking your life and limb?' So," she said, turning to him with the same smile he had been trying to get her to duplicate all evening, "do you want my standard cocktail party answer or the real story?"

"Let's see if I can handle the cocktail answer first," Cockran answered with a grin, pleased he had her answering questions now, instead of asking them.

"Well, Mr. Cockran, I do it so brave men like you can keep informed while your tender little backsides are safe at home doing more manly, risky things, like buying stock on margin."

Cockran grinned again. "So, that usually works?"

"You bet. Especially when they've got some other pretty little thing draped over their arm and dripping with jewelry bought from the proceeds of those margin accounts."

"Not bad," Cockran admitted. "I'm happy I came alone tonight. What's the real story?"

"It's simple, actually. I love my job. I love what I do. Only it's not a job, it's an adventure. I'm good at what I do. I make a difference and I'm paid quite well, especially since I went to work for the Chief."

"You mean Hearst?" Cockran asked.

"Yes. It's what we all call him."

Cockran nodded. "But what about the photojournalist part?"

"Don't make too big a meal of that," she said. "Most photo-journalists are photographers first and journalists second. They couldn't write to a deadline if their lives depended on it. They think I'm some babe who took a few lucky photos and won some awards." She laughed. "And they're probably right. I'm a writer first. But I'm going to get shots they never will because all they can do is react and record what they see. That's not me. The story comes first. And, because it does, I know where to be to nail the photos I need to illustrate what I write."

"Exactly how did you become a photojournalist?" Cockran asked.

Mattie's face darkened. "I get that question a lot also. I think it's because I'm a woman. But it's not something I like to talk about. It was Munich in 1923. My photographer, a smart, delightful man named Helmut Stein and I were working for *The Daily Mirror,* covering what has now become known as the Beer Hall Putsch. Unfortunately for us, we were literally caught right in the middle of it. I made it. Helmut didn't. He was killed that night by Nazi thugs."

"Nazi?"

"Sorry. National Socialists. A small political party with their own military wing, the SA. Brownshirts."

"I've heard of them." Cockran said. "Their leader is a guy named Hitler?"

Mattie paused, her eyes moist. "That's the one. Anyway, Helmut had taught me enough about photography that I was able to get by without a photographer while my paper searched for a replacement. Finally, after a few months of taking my own photos, I decided I didn't need my own photographer. If I had made better decisions that day, Helmut might still be alive."

Cockran nodded in sympathy. "I understand. It's never easy when others you care for and who depend on you are taken." Then he quickly brought the conversation back on track. "Does this mean you're a self-made man, then, when it comes to photography?"

Mattie chuckled. "Hardly. Helmut taught me a lot before he was killed and introduced me to his peers and they were enormously helpful. Erich Salomon especially, but also Alfred Eisenstaedt and Fritz Goro. Brilliant artists, all of them. I'll never be in their league but they persuaded me to buy a Leica and a Contax and that made all the difference in the world."

"How's that?"

"They're small. They use 35 mm motion picture film in rolls which give you 36 exposures. I only need one bag over my shoulder, two cameras, and lots of film. A telephoto lens, a supply of flashbulbs for those few occasions when natural light won't do, and I'm good for weeks. With his equipment, Helmut sometimes needed an assistant to carry it all."

"Why did you go to work for a tabloid like *The Daily Mirror*?"

"Easy. They hired women reporters. It originally started way back when, 1903 I think it was, as a paper for women. And as Lord Northcliffe himself told me, they had to hire women if it was going to succeed. It didn't, not as a women's paper, but even after it became a tabloid, they've always had an open attitude about hiring women."

They walked along companionably like that for another twenty minutes. Washed by the rain, the air smelled fresher and cooler. Cockran couldn't explain his attraction to this woman but it was undeniably there, just as it had been with Nora. It had started out as a favor for Anne. A photojournalist from Scotland, for God's sake. How sexy could someone like that be? Well, a lot actually. Too soon for Cockran, they arrived in front of the Essex House. He had enjoyed her company a lot more than he had expected.

"Bourke, it's been a pleasure to meet you," she said, "and you've been so sweet to walk me home and listen to me chatter on. Do have a pleasant journey tonight. I don't know when I'll next be in New York, but I hope we may meet again."

"Sure, I'd like that too," he said, handing her his card.

"You're a dear," she said, as she took his card, leaned over and kissed him softly on the cheek. "Who knows? We might even run across each other somewhere else before then. In some things, it's better to be lucky than good."

10:00 p.m.

Cockran crossed the street and headed into Central Park with a smile on his face. He soon took off his jacket, slinging it over a shoulder as he felt the humidity in the rain-soaked air.

As he walked, Cockran couldn't keep his mind off Mattie. Anne Dawson had chosen well. He smiled at how irrepressible she was, always trying to set him up. Normally, this would be the first and last time he saw an Anne Dawson introduction. Maybe one date but then never again. But something about her made him want to see Mattie McGary again. So far as her visits to New York were not too frequent, he believed it would be safe to see her the next time she was in New York. Why he even worried about something like this was complicated.

After Nora's death, Cockran had no intention of ever marrying again. Having achieved perfect happiness the first time out, Cockran did not believe in tempting fate. He was not going to share his life with another woman, always comparing her unfavorably in his mind to Nora. On the other hand, Cockran was a healthy young man with an equally healthy interest in female companionship. After a period of mourning, he had allowed Anne to coax him back into the market because he was, in fact, a highly eligible bachelor whose father had left him fairly well fixed financially with blue chip bonds as well as homes on Fifth Avenue and Long Island's Gold Coast. He wasn't rich like his Gold Coast neighbors but he was comfortable.

He developed a simple formula for avoiding marriage, less out of calculation than intuition inspired by the memory of his former relationship with Emily Farnsworth. High-born Protestants didn't marry Catholics. So, he politely declined Anne Dawson's occasional attempts to introduce him to a Catholic girl and limited himself strictly to Protestants, the higher born the better. The 1920s were a liberating era for women. Sexual permissiveness and even promiscuity were well in fashion. And parties at the Gold Coast mansions often matched those described by Scott Fitzgerald in *The Great Gatsby.* Cockran went to them all with his girlfriend of the day, confident that women of that background might sleep with a Catholic but never marry him.

It had worked. Cockran moved from one Protestant girl to another among the people he had grown up with and he had been pleased with himself right up until the day it stopped working. He had been dating and sleeping with a stunning debutante eight years younger and things were proceeding just fine, thank you, or so he thought. But, as it often does, the world was changing and he had not noticed. What happened was that not one but three attractive women he had dated, Protestants all, fell in love with him and were unintimidated by what was, in fact, his feigned Catholicism, riding on the coattails of his father's reputation as a pillar of the Church. All had been willing to be married in the Church and to raise all their offspring in the one True, Holy, Catholic and Apostolic Church in the event her spouse predeceased her.

Cockran was appalled when he saw this, bringing pain into another's life where once he had brought only pleasure. The first time it happened, he laid it off to bad luck which could happen to anyone. The next time he wasn't so sure and that parting had been more painful than the first. There would not have even been a third had she not been a Vanderbilt. Who would have thought that a Vanderbilt would be willing to marry an Irish Catholic, let alone convert? Each time he ended things with the three women became a variation of what, in his mind, had turned into "the speech." The one where he held her face in his hands, stared deeply into her eyes and told him what a wonderful woman she was, a woman who should be loved above all others and how Cockran would never be able to do that because he loved his late wife Nora above all others and always would. Forever.

The speech wasn't bad. In fact, it was pretty damn good. Why? Because he meant every word. He wasn't in love with any of them, not the way he had been with Nora. But he had hurt those three women deeply and was sorry for it, the Catholic guilt of his childhood creeping back into his adult life. Also, his father had raised him as a gentleman and he knew if he kept doing this with single women, he was in danger of becoming a cad. He believed that would have disappointed his father even more than his fallen away status with the Church.

A modification of his relations with the opposite sex was in order because he was not going to allow himself to continue causing pain in others. Quite by accident, Emily Farnsworth came to his rescue. They had remained friends and, over the years, the two of them would occasionally have lunch together. At one lunch though, he had seen she was distraught for it turned out that her extremely wealthy husband had been sleeping with a series of attractive young Irish underhouse parlor maids, turning them over at a rapid clip and refusing to stop despite Emily's insistence that he do so.

Cockran agreed that her husband was a rotter and, for the sake of their old friendship, he was more than willing to honor her request to make him a cuckold as well. She didn't state it in exactly those terms, of course. After all, she was a well-bred young lady and he was a gentleman. But the message was unmistakable. There was no question of a divorce, as Cockran well knew. Emily had two beautiful children to whom she was devoted. The affair lasted for six months until she and Cockran resumed a platonic friendship after she seduced a tennis pro at one of the local country clubs. After all, Cockran had been exceptionally discreet in their affair, whereas Emily wanted something which would set the tongues wagging at their own Club and rub her husband's nose in it.

Cockran wasn't saddened by this but rather was happy for his old friend. He hadn't intended to establish a pattern but, as it turned out, there was no shortage of other well-bred young Gold Coast matrons in exactly the same position as Emily, eager to get even with their philandering husbands. Cockran, his reputation as an eligible bachelor preceding him, had plenty to choose from. With them, neither love nor marriage were on the table and Cockran found that comforting because to him, both words meant pain. Pain he had spent seven years trying to cope with; pain he did not wish to inflict on others.

Mattie McGary did not fit this pattern. She appeared to be single in that she wore no ring, which was one of the first things he noticed. Still, the fine wrinkles around her eyes when she laughed led him to believe she was in her late twenties. She was obviously a woman who was dedicated to her career so he was fairly confident marriage would not be on her mind. But he would be careful. He had no desire to resurrect the speech. A fling or two with her would be nice but at the slightest hint their relationship might become serious, he would end things before it went further just as he already had with several of the revenge-seeking young Gold Coast wives.

Thinking about Mattie had distracted him, he realized later. Others were walking along the broad sidewalk when he had entered the park but now he was alone, walking through the gloom illuminated by the circles of light cast by street lamps, moving from one bright pool of light to another, humming softly to himself.

It happened swiftly before he had a chance to react. There were three of them. He heard a rush of footsteps behind him and turned in the direction of the noise. It had been a long time since he had been surrounded by danger and his defenses were down. Before he could react, a heavy fist struck him a blow squarely in the kidneys, causing him to gasp with pain. It was soon followed by another blow that forced him to his knees. A boot hit him in the back and he fell forward, his coat flying out in front of him. Before he could even get to his knees, the other two men rolled him over and began raining fists at his ribs. Once, twice, three times. He felt rather than saw the initial aggressor grab his hair and lift his head up painfully. The man spoke in a hard, County Cork-tinged accent. "You stay out of our business, boyo!" slamming Cockran's head back into the soft glistening grass.

An angry Cockran stood up, his ears burning as blood rushed to his head, and looked around for his assailants, eager to find them and pay them back. But he was dizzy and he knelt on the grass as he felt his anger ebb, replaced by embarrassment. As an Army MID agent both during and after the war, he had been trained to handle situations like this and, had he been alert, all three of his attackers might now be limping away with broken limbs and noses. Two break-ins and now an attack? It was a warning, not a coincidence. And he wasn't going to let it happen again.

7.

Tommy McBride

New York City
Friday, 9 August 1929
10:00 p.m.

Kurt von Sturm's unfavorable impression of Philip Cromwell remained even though he was now sitting in the back of the man's chauffeured Rolls Royce limousine. Three days together on an airship was more than enough time to make that judgment. Cromwell's chauffeur had met them when the airship landed in New Jersey. They stopped briefly at the paneled offices of Wainright and Cromwell on Wall Street before his chauffeur had dropped Cromwell off for an engagement on the upper West Side and left the motorcar at Sturm's disposal for the evening.

Sturm had investigated Cromwell for membership in the Geneva Group four years earlier when it had determined to take on an American member. During their brief stop at Cromwell's offices, Sturm had noticed a portrait of Cromwell's father. The family resemblance was strong although his father, when he sat for the artist, was probably ten years older than Cromwell today. The father looked proud and confident, one hand resting on a globe beside him, his head high and eyes fixed on a distant point on the horizon as if he were looking forward to a century in which American financial interests would dominate the world. He committed suicide two months after the portrait was painted, wiped out in the panic of 1907.

Sturm knew the son was more formidable than the father. A 1902 Princeton graduate with a degree in history, Cromwell's faculty advisor had been the Department Chairman, Woodrow Wilson. He was well-connected socially and in financial circles, his father's death notwithstanding. As a young man, he held a succession of high government positions during the war. A protégé of Col. Edward House, he was given a prominent place on the American delegation to Versailles and was also close to the American Attorney General, A. Mitchell Palmer. Some said he would have become Treasury Secretary in a Palmer administration. Once Palmer did not receive his party's presidential nomination in 1920, Cromwell determined to leave government service.

Sturm also knew that Cromwell had been rejected for a partnership at J.P. Morgan. Not even his patron, Colonel House, had that much influence, especially after Wilson's stroke. It's not that Morgan partners hadn't committed suicide before, but they had always had the judgment and good taste to do so quietly. Those weren't the words Sturm would have used to portray the very public deaths of Philip Dru Cromwell, III and his naked blonde mistress. It did not matter a short fourteen years later how brilliant and promising a career young Philip had in front of him. Jack Morgan was a prudent and cautious man. He was not going to take a chance on another messy Cromwell suicide. He wished Philip well, and even put in a good word for him with old Marcus Wainwright, the founder, now retired, the firm renamed as Wainwright & Cromwell.

The revival of the old-line firm under Cromwell's leadership was nothing short of spectacular. Though obviously tied to the previous Democratic administration, Cromwell's contacts and influence with the two Republican administrations which succeeded Wilson belied that fact. Fixed firmly at the intersection of the growing cooperation after the war between business and government, Cromwell was the man to see if you wanted anything done in Washington. His connections in the Commerce and Treasury Departments were exceptional. His reputation was such, Sturm knew, that he charged

$25,000, in cash or securities, simply for an initial consultation, plus ten per cent of all profits generated should his efforts prove successful. In five years he had become one of the wealthiest men on Wall Street and one of the first on Wall Street to steer hundreds of millions of dollars of investment into Weimar Germany.

Sturm directed the driver to stop as the long motorcar drew up in front of his destination on the Bowery in Lower Manhattan.

"Are you entirely certain this is where you wish to go, Sir?" the driver asked. "This is a rough neighborhood."

"It is bad?" Sturm asked.

"The worst. Dressed like you are now," the driver said, referring to Sturm's grey worsted three-piece suit with a razor-sharp crease in his trousers, "you'll be mugged for sure."

The driver came around to open the car door for Sturm. "Good luck, Sir. But you'd have better luck if you carried a weapon."

Sturm smiled and opened his jacket, revealing a polished leather holster which held his Mauser C-96 automatic pistol, chambered for 9 mm Parabellum cartridges. "I always do."

Sturm walked down the short flight of steps to the speakeasy's entrance. This would be the third time he had met the Irish team leader. He wasn't impressed by him either.

10:15 p.m.

Tommy McBride missed his Guinness. The flat, watery beer in Prohibition America just didn't match up to any beer in Ireland, let alone Guinness. McBride was sitting at a table in the rear of a long room, a speakeasy beneath the Blossom Restaurant on the Bowery in lower Manhattan. It was a workingman's saloon, a loud piano playing in one corner, a long wooden bar running along the right side of the room. The noise level was raucous. McBride pulled his pocket watch out of his vest pocket. Most of the men had been drinking steadily since they arrived when their shifts at the docks ended at 4:00 p.m. or 5:00 p.m. Ten p.m. was far too soon for most of them to stagger home to their families, those that had them.

McBride and two of his men had arrived thirty minutes earlier. Tommy had tipped the bartender well for a secluded booth in a corner of the room. McBride had positioned himself so that he could observe the entrance. The two men with him sat at an adjacent table. They were dressed in work clothes, unlike McBride, who wore a suit. It was well-pressed and had seen many years of service. It easily could have come from a Sears Roebuck catalog ten years ago.

McBride had met Sturm on two other occasions in Europe, once in Berlin and again in London. He was uncharacteristically late for this meeting. McBride looked again at his watch. As he returned it to his pocket, he saw the entrance door being opened by the burly guard who determined who would be permitted access.

Sturm had arrived. Tall, blond, good-looking, self-assured to the point of arrogance. McBride couldn't stand him. He watched as Sturm slipped a bill to the doorman and began to make his way across the room to McBride's booth. Halfway across the room, McBride saw Sturm bumped by one of the men at the bar. The noise was too loud in the room for McBride to hear what was being said, but it was obvious the Irish laborers were making fun of Sturm's Saville Row clothing. Sturm did not appear disturbed and was taking the ribbing with a good nature. Then, one of the men behind Sturm shoved him hard. Instantly, Sturm whirled and before the man's laugh had faded into silence, Sturm grasped the man's wrist with his right hand, the elbow with his other, and with one wrenching movement, using the elbow as a fulcrum, fluidly pushed the man's wrist back until it snapped. McBride thought he had heard the snap, but he certainly heard the howls of the man as he bent over in pain, clutching his dangling wrist.

Two of the injured man's companions grabbed Sturm from behind. Sturm's right elbow immediately flew out, smashing into the face of the man holding him on the right. McBride then watched in amazement as Sturm dipped under the man on his left, threw him over his shoulder so that he landed on his back, and then, with the same maneuver of grasping the wrist and the elbow, snapped that man's wrist as well, a sound clearly heard by McBride and everyone else in the room. The time elapsed since the first man had pushed

Sturm until the second wrist was broken was fifteen seconds. That was enough time for the doorman, a baseball bat clutched firmly in his meaty right hand, to have approached the huddled group of three broken men and Sturm, who by now had drawn his Mauser, holding off three other men advancing on him, one of whom had pulled a knife.

"Here, now, we'll have none of that," the bouncer said, taking a left-handed swing of which Babe Ruth would have been proud and slammed it against the shoulder of the man holding the knife. The man cried out, his arm numbed by the force of the blow and the knife clattered harmlessly onto the floor, his fingers no longer functioning.

"I'm sorry you were bothered, sir," he said to Sturm, who holstered his weapon and picked up the knife, handing it butt first to the doorman.

"I'll be taking care of this lot for you, sir, you won't be bothered again." Whereupon, using the bat as a prod, he moved the four men up to their feet and marched them out.

Sturm slid in the booth across from him and McBride noted that he had not worked up a sweat, hair still neatly combed, tie still held firmly in place by the collar pin beneath it. McBride still couldn't stand him but reluctantly admitted that he had been impressed. The Kraut could take care of himself. On McBride's previous two encounters with Sturm, he had sensed Sturm's competence if only from his rigid military bearing. He now knew there was both skill and ruthlessness to go with it. He wondered for a moment if the show had been for his benefit. But the thought quickly passed. McBride knew he could be just as ruthless as the German bastard sitting across from him casually ordering a Ballentine's and water from a hovering waiter.

"Charming place you chose for our rendezvous, McBride. The real New York."

"My fault," McBride said. "Wasn't it me who never thought to tell you not to dress like you were going out for fucking afternoon tea?"

Sturm ignored the comment and stared evenly at McBride. "To business, then. The money. I want to know about the money, Irishman."

"And I want to know about the fucking guns," McBride shot back, tensing to reach for his own pistol as he saw Sturm place his hand inside the jacket of his suit. He relaxed again when Sturm pulled out a long suede leather envelope and slid it across the table.

McBride picked up the soft leather envelope and removed the papers from inside. Invoices and purchase orders: Pacific Arms Corporation, San Francisco. Colt Firearms in Hartford, Connecticut. Winchester & Marlin in New Haven. Remington, and Savage in New York. Hercules Powder Company in Wilmington. Austin Powder in Cleveland.

McBride couldn't believe it. Jesus, Mary and Joseph! It was fucking Christmas Day and Jolly Old Saint Nick had just filled their bloody stockings to overflowing. Grenades. Browning automatic rifles and machine guns. Model 1911 Colt .45 automatic pistols. Thompson submachine guns. Rifle grenade launchers. Mortars. Browning M2 heavy machine guns. Pack Howitzers. They could start a bloody war with all this. They bloody well *would* start a war.

McBride returned the papers to the leather folder and pushed it back across the table to Sturm. "Impressive. Quite thorough. It will do nicely."

"Yes, it will," said Sturm. "But only if the funds are properly transferred to the correct accounts in Cleveland, Chicago and San Francisco. If that doesn't happen, the weapons will go nowhere except straight back to their manufacturers."

McBride didn't like being lectured and replied impatiently, "I know. Don't worry."

"Ah, but I do worry, my Irish friend. My superiors pay me well to worry about all the details. I will say this only once. You will take me to the man who is to arrange the wire transfers. You will demonstrate to my satisfaction that he understands completely the order, sequence and timing of the transfers," Sturm said in a slow and careful voice.

McBride knew Sturm was addressing him as if he were some retarded relative who had to have things explained in a simple way. He struggled to keep his anger beneath the surface. No need to complicate things. "It's our money, not yours. I know what the instructions are."

"You are wrong, Mr. McBride. At the end of the day it is *our* money. You know what's been arranged. But our time table is rigid. We can afford no delays. We meet with your Mr. O'Brien tomorrow night. If he is as well-instructed as you claim, it should not take long."

McBride did not like taking orders from anyone. Not the IRA. Not Sinn Fein. Not Dev. And certainly not this arrogant German. But in the end, German money was going to buy the arms and the money he had helped de Valera raise in America for the war with the British was going to be returned. With interest of $1 million going to Dev. Still, he didn't have to like it.

"Okay, okay, you win. He's a busy guy, our Mr. O'Brien. I'll give him a call tomorrow and see what we can work out."

"Tonight, Mr. McBride. Call him tonight. Schedule the meeting at O'Brien's home in White Plains at 7:00 p.m. tomorrow. Make it so," Sturm said, as he rose from the table, picked the leather envelope up from the table and smoothly slide it into his inside coat pocket. Turning on his heel, he walked out of the speakeasy. As he left, McBride saw Sturm slip another bill to the burly doorman whose crooked features broke into a smile as he pocketed the currency.

11:00 p.m.

Sturm quickly located Cromwell's waiting limousine and settled in for the ride uptown to the Plaza. The Irish were so easily fooled. At the end of the day, it was their money at risk, not the Geneva Group's. And the risk was real. Sturm had persuaded his masters that the *Graf Zeppelin* was the safest ship in the air. Which it was. But the voyage on which it was to embark tomorrow from Lakehurst was unprecedented and fraught with peril, especially the portion over the vast, uncharted wilderness of Siberia. If the ship went down there, it was doomed. Sturm hadn't told the Geneva Group that, just as Dr. Eckener hadn't told his partner, Mr. Hearst. If the *Graf* and the gold bearer bonds were lost, however, Geneva had no intention of doubling its bet. The Irish would have to pay for their own revolution and he would find a new diversion for the British.

Sturm had debarked from the *Graf* a few hours earlier with a sense of regret. He had conceived the mission to America as well as the unique method of delivering the bearer bonds. He fully intended that his capable second-in-command, Bruno Kordt, would lead the mission on the ground here while Sturm kept the bonds safe as they journeyed with him around the world.

Regrettably, a higher authority had intervened, persuading Sturm that he would be more useful in America than on the *Graf*. A disappointed Sturm had agreed with the logic of this and the short voyage to America just ended had been his consolation prize. Zurich, the chairman of the Geneva Group and Berlin, not Sturm, would have the high honor of being passengers on the first airship to circumnavigate the globe. Sturm was left with newspaper accounts and newsreels.

8.

The Night Train to Montreal

New York City
Friday, 9 August 1929
11:15 p.m.

Cockran walked briskly across the concourse of Grand Central Station toward Track 28 where the New York Central Montreal Limited, Train Number 61, was waiting to depart. The fracas in Central Park had made him late and the pain in his ribs slowed him down. He passed through the entrance to Track 28, showed his ticket to the gatekeeper and was directed to the second Pullman car on the train. He stepped up onto the train, and handed his overnight bag to the Pullman porter who, glancing at the ticket, said, "This way, sir. Compartment Seven."

In his haste, Cockran did not notice the man who had followed him into the station and saw him enter the gate on Track 28. Once the man saw Cockran board the train, he hurried back out to the row of telephone booths in the main concourse, entered one, closed the door and placed his call. "He's on the night train to Montreal, like we thought."

Cockran followed the porter down the narrow passage. He opened the door to Number Seven and stepped back to let Cockran enter. The porter followed and placed his bag on the floor beside the wash basin. "We leave promptly at 11:30, sir, and we arrive in downtown Montreal at 8:37 a.m. The dining car will be open for breakfast at 6:00 a.m. Is there anything else I can do for you?"

"Yes, please," Cockran said, handing him a quarter. "Some ice and a pitcher of water."

"Very good, sir."

Cockran opened the satchel and pulled out a clear crystal tumbler and a fifth of Johnnie Walker Red. A moment later, the porter knocked on the door and delivered the ice and water. Cockran pulled the blind down to shield his compartment from prying eyes outside and poured two fingers into the tumbler, added ice and water. Taking four aspirin, he took a long sip and gingerly settled back in the compartment's comfortable seat. A few moments later, he heard the conductor's "All aboard!" cry and felt the first lurch of the engine as the train slowly pulled out.

Cockran thought back to the cocktail party. Obviously, Cromwell didn't remember him. They had never met but Cockran knew too well who Philip Dru Cromwell was. A prominent fund raiser for Hoover in the last election, Cromwell had held one of the top three posts in the Inquiry. Located in unmarked offices at the American Geographical Society's headquarters at 155th Street and Broadway, the Inquiry had been formed in the fall of 1917 at the direction of President Wilson and his right-hand man, Colonel House. Anticipating victory, the President set up his own intelligence arm, independent of the State Department and operated in strict secrecy, to prepare him for dealing with post-war issues which would arise at the peace conference. It was the Inquiry which had drafted Wilson's Fourteen Points.

Cockran's position at the Inquiry was more modest. After Cockran had been wounded in the war, both Cockran's father and Bill Donovan had used their influence to have the young infantry intelligence captain transferred back to the United States where, after his leg had healed, he eventually was assigned to the Inquiry's Irish Section. Authors of the staff reports produced by the Inquiry for the President were never identified. Once a report made it past the Section Chief, one of three men had to approve its transmittal to Wilson's Chief of Staff and alter ego, Col. Edward House. Without approval, the report died. Cromwell was one of those three men and Cockran had written the Irish Section's report, containing modest suggestions for Irish self-determination which mirrored those which the Inquiry had proposed in central Europe for the Czechs and Slovaks, carving an entirely new country, Czechoslovakia, out of the old Austro-Hungarian Empire.

Cromwell had vetoed the report "The U.S. cannot possibly side with the Irish against the English as it would place in severe jeopardy repayment of U.S. war loans to the Allied Powers. Besides, the Irish have demonstrated no capacity for self-government. REJECTED— PDC"

That little sojourn working for the Inquiry had been Cockran's only foray into politics and the internecine warfare rampant in wartime Washington. Watching his father while growing up, Cockran had not been attracted to the political life and the time he had spent with the Inquiry had confirmed his initial impressions. When the war was over, he had not returned to the law. Instead, he went to work for William Randolph Hearst's New York *American* where, as an investigative reporter, he could expose politicians; hold them up to the light of day; and occasionally send them to prison where he believed most of them belonged. Cockran smiled. He had been so good at it that Hearst had sent him to Dublin to be his chief European correspondent. There, he met Nora who was also a journalist.

Cockran winced once more as he shifted his weight and the pain returned. The assault wasn't an accident. It was a warning. They weren't out to rob him. They left his billfold behind. But a warning about what and from whom? The IRA? Probably. He was certain now there was a link between the attack and the break-ins at Columbia and The Cedars. Anyway, morning would come soon enough and, with it, his meeting with Winston. What did Winston know about the IRA? And what did he want? His mind wandered as he thought of Mattie. Red hair and a journalist, just like Nora. And with both Mattie and Nora on his mind, he turned down the covers and drifted off to sleep, lulled by the comforting sound of the train and the rails.

9.

Can You Ask Around?

Montreal
Saturday, 10 August 1929
9:00 a.m.

The taxi dropped Cockran off at the Mount Royale Hotel on Rue Ste. Catherine near Peale Street. With 1046 rooms, it was the largest hotel in the British Empire. The lobby was three stories high with vaulted ceilings, skylights and a balcony running around three sides of the room. Huge potted palms, themselves over a story high, were massed at either end of the room. The doorman greeted him, took his overnight case and handed it to a nearby bellhop, who held the brass-plated door open for him as he walked to the front desk and asked for Mr. Churchill. Five minutes later, Cockran was sitting across from his old friend in the spacious living room of Churchill's tenth floor corner suite with a commanding view sweeping from the foot of Mount Royal down to the St. Lawrence River, a full English breakfast between them..

"Bourke, my boy! How are you? How was your journey? It's so good to see you again," Churchill enthused.

He was fine, Cockran assured him, as was the trip.

Then the monologue commenced. "I have a delightful lunch planned for us. It's in the old section. Auberge Le Vieux Ste.-Gabrielle. Authentic Québécois food. My brother, Jack, has the other bedroom here. He and our two sons, Randolph and Johnny, are out this morning exploring Mount Royal Park. Did you know that the architect who designed the park is the same one who did your Central Park in New York? What was his name?"

Cockran nodded. "Frederick Olmsted. He's done parks in Boston and Philadelphia as well. You really should see it yourself. Montreal is his best work by far. So much of Central Park is artificial. But here he worked with what nature gave him and harmonized it."

The conversation continued in this vein for ten minutes, Churchill's mind flitting from one topic to another with Cockran along for the ride, exchanging information about their sons, the weather on Churchill's ocean voyage, the wonders of Quebec City where Churchill and his party had stayed the night before, the American stock market and how wealthy it was making him, the lucrative writing contracts Churchill had with several London publications, and the sales of *The Aftermath*, the final installment in Churchill's history of the Great War.

The reference to *The Aftermath* prompted a comment from Cockran regarding the three chapters in it on Ireland and Michael Collins. Cockran briefly sketched for Churchill the nature of the book he was writing on his time in 1921 as a go-between and asked whether he could review the correspondence between Collins and Churchill after the war.

Churchill readily agreed and was soon off to other subjects. He abruptly stopped, however, when he reached a description of his plans in California, including a stay at Hearst's country home, San Simeon and his offer to Churchill of $2,000 an article.

"There's more than money involved in my visit to Hearst." Churchill paused, pursing his lips. "It's bad business, Bourke." Churchill then proceeded to outline for Cockran all that he had learned from the Prime Minister about the IRA and what he hoped to accomplish in his meeting with President Hoover at San Simeon. "The President is going to be in California to welcome the airship crew which Hearst is sponsoring on their journey around the world. I hope to have a full report for Mr. Hoover by that time."

While Churchill talked, Cockran's face conveyed no emotion. His courtroom face. Inside, he was skeptical. It couldn't be happening. The sums were staggering. They were talking millions of dollars. Still, what did Churchill want from him?

"We've alerted the Free State authorities," Churchill said. "They are grateful for our concern, but their resources are quite limited, their army almost nonexistent and their intelligence capability even worse. They said they would be grateful for whatever we could do."

Cockran eyed Churchill warily. "Exactly how do you think I can help, Winston?"

"A team of SIS agents traveling with me," Churchill replied, "will be conducting a fact-finding mission while I tour Canada. They are to meet me in San Francisco to brief me on what they have found so that I can enlist your President's aid."

Churchill had evaded his question but Cockran persisted, "Where do I come in?"

"As you can appreciate, I am not without my own resources in America and I would like to supplement what the SIS are doing. Some of my own people. Ones I can trust." Churchill paused and lit a cigar. "We were always concerned about the strength of American support for the IRA during the war with Ireland, and it was most gratifying after the Treaty to find most of your countrymen supporting Michael Collins and the Free State. Our people thought there would be bitter division between Irish Americans just as there was between the IRA and the Free State. Collins told me it would never happen. He was right and it made all the difference. The Irregulars were cut off from their major sources of funding. They got no money from America ."

Exactly, Cockran thought, because I killed the three men who had the checkbooks.

Churchill paused again, taking a sip from a very weak whiskey and water.

Cockran took advantage of the pause. Who knew how long the monologue would last otherwise? "Winston, for the third time, what do you want from me?"

"What I want, Bourke, is for you to help us find where the money is coming from. How can the Irish in America be doing this now when seven years ago they wanted no part of the IRA? I know you have contacts in the Irish American community, just as your father did. Possibly even the *Clan na Gael.* Can you ask around? Make a few inquiries?"

Cockran chose his words carefully. He didn't want to offend his old friend. "Your intelligence wasn't that good in the war, Winston, and it's no better today. The IRA is not and could not be raising money in America. Someone sold your SIS boys a bill of goods."

"I disagree," Churchill said quietly. "Your point is well taken about the quality of our intelligence, but we still have some good sources. Michael Collins didn't kill them all. The information is from one of those sources, and we take it very seriously. Please reconsider."

Cockran shook his head firmly. "I'm out of that business, Winston. I can't save the world. I'm thirty-four years old. I have a son and I once promised his mother to turn my *Atlantic* articles into a book. But that's all I'll ever have to do with Ireland. Write a book. I'm not going back. Ever. The memories are too painful. And I'm certainly not going off on a wild goose chase for the SIS."

"I understand your feelings, and I sympathize with them," Churchill said, his voice softer. "I did not mean to unduly impose on an old friend whose grief I still share. I feel deeply about the Free State. As one of its founding fathers, I feel the same concern of any parent to see his child grow, prosper and live well in peace and harmony. You have been very kind to come all this way, Bourke, and I appreciate it. Think over what I have said, and if you reconsider, please tell me after lunch. Otherwise, I shan't bring it up, and perhaps we can begin our talks for your book. I have many stories about Michael Collins I haven't told you."

10.

Blood and Steel

Lake Constance, Germany
Saturday, 10 August 1929
7:30 p.m.

A series of long closed motor cars, Mercedes and Daimlers mostly, began to arrive at a large estate on the shores of Lake Constance. It was a clear, crisp evening and the sound of the tires of the cars crunching the carefully combed stone in the driveway was louder than the silent purring of the engines in the expensive vehicles. Each motor car contained only one passenger. A total of nine vehicles were scheduled to arrive, precisely two minutes apart.

This was a special meeting, the first of four scheduled in the next twelve months to outline and help refine the plans for implementing the Dresden Protocol. The initial arrival, known to the others as Zurich, was greeted warmly by his host, Berlin, who maintained the Lake Constance house as a summer retreat. Zurich watched as each new man was greeted in turn by those who arrived before him. The servants were there to take their outer garments and serve them Pol Roger champagne in tall, crystal flutes. The meeting had been arranged at this location for the convenience of both Zurich and Berlin who would be departing in a few days from nearby Friedrichschafen on the German portion of the *Graf Zeppelin*'s around-the-world flight. The two would have with them $4 million U.S. in gold bearer bonds for delivery to the Irish terrorists in

California, the Geneva Group's insurance policy for the success of the invasion of Poland. The only ones missing today were the two men in charge of the IRA arms deal—Geneva's U.S. member, Manhattan, and its executive director, Kurt von Sturm.

After gathering in the large, octagonal foyer, Berlin directed them into the Great Hall where they continued to converse in small groups. The room had a massive, barrel-vaulted ceiling, two stories high. Paintings and tapestries lined the wood-paneled walls on the first floor. There was a balcony on the second floor on all four sides of the room. The second-floor walls were lined from floor to ceiling with bookcases, indirect lighting casting a warm glow on the figures talking softly below. A fire was blazing in a huge fire place at the end of the room.

Zurich accepted a single malt as more substantial drinks were served. Like all the men, he was in black tie. They varied in age from their mid-forties to late seventies. Together, Zurich knew, they provided the financing, the tooling, the raw materials for the manufacture of armaments. Zurich was the chairman of the largest private bank in Switzerland. Tall and white-haired, with a trim black moustache, he had served as Chairman of the Geneva Institute for Scientific and Industrial Progress, known internally and informally as the Geneva Group, since shortly after its founding over thirty years earlier.

The Geneva Group had been formed in the early 1890s as a secret society of European financiers and industrialists ostensibly dedicated to scientific research. Initially, and what all conceded by now was merely a nineteenth-century affectation, they had given themselves code names. Nothing complicated nor difficult to penetrate. They merely adopted the names of the great cities from which they came. Amsterdam, Stockholm, Brussels, Milan, Madrid, Berlin, Munich, Vienna, and Zurich. It was a tradition that had been passed down to the current group.

Zurich knew it was fortunate he had assumed his position at such a young age. Unlike his elders and his ill-fated predecessor, he knew what had to be done. Control change. Guide the future. Stabilize profits. Not for them the laissez-faire example pioneered by

Great Britain. There were better and, for the men of Geneva, more profitable models.

Business had to form a partnership with government as had happened by the end of the century in both America and Bismarck's Germany. An arms build up, even an arms race between countries was an important and profitable part of this program. What were weapons for if not to be used? So, wars were to be encouraged. But only by proxy, through smaller nations who depended upon the "civilized" powers of Europe for their weapons and munitions. Supplies which members of the Geneva Group were happy to provide. For a price. In turn, as government stocks of arms and weapons were depleted in this manner, either in colonies or in small, faraway countries, newer generations of weapons would be created. Profits would continue. Their success, if not quite final, would endure.

Zurich glanced at his watch and signaled a nearby waiter for another single malt. One more wouldn't hurt, he thought, and then the meeting could begin. Zurich still felt a pang of regret for 1914. Zurich and the rest of the Geneva Group never saw the war coming. 1914 was a mistake. A profitable mistake, but a mistake nonetheless because the chaos created in the war's aftermath threatened to undo all that they had built.

When the carnage was over and the profits had been made, Zurich vowed it would never happen again. He recognized that changes had to be made and he moved swiftly, decisively, brutally. When he was finished, over half the members of Geneva were removed and younger members were chosen. Even an American member to replace the purged French member as well as a ruthless executive director with equally ruthless men at his disposal. And so it started again. The same formula, the same results. The war to end all wars had not and the Geneva Group was back. Small conflicts. Little wars. Controllable. Profitable. The ancient hatreds were still intact; money was still there to be made. The business of the Geneva Group was blood and steel and business was good.

Zurich drained the last of his single malt, placed it on a silver tray held by a hovering servant, and started to move to the large table which dominated the center of the room. He had taken only two steps when he was intercepted by the member known as Munich. Zurich sighed inwardly. He knew what was coming. He had heard it all before. A plea to place on the meeting's agenda the issue of financial support for Adolf Hitler's National Socialists. After removing the Jew Trotsky from the Ministry of War, Stalin was now a confirmed anti-Semite. Support for Hitler, Munich claimed, would no longer jeopardize the Dresden Protocol.

Zurich feigned attention as Munich babbled on. For four long years, Munich had been regularly raising the tiresome subject of the Austrian corporal. Zurich wondered, not for the first time, if he had made a mistake ten years ago in not purging Munich from the group as he had with the others. Zurich motioned to Vienna to join them and repeated what Munich had said.

"What is your opinion?" he asked.

"With all respect, Munich has been bringing up this topic every year since Hitler was let out of jail in 1925, and we have always given him the same answer," Vienna replied.

"That doesn't mean the answers were correct," Munich responded. "You've never seen this man handle a crowd. He's masterful. A coming force! *Herr* Hitler is a great leader."

"Nonsense," Vienna said. "Austria was happy to see him leave. I mean, what has he done, really? Attempted a *coup d'etat* in 1923 from a beer hall in Munich, only to have his pitiful band of 3,000 storm troopers routed by a Bavarian police force of a few hundred men? He took a sabbatical in jail and wrote a barely literate book blaming all Germany's problems on the Jews. Of course, he does wear decent suits; he's learned to use a fork properly; and he speaks well enough to render peasants in Bavaria spellbound." Vienna took a breath, visibly calming himself. "But he is still a rabble rouser, a small-time politician. Nothing more."

"Apparently not a very good one either," Amsterdam added politely, as he joined the group. "The undeniably enthusiastic crowds which greet his speeches apparently do not vote in very large numbers. Only twelve seats in the Reichstag election a year ago last May."

Zurich had heard enough. "No one agrees with you, Munich. Hitler is all talk, no substance. He has had four years to prove himself since restrictions were lifted on his party and he has done nothing. Such men rarely affect history. They are carried along by the currents of time. So the answer with respect to *Herr* Hitler is simple. Do nothing. Ignore him if you wish, watch him if you must. He will soon be carried along by the currents, like all politicians."

Zurich took a puff on his cigar, and exhaled the smoke toward the ceiling. "Perhaps he will bob to the surface from time to time. Perhaps he will drown. But we have far more important matters to attend to than petty German politics. They will sort themselves out in due course. Of that you can be sure."

Zurich excused himself and took his place at the head of the table. He rapped his heavy fountain pen on its mahogany surface to gain the group's attention. The servants withdrew. Social amenities were over. The meeting of the Board of Directors of the Geneva Institute for Scientific and Industrial Progress had begun. There were only two items on the agenda. Both concerned the Dresden Protocol. First was an update on their plans for a *coup d'etat* in the Irish Free State. Second, and far more important, was Zurich's projection for the profits to be made from supplying the weapons and munitions to the Reichswehr and the Red Army as they finalized their secret plans to erase Poland from the map of Europe—the first step in Germany's revenge for what had been done to it at Versailles.

11.

A New Request

Cockran and Churchill walked along Rue Sherbrooke over to Rue Ste. Laurent where they turned right and continued down towards the river and their luncheon engagement, Churchill's walking stick tapping the pavement in time with his steps. The street was wide, tree-lined and the sun glistened off the pale green copper-peaked roofs of the six story high buildings. Neither noticed the well-dressed man behind them making notations in a small notebook.

Fifteen minutes later, they arrived in front of Auberge Le Vieux Ste.-Gabrielle, which occupied a large building of rough stone, old wood and gabled roofs. Churchill gave his name to the *maitre d'* who directed them to a large high-ceilinged room with exposed rough-hewn beams. Along the walls were a collection of snowshoes, a Wurlitzer music machine and carved wood reliefs from St. Jean-Port-Joli. Churchill spoke French to the waiter and, while Cockran didn't know French, he could tell from the waiter's expression that Churchill was speaking it badly.

Cockran had not changed his mind. He wasn't going to get involved. While in Ireland, he had his fill at being a chess piece in someone else's game, usually a pawn. That was why he had left

Hearst and taken the job teaching international law at Columbia. There, it was his game. They were his courses, his students, his research and his articles. He was responsible. He was in control. When things went wrong, he had only himself to blame. He didn't depend on others. That was just how he liked it.

Churchill's request was innocent enough on its surface but he knew Winston and he knew that, however innocuous it seemed, it was only the thin edge of the wedge. Basically, Churchill's plan was flawed. Too many others to depend upon. Two weeks was not nearly enough time to do any good if the IRA really were mounting a major arms buying operation.

Cockran touched his still tender ribs to remind himself he might be wrong. It could have been the IRA. But how had they known of Churchill's cable? Had the Brits been careless? "Even if your intelligence sources are correct, why do you think the American government will care?" Cockran asked as Churchill took a bite of Galantine of Pheasant Aux Chanterelles.

"This is excellent, really excellent!" Churchill said and took a long sip of champagne. "Why wouldn't the Americans care? Hasn't Ireland always been important to them?"

Cockran was becoming impatient. Ireland important? Not really. After all, every U.S. President after Grover Cleveland, his father once told him, had been in bed with big business, the only possible exception being his father's Long Island friend and neighbor, Theodore Roosevelt. Cockran, Sr. would have made the point in a more partisan way by simply referring to Republican administrations which had been in power continuously since Cleveland left the White House in 1896. Except for the brief and lamentable eight-year reign of the man H. L. Mencken once labeled the "Archangel Woodrow." Big business so loved Woodrow Wilson and all he did for them that he might as well have been a Republican for all the good it did the common man. At least that's what Cockran's father had said. Given the unprecedented prosperity which had prevailed during the 20s, Cockran didn't think Hoover cared whether American arms makers reaped whatever profit they could from any new blood that might be shed in Ireland. Catholics in general and Irish Americans in particular simply weren't that important politically to Hoover. They had backed the wrong presidential candidate last fall. Why couldn't Churchill see that?

"Only the politics, Winston. The Democrats never objected to IRA fund-raising when Wilson was in power because Irish Catholics in the big cities were an important part of their power base. They weren't about to interfere with a key constituency. The Republicans have been in power for the last eight years, and they don't care for the opposite reason. Their strength is not in the big cities. It's in big business. The manufacturers who make the arms. So they're not going to lift a finger to stop this commerce, especially when they think all you Brits want to do is renege on your war loans. Let's face it. If we didn't care when Ireland was part of the United Kingdom, why should we care now when it's only a dominion like Canada or Australia?"

"That's not fair," Churchill protested. "Great Britain has done its best to be a good friend to the United States. I can't begin to tell you how much valuable time I wasted as Chancellor on that subject. And unlike the French or the other Allies, we British have made all of our interest payments to you on time. Every single one. No one else has done that. No one. And if your government had listened to your father's wise advice in 1917, the loans would have been treated as gifts and reparations wouldn't be the obstacle to genuine reconciliation they are today."

"That may be...," Cockran said.

"Wait, there's more," said Churchill, interrupting. "You Americans foolishly have it in your mind that disarmament is the way to achieve peace. Your father knew better. And yet your country's latest idea of disarmament is to decommission more British ships of the line in exchange for you Americans building fewer new ships. Our Admiralty resisted and, privately, I thought them right. But at the Exchequer, I was responsible for our budget and I had to cut expenses wherever I could. You Americans made it easy for me. But mark my words, you'll pay a terrible price some day. You have lived well and prospered in this country because of the strength of the British Navy, not your own."

"Actually, I don't necessarily disagree with you" Cockran replied, "but I don't see what that has to do..."

"Don't interrupt me," Churchill said, "and you'll soon understand. Our Prime Minister is visiting the President in October specifically on the subject of more naval disarmament. You Americans have sunk more British battleships than the Germans, and now you want to go after our cruisers. We're not going to be as easy as before but we will make a few concessions. I don't know how far Ramsay will go. But, with me as Ramsay's representative, your President can hardly turn down this small favor, not when he needs our good will in October."

"Why not have the Prime Minister make the request himself?" Cockran asked.

Churchill looked up at Cockran with an expression on his face conveying utter disbelief. "I thought you taught international law. Don't you understand that if the Prime Minister makes the request personally, a *quid pro quo* is certain to follow? We could well have to give up two cruisers in exchange for the President's help. That just wouldn't do. It wouldn't do at all. Besides," Churchill continued, "your economy is the marvel of the world and your President Hoover talks seriously of ending poverty as we know it. He treasures his role as a man of peace. Why would he not want to keep Ireland at peace?"

"His power is not that great in this area," Cockran replied. "He can't even stop Chicago gangsters from buying Mr. Thompson's submachine guns. So, if the IRA is out to buy weapons in the U.S., there's not much the federal authorities can do to stop them. American arms makers have a long history of selling their products to South American countries and revolutionaries alike. All it takes is cold, hard cash. Don't forget what Coolidge said, 'the business of America is business.' Even Democrats don't disagree with that, and I can guarantee that President Hoover doesn't disagree. He's more in bed with business than Coolidge ever was."

Their main course arrived, tournedos of rare beef for Churchill, rack of lamb, medium rare, for Cockran. Churchill switched from champagne and ordered a bottle of claret while Cockran continued to press his position with Churchill. "You know more of politics than me, including international politics. But if the IRA are buying guns and ammunition in America, they're not doing it with money they raised here. I know that for a fact."

"Why is that, pray tell?"

"John Devoy," Cockran replied.

"I've heard that name." Churchill said.

"You have. He's the old Fenian who was the secret head of *Clan na Gael* throughout the Anglo-Irish War." Cockran said. "You would think he would be the first to be behind something like this. And not for the first time about the Irish would you be wrong."

"I didn't even know he was still alive," Churchill said, "Tell me more."

"It all goes back to de Valera's fund raising in America in 1920. Devoy and Judge Cohalan had united all the Irish American groups." Cockran paused, sipped his wine, and continued. "You British and your Black and Tans had brought us together in a way we had never done. Devoy and the Judge had it lined up so that both major U.S. parties were going to pass planks at their conventions that summer for Irish self-determination. Both the conventions were wired. Even though Wilson had betrayed us, the Democrats had to go along because they couldn't publicly denounce self-determination. Republicans were in the same boat."

Churchill nodded thoughtfully. "I wasn't aware of this. That would have been decidedly untimely. Please go on."

"Exactly. Until de Valera stepped in. He couldn't stand to share the credit with anyone else, even an old Fenian like John Devoy. Anyway, de Valera quibbled over the language drafted by Devoy and Cohalan. It was carefully written to pass muster with both parties. They couldn't change a word without jeopardizing support. Once one party passed it, the other would have had no choice. But de Valera insisted upon submitting his own resolution to both conventions in competition with Devoy and Cohalan. Same purpose. Different words. Dev's words. So the Irish lost unity once again and neither convention passed a resolution on Irish self-determination."

"Well, you have had the floor for some time, my young friend." Churchill said gently. "Pray explain what all of this has to do with the problem at hand."

"It's easy. When the Irish delegation to the peace negotiations had produced no more than the Free State, a member of the British Commonwealth taking an oath to the King, no one here expected Devoy to support it. Without a Republic, everyone thought the old man would condemn the Treaty. They were wrong and nothing pleased Mick more than when Devoy endorsed it. He had the same vision as Mick. The treaty was a stepping stone to freedom. He condemned Cathal Brugha, Connie Markowitz and Dev in his weekly newspaper for placing their egos above the cause of Irish freedom."

Cockran brushed a thick lock of hair from his forehead and then continued. "John Devoy is very much alive, and there is no way that the IRA could begin to attempt to raise money in America without Devoy finding out. John Devoy is fearless. Once he found out IRA fund raising was going on, nothing could stop him from broadcasting it all over the Irish American community through his newspaper and condemning the IRA for the lunatics they are. But John Devoy has written nothing. If your sources are right about arms buying in America, and I don't think they are, the money wasn't and isn't being raised here."

"I had no idea you and Devoy were so close," Churchill replied. "You know him well?"

"I do. He and my father were good friends despite their differences. I've probably seen more of him since Dad died. He's a grand old man and I enjoy his company."

Churchill pursed his lips and then locked his eyes on Cockran. "I promised I would not bring the subject up again without your leave. But you have given me information of which I was previously unaware and, had I known it, I would have made a different request than I did earlier. May I make a new request now?"

Cockran nodded his assent and Churchill continued. "Our intelligence sources are of the highest quality. I have made my own inquiries and am satisfied of that. But your point on John Devoy is well taken. Would you be so kind as to lodge an inquiry with him?

Nothing more. He may have heard things but discarded them because of their improbability. But if there are rumors circulating out there which have not been enough for him to go public in his paper, perhaps confirmation from British intelligence will crystallize these rumors. And if he has heard nothing, I agree with your conclusion that money is not being raised in America. Will you at least do that? Talk with John Devoy?"

Cockran shook his head. Winston was clever. He had deliberately not disclosed his meeting yesterday with Devoy and now Churchill was asking him only to do what he had already set in motion. How could he say no? After all, he was meeting Devoy anyway.

"Well, I'm having a dinner with him Sunday. I'm sure I'll be able to find a way to bring it up in the course of an evening."

"Splendid, Bourke, splendid! Thanks ever so much. Send a wire or telephone me in Toronto. We'll be at the Royal York."

12.

You Were Warned

Montreal
Saturday, 10 August 1929
3:50 p.m.

A taxi took Cockran to the rail station where he boarded the Montreal Limited Number 10 and made his way to the club car and settled into a comfortable leather chair. Given the abundance of available brands arrayed behind the polished mahogany bar, he ordered a Bushmill's with water and began to make notes on Winston's stories about Michael Collins.

Cockran glanced at his watch. It was 3:55 p.m. and the train had left Montreal at 2:50 p.m. Within ten minutes they would cross the border and switch engines at Rouses Point, New York. He finished his Bushmill's, ordered a refill and returned to his Pullman compartment.

Cockran opened the door to his compartment and saw the contents of his suitcase strewn on his bed and a large man bent over the bed. "Hey! What the hell do you think you're doing?"

The man turned and Cockran caught a glimpse of a weapon in the intruder's hand as he quickly closed the gap between them and pressed the weapon's barrel firmly into Cockran's side.

"You were warned but you . . ."

The sentence went uncompleted as the train lurched and Cockran felt the barrel move off the mark. He brought his right foot down hard on the man's ankle, knocking him off balance. Turning, Cockran grasped the wrist of the man's hand which still held a Walther P38 with a long six-inch silencer attached to the barrel. As the train lurched again sending them both into the side of the compartment, he pressed his thumbs into pressure points on the man's wrist and slammed the gun into the wall. The man tried to lift his knee to force Cockran back but his weight kept the man in place as he slammed the gun against the wall for a third time. The pistol dropped to the floor and bounced through the still open compartment door. The intruder bolted after his weapon but only managed to kick it with his foot down the corridor. Before he could retrieve it, Cockran leaped on his back but the man slipped from his grasp. Cockran jumped to his feet and found himself standing in the passageway between the man and his weapon.

Cockran had a good look at the man now, his narrow face twisted in anger. He was several inches taller than Cockran and easily outweighed him by thirty pounds. The top half of the rail car door was open and Cockran could feel the cool air on his back as the man lowered his head and rushed at Cockran just as the train entered a long dark tunnel. The impact of the collision drove Cockran back several feet and pain lanced through his tender ribs. The man's hands reached out and Cockran felt them close around his throat. As the man's grip tightened, Cockran jabbed two of his fingers stiffly into the man's right eye, the man howled in pain and slapped a hand over his eye. Cockran reversed their positions and threw the man against the half-open door. Before he could recover, Cockran grabbed him by the knees, lifted up until the top half of the man's body was leaning precariously over the door. Then, with one last heave, Cockran pushed him over the top with arms flailing. Cockran heard a dull thud in the dark as the man hit the ground below. He picked up the gun and threw it out just as the train left the tunnel and emerged into sunlight.

The time elapsed was less than two minutes. Cockran was astonished their struggle had not attracted the attention of the porter or his fellow passengers. Thirty seconds later, Cockran was back in his own compartment. He poured himself two fingers of scotch and pulled out a fountain pen to see if it was possible to make more corrections to his manuscript. It wasn't. His adrenaline level was too high, his suspicions even higher.

13.

You Arrested Herbert Hoover!

Mattie McGary was not happy. The reason why blared out at her in bold headlines from an air mail copy of Hearst's *New York American* sitting there on the coffee table of the Churchill brothers' suite at the Mount Royale.

GRAF OFF ON WORLD TOUR
AIR GIANT HEADS TO SEA FOR EPOCHAL SKY VOYAGE

EXCLUSIVE BY LADY HAY-DRUMMOND

FAMOUS CORRESPONDENT WHO IS TAKING
THE HEARST-ZEPPELIN ROUND-WORLD FLIGHT

Famous correspondent, my ass, Mattie thought. That trip should have been hers, not "Lady Grace", that social-climbing columnist with the double-barreled name acquired by marrying a man nearly fifty years older who conveniently passed away soon after. And it would have been hers had she not let Winston talk her into joining his adventure instead.

Mattie wondered when Winston's monologue would end. Churchill, dressed in a navy, pin-striped vested suit, wearing his ever-present blue polka dot bow tie, paced back and forth, pausing only occasionally to interrupt his flow of words by taking a sip of champagne, the chilled bottle sitting on the butler's table in the corner of the room.

"I've known Bourke since he was a small boy. His father was one of the wisest and most principled men I've ever known. That's why I don't understand Bourke's reaction. Look how helpful he was back in '21. I mean, we knew he worked for Collins. What young Irish American wouldn't? Even I would have worked for Collins had I been in Bourke's position. So I don't understand his reluctance to help the Free State in its time of need. Nay, his lack of enthusiasm." Churchill said as if, Mattie thought, that were a mortal sin in Churchill's eyes.

"What do you mean?" Mattie asked.

"Bourke is not as sound as his father. I can't quite put my finger on it but there's something there I don't completely trust. It probably started with his articles."

His articles?" Mattie asked. "What is it about his articles?"

"They betray a certain mind set common among Americans today of holding themselves aloof from the problems of Europe. Of calling for 'a free hand' in foreign policy. No allies. But it's no better for a country to cut itself off from the world than it is for a man."

Churchill paused and lit a cigar. "It's the articles about the Great War which give me the most pause. Let me show you. This one, from *American Mercury*, argues that United States sovereignty was infringed by the Royal Navy's blockade every bit as much as it was by German submarines. Imagine! Equating us with those wolf packs that killed innocent civilians.

"Or this one from *The Atlantic Monthly* which argues that America's and England's vital interests were not at stake in the war and that we both should have sat the war out. Without English or American intervention, he claims there would have been a negotiated peace in Europe. No Bolshevik revolution. No German revolution. No monarchies forced into democracy only to descend into dictatorships a few years later.

"I know the primary focus of his attack is on President Wilson's policies," Churchill continued, "but it tells me that we had best keep a close eye on young Cockran even if his help proves beneficial, however reluctantly it is offered. He lost his wife in that unnecessary civil war. A tragedy, but we simply can't know how committed he still is to the Free State."

Churchill paused and picked up his champagne flute. Mattie seized the opportunity, knowing that Churchill's monologue would otherwise continue unabated. "Winston, I only met Mr. Cockran at your request for a few hours the other night. He seemed to be a sensible, level-headed fellow with a good sense of humor. I don't find it at all surprising that he is reluctant to become involved in what you obviously perceive as an adventure. It's a considered, rational response. He has an eight-year-old son, for goodness' sake!

"But we're off the subject." She continued, "I think your Mr. Cockran is right."

"Pray tell me why," said Churchill as he resumed pacing.

"Apart from Cockran's excellent point that no American laws are being broken is the issue of Hoover himself." Mattie replied.

Churchill's face took on a quizzical look. "What issue is there with the President?"

Mattie laughed out loud and threw her napkin down on the table. "Don't you remember? I was only fifteen, but I remember it clearly. Like my first day of school as a child. It was all great fun because I knew the man who was First Lord of the Admiralty."

Mattie saw that Churchill's quizzical expression had vanished but the light of recognition had not blinked on in his eyes. "You don't remember, do you, Winston? You really don't."

"Well...," Churchill began, but Mattie interrupted.

"You arrested him! You arrested Herbert Hoover! You had bloody Naval intelligence arrest the future President of the United States in 1915 on corruption and espionage charges!"

An embarrassed look crept over Churchill. "My dear, I had nothing to do with that. Some over-enthusiastic intelligence agents As soon as the matter reached my desk, I put things right. We were in the middle of the Dardanelles operation. I had far more important matters on my plate than some do-good American trying to bring food to the starving citizens of Belgium."

Churchill paused for a moment and turned to Mattie, a sheepish look still on his face, and said, "You don't suppose the President remembers that, do you? Or would hold it against us? "

Mattie stood up from the damask-covered chair in which she had been dining and smoothed the front of her khaki trousers. She walked over to Churchill and gave him a hug. "You're a dear old man, Winston, and one of the nicest people I know. But you're really quite naive when it comes to how Americans think, especially for someone whose mother was an American."

"I'm not that old," Churchill replied defensively.

"No, my dear godfather, you're not," Mattie said. "But you still don't know Americans. Until your Navy did it fourteen years ago, I don't believe we Brits had ever arrested a future American president. He'll remember. Herbert Clark Hoover has never received a slight he didn't remember. That's what the Hearst reporters who cover the White House tell me."

"Well," Churchill began, his lower lip pushing forth in the beginnings of a pout, but Mattie interrupted again, clearly upsetting a man who was not used to being interrupted.

"Don't worry, Winston. I'm certain he would not let his personal feelings influence him in matters of state. But tell me more," she said, "about your Mr. Cockran. What will you do if he can't find where the IRA are raising their funds? Given what you told me a few moments ago, would you trust him to do anything more?"

Churchill smiled, and Mattie could see that he was happy she had given him an easy opportunity to resume the initiative in their conversation.

"I believe so. Anything more I ask Bourke to do will be strictly compartmentalized. Information will be given him on a need to know basis only. We will do so until we are certain, beyond doubt, of his commitment. Bourke will be fine. Mark my words. He comes from good stock. I am confident he will run to ground the funding question. Just as I'm equally confident, my dear, that you will be able to track down the companies who are in league with the devil against the Irish Free State. Once we do that, the President will do his part, I assure you. It is a good plan, and we have good people to carry it out. You know most of them and in a few moments, you'll meet the newest member of the team, Sgt. Rankin. It should be all we need. If we require more resources, I have some more in reserve to draw on as well."

Mattie grinned mischievously. "You mean Mr. Smythe and his men from SIS?"

"Hardly," Churchill snorted. "Ramsay may be fooled by people like that, but not me. Anything Smythe or his men bring us will be an unexpected gift. Their tactics may have worked for a while in Ireland in 1920 and 1921, where they had few civilized restraints. America will be something else entirely for them. Besides, you knew perfectly well who I mean."

A knock on the door interrupted Churchill, who walked over, opened it and brought in his visitor. "Martha McGary, meet Detective Sgt. Robert Bruce Rankin," said Churchill.

"Pleased to meet you, Ma'am," said Rankin, waiting until Mattie had extended her hand before grasping it in what Mattie could only consider to be a large paw. Rankin was a giant, six feet, five inches, at least, with an unruly mass of reddish blonde hair and over 220 pounds distributed solidly over a brawny frame. He appeared to be in his early thirties but his full beard made it difficult to tell.

"Please call me Mattie."

"Yes, Ma'am."

"Please have a seat, Robert," said Churchill, and the large man delicately sat down in one of the side chairs. Churchill continued to pace. "Here's what you do, Robert. Travel across the United States while we do the same in Canada. Keep pace with us. New York, Philadelphia, Cleveland, Chicago, St. Louis, Denver, San Francisco. All the Fenian strongholds. Use your Scotland Yard credentials. Visit all the police departments in those cities. Track down every rumor you can regarding arms purchases. Keep in touch with Mattie also. Give her whatever assistance she needs in Chicago where we have a solid lead. Then meet us in San Francisco. Can you do that for me, Robert? There is no time to waste."

"Yes, sir, Mr. Churchill," Rankin said, a look of puzzlement coming over his broad face. "But I thought, sir, that I was to assist Inspector Thompson in serving as your body guard."

"No need for that in Canada, my boy, I'll be perfectly safe with Inspector Thompson. No real danger till we reach America. You can be more valuable tracking these rumors down."

"Yes, sir, Mr. Churchill. I'll call as soon as I'm packed. Pleased to meet you, Ma'am," he said, almost bowing in Mattie's direction. "Good evening, Mr. Churchill."

Mattie picked up her photographer's vest, slung it over her shoulder, turned to Churchill and laughed out loud. "My god, Winston, wherever did you find such a boy scout ? That man is as big as an elephant and about as graceful."

Churchill smiled back at her. "Now, Mattie, be nice. He's a bright, clever lad. Don't be fooled by his appearance. He was a commando in the Middle East in the early 20s. I've read the field reports—many who underestimated him are now dead. He's filled in for Thompson before and Clemmie thinks highly of him. Trust me, his demeanor and his accent will bring us more cooperation than Smythe's condescension," Churchill said. "I know more about my mother's country than you give me credit for. Did I ever tell you she was one-eighth Indian?"

"Many times, Winston, many times," Mattie said, rolling her eyes as she leaned over and kissed his rosy cheek. "Stay safe until I see you in San Francisco. I'll find what you need."

"I know you will, my dear. You take care as well. These are rough people."

6:30 p.m.

Mattie took the elevator down and walked across the palm-laden lobby. She wondered how safe any of them were going to be. Danger never bothered her. It went with the territory. She knew how to take care of herself. But Cockran? He was a law professor for goodness sakes! She had covered Ireland in 1921. She knew the IRA could play rough. So could the SIS. Add Churchill and Hearst and their separate agendas to the mix and it all became quite complicated. With more to come and much to do. Cockran's role would be small if she had anything to do with it. And she did. Was he up to it? She didn't know. But the manipulation of Cockran was not the only thing about him on her mind. Mixing business with pleasure was usually not a good idea but Mattie had always liked to live on the edge. Taking risks was second nature to her.

Mattie's career and travel demands made relationships difficult to sustain. At 29, she rarely went out of her way looking for romance on assignment but Cockran showed promise. From her first glimpse of him outside his town house, she had thought it possible but the cocktail party had convinced her. For him, she would definitely make an exception. Could she seduce him while otherwise keeping him in the dark as her people wanted? Maybe. Finding out was going to be interesting.

7:00 p.m

Churchill sat comfortably in a large upholstered chair in the observation room of the palatial private rail car placed at his disposal by the Canadian Pacific Railway, a small whiskey and soda on the drink table at his right hand, the liquid in the glass gently rolling in time with the swaying of the train. David Brooke-Smythe sat across from him, reluctantly outlining for Churchill his intelligence-gathering plans. Two of his men were already visiting east coast cities.

"We're going to fan out around the country in teams of twos. We'll lift these Irish bastards one by one and, by God, we'll beat the truth out of them, if that's what it takes."

"Are you quite certain that's a wise approach?" Churchill mildly inquired.

"The Americans might be friends of yours, Mr. Churchill, but they aren't friends of mine. The Lord spare us if those are the kinds of allies you want our country to have in the future."

"Well, my dear Smythe," Churchill said, "you have your job to do and your own masters to answer to. It's comforting to see that you approach the task ahead of you today with the same insight and intelligence that you did ten years ago. Now, if you'll excuse me, I still have a few letters I must write. Good luck to you, then," Churchill said, as he rose without shaking his hand and padded down the hall towards his bedroom, his whisky in one hand, his cigar in the other.

Once there, cigar clenched firmly in his mouth, Churchill picked up his fountain pen.

My darling,

We are now on the way to Ottawa in our wonderful car furnished to us by the Canadian Pacific. This car is to be our home for three weeks so we have unpacked all our clothes and arranged them afresh. The car is a wonderful habitation. Jack and I have large cabins with big double beds and private bathrooms. There is a fine parlor with an observation room at the end and a large dining room, which I use as the office and in which I am now sitting, with kitchen and quarters for the staff. The car has a splendid wireless installation, refrigerators, fans, etc.

The immense size and progress of this country impresses itself upon one more every day. The sentimental feeling towards England is wonderful. The United States are stretching their tentacles out in all directions, but the Canadian National Spirit is becoming so powerful that we need not fear the future.

After I brought Martha and Sgt. Rankin together for the first time, I saw my old painting instructor again before her train departed for Chicago. Events are moving rapidly here. I will write again from Toronto.

Always, my darling one, with fondest love, Yr. devoted,
W.

14.

I've Had A Break-In

New York City
Saturday, 10 August 1929
9:00 p.m.

Supper with Bill Donovan at the Stork Club went better than Cockran had expected. After his train arrived from Montreal, he had headed there straight from Grand Central so as not to be late. Donovan was a proud man, used to getting his own way. Being passed over by Hoover for Attorney General had been a humbling experience. The Stork Club's owner, Sherman Billingsley, however, had a way of making the most humble man feel more important. And if that man had earned the Congressional Medal of Honor, so much the better for the Stork Club's reputation. A striped awning ran from the curb to the basement entrance protecting them from the rain. Billingsley knew Donovan and fawned over him. Almost everybody did.

"Colonel, how good to see you again. And you as well, Mr. Cockran. Welcome."

That ought to be good for a mention in Winchell's column, Cockran thought, as Donovan responded, "How are you doing, Sherman? Keeping out of trouble?"

"Can't complain," Billingsley replied.

Donovan pulled Billingsley close to him and Cockran could barely hear Donovan's whispered words. "I've heard about your new

partner. Watch out for him. Frank Costello is not someone you want
to get close to."

Billingsley laughed nervously, saying to the *maitre d'* "Our best
table for Col. Donovan."

Over iced tea for Donovan, dry martinis for Cockran, and thick
rare steaks for both, Donovan laid out the plan for his new law firm.
America's business interests in Europe had grown dramatically in the
1920s. Investment houses and the big banks had their lawyers. But
Donovan saw an opening and a need for representing American
manufacturing and trading interests in Europe, South America and
the Far East. He could use Cockran's expertise in international law.
It wouldn't involve travel—unless Cockran wanted it—and
assignments would be on a case-by-case basis. But it would pay well,
he said, and keep Cockran in those English-cut flannel suits he had
grown accustomed to. By supper's end, Cockran had agreed that
Donovan could carry his name as "Of Counsel" to the firm in both
its New York and Washington offices. Cockran would remain a free
agent, able to accept or turn down any case.

10:30 p.m.

Cockran walked home from the Stork Club, crossed over Fifth
Avenue at 53rd Street, and headed north toward his townhouse in
the 60s. He knew something was wrong when he inserted the key in
his front door. The deadbolt was no longer in place, and he had
locked it himself last night before leaving. The small lamp in the
foyer cast a yellow glow over the honey-colored wood and the small
Oriental rug. Cautiously, Cockran made his way to the back of the
house and the kitchen, the only other entrance to the house. He
flicked on the overhead light and his suspicions were confirmed. A
small pane of glass in the back door had been knocked out, shards of
glass glittering in the harsh electric light. Cockran walked quickly
back through the house to his study and the downstairs telephone
where he called the district police station to report the break in. The
Desk Sergeant promised to dispatch an officer immediately.

Cockran sat in his chair behind his desk after he hung up the phone and surveyed the devastation around him. Like the break-ins at the Cedars and the law school, the intruders had made no effort to conceal their presence. Books were pulled off the shelves and strewn on the floor. The pair of two-drawer mahogany filing cabinets adjacent to his desk gaped open, the files strewn carelessly around the room, lying against the books on the hardwood floor. He knew what they had been looking for. Michael Collins' journals. But he didn't know why. What was in them that made the IRA want them so badly? Thorpe's identity? Blackthorn's? Even John Devoy had not been able to figure out who the men behind those code names were.

The six Collins' journals began late in the early spring of 1920. Kept on an almost daily basis, they reflected a man as obsessed with rooting out spies in his own midst as he was in neutralizing British intelligence agents. Collins' journals conveyed his suspicions that the British had an informer high in the echelons of Sinn Fein, if not the cabinet itself. Possibly even two. His own intelligence sources could only uncover code names. The conduit between the Sinn Fein informer and the British was named Blackthorn. The Irish spy was code-named Thorpe.

Less than fifteen minutes had elapsed after Cockran's phone call to the police when the front doorbell rang. Cockran walked out, exchanged introductions with Officer Johnny O'Connell, and led him to the kitchen, telling him on the way about the other two break-ins. From there, Cockran led him on a tour of the house, intending to take an inventory of what the burglars had stolen. Cockran wasn't surprised that nothing was missing. His silver was intact. His father's nineteen century impressionist paintings were still on the damask-covered walls, the gun case which displayed his father's collection of shotguns and revolvers was untouched.

Nothing touched except the study. The same pattern as the Long Island break-in.

"And were you keeping any money in the study, Mr. Cockran, that the thieves might have been interested in?" asked Officer O'Connell.

"No, I'm afraid not, Officer. This is the third one after my home on Long Island and my law school office. All these break-ins have me puzzled," Cockran replied, as he showed the policeman out. The officer promised to file his report promptly but indicated to Cockran that the absence of anything valuable missing would make it well nigh impossible to ever locate the perpetrators.

As he walked down the hall toward the stairs, the telephone rang in his study. He picked it up. It was Devoy. "I've been trying to reach you all evening, Bourke, where have you been? We've got to meet right now."

"I'm sorry, John. I just got back from Montreal. I've had a break-in here. Can't this wait until tomorrow?"

"No, it can't. We must meet now. Can you please come over?" Devoy's voice sounded worried.

Cockran pulled out his watch from his pocket. "It's 11:30. If I can find a taxi, I'll be at you're apartment in fifteen minutes."

"No, not there," Devoy replied. "Meet me at the office. Make sure no one follows. It'll be safe to talk there."

Cockran shook his head as he hung up. The habits of a lifetime die hard. The old man might be paranoid, but it was clear Cockran had some enemies. The assault in Central Park, the attack on the train and now another break-in. He left through the back door and walked down the narrow, dimly-lit alley through to Madison Avenue where he hailed a taxi. He looked around. No one was following him.

15.

My Regards to Your Lovely Wife

White Plains, New York
Saturday, 10 August 1929
9:30 p.m.

James O'Brien was a bigger fool than he had imagined, Tommy McBride thought, as he shook hands with O'Brien's wife, Elizabeth, and introduced her to Kurt von Sturm. The balding O'Brien was stout and in his forties. His lovely wife was neither.

"Please call me Betsy," an invitation McBride promptly accepted. Betsy was wearing a low-cut blue silk dress that matched her high-heeled shoes and showed off her long, shapely legs. Betsy wore her hair long with loose light brown curls framing an attractive oval face, brown from the sun as was the rest of her body, much of which was on display. The scooped bodice of the dress made it difficult for McBride to avoid seeing an ample portion of her pale breasts as he walked beside her. He didn't try.

They were shown into O'Brien's study, McBride and Sturm sitting at opposite ends of a dark green leather Chesterfield sofa. Betsy asked if they would like coffee. McBride smiled and said yes. With something like that waiting for you at home, McBride thought, why would James O'Brien keep a mistress whom he regularly visited every Monday and Thursday in a midtown Manhattan *pied-a-terre* and who, in turn, entertained other men when O'Brien was not there?

McBride had been impressed with the ten-page report Sturm had given him on O'Brien. For all his outward bluster and bonhomie, O'Brien was a weak man who'd unwittingly provided his mistress with the perfect location for a high-class call girl plying her trade in Manhattan's expensive hotels and in the exclusive, member-only "clubs", as the high-priced speakeasies selling only premium branded liquor referred to themselves. Cote d'Or, Club New Yorker, the Stork Club and Parrouquet. If O'Brien was so careless in one part of his life, they had to make sure he was not equally careless in the one area that mattered to McBride—the wire transfer codes. Sturm was right. Once the funds were wired, O'Brien had no further use. A loose end.

McBride was going to be a busy man in the next few days. The wire transfers on Monday were crucial. They had to be done perfectly. But once all his business was concluded, he looked forward before leaving New York to consoling Jamie O'Brien's wife who had just returned with a silver coffee service. Bending over at the waist so her breasts once more enticed him, the view even more generous than before, she proceeded to pour cups for him and Sturm while a white-coated servant entered behind her with a large whisky for her husband.

It was obvious that her husband, flush in the face, was drinking something more than his second whiskey that night. When O'Brien asked her to leave them alone, promising her he would return to their guests in half an hour, McBride decided to show him up.

"Betsy, 'tis a lovely cup of coffee you make. Would you be so kind as to pour me another before you leave?" McBride said as he drained the cup quickly and placed it back down.

"Of course, Mr. McBride," said Betsy, who clearly had also enjoyed more than two cocktails that evening. The coffee pot was no more than two feet from McBride's hand and he could easily have refilled his own cup but he was looking for a repeat performance from the engaging Mrs. O'Brien and she didn't disappoint. As she bent over to carefully pour the coffee, she leaned forward so that the front of her dress fell away, her right breast entirely exposed.

"Thank you, Betsy," he said with a smile, staring at her breasts and making no effort to conceal it. "You're very kind. Please call me Tommy."

Facing away from her husband, McBride watched while Betsy's eyes followed his to her breasts as she placed the coffee pot down and blushed as she stood up. "I'm delighted to entertain friends from Ireland in my home, Tommy. Please come back and see us." Betsy said.

"Oh, I'll be back, Betsy," McBride said, as he took a last lingering glance at her bottom moving provocatively beneath the silk as she walked out. "I wouldn't miss it for anything."

McBride returned his attention to O'Brien who had noticed and not appreciated Betsy flashing her tits. Get used to it Jamie. A lot more than her tits would be showing the next time.

"See here, McBride. I don't like being interrupted in the middle of a dinner party. This better be important," he said, taking a gulp of the whiskey from the Waterford crystal glass.

McBride's eyes narrowed and he paused, letting the silence fill the air until O'Brien took another gulp of whiskey and blurted out, "Come on, man, I can't take all night!"

McBride took a sip of coffee and said in a low, quiet voice which caused O'Brien to lean forward in order to hear him, "You'll bloody well take as long as I want you to take. The IRA thinks it's important. And if the IRA thinks it's important, your life depends on it. Are we clear?"

O'Brien flushed and reached for the glass a third time, nervously taking another gulp before responding. "Of course. I understand. I didn't mean..."

McBride raised his hand for silence. O'Brien's babbling ceased. Tommy had been dealing with self-important men like this all his life but he had settled the score and taken them all down a peg or two. A few moments earlier, McBride had been content with the knowledge that, before he killed him, he was going to humiliate Jamie O'Brien by shagging his sexy wife right in front of his face. But now, after his pompous little lecture, that wasn't enough. He stood up, took a step forward and moved around the coffee table between him and

O'Brien and, with his left hand, grabbed the insurance executive by his necktie, pulling him awkwardly to his feet.

O'Brien sputtered but the pressure on his necktie kept him from uttering any words as McBride drove his right fist firmly into the insurance executive's soft belly which caused him to bend over, gasping in pain. McBride straightened him up with a tug on his tie and hit him in the belly again before he let the bulky man fall heavily back on his leather chair.

"My colleague, here," McBride said, "wishes to be reassured that you understand the instructions I gave you this afternoon. After seeing how much you've had to drink, I do too."

McBride watched as Sturm, in his flawless, unaccented English, began to cross examine the insurance executive. Despite his fear and the whiskey, it quickly became obvious O'Brien knew what he was supposed to do. He had already placed in his office vault the notarized letter of authorization from de Valera in his capacity as President of the Irish Republic to transfer the funds in the trust account as directed by the bearer of the letter. He would keep the letter in his vault until he received further direction from de Valera or his successor as President of the Irish Republic. The sequences. The amounts. The banks. Even the account numbers.

Sturm turned to McBride. "I am satisfied, Mr. McBride. Everything is in order."

McBride nodded, turned to O'Brien, a large smile on his face, leaned down and patted him softly on his cheek. "Well, then, Jamie, things are fine now. I'll be back here Monday."

O'Brien wiped a handkerchief over his perspiring forehead and passed it beneath the soft underside of his chin as he responded, in a nervous voice, "I didn't mean to be so abrupt earlier, Mr. McBride. It's just all so unexpected. You showing up this afternoon. The letter from President de Valera. All those years which have passed since the war. I mean, I was concerned about taking on all this responsibility. Ever since those three men who had control over the funds before me were killed in the summer of '22. And then nothing's happened for so long, I thought there was nothing left for me to do. I figured, what with Dev taking his seat in the Dail and all..." O'Brien continued, until silenced once again by a raised hand from McBride.

"You figured wrong," said McBride coldly. "Don't make the mistake again. Give my regards to your lovely wife. Tell her I'm looking forward to seeing her again."

10:30 p.m.

McBride stepped into the back seat of the Model A. Timothy Cronin and Sean Russell were in the front. "Let's be on our way, boys. We've got a long night ahead of us."

Back in Dublin two months ago, when Dev had told him about the new arms deal and McBride's role in securing the safe passage of the weapons back to Ireland, Dev gave him another assignment—locating six critical missing volumes of Michael Collins' private journals. Dev knew that Collins kept a meticulous daily record throughout the war; that there were many volumes; and they had been mysteriously spirited away from Collins' rooms the day after his death. Dev said Blackthorn managed to intercept most of them before they were sent out of Ireland. The others were tracked to America and destroyed. All but the six that mattered most.

McBride had tried to pry more out of de Valera but he refused. Instead he told McBride where he believed the six missing Collins' journals could be found—in the possession of a Columbia Law School professor named Bourke Cockran. Dev had explained that his sources had traced the journals to Cockran's father in America. He believed Cockran had inherited them and was writing a book about Michael Collins where the journals would be an important source.

McBride had not been impressed. Thanks to Blackthorn, he knew all about Cockran and his dead whore of a wife as well. Who cared what one bastard wrote about another? After warning McBride to watch his language, de Valera had said he didn't want Collins' blackening his name with lies from the grave. The six journals had to be destroyed. "History will record Michael Collins as a great man," Dev had said. "And I don't want it done at my expense."

So, earlier that evening, McBride had searched Cockran's Fifth Avenue townhouse to no avail just as he had found nothing at Sands Point or Columbia's law school. Cockran's apartment in Cleveland was next. The Model A began moving and McBride grilled Timothy Cronin and Sean Russell.

"How many friends did O'Brien talk to?"

"Four that we know of," Sean replied. "We have their addresses."

"Any others?" McBride asked.

"Only the two reporters."

"Fine. You know what to do. Take care of them all. I'll do the last one myself,"

"What about O'Brien and his mistress?" Timothy asked.

"We need him for the wire transfers but we'll take care of both of them after that. Bring her to his house first thing Monday."

"And Mrs. O'Brien?" Timothy asked with a smile.

McBride waved his hand. "We need to know how much our Jamie told her. If she knows nothing, she'll be fine. Otherwise, we take care of her too. Either way, no gentleman would pass up the opportunity to leave such a lovely lass with a smile on her face."

The men laughed. "But we'll each take a turn with her when you're done?" Timothy asked eagerly.

McBride laughed. "Always ready to do the Lord's work aren't you Tim?"

16.

Tommy McBride Is In Town

New York City
Saturday, 10 August 1929
11:45 p.m.

Cockran walked up two flights of well-worn stairs in the shabby building in lower Manhattan which housed the offices of *The Gaelic American,* modestly subtitled "America's Finest Weekly". Visitors to the crowded third-floor editorial offices were reminded of this in gold letters at the entrance to the newspaper's suite of rooms. Cockran had only met Devoy here on a few occasions and each time it had been during working hours with the clatter of typewriters, the shouts of copy editors and the pleasant anarchy of a newsroom.

He turned the door handle and, to his surprise, it wasn't locked. The newsroom was silent, the typewriters covered, and the only illumination came from Devoy's corner office. "John, are you there?" Cockran shouted, mindful of Devoy's fading hearing.

"Over here, Bourke," Devoy replied. "In my office."

When Cockran found him, Devoy pulled out a drawer in the ancient desk and brought out a bottle of Jameson's and two scarred but serviceable glasses, pouring two fingers of whiskey into each, and handing one to Cockran. "To hell with the King and de Valera, too!"

Cockran raised his glass in reply and took a sip. "So what have you found?" he asked.

"No fund raising of any kind, anywhere. I knew that but I made the inquiries I promised. Everything is quiet, just as it has been since we won our freedom."

"That's a relief," Cockran said. "I was starting to believe Churchill had something ."

"Not so fast, laddie," said Devoy. "Just because your information comes from Winston bloody Churchill doesn't mean it's wrong."

"What do you mean?"

"Just what I said. You remember, back in 1919, when the black coward himself came to America to raise money and keep his Spanish arse safely out of the way of British guns?"

Cockran nodded while Devoy launched into his version of de Valera's fund raising efforts in the United States and the millions of dollars he had left behind in trustee accounts.

"Those accounts are frozen, John," Cockran said. "Ever since..." Cockran caught himself, "...since the unholy trinity were killed when they tried to buy weapons during the civil war. No one would dare try again."

"If you think that, lad, you think wrong," Devoy replied. "When the IRA got Kevin O'Higgins two years ago, that was the end of it. No one's afraid of the Free State now." Devoy paused, took a sip of whiskey and continued. "There's an operation on. I'm sure of it."

"Why do you think so?" Cockran asked.

"Two reasons," the old man replied. "For one thing, I asked around about James O'Brien. He's the sole trustee Dev eventually named to look after the money. He spends a lot of time at Parrouquet, a club on the east side, where he's got himself a girlfriend. I sent a couple of the boys over this afternoon to see what they could learn. It was child's play. The boys pretended to be old IRB men from Cork and, inside of three drinks, our Jamie was telling them everything. He says he's going to transfer $3 million from the trustee accounts on Monday."

Cockran was stunned. Monday? Just like that, the money would be gone? Cockran had killed three men seven years ago. Wasn't that enough? How many more people did he have to kill? "Where will the funds be transferred?"

"We don't know. O'Brien was drunk but Seamus didn't want to make him suspicious."

"What's O'Brien's background?"

Devoy snorted. "Insurance broker. Rich, too. Divorced his first wife. Lives in sin with his second. A good looker and a lot younger. He's trying to buy an annulment. Has the big house in White Plains. Risen above his station. His father was a butcher, always ready to contribute."

"So how do we find out where the money is going?" Cockran asked.

"I'll know soon." Devoy said. "I have an old friend who's an assistant teller."

"You said there were two reasons you knew there was an operation."

Devoy nodded. "Tommy McBride is in town."

Cockran froze.

"He's in New York. Someone saw him at the speak underneath The Blossom restaurant last night. He met with some well-dressed German gent who can take care of himself. The Kraut broke two arms, a cheek bone and one nose when some of the boys tried to roust him."

"Are they sure it was McBride?" Cockran asked.

"Yes, laddie," Devoy sighed. "They're certain. McBride's a big man, not easy to miss that red nose of his. These are boys who knew him by sight in Ireland."

Tommy McBride! Cockran clenched his fists and audibly exhaled. This changed everything. McBride was the man whose IRA squad robbed the bank in Galway and taken Nora hostage. After he returned from San Francisco, his mission for Collins complete, he had banished all thoughts of Ireland except for one last thing—to find McBride and make him pay for Nora's murder. After Collins was assassinated by the IRA in August of 1922, Cockran had continued to correspond with contacts he had in the Free State. To no avail. No one could find McBride. He couldn't blame the

Apostles, Michael Collins' squad of assassins, for not redeeming Mick's promise to have McBride killed. They may have been hardened killers, but they were still boys and unless someone were leading them, that's all they ever would be. Boys. Collins' promise of revenge for Nora's death had died with him.

Tommy McBride! Revenge had been a concept alien to Cockran's father who had tried to pass on his wisdom to his son. But he had lost two young wives to natural causes, Bourke's mother the last, and that made all the difference. A devout Catholic, his father couldn't very well blame God now, could he? Cockran didn't have that problem. His wife hadn't died of natural causes and he knew who was responsible. Tommy McBride. Some might say healing was brought by the passage of time. Cockran knew better. The wound was still there and the layers of scar tissue over it were still tender to the touch. The aching need for revenge still smoldered.

Cockran's own guilt over Nora's death had been a twin companion to his desire for revenge. Of the two, guilt had proved to be the stronger companion. It had given him nightmares for years, something even the Great War and its killing never did. Gradually, long talks with John Devoy helped persuade him that he could have had no way of knowing that staying in Dublin to interview a ranking IRA army council member would have taken place on the day the bank in Galway was robbed, Nora taken hostage and killed. His guilt quickly found a new home after that. He had become too close to Mick Collins, he decided. He had lost his objectivity as a journalist. His *Atlantic Monthly* articles, while factually accurate, were critical of Collins' enemies, especially the IRA. Cockran had no proof one way or the other that his association with Collins had anything to do with Nora's death but the guilt stayed with him.

Cockran often wondered whether Collins had sent him to America knowing Nora's enduring influence would reassert itself once the breadth and depth of the Atlantic was between Cockran and revenge. Mick could have sent any of the Apostles and the three IRA moneymen would have been just as dead. But sending Cockran kept him from going after McBride and gave him another target for the revenge he craved. After that, Nora's voice had whispered in his subconscious that raising their son was more important than seeking more revenge for her death and his father had said the same to his face.

Indeed, Cockran could still hear Nora's lilting voice today, echoing his father's golden baritone. He consulted them often and he would play out their conversations in his head. He still could hear his father's voice: *"Revenge is the most expensive luxury known to man. Anyone can generally attain it, but it is all that he is ever likely to accomplish."*

His father might be right, Cockran thought, but the fact was that he hadn't even accomplished that much—the revenge he had denied himself for seven long years by listening to the better angels of his wife and father. And now, revenge was well within reach. Tommy McBride was in America. Cockran's home field, not McBride's. He didn't need the Apostles now. Tommy McBride had made a mistake at last and Cockran was going to make him pay.

Cockran rose from the chair and walked to the window. It had started to rain. The pavement outside glistened in the glow of the street lamps. He heard the old man's voice behind him. "You know what you have to do, lad."

Cockran turned from the window to face Devoy, who continued, "You won't have much time. I'll soon find where the money's going to be sent. But if there's an operation on and arms are being purchased, the money's not going to stay in one place long. You and your British friends are going to have to move and move quickly."

But Cockran's thoughts were elsewhere. On finding Tommy McBride. Stopping the IRA from buying arms no longer seemed as important. Besides, if the IRA were active here, then they must be so in Ireland as well. Where he had just sent the one person who meant more to him than anyone. Patrick. No one in the IRA would hold it against Cockran if he killed McBride. They'd understand. But queering an arms deal? That was different. He shook his head. "No, John. I'll pass on to Winston whatever you find out. But that's all. I'm not going back in, especially since Paddy's not here where I can protect him."

"There'll be more sons than yours put at risk if we don't stop those bastards."

"They're not my responsibility. I failed Nora once. I won't let it happen again."

Devoy got up and walked to where Cockran stood beside the window, looking down at the street below. "I understand, lad. Believe me, I do. But leave nothing to chance. Evil never sleeps. I still have many friends in the Free State, lad. From the Clan and the Brotherhood. I'll send a cable tonight. Tell me where the boy and his grandmother are staying. By tomorrow morning, there will be two armed men with them around the clock for the rest of their holiday."

"I appreciate it, John. But it's not enough. I can't risk Patrick's safety."

"You've been attacked twice," Devoy said, his old gnarled hand grasping Cockran's arm with surprising force. "The boy's already at risk. Let me do this for you. And for Paddy."

It's not enough, Cockran thought, but it can't hurt. "Okay, have your men explain things to Mrs. Morrissey. Ask her to send a cable to me telling me she will accept their protection."

"Don't you worry," Devoy said. "I'll make that clear."

"How soon will you have the bank information?"

"Soon." Devoy glanced at his watch. "I've got an appointment in fifteen minutes."

"Should I wait here for you?"

"No, I'll be going uptown. There's a neighborhood speak two blocks away from my flat. O'Connor's at West 105th and Broadway. Tell the man at the door the 'old Fenian bastard' sent you. Be careful. Meet me there in an hour."

17.

You're Too Nosy, Devoy

New York City
Sunday, 11 August 1929
12:45 a.m.

"The 'old Fenian bastard' sent me," Cockran whispered through the four-by-four inch space which had opened in the black lacquered door after his knock. The space quickly shut again and the door opened. Cockran entered into a small antechamber where an exceptionally large and well-muscled doorman patted him down for weapons. Finding none, the man jerked his head over his shoulder. "In the back. Beyond the bar. Last door on the right."

Cockran walked past the bar, stopped at the designated door and opened it. He saw Devoy sitting in the corner, two glasses and a bottle of Bushmill's open before him. They were alone. The walls of the room were covered in posters from long ago fund raising events to support the Irish Revolution. New York, Philadelphia, Cleveland, Chicago, San Francisco, Buffalo, Detroit. All the Irish American strongholds. Conspicuous by their absence were any posters advertising rallies featuring the appearance of Eamon de Valera. Cockran smiled. John Devoy was a man to hold his grudges, nurturing them carefully. Cockran sat down and poured himself a drink from the bottle, adding water from the pitcher beside it.

"What did you find?" Cockran asked.

"It's for real. It's not loose talk or rumors," Devoy replied. "It's all here."

Cockran picked up the paper which Devoy had pushed across the table to him. "Wire transfers," said Devoy. "Dates and account numbers. Crocker Bank in San Francisco. First Union Trust in Chicago. National City Bank in Cleveland. A million dollars will be transferred Monday morning to each of those three accounts. There's to be less than two hundred thousand left in the Guaranty Trust account."

The old man stopped, putting his hand over his eyes, massaging his temples. "I helped raise that money, Bourke, and I've bought more than my share of weapons in my life. Do you have any idea how much $3 million will buy today?"

Cockran shook his head and Devoy continued. "That man has to be stopped. He's a monster who should have been punished for his crimes. They should have eliminated him when they had the chance. He's not Irish in blood, character, temperament or outlook."

"De Valera?" Cockran responded.

"And who the hell else do you think I would be meaning!?" Devoy shouted, slapping the table with the flat of his hand. "If Dev has ordered the money to be moved, he's already cut his deal with the IRA. Good God, man, look what he's done! He drenched Ireland in blood in 1922. Destroyed its military and economic resources. He has no qualities of leadership and his record should bar him forever from any responsible position. Mark my words, once he comes to power, however he obtains it, he'll never give it up. He'll bribe the Church by turning education over to it and Ireland will be doomed to generations of poverty, just as it was under the British."

Devoy paused, and Cockran could see he was having trouble breathing. Cockran moved as if to help, but the old man waved him off. "I'll do what I can, Bourke, but I'm old and I'm tired. I'll run a front page editorial in next week's paper exposing all this and blasting de Valera, but I don't know if it will be enough. And if it's not, then I've wasted my life."

"Nonsense," Cockran responded. "Ireland is free and no one did more than you."

"Aye, Ireland is free." said Devoy. "For now. But how much longer?"

Devoy reached out and Cockran felt the warmth of his wrinkled hand as it grasped his wrist. "You helped us in '21 and '22, Bourke, you did good things. The Big Fella told me so in his last letter. I've sent the cable.Your son will be safe but you've got to stop these people."

"I will," said Cockran. "I'll get the information to Churchill by telegram first thing tomorrow. This is exactly the information he said the British Secret Service needed."

Devoy laughed, a laugh which broke off into a hacking cough. "The British? You trust the British with Ireland's future? Are you daft, lad?"

"What more can I do, John?" Cockran asked.

"Do what I tell you, lad. Just do what I tell you. Here," he said, pushing another sheet of paper across the table at Cockran. It contained a list of three names, addresses and phone numbers. "These are all good men in Cleveland, Chicago and San Francisco. All *Clan na Gael.* All of them backed Collins and the Free State against that Spanish bastard!"

Devoy paused, sipped his whiskey, and continued. "All hell is going to break loose on Wednesday when the next edition of *The Gaelic American* hits the streets. Between now and then, you get your sorry arse on a train and you see each of these men. I've talked with them briefly earlier tonight. They will be expecting you. They are all prominent citizens. Powerful, each in his own way. They know me and they'll know who your father was. You tell them what we've learned about this and what's going to be in next week's edition. They'll make sure the story gets picked up by all the local newspapers. Each one has important political contacts in local government. We'll use publicity and political pressure to smoke out what's going on."

Cockran appreciated, not for the first time, Devoy's creativity. "Why do you suppose that will work? The newspapers may eat it up but will the politicians notice?"

Devoy cackled until his laugh dissolved into a cough. "That's the beauty of it, lad."

"What do you mean?"

"The best part of my story is *not* going to be true. I'm going to write that, in each of those cities, de Valera and the IRA have made a pact with local gangsters and that the gangs are putting together the arms for the IRA."

"But if it's a lie, what good will it do?" Cockran asked.

Devoy gave him an exasperated look. "Do I have to explain everything? I know it's a lie, and the gangsters and racketeers will know it's a lie. But the politicians won't. And the good city fathers won't like that publicity. Most of them are on the pad from gangsters anyway and they'll put pressure on the mob for turning their city into an arms bazaar. And since the mob isn't behind any of this, the gangsters will do all our work for us. They won't want their profitable enterprises of booze, gambling and prostitutes disrupted so they'll find out where these arms are being assembled and tip off the authorities. The authorities then will find some pretext to confiscate the arms. And even if they don't, we'll create enough of a firestorm that even the bloody British will be able to track the weapons. What the hell else is their goddamn navy good for!?"

"That's not a half bad plan." Cockran. said. "I wonder why Churchill didn't think of that."

Devoy smiled. "Because he's not me and the only publicity he knows how to generate is for himself. Will you do it? Will you do this for me? For your father's memory?"

Cockran was torn. His son would soon be safe and Devoy had a good plan. The old Fenian hadn't lost a step. His idea made sense. But he had to find a way to reconcile his role in Devoy's plan with what Nora would want. If he got involved again, would he be putting Paddy at risk as he had with Nora? More importantly, what would he do about McBride if their paths crossed? And what were his real motives? Stopping the arms deal? Or revenge on McBride? Both? He really didn't know. He would have to think about that.

"I'm not sure, John. Let me sleep on it." Cockran said and told the old man about the break-in at his house and his suspicion that they were after the six remaining Collins journals.

Devoy agreed. "I think you're right, lad. Perhaps I should read the journals again. Maybe something will jar my aging memory. Would you be able to drop them by tomorrow?"

"I can't. They not in New York. But I can have them mailed to you within the week."

"That's good. Get on with you now and let me finish my drink in peace."

"You sure I can't walk you home?" Cockran asked.

"Thanks very much, but no. It would not be good for us to be seen together. You run along now and let me finish my drink. My flat is just around the corner."

Cockran bade the old man goodbye and walked out through the bar, tipping his hat to the bouncer at the door as left. Behind him, a tall, dark-haired man with a jagged scar on his receding chin, wearing a blue work shirt and dungarees, got up from a stool and headed towards the restrooms, stopping at the phone located adjacent to them. He put a nickel into the slot, looked at a phone number, scribbled on a piece of paper in his left hand, and gave it to the operator who put him through. "It's me, Timothy. He just left. The old man's still here."

1:30 a.m.

Tommy McBride put the telephone down and fondled the .45 caliber Colt automatic pistol in his gloved hands as he sat in a soft, sheet-covered armchair, a bath towel beside him. He ran his fingers along the barrel and noticed again the intricate engraved "W.B.C." on the polished walnut handle of the pistol. He smiled inwardly with satisfaction at his decision earlier that night to jimmy Cockran's gun case and lift the weapon from its honored resting place. It was so easy to take things that belonged to Cockran. And oh so sweet when you did and all your plans fell together like this. The two reporters O'Brien talked to were already dead. So were the four other men O'Brien had bragged to at the fancy club. He looked at his wrist watch. Just about now, Sean Russell would be torching the editorial offices of *The Gaelic American*. With any luck, the whole damn building would go up in smoke. McBride smiled. By the time the paper ever got back in business, the IRA would have its arms and he would be out of the country.

McBride's ears picked up the sound of shuffling steps on the stairway outside. He lifted himself from the chair and walked over to the door, standing behind it. He heard the key rustle in the lock and the door opened, effectively shielding him from sight. The door closed and he saw the gray-haired old man advance haltingly toward the nearest lamp. Before Devoy could reach his destination, McBride stepped forward, wrapped his left arm around the old man's neck and mouth, preventing him from crying out. He roughly pushed Devoy to the floor and knelt with his full weight on the old man's back, hearing him groan in pain. He leaned down and whispered into his ear. "You're too nosy, Devoy. You should have minded your own business."

With his left hand, he put the towel over Devoy's head, pressed the pistol firmly into the back of Devoy's head, and pulled the trigger. The muffled shot echoed softly through the apartment and the towel slowly began to turn a crimson color. Devoy wasn't the first man—or woman—McBride had killed with a bullet in their brain nor would he be the last. He dropped the weapon beside the body and made his way out the back door, down the stairs and into the alley beyond.

18.

My Decision Is Final

New York City
Sunday, 11 August 1929
9:00 a.m.

It was a warm summer morning and the sky was overcast as Cockran walked down Fifth Avenue to the Western Union office at the corner of 51st Street. Up late, he hadn't even taken the time to read the morning newspaper. Most New Yorkers had fled the heat of the city for the cool breezes of Long Island and the Jersey Shore, their places in the city filled by tourists.

Mary Morrissey's cable had been delivered at 7:30 a.m., agreeing to Devoy's protection. He hated like hell to trust anyone else with his son's safety but he had no choice with an ocean between them because he had decided to do what Devoy wanted. His hand would be hidden as he visited the three cities. Devoy's reporters could have done the same thing but they wouldn't have carried the same weight as the son of Bourke Cockran, the most honored Irish-American of his generation, as welcome and respected in the posh clubs of New York and London as he had been in Tammany meeting halls. But Cockran would take care to leave no footprints that might draw the further attention of the IRA. He would tell Winston what he had learned but he would also say he would be involved no further. As for discreetly seeing Devoy's contacts in Cleveland, Chicago and San Francisco? Well, what Winston didn't know wouldn't hurt him.

Cockran made one more pledge. To his father. And Nora. No revenge. No special efforts to seek out and kill Tommy McBride.

Expose the IRA and its arms deal. Period. After that, a retreat to Sands Point and his new book, waiting for Paddy's safe return. Right. But he was not going to make this journey unarmed. The only question was whether it would be his old Army Colt .45 automatic or the Webley revolver. And while he wouldn't seek McBride out, he thought the odds of their paths crossing were fairly good. Then, all bets were off, weren't they?

Cockran left a message at Churchill's hotel and was working on his book in the study of his town house, his fountain pen flowing smoothly over the long legal pad in front of him when the telephone rang. Churchill.

"Bourke, how good to hear your voice. I understand you have news?"

After telling him briefly of the two assaults and the break-in the night before, Cockran recounted for Churchill his meetings with Devoy and the information he had secured. Banks. Account numbers. Devoy's forthcoming front-page story and editorial.

"Splendid, Bourke, splendid. I could ask no more. The publicity in Devoy's newspaper should help immensely. My people are off to Chicago and we will be in San Francisco within ten days. Even if the publicity drives them underground, we still should be able to persuade the Americans to impound the funds. All will be well, Bourke, but..." Churchill's voice trailed off.

Picking up the tone in Churchill's voice, Cockran was on guard. "What is it, Winston?"

"It would be so useful, Bourke, if you could go to Cleveland yourself and check things out from that end. Speed things up. Shouldn't be too difficult."

Cockran sighed. "Nice try, Winston, but no sale." Cockran would not be Winston's pawn.

"Are you sure you won't reconsider?" Winston asked.

"No, Winston, my decision is final. I've done more than you asked. I've found more than you could possibly have hoped. I've been assaulted twice. Both my houses and my law school office have been ransacked. I've had enough. I'm going back to writing. Nobody beats you up for what you write."

19.

An Anonymous Tip

New York City
Sunday, 11 August 1929
1:30 p.m.

Cockran was in his study, at work again on his book, when the phone rang.

"Mr. Cockran, please."

"Speaking. Who is this?"

"It's me, sir, Aloysius McFadden. I'm the bartender at O'Connor's. I tried to call you this morning. As soon as the police left. But you weren't home," the man said breathlessly.

"Slow down, Al, slow down," Cockran said. "What's this about police?"

"It's about Mr. Devoy, sir. They were asking about Mr. Devoy."

"Why were they asking about Mr. Devoy?" Cockran asked.

"It's terrible, sir, terrible. Mr. Devoy's been murdered."

Cockran was stunned. "When?! Where? How?!" he demanded.

"I don't know, sir. The detective who was here, Terence Sweeney, wouldn't tell me. But I saw our beat patrolman Billy McGurn this morning. He told me it was likely an intruder in Mr. Devoy's apartment. Shot him in the back of the head. Neighbors found him early today, face down. There was blood all over. Terrible, terrible. Mr. Devoy was such a gentleman."

Cockran collapsed in his chair. "Do the police have any

suspects?"

"I wouldn't be knowing, sir. I never saw Sweeney before so I didn't give him your name, sir, but I can't be certain about our other customers who saw you here last night."

"Thanks, Al. I owe you one," Cockran replied.

"Sure thing, Mr. Cockran. It's a terrible thing, himself being killed the same night the building where his newspaper was published burns to the ground. They're saying it was arson."

"What's that? Arson?" Cockran asked.

"Yes, sir. Didn't you know? It was all over the newspapers today."

Cockran replaced the receiver and stared blankly into space, his eyes fixed, but not focused, on the miniature soldiers arrayed in battle formation on the fireplace mantle. *The Gaelic American* offices destroyed. John Devoy killed. He knew what the MO would be. Collins told him you could always tell a Tommy McBride operation. A single shot in the back of the head, the victim lying helplessly on the floor. Usually innocent civilians, not British troops.

Cockran focused on his anger as it grew inside him, making no effort to control it. Nora would insist that two wrongs didn't make a right, but now, all bets *were* off. Just as was the scar tissue. The wound was wide open. It would not begin to heal until McBride was dead.

Cockran knew Devoy's plan would not work without his newspaper but he still would meet Devoy's friends and pass their information on to Churchill. Churchill had the only game in town with the IRA but Cockran was starting his own game. Hunting Tommy McBride.

1:45 p.m.

"Colonel, this is Bourke. I need a favor." Cockran toyed absentmindedly with the letter opener he had picked up from the green leather surface of his writing desk while he told Bill Donovan about Devoy's death, the arson at his newspaper, and the break-in at his town house.

"See if your friends at City Hall can identify the detective assigned to the investigation."

Donovan's voice echoed in the receiver. " I'll make the calls. But what's this all about?"

"Not now. I'll tell you later if my hunch is correct. For now, I want to make sure that a homicide detective is on the up and up. His name is Terence Sweeney."

An hour later, Cockran had just finished a sandwich when the phone rang. "Jesus, Mary and Joseph!" Donovan said. "What in the good Lord's name have you gotten yourself into?"

"I take it you found something?" Cockran asked.

"You bet," Donovan replied. "There is no Sweeney in Homicide."

"Who is he?"

"You've got a lot more trouble than a fake homicide detective."

"And that would be?"

"I talked to the head of Homicide himself. Ed McCracken. They have the murder weapon on John Devoy and they received an anonymous tip this afternoon that it belongs to you. If that proves accurate, you're going to the top of their suspect list. Do you own any guns?"

"A whole case full. My father's collection. It's just down the hall."

"Was anything taken from it during the break-in?" Donovan asked.

"Not that I could tell."

"So you didn't report any stolen weapons to the police?"

"No."

"Check again. If it turns out the murder weapon is yours, you're going to be needing my services and not just a favor. Are you going to tell me now what this is all about?"

So Cockran did. Churchill and the IRA. The two assaults. All three break-ins. McBride. Devoy. De Valera's money. The wire transfers. The works.

"I've sent the information on to Winston this morning. He wanted me to check out one angle myself in Cleveland but he thinks I turned him down."

"The first thing you should check out is your own gun case. Then call me back."

Cockran pulled open the drawer to his writing desk and took out a small ring of skeleton keys and made his way down the hallway to the glass-fronted mahogany cabinet which housed his father's gun collection. He unlocked the door and opened it, mentally scanning the contents. The matched set of Purdy shotguns. A Winchester .30 caliber repeating rifle. Two antique Colt revolvers...Yes! It was missing! His own .45 caliber Colt automatic pistol he had delivered to his father on his return from San Francisco, an unspoken promise that killing was behind him; that Patrick and the future were his priorities; that revenge was in the past.

Cockran examined with care the cabinet's brass lock and there indeed were small scratches where there had been none before. McBride! The IRA and fucking Tommy McBride! John Devoy had been right. Churchill and British intelligence were not going to be able to stop the IRA. Devoy's plan could have worked. But no true Fenian, was going to cooperate with British agents. Ever. But they would listen to Bourke Cockran's son. Of that much he was certain.

Nora's voice in his head was silent as he walked up to his bedroom, heading directly for the space beneath his closet floor. Cockran took this as a good sign. He pried up two floor boards in the right rear, reached inside and pulled out a bulky package covered in cloth. A large Webley revolver, a shoulder holster made of belting leather, and two cartridge boxes of heavy .455 caliber shells, all sitting unused since their last engagement in San Francisco seven years earlier. Michael Collins' parting gift that rainy night in Dublin on the day of Nora's wake. His father's advice might well be correct. In killing McBride, he might accomplish nothing more than revenge. But he would settle for that.

20.

Jumping Bail

New York City
Sunday, 11 August 1929
3:45 p.m.

A detective rang the doorbell a little before four but his name was Hagan, not Sweeney. Donovan had not gotten back to him on Sweeney's identity so Cockran inspected Hagan's badge closely. Someone had obviously recognized Cockran last night at O'Connor's because Hagan began asking questions about why he met with Devoy; when he had last seen him alive. Instinctively, Cockran decided he didn't trust the detective and wasn't going to educate him.

Hagan wasted little time before he asked whether Cockran kept any firearms on the premises. Cockran answered affirmatively and Hagan insisted on inspecting the antique gun case at the end of the hallway. Cockran could smell the set-up coming but, seeing no way around it, he told Hagan of yesterday's break-in and theft of his service automatic.

"You didn't report it as stolen to the police?" Hagan asked.

"No, I didn't realize it was gone."

There was an uncomfortable pause as Hagan shot him a look. "Mr. Cockran, I believe you ought to come down to the station with me and answer a few more questions about this missing .45 caliber automatic you claim was stolen from you."

"That's absurd," Cockran replied. "I'm not going anywhere."

Hagan arched his neck to look past Cockran to the foot of the stairs at his suitcase and trench coat. "From the looks of it, Mr. Cockran, you're planning to go somewhere quite soon."

"To my home in Long Island. I was planning to spend the next few weeks there. It's part of New York City. You can look it up."

"Look, Mr. Cockran, we can do this one of two ways. Either you come with me now or I go back to the station and swear out a warrant for your arrest as a material witness."

"Don't make hollow threats to me, Detective Hagan. If you want to ask me more questions, do it now. Otherwise, get the hell out of my house."

7:00 p.m.

A little more than three hours later, Cockran's view of Bill Donovan's ruddy face was obscured by the iron bars of the local precinct's holding cell. Less than an hour after he left, Hagan had slapped him with an arrest warrant as a material witness. He called Donovan immediately but it took several hours before Bill was able to post bail. The grim expression on Donovan's face showed his unhappiness with Cockran.

"This gets stranger by the minute," Donovan said as an officer slid open the bars to his cell. He leaned close and spoke in hushed tones as they were escorted to a desk for processing. "I found your Sweeney. He's an undercover agent working for the Department's Red Squad, investigating subversives. I knew a Terence Sweeney once. Worked for Edgar Hoover at the old Bureau of Investigation in Washington. Make no mistake, Bourke, these are nasty enemies."

Cockran scanned the room as they walked, expecting to see Detective Hagan but he was nowhere around. As they reached the processing desk, Cockran saw a familiar face waiting for them. Ed McCracken, head of Homicide. He looked tired. He always looked tired, Cockran thought. A short, balding man in his fifties who could pass for sixty-five. It was a tough business to be in, especially when it involved the son of an old friend. Like most of the Irish in town who'd gotten somewhere in life, McCracken had known Cockran's father and been a family friend. He was one of the few authority figures who had earned Cockran's respect.

As Donovan took care of the paper work, processing Cockran's bail, McCracken placed a soft hand on his shoulder. "Bourke, can you tell me what's going on here?"

"You tell me, Ed. My homes and my law school office are broken into, my service automatic stolen, and I'm arrested in the murder of one of my closest friends."

McCracken rubbed his forehead in frustration. "I don't know what to say. My folks here are just doing their jobs. You were one of the last men to talk to John. With all the evidence...look, we had to arrest you, Bourke. At least as a material witness. I'm sorry."

"I understand."

"At least you were able to post bail. I'd hate to see you spend the night in one of these cells," McCracken swallowed and then paused, clearly upset by something. "Bill tells me that one of our boys in the Red Squad is asking after you."

"Sweeney. What's he doing in your business?"

"Ah well, the boys in the Red Squad have a free leash of sorts. Undercover and all. Not much I can do about it in Homicide. But why are they asking about you and Devoy?"

Cockran shrugged his shoulders.

"Just tell me you didn't do this, son."

"I didn't."

McCracken nodded silently, trying to hide the doubt in his face. This was not good. There must be a lot going against him if Ed McCracken was not convinced he was innocent.

"I'll put one of my best men on the case, Bourke, but there's only so much I can do."

"What do you mean?"

McCracken rubbed his forehead again. "I'm getting pressure from upstairs to put someone else on the case. Someone hand-picked. Not one of my favorites."

"Detective Hagan?"

"Who?"

"The detective who brought me in here. Hagan. Is that who they want?"

"There's no detective named Hagan in my department."

Cockran turned to the officer processing his bail, "Where is the man who brought me in here? Detective Hagan."

"Hagan?" the officer said. Cockran nodded. "I never heard of him."

"Could be another Red Squad boy," Donovan ventured. "Wouldn't surprise me."

"Bourke, listen," McCracken was saying. "Would you mind if I stopped by your townhouse later? Say about 9? I don't like the way all this sounds and there are some things I'd like to ask you in private. Does that sound O.K.? I mean, with your lawyer there, of course."

"That's fine, Ed. Come on over. Bill doesn't need to be there."

8:45 p.m.

It was raining heavily outside, a mid-summer thunderstorm, by the time Cockran returned to his townhouse. He regretted agreeing to have McCracken stop by. If he persuaded McCracken he was innocent, that would vanish once he skipped town. Which is precisely what he intended to do. While he waited, he went back into his study and placed a long distance call to Devoy's contact in Cleveland. They talked quietly for ten minutes.

Finally, just after nine, there was a knock. on his door. "Be there in one second, Ed."

He reached the door and opened it to the grim face of Detective Hagan, rain pelting off his soft hat. A pistol rested in his gloved palm was trained squarely on Cockran's chest.

"Step inside, Mr. Cockran. Slowly and quietly."

Cockran did as he was told. Hagan closed the door behind him, keeping the weapon aimed at Cockran. Water rolled off his hat and onto the polished mahogany floor.

"Couldn't stay put, could you Mr. Cockran?"

"I don't know what you mean."

"I would've left you alone if you'd simply stayed where I put you. In a cell."

"I'm not going anywhere."

"Damn right, you're not. Where's your whisky?" Hagan asked.

"My whisky?"

Hagan nodded. Cockran stalled, "I normally reserve that for guests, not intruders."

"Grab a bottle and move into the study."

Cockran looked again at the pistol in Hagan's hand. It wasn't standard police issue. More than that, it looked familiar. It was a Colt New Service from 1917. They had arrived at the front before Cockran was wounded. Cockran had kept his Colt semiautomatic but having an M1917 revolver wouldn't have been unusual for a veteran like Cockran. It was clear Hagan was going to kill him and make it look like suicide in drunken remorse for having killed Devoy.

Hagan raised his voice, "I said, grab a bottle of whisky and move into the study."

"No." Provoking him was all he could do. He had to get to Cleveland.

"I'm not asking you, Mr. Cockran. You have no say in this matter. Grab a bottle—"

"No."

The color rose in Hagan's cheeks and he took a menacing step forward but stopped when there were several loud knocks at the front door. Hagan's reflexes betrayed him. As his head twisted towards the noise, Cockran bolted directly at him, catching him in the mid-section and forcing him to the floor. His momentum carried them both into a cabinet in the front hall, Hagan's backside taking the brunt of the impact, the pistol falling from his hand.

The knocking resumed, even louder this time. He could hear McCracken's agitated voice, "Bourke? Bourke?!" Before Hagan could shake off the cobwebs, Cockran made a dash for the kitchen, snatched up his suitcase and coat, and burst through the kitchen door.

The rain was still pouring down and it was difficult to see in the dark, but he knew there was a narrow alley behind the townhouses through which he could reach East 79th. Behind him, he heard his kitchen door flung open, a pane of glass shattering from the impact.

Holding his suitcase in one hand, he hit the alley and bolted right towards 79th. As he neared the street beyond, he turned his head back to see Hagan enter the alley, gun raised. Cockran flinched as a shot sailed over his head and then he was through the last few feet of the alley and into the street.

Cockran turned right and ran down 79th, towards 5th Avenue, which was his best chance for a taxi, but Hagan would be onto him quickly. Just before the last brownstone, his feet slapping on the wet sidewalk, his heel caught on the raised edge of a concrete slab and sent him sprawling to the ground. Scrambling to his feet, with his suitcase still intact, he didn't wait to see if Hagan was following. No time, he told himself. Just run like hell.

Back on 5th Avenue, Cockran sprinted up toward 80th Street until he saw a taxi, flagged it, swung the door open and tossed his suitcase in..

"Bourke!!"

Cockran froze. His hand on the taxi door, hair dripping with rain, he turned to the voice. It was Ed McCracken, standing at the door to his townhouse, staring at him with wide eyes.

"Bourke, stop!!"

This looked bad, Cockran realized. But there was nothing else he could do. He was jumping bail. He gave McCracken a salute, tossed his bag into the taxi and hopped in.

"Grand Central Station. Step on it. I'm late."

Cockran tried to recall the lessons Michael Collins had taught him during the war with the British but it had been a long time. Longer still since he had been trained in evasion by MID. He peered out the back window of his taxi. It looked as if no one was following. No sign of Hagan but it was difficult to tell cars apart at night. Most headlights looked the same.

By the time Cockran's taxi reached Grand Central Station, the rain had subsided, and the streets were still steaming as they glistened in the glare of the overhead lights. Cockran bought a Pullman compartment ticket on the New York Central's Cleveland Limited

No. 57 leaving at 11:35 p.m. He felt safer with the sizable crowd in the terminal but still kept a low profile. In the half hour left before departure, he walked over to the Western Union office and penned his second telegram to Churchill that day: PROCEEDING CLEVELAND. STOP. MORE LATER.

11:20 p.m.

Tailing Detective Terence Sweeney was not a problem for the tall, dark-haired man with the cold blue eyes and a nose which once had been broken. Sweeney was preoccupied with following Cockran and that made it easy for the man to get as close as he liked. He followed at a discreet distance as Sweeney shadowed Cockran to the Grand Central ticket windows, then to the Western Union office. As Cockran headed to the waiting train, Sweeney had a few words with the Western Union clerk and then caught up with Cockran just as he stepped up into the last car on the train.

Sweeney then abruptly turned and walked back towards the tall, dark-haired man who kept walking straight ahead, past Sweeney and on for another ten yards until he came to a pillar behind which he stepped. Peering cautiously around it, he saw Sweeney had almost reached the exit. The man walked rapidly to catch up and got a glimpse of Sweeney going into a telephone booth.

The man folded his six foot two inch frame into the booth adjacent to the one Sweeney had entered, closed the door, picked up the receiver, and cupped his ear against the thin wooden partition separating him from the next booth. He heard the man say, "Manhattan? Sweeney. Hagan failed. Cockran's alive. He's on the Cleveland Limited. It arrives there at 7:52 a.m."

There was a pause and then Sweeney said, "No, he didn't. But he sent a telegram. Yes I got a copy. Western Union always helps the police in their inquiries. To someone in Toronto named Chartwell. Told him he was going to Cleveland. Nothing more. Just that."

Sweeney hung up the phone and the blue-eyed man with the once-broken nose waited a full thirty seconds before exiting the booth and heading for the ticket window. Only ten minutes were left until the train departed. "One way to Cleveland, please. Yes, coach will be fine."

The man smiled. It wasn't a pleasant smile. Wouldn't it be grand, he thought, if luck were with him now? He had been waiting for so long. It was time to put things right. He smiled again. It still wasn't a pleasant smile

21.

She Was Nothing Special

En Route to Cleveland
Monday, 12 August 1929
11:45 a.m.

McBride poured whiskey from the small silver flask he had produced from inside the jacket of his suit and offered it to Sturm who declined and silently stared past him to the scenery outside their Pullman compartment's window.

"Your plan failed, Irishman," Sturm said at last

"What do you mean?"

"Your Mr. Cockran has taken it on the lam, I believe the Americans would say," Sturm replied. "He was arrested as you asked but he made bail. We sent someone to silence him but they failed. Now, he's skipped town. It seems that our Mr. Cockran is a formidable opponent."

"At least he'll be out of our hair," McBride said, annoyed his frame to stick Cockran in jail had failed. Still, his clever little frame of the widow O'Brien this morning should fare better.

"Perhaps not. Our paths may cross again. We share the same destination."

"You mean Cleveland?" McBride asked.

"Yes. He took a train to Cleveland last night. We have him under surveillance there."

McBride's eyes narrowed and a smile creased his face. Sod Blackthorn. He'd kill Cockran too. Why not? He'd already done the wife. "I'll take care of him. Goddamn American reporter. Never knew when to mind his own business. If he had, his wife might be alive today."

"His wife is dead?" Sturm asked.

"Yes, back in Ireland. She got caught up in a bank robbery," McBride replied.

"Unfortunate. Did you know her well?"

McBride smiled and looked out the window at the passing countryside. A lot better than you might imagine, he thought. "Why? What does it matter?" McBride asked, turning to Sturm.

"Everything about your adversary matters. His likes. His dislikes. The woman a man chooses often reflects his character. Even his strengths or weaknesses."

McBride just shook his head. If Sturm believed that, he was a fool. Men chose women for one thing only as that sexy tease Betsy O'Brien had discovered a few hours ago. He knew she had wanted it bad ever since she flashed her tits at him the other night. So he had given it to her good. She had struggled at first, kicking and protesting when he folded her over the high arm of the green leather sofa in her husband's study but a few hard cuffs on the side of the head soon set her straight.

Flipping her yellow sun dress up and yanking her lacy knickers down, weak whimpers were the sum of her resistance as a smiling Tommy had promised the squirming young matron he meant her no harm. "Be still, lass. T'is only fair we pay your husband back for his two-timing ways," the IRA man had said right before he breached Betsy from behind with the faithless husband looking on, a bound and gagged witness to the shagging of his spouse.

Tommy had laughed in triumph as those damn whimpers gave way to groans when Betsy's body betrayed her. Women were like that, he knew, once their knickers were off. After all, he reasoned, was it still really rape once a lass helplessly began to enjoy what she couldn't avoid? Tommy thought not. "Your woman fancies me, Jamie. Sopping wet inside, she is. Do you fancy a wager I bring her off? Say ten quid? Does she ever sound this way when you're in the saddle?"

The sorry cuckold had turned his face away at the sight but he would have had to be deaf not to hear his wife's sharp cries echoing in his ears until Tommy had reduced her to just another receptacle where the warm remains of his lust were left to linger. A cruel reminder she was nothing special. No woman was.

When he withdrew at last, she had stayed limply bent over the sofa, gasping for breath. As she began to weep, Tommy had noticed a swelling on Betsy's face where his big fist hit her and he lightly stroked her bruised, tear-stained cheek, causing her to wince. "We better put some ice on that," he'd said. "Wouldn't want the neighbors thinking Jamie was beating you now would we?"

After his men had taken their turn with her, McBride had brought ice for Betsy's face and coldly dispatched her husband with the same pistol used to eliminate his mistress. No witnesses. Well, no believable witnesses. McBride didn't think himself a beast. Once he learned she knew nothing of the wire transfers, a dazed and re-clothed Betsy had been placed in a nearby chair, exhausted by her ordeal and staring with blank eyes but obeying and closing her fingers when Tommy placed the empty weapon in her hand—a faithless husband and his mistress killed by a jealous wife. The lads had laughed when he said the police might not be entirely persuaded by her protests of innocence.

The train passed through a tunnel, throwing the compartment into darkness as McBride pondered Sturm's question, his smile even wider at all the sweet memories it stirred. Had he known Cockran's wife well? Aye, that he had.

McBride believed that any good leader, intent on maintaining morale, should always selflessly share the spoils of war with those serving under him. Under wartime conditions, women were fair game. It had been true for Tommy during the Irish war for freedom from the British where shamefaced young Anglo-Irish women were stripped and shagged by McBride and his men in full view of horrified relatives as their spacious country houses burned in the night, flames illuminating the fused spectacle of passion and reprisal.

After the truce with the British in '21, such easy opportunities vanished only to return in the Irish Civil War in '22 where even well-to-do Free State women were not spared the lusty pleasures of a slap and tickle courtesy of the IRA. Planning made it possible. Stalking their chosen prey. Blackthorn had taught him that.

More than maintaining his men's morale, Blackthorn had told him, violation of the fair sex was a key tactic for demoralizing the enemy. "Target their women, Thomas. Turn them into trollops. Return them as damaged goods. God approves. The Book of Deuteronomy. The women of your enemies are the spoil of war delivered by the Lord which He *commands* you to enjoy. All is still fair in love and war. Supply the lasses with a generous sample of both and boast about it in the pubs. Make their menfolk hang their heads in shame as they face the proof their precious Free State can't even keep the honor of their wives and daughters unstained."

Encouraged by Blackthorn and the Bible, Tommy and his lads were happy to force favors of the flesh from Free State women—the spoil of their new enemies—just as they had from the Anglo-Irish. Praise the Lord and pass the list. Yes, Blackthorn had given him a list—a long list—and told him to start at the top. "Don't save the best for last. The first two lasses come from well-known Free State families. I once knew one of them myself." he had said with a cold smile. "Their spouses may have loosened them up a little but I daresay they'll still supply you and the boys a rewarding romp."

Real lookers the two women were and, predictably, Tommy felt his disdain and desire for both growing in equal measure as he followed them around town and learned their patterns—one in Donegal, the other in Galway—while they ran errands, shopped and lunched with friends, their noses always looking down on common Irish lads like him just as if they were as good as the Anglo-Irish themselves. Free State bitches both. He vowed they'd soon see, once all their charms were indecently on display, that they weren't so high and mighty as they thought.

The two wives had been taken hostage during IRA bank robberies, one in Galway, the other two weeks later in Donegal. His men had worn masks and blindfolded their victims on the way to a safe house by a stream in the Connemara Mountains where the women proved to be neither high nor mighty. Naked and on their knees, pretty faces forced flat on the floor, helpless backsides hoisted up in the air, their noses had been in no position to look down on anyone.

Thanks to Blackthorn, Cockran's wife was the first. He betrayed the Republic but his mate paid the price. Taming that wild lass from the west of Ireland was a challenge but the outcome inescapable. Held tight by Sean and Timothy, Tommy had mounted her married bum and made it all his own. Afterwards, her new riding master had leaned forward to wipe the tears from her face and, with a laugh, whisper in her ear "T'was a fine shag, my sweet, and a fine fit you were. But let's keep this our little secret. And wouldn't you be agreeing with me that a husband won't be happy to hear that his wife's next wee one might not be his? Men are like that, don't you know?"

When, after a last caress, Tommy had finally tugged free from the snug embrace of his first Free State spoil, who knew the daft woman would show so little gratitude? She had ripped off her blindfold and come at them with a nearby fish-scaling knife leaving Timothy bleeding from a slash on his jaw. They hadn't wanted to kill her but after the mad bitch sliced up Sean as well, she left them no choice. Naked with a knife had proved no match for a man with a gun. Sean and Timothy had begged him to wait until they could take their turn with her but, cut and bleeding like stuck pigs, he knew they were in no shape for tupping. It was quick and Tommy made sure she didn't suffer. He wasn't a beast but what else could he have done? She had seen their faces.

Their second Free State spoil, Mary Sullivan Flaherty, had furnished almost as fine a ride as the first but she had displayed more sense. After they all finished, she had left her blindfold on. This had spared her the fate of the unfortunate Mrs. Cockran and afforded her safe return to her cringing bank clerk of a husband. He had stood there quivering during the robbery, his cowardice permitting the pillaging first of his father-in-law's bank, then his new bride's body and, finally, her reputation for virtue, ruined by the gossip slyly spread in the pubs that she had given as good as she got.

McBride turned his head back from the window and, in reply to Sturm's initial question, shook his head again and said, "Two of the boys and I once spent a little time with Cockran's wife. You might say I got to know her a lot more than most. I've met many like her. They put on airs but aren't they all alike on the inside? Just a girl from Galway. She was nothing special."

Part II

Cleveland and Chicago, 1929

Cleveland was known as a haven for racketeers, most of whom had used the profits of bootlegging and gambling during Prohibition to purchase political power.... [T]he city was honeycombed with brothels and gambling dens, and its police department was widely acknowledged to be corrupt and ineffectual, its equipment obsolete.

* * *

If there was one moment in Al Capone's racketeering career where he appeared absolutely invulnerable, it was [during] 1929....The Capone bootlegging network reached from New York's Long Island to Lake Michigan, and he controlled the flow of alcohol from Europe, Canada and the Caribbean.... Political circumstances continued to favor him: the mayor was afraid of him, he had bribed the Chicago Police Department into a state of compliance, and Prohibition, the chief cause of his good fortune, was entering its tenth year, turning millions of otherwise law-abiding Americans into lawbreakers.

Laurence Bergreen
Capone, The Man and the Era

22.

My Old Friend!

Cleveland
Monday, 12 August 1929
8:00 a.m.

Cockran walked up the familiar ramp of Cleveland's Union Terminal, a sprawling complex of buildings on Public Square which had been under construction since 1925, billed as the world's most massive construction project since the pyramids in Egypt. Already, its Terminal Tower was the tallest building in the country outside New York. On the horizon of Lake Erie, he saw the swiftly moving black clouds of a summer storm moving in. He handed his suitcase to the cabby, settled in and stretched out his long legs in front of him.

"Where to, mister?"

"The Alcazar. It's right off Cedar..." Cockran said before the cabby interrupted him.

"Fancy hotel. Owned by Arabs. The only place in town a fellow can't get a drink."

Cockran smiled. The Arab owner had a taste for Irish whiskey he learned from Cockran.

The rain had started to fall by the time the taxi pulled up under the Alcazar's canvas awning. Cockran tipped the doorman who opened the door and secured his bags.

"Welcome back, Mr. Cockran. Good to see you again."

"Likewise, Safir." Cockran said to the tall uniformed man wearing a fez straight out of a comic opera. All that was missing was the curved steel of a scimitar through his belt.

Cockran walked into the hotel lobby and was instantly transported into a room right out of the Arabian Nights, one in which a Moroccan chieftain would have felt at home. Opened in 1923, the hotel was modeled after the Alcazar Hotel in Seville, Spain and the Ponce de Leon Hotel in St. Augustine, Florida. It was a five-story, irregular pentagon of eclectic Spanish Moorish design featuring a lush botanical courtyard with a fountain at its center.

Cockran stopped at the front desk and was pleased that, unlike the doorman, he was not recognized by either the desk clerk or the bellhop. He registered under a false name and asked, "Is Hasim in this morning?" referring to the patriarch who owned the hotel. "I'm an old friend."

Cockran watched as the clerk walked over to a door marked "Private", knocked softly and entered. Cockran followed, placing himself in front of the door at a discreet distance of twenty feet. The door opened and the great bulk of his friend filled the door frame, bald head glistening, the tips of his waxed black mustache curved upward. His greeting died in his throat as Cockran put his finger in front of his lips then beside his nose.

"My old friend," said Hasim. "Good to see you again. Let's talk in my office," gesturing expansively with his hand. Once inside the office, Hasim embraced him in a bear hug. "Bourke, old fellow! How have you been? How's your son? What's all this about? Why the incognito?"

Cockran laughed. "One at a time, my friend, one at a time. Where's that famous Arab hospitality? Do I have to beg you for a thimble full of that thick black syrup you pass off as coffee? Do I make you beg for Irish whiskey in my home?"

Now it was Hasim who put his finger to his lips. "Not so loud, my friend. Only Allah knows that. My wife does not. Besides, it would have been a grave breach of diplomatic etiquette to decline a sip of whiskey in an Irishman's home. And, above all, I am a diplomat."

Hasim walked over to the corner of the large office and pulled the wooden blinds shut on the window which overlooked the hotel's courtyard. He returned, holding two small, handleless cups, each half-filled with a thick, sweet-smelling brew. "Here, my friend," handing Cockran a cup. "What brings you back to Cleveland? Fall semester must be at least six weeks away."

He paused, arched a thick, black eyebrow and said, "Could it possibly be that you are checking up on me to see if I am giving proper care to that formidable green Auburn speedster you so graciously left in my care for the summer? The attendants in my garage below treat her as if she were my own. And I have taken her out every Sunday for long drives in the country."

Cockran laughed. "Nothing like that, Hasim. I'm sure the Auburn is well-cared for. I'm here on business. I'm meeting an old friend and, alas, she has an exceptionally jealous husband who may have private detectives following her. I don't want to embarrass her and it would be indiscreet if we were to meet at my apartment. You will not recognize the name under which I registered and I would appreciate if you would ask Safir to exercise the same discretion as you."

Hasim smiled broadly. "You devil, Bourke. A married woman? You may rely on me."

In fact, there was an attractive married woman from Shaker Heights with whom Cockran had been sleeping during the previous semester but he was not going to see her this visit as she was on holiday in Italy with her husband who had promised to stop his philandering ways. He and Susan had spent many a rainy afternoon in his apartment on Derbyshire while Patrick was in school and her wayward husband was at his law offices in the Union Commerce Building.

After another coffee in his room, Cockran went for a walk. It was still overcast, but the rain had stopped. He headed east, past the left-hand side of the Alcazar and paused at an intersection two blocks later. He turned right onto Derbyshire where his apartment was located and then he stopped in mid-stride. A black, four-door

Buick was parked up the street, facing away from him, barely a hundred yards away. Two men, both smoking, sat in the front seat. A stake-out. Cockran paused and looked up at the apartment building in front of him. Nodding to himself, as if he had found the right place, he walked toward the front door.

Upon reaching the door, he was out of the line of sight of the men in the car. Cockran quickly moved off to the right and down the adjacent alley. It had begun raining again and Cockran pulled the collar of his trench coat higher. He reached the intersecting alley at the rear of the building and turned left, keeping his eyes peeled for either of the men in the Buick. In a few moments, he had reached the rear of his own apartment building. Using his key to the service entrance, he sprinted up the three flights of stairs to the fourth floor. He cautiously opened the fire door and looked in. The hallway was empty. He silently closed the door and walked back over the fourth floor landing to the rear entrance to his apartment. The door appeared to be undisturbed. He let himself into a kitchen looking the same as he had left it.

The living room, however, was a shambles. His bedroom and the adjacent bedroom of his son were relatively Spartan affairs and not much damage was done. But the third bedroom, which doubled as his library and study, was unrecognizable. Much worse than his homes in New York. Papers were strewn all over the floor, drawers and their contents upside down, books ripped from their shelves, spines broken. The IRA boys were obviously frustrated.

It had grown darker in the apartment and the rain had increased in intensity. Cockran walked back into the kitchen where he searched through a large ring containing an assortment of skeleton keys until he found one which fit the door to his unmarked office at Western Reserve University's law school. Unless the IRA searched there as they had in New York, he would pick up the Collins journals at the law school before he left town.

Cockran stopped at the front desk of the Alcazar to retrieve his room key and was given a message to see Hasim. Upon knocking and entering Hasim's office, he saw that his friend's face held a worried look. "You wished to see me," Cockran said.

"Your jealous husband must have friends in very high places," Hasim said. "Shortly after you left for your walk, we received a visit from two men who demanded to know if a Mr. Cockran was registered here. We told them no and showed them the guest register. But they weren't private detectives, Bourke. My desk clerk is still learning English, but he swears they were government agents. Federal agents." Hasim paused. "She must be very beautiful."

"She is, Hasim. Very beautiful. I appreciate what you have done. Thank you, my friend."

Once back in his suite, Cockran picked up the telephone from the desk in the sitting room. He gave a number to the switchboard operator who placed the call for him. "Mr. Greene? Johnny Greene? This is Bourke Cockran. We spoke yesterday."

"This is Greene. I remember you, Cockran," a gravelly voice replied. "As I told you yesterday, if you're a friend of John Devoy's, you're a friend of mine. What can I do for you?"

"I'd like to meet, Mr Greene. I'm on the assignment which Devoy gave me before he was murdered. I intend to complete it. I hope you have information for me which will help."

"Call me Johnny. It's not that easy for me to get out in public much right now. Nor safe, either. Tell you what. Come on down to the warehouse district tonight. The Flat Iron Café. One of my people will pick you up and bring you to me. How're you going to be dressed?"

Cockran told him and Greene responded. "A trench coat is fine, especially if this rain don't let up. But it would be better if you didn't wear no tie. Draws too much attention."

"I understand," Cockran said. "How will I identify your man?"

"Don't worry, Cockran, we'll find you. Just be there by half past eight."

Cockran rarely ate lunch and it had been a long time since breakfast on the train. He called down to room service and ordered a light supper. The hotel kitchen specialized in Middle Eastern cuisine so Cockran ordered a small lamb kebob, roasted squash and lemon cous cous. Cockran would have liked a half bottle of Bordeaux but the Alcazar didn't have a wine cellar whose stores it could draw upon for favored guests while waiting for America to awake from the nightmare of Prohibition. Ever his father's son, Cockran knew it some day would. Republicans couldn't stay in power forever.

Speaking of Republicans, Cockran thought as he pulled the bottle of Johnnie Walker Red from his suitcase and fixed a drink, it was time to check in with Wild Bill Donovan.

"Colonel, sorry to bother you at home."

"Where are you, Bourke?"

"It's better you don't know."

"I agree. You jumped bail. You can't expect me to defend you with one arm tied behind my back. With you on the run, it's only going to make things worse."

"I'm not on the run..." Cockran began, but Donovan interrupted.

"It sure as hell looks that way. Ed McCracken himself told me he saw you running."

"I can't help that. Hagan was shooting at me, for God's sake. Look, I've had my bank send you a check for $10,000. Use it to cover the bond and keep the rest as a retainer. I have to do what Devoy asked before he died, before McBride killed him"

"You're letting your emotions cloud your judgment."

Cockran paused and softly replied, "I really don't think I am, Bill. I wanted to go after McBride with every fiber of my body but I didn't. I was only going to help Devoy. His plan would have shone a bright spot light into the dirty little corners where McBride operates. But the bad guys were one step ahead of me. And of John. Now he's dead. It's my fault. I owe him."

There was a long pause from Donovan before he replied. "All right, Bourke, you win. For now, you're only a material witness. But if an indictment for murder is issued, all bets are off. You'll have to come home. Watch yourself. Make sure those guys aren't one step ahead."

The tall dark-haired man with the cold blue eyes and a crooked nose who had followed Cockran from New York sat in a corner of the Alcazar's spacious lobby, a newspaper in front of him, attempting to remain as inconspicuous as his six foot two inch height permitted. He was positioned to give himself a clear view of the elevators and he had been waiting patiently for the past two hours for Cockran to appear.

The Alcazar lobby's level of activity had picked up in the early evening. The man heard the bell of the elevator and saw Cockran emerge in casual clothes, tan pants and a navy blue blazer with a trench coat over his arm. As he watched Cockran , he saw two other men rise from their chairs and follow Cockran, no more than ten feet behind. He smiled. Luck was with him. One of them was McBride's man Sean Russell. Revenge was coming closer.

The tall man saw the valet pulling up with a motorcar for Cockran. It was dark emerald green on the sides, shiny black on its long hood and tapered tail. While Cockran tipped the valet, the man asked the doorman to hail a taxi. The doorman blew his whistle and the taxi at the head of the long yellow queue which curved to the right around the building's corner began to move forward. Before the taxi could pull in under the hotel's awning, a black four-door Buick pulled in front, cutting it off. Sean Russell and his companion quickly hopped in and the Buick accelerated, taking a left at the same corner as Cockran's motorcar had done.

The taxi now in front of him, the tall man entered. "Would you be up to following that small green roadster and the large black motorcar behind it?"

23.

Sheila Greene

Cleveland Heights
Monday, 12 August 1929
8:00 p.m.

Cockran peered through the Auburn's windscreen, stuck his arm out the window, and signaled a right turn onto Cedar Hill, keeping an eye on the two cars which, trailing in his wake, appeared to be following him. The Auburn was faster and many turns and twenty minutes later, he arrived at Public Square where he valet-parked the Auburn at the Hotel Cleveland and hailed a taxi. He gave the cabbie the Flat Iron Café's address and they headed down a hill to the warehouse district on the banks of the Cuyahoga River. Half the street lamps were out. The nondescript Flat Iron Café was the lone beacon of bright light in a scene punctuated by a series of ill-disguised speakeasies and small groups of sailors who stumbled along in the young night.

Cockran sat at a booth in the rear of the Flat Iron Café nursing his second cup of coffee. The café had a long counter on the left with eight stools, half of which were filled, a short-order cook behind the counter working on the grill. Booths lined the right-hand side of the room.

Cockran looked up as an attractive young woman in her early twenties with short dark hair framing her face entered the room. She wore a white cotton sweater, a short plaid skirt, and white socks with sport oxfords. She looked as out of place as Cockran felt but she knew half the customers, greeting them all by name before she slid into Cockran's booth, extending her hand.

"Hi, Mr. Cockran. I'm Sheila Greene. Daddy sent me."Cockran returned her infectious smile. "I was expecting one of your father's men."

She laughed. "No, Daddy just said he would send one of his "people". I was there when he took your call." She shrugged her shoulders. "Besides, I've always been one of his boys."

"So, I understand you'll be taking me to your father?"

"Not exactly. He's sleeping now and I persuaded him that I can handle this."

Cockran was confused. "I'm not sure I understand."

"It's simple," she said. "he's in a wheelchair. He was hurt in a strike this spring. He heads one of the largest Teamster locals in Cleveland and the company guards and some off-duty police had more baseball bats than the pickets. They broke his legs. He's had two operations, but the doctors say he won't be able to walk again for another month or so. Mom died after the war. The flu. I'm his only kid. I was in college back east. When he got hurt, I dropped out and came home right away to take care of him. I'll probably skip the fall semester, too."

"So exactly how do you intend to handle this? Do you know what information I need?"

"Sure, let's get down to business," she said, shoving papers across the table's surface.

Cockran read the papers. "Who is this Charles Westwood and who is he trustee for? The account shows receipt of over $1 million today. Yet there is barely $50,000 left in the account."

"Charles Westwood used to be the publisher of the *Cleveland Chronicle*. Owned by Hearst. He retired six months ago."

"Does your father know him? Is there any way he could arrange for me to see him?"

"Oh, Daddy knows him, all right. Daddy knows everyone. He's made you an appointment for tomorrow. Nine a.m. at the Westwoods' home in Shaker Heights."

"Please thank your father for me," Cockran said. "Did you find out where the money went after it left the trust account?"

Sheila reached inside her purse and pulled out another sheet of paper. "Here. Five checks in amounts anywhere from $76,000 to $325,000, all payable to Great Lakes Art Brokers."

"Art brokers," Cockran asked. "What do you know about them?"

"Nothing, I'm afraid. Cleveland's a nice place. Lots of culture. Lots of art brokers. But no Great Lakes Art Brokers. Nothing in the phone book. Nothing in the city directory. Sorry."

"Don't be sorry, Sheila," Cockran replied. "You've been enormously helpful. Please tell your father how much I appreciate this."

"Wait," she said brightly. "It gets better. Daddy thinks he's found where those weapons you're looking for are stored."

"Really?"

"Yep. Not more than half a mile from where we sit. That's why we're meeting here."

Cockran listened as Sheila explained. It was an old warehouse. Still bonded but vacant up until two weeks ago when someone leased it for a month. Nothing happened in Cleveland with a warehouse that her father didn't learn of immediately. Her father talked briefly to the landlord who agreed to insist that Teamsters be hired to perform the work.

"Daddy says the lease is up next week. He talked to the foreman who heads up the crew that's been working there. The place is almost full. Daddy says there's enough guns and ammunition in there for a small army. The manifests alone are near a million dollars."

"I need to get inside the warehouse," Cockran told her. "I want to see those manifests. Verify what's in there. Can you arrange that for me?"

"Why, Mr. Cockran, I thought you'd never ask," Sheila said, playfully batting her eyelids. "Of course I can. Are all these weapons really going to be used in Ireland?"

"Call me Bourke. Yes, the arms are headed for Ireland. How soon can I get in?"

"Soon, but not right now. The warehouse is working late tonight and the swing shift doesn't end until 11:00 p.m. There's no overtime scheduled this week. So if we wait until, say midnight, there shouldn't be a problem. Here," Sheila said, giving him a set of keys. "I'll meet you there. This one opens the rear door; this one opens the inside office where they keep the manifests; and this little one opens the file cabinet where you'll find the manifests."

Cockran hesitated. "But if you're going to meet me there, why give me the keys?"

"As soon as we're done here, Bourke, I've got a hot date. You don't think I normally dress like this to visit the Flats, do you?" she asked, referring with a gesture to her collegiate clothing. "Anyway, midnight should give me plenty of time but, just in case I'm late, you go ahead. I'll catch up later. If you go in without me, leave the door unlocked. I won't be long."

"Are you certain it's safe for a girl like you to be down here alone in such a rough area?"

Sheila laughed again, shaking her head. "I'm not a helpless young thing. Appearances to the contrary, I can take care of myself. Besides, there shouldn't be a problem when I've got a big, strong man like you to take care of me."

"These are ruthless men we're dealing with, Sheila."

"Well, not to worry, Bourke. So is Daddy. Everyone down here on the waterfront and in the warehouse district knows who my Daddy is. And I am," she said proudly, "the apple of my Daddy's eye. No one messes with Daddy's little princess," she said with a grin.

"Come on. I'll give you a ride back to your car and take you past the warehouse and show you where we'll meet."

Cockran followed Sheila and held the door open for her as she slipped behind the wheel of a deep maroon Cadillac convertible. "Nice. Too nice for this neighborhood."

Sheila laughed again. "Everyone knows it belongs to Daddy. It's almost as precious to him as I am. I kid him sometimes that he pays more attention to her than me, but then he always reminds me of how much tuition he pays Vassar every year."

She pulled the Cadillac to a stop on the far side of the street across from a faded brick building with high windows. "That's the swing shift now," said Sheila. "Once they finish tonight, the warehouse should be deserted for the next eight hours."

"Won't there be any security?" Cockran asked.

"Only a night watchman. He's a member of the union. Old Charlie Mahoney. I've known him since I was in grade school. He's retired now, but Daddy thought he could use the money."

She eased the big convertible forward until they were adjacent to the building's edge. She gestured to a single bare light attached to the right side of the warehouse at the rear.

"Down there. Underneath the light. The big key opens that door. That's where I'll meet you later tonight, hopefully around midnight. Remember, if I'm not there on time, don't worry, just go ahead without me. I'll make sure Charlie knows we're coming. Just tell him you're with me."

Five minutes later, Sheila dropped Cockran off in front of the Hotel Cleveland's Superior Avenue entrance. Neither of them paid attention to the black Buick sedan which had been following them from the flats and which now drove past and turned right, stopping at the hotel's Public Square entrance.

24.

Fair Game

Cleveland
Monday, 12 August 1929
10:00 p.m.

Cockran adjusted the Webley revolver in the shoulder holster he had not worn in seven years as he paused at the traffic light on Euclid Avenue adjacent to Severance Hall. Moments later he turned the Auburn right on Adelbert Road and slowed to a halt beside the No Parking sign in front of the darkened limestone building which housed Western Reserve University's School of Law. Cockran knocked on the window of the Law School's front door and caught the attention of the uniformed security guard, a tall, elderly, dark-skinned man, with a fringe of white hair forming a halo around his shiny black scalp.

"Mr. Cockran! A pleasure to see you. Didn't expect you back so soon."

"Just in town for a few days, George. I thought I would pick up some materials for my fall classes," Cockran said as he signed the security log.

Once in his unmarked third-floor office, Cockran turned on the desk lamp and wheeled his worn wooden desk chair over to two wooden file cabinets adjacent to the window. He unlocked the one on the left and pulled the bottom drawer completely out of the cabinet. He reached inside and retrieved from the floor of the cabinet a package still wrapped in the oilcloth in which he had bound it over six years earlier when closing down his father's law office.

Cockran placed the package on his desk and untied the twine which bound it. Within were six worn leather notebooks, none of them alike, linked together only by the small, neat accountant's longhand of Michael Collins. Cockran sat there for an hour, taking careful notes. At last, he stood up from the desk, and stuffed the notes deep into one trench coat pocket and the six volumes in the other. He would store them in Hasim's safe tonight.

Back at the Alcazar, Cockran gave the notebooks to Hasim and took the elevator down to the garage. He walked over to the battered black Chevrolet sedan which Hasim had lent him. It would draw no attention. Cockran parked the Chevrolet two blocks from the warehouse and walked the rest of the way to the corner of the building and ducked into the alley, walking down to the light at its far end. He ducked into a doorway in the building adjacent to the warehouse and waited. Cockran again didn't notice the black Buick drive past and turn into the next alley.

Cockran looked at his watch. 11:45 p.m. Cockran was rarely on time for anything and Sheila had been self-assured but he didn't want her alone in this alley so he had come early. Thirty minutes later, Cockran decided he had waited long enough. He would leave the door unlocked, as she had asked, so she would spend no more time than necessary outside.

Cockran approached the door, keys in his right hand. He grasped the handle and began to insert the key when, to his surprise, the doorknob easily turned in his hand and he pulled it open.

Once inside, Cockran pulled out a hooded electric torch. He waited for his eyes to adjust to near pitch-black darkness before he switched on the torch and proceeded down the nearest aisle, stacked high above him with crates. He flashed the beam randomly at the stencils on the sides of the crates. Colt. Winchester. Thompson. Austin Powder. Sheila's information was solid. He turned left at the next aisle and headed toward the back of the building, along which ran a rail spur where the cargo bays for loading and unloading were located. Once he reached the wide area of the cargo bays, he turned to the right and proceeded toward the area where Sheila had told him the glass-enclosed office was located. Cockran pulled the keys from his pocket, unlocked the office and went in.

File cabinets were arrayed against the far wall. Using another key, he opened all three of the wooden file cabinets. The first two cabinets were empty but the third contained what he wanted. He pulled out the folders and sat down at the scarred wooden desk. Illuminated only by the electric torch, he began to make notes from the invoices. The names of the manufacturers. An itemization of the weapons. The dates they had been shipped. The cost. Then he heard a sound. Perhaps Sheila has finally arrived, he thought, but he switched off the torch and waited in the dark. It wasn't Sheila. It sounded like a moan. Someone in pain. Cockran reached inside his jacket for the Webley and walked through the office door back into the warehouse.

The sound was coming from the nearest aisle, the one immediately parallel to the one Cockran had come down to reach the loading bays and the office. He reached the corner and cautiously peered around but, even though his eyes had again adjusted to the darkness, he could not tell who was making the noise. He decided to risk it and flicked on the torch again, pointing it in the direction of the noise. Halfway down the aisle he saw a crumpled, white-haired form slumped against one of the crates. He knelt beside the man. Up close, his white hair was matted and streaked with blood. He wore the uniform of a security guard, but his holster was empty. "Charlie. Wake up, Charlie," Cockran said. "What's happened here?"

The man was too dazed to respond. Then Cockran saw why. The guard's hand fell limply away from his stomach where it had been covering three small dark holes in the fabric of his uniform. And, surrounding it, a stain even darker than the blue uniform. Cockran felt for a pulse, but it was faint. Cockran had been in combat with the 69th only three months before he was wounded. But he had seen several belly wounds like this one. Charlie Mahoney was dying.

And then he heard Sheila scream, followed by the sound of four gun shots. He pulled the Webley out, cocked it and ran toward the sound. He stopped behind one of the crates and carefully peered into the space lit by a single bare bulb. It was a break area. A small, battered wooden table pushed against the wall on which sat several scarred and chipped coffee cups, a hot plate at one end, a coffee urn at the other. There were three unmatched chairs in front of the table and Sheila Greene was in one of them.

Blood trickled from a corner of her mouth and she was rubbing her wrists as if they had recently been bound like her ankles still were. Her sweater had been ripped, exposing her brassiere beneath, both spattered with blood, as was her skirt. The source of the blood was obvious. The bodies of two men were sprawled on either side of her chair, both quite dead. A massive gunshot wound to the head for one and three well-placed bullets in the belly of the other. The spray pattern of the blood made it evident that both men had been standing in front of her.

"Sheila! What happened? Are you hurt?" Cockran asked.

"I'm okay...I think," Sheila said. "Did you see him?"

"See who?"

"The man who saved me. He shot these two men. He had just finished untying my hands when he heard your footsteps. He ran off that way," she said, pointing one aisle away.

"What did he look like?"

"I couldn't see much. He was tall, over six feet. Very blue eyes. An Irish accent."

Cockran knelt in front of her and began untying the rope around her ankles.

"Tell me what happened," Cockran said.

"There were four of them," Sheila said. "Two of them got away. I think one was the leader. He certainly acted like it. His name was Tommy. Can I borrow your handkerchief "

Cockran handed it to her. "We need to get out of here Sheila. Someone may have called the police."

Sheila laughed, short and sharp. "Police? I don't think so. Not in this part of town. Not at this time of night. This is Cleveland, for goodness sake. Gunshots in the warehouse district are not a big deal and no copper I know is going to risk his neck investigating them."

"All the same, I need to get you out of here. Let me check these two bodies for any ID."

Cockran walked over to the nearest body and looked down, recoiling in shock and recognition. The man's features were unmistakable. Sean Russell! Tommy McBride's second-in-command. Cockran had watched from behind a two way mirror as Free State police, the Gardai, had questioned him in connection with the bank robbery and Nora's murder but he had a solid alibi which Cockran hadn't believed for a minute. He was still alive, his hands clutching his stomach, groaning in pain, arterial blood attesting to the shooter's accuracy. He would die in the next few agonizing moments. Good, he thought, as he checked for ID but found none.

Turning his attention to the other body, clothed in a suit and tie, he found a .38 special police revolver in a shoulder holster. The man's billfold had a badge pinned to one side and an identification card on the other. William Miller, Special Agent. Office of the Inspector General, U.S. Department of Commerce. A Fed! What in hell was a federal agent doing with Sean Russell in a warehouse loaded with weapons and ammunition for the IRA? Just then, Russell's eyes rolled back in his head and the groaning stopped. Cockran felt for a pulse and found none. Rot in hell, you bloody bastard, he thought as he let the man's wrist fall limply to the ground.

Cockran turned back to the girl and took off his trench coat and put it over her shoulders. "Come on, let's get you safely home."

Back in the battered motorcar, Cockran took his eyes off the road and looked at Sheila. Color was returning to her face. He didn't notice the black Buick following them.

"Why didn't you wait for me tonight?" Cockran asked.

"I'm sorry. I know it was stupid of me. I'm so used to being my father's daughter that I didn't believe any harm could come to me. Not in my town. Not like this."

"So, what happened? How'd they get you?"

"I heard them talking in the office. The two Irishmen."

Cockran nodded.

"They were arguing. One of the guys was supposed to meet someone in Chicago in a couple of days. I forget his name. Something like Blackburn, Blackleaf. I'm not sure."

"Blackthorn?" Cockran asked.

Sheila shook her head affirmatively. "Yes. That's it. Blackthorn. The other Irishman, the one who was killed didn't like it. He said Blackthorn couldn't be trusted. But the other guy?"

"Go on," Cockran said, certain now that it had been McBride.

"Yes. Well, he didn't agree. He said this Blackburn had all the right codes. He said that he clearly had a message from the 'Council', whatever that is. Seeing as how they hadn't found 'the bloody notebooks', he said, they couldn't ignore a message from Blackburn. I remember what he said, word for word, because that's when Charlie found me and tipped them off."

Her face darkened. "That's when it all happened. They shot poor Charlie and grabbed me, tied me to the chair, tore my sweater and hit me. Told me weird stuff like I was fair game, and the spoil of war. After that came the shots. The two men killed." Sheila paused. "Blackburn? The Council? What's it all mean?"

"Blackthorn. The name you heard was Blackthorn. And I'm not sure what it means either. And if I were, I wouldn't tell you. I shouldn't have put you in danger like this. Your father shouldn't have, either. What we've got to do right now is get you home safely."

"No, Bourke, if you really want to stay on my good side, take me back to your hotel."

Startled, Cockran stared at her sidewise, raising his right eyebrow. She laughed. "No, silly. It's not like that. I just can't go home looking like I do. I'm a big girl but Daddy still doesn't like it if I stay out all night. He's a light sleeper. Whenever I come home, whether it's one in the morning or after breakfast, I have to either give him a kiss goodnight or good morning. If he sees me like this, and I have to explain, then he's going to send me back to school in the fall before he's really strong enough to fend for himself." She paused before continuing. "So, it's simple, really. You take me back to your hotel. I'll wash up and spend the night there. I'll call one of my girl friends first thing in the morning. She'll bring a fresh change of clothes over and I'll take a taxi home. Daddy is none the wiser and I'm still here to take care of him."

Cockran and Sheila rode in silence in the Alcazar's elevator up from the basement garage to Cockran's suite of rooms. He showed her into the bedroom. "The bathroom's in there. You take the bedroom. I'll use the Murphy bed in the sitting room."

It was 2:15 a.m. It was late but Cockran knew Churchill's habits. He placed a phone call and the great man was still awake, working on an article for a London newspaper. Cockran gave him a short version of the night's events. Cockran then used the suite's second bathroom to put on his pajamas, pulled down the Murphy bed, and quickly fell into a deep sleep. .

Cockran was roused from his sleep twenty minutes later when a wet-haired, terry-cloth clad figure, smelling of soap, climbed into bed beside him, pulled his left arm around her and snuggled in. "I'm not being fresh. Really. I just want someone to hold held me while I fall asleep."

Cockran, barely awake, mumbled his assent and left his arm where she had placed it. His last thought before he quickly fell asleep again to the sound of her soft breathing was that Sean Russell was dead. Good. Tommy McBride was next.

25.

We Don't Need Help From Amateurs

Toronto, Ontario
Tuesday, 13 August 1929

The train rumbled through the countryside. To his left, Churchill could see the vast expanse of Lake Ontario. He put down his cigar and picked up his fountain pen.

> *My darling Clemmie,*
> *I have just come back from the Toronto meeting—a tremendous affair. I made my best speech so far. Tonight we go to Niagara—see the Falls tomorrow.*
> *Puzzling conversation yesterday with Smythe. I shared with him some of the information about the bank accounts and the transferred funds. He didn't seem interested. Dismissed out of hand my suggestion he ask the P.M. to authorize reinforcements.*

"Out of the question, Mr. Churchill. My men are more than adequate. No need for reinforcements." Churchill leaned over, picked up the crystal tumbler filled with a light scotch and water and looked out the window at the soft, green blur of the Ontario countryside.

"See here, Smythe, we've got perfectly good intelligence on where the IRA is assembling weapons and we should act on it." Churchill took a sip of the whiskey and placed it back on the low table between them, the contents of the glass rolling gently back and forth in harmony with the swaying of the train on the tracks. "We need to have an alternate plan if the Americans are not persuaded. We don't have enough men to use force to stop the shipment. Even if you use my two men, Inspector Thompson and Sgt. Rankin, it won't be enough to mount a proper operation." Churchill paused and watched the color rise in Smythe's cheeks as he sought to contain his anger. Pleased with Smythe's reaction, Churchill took another sip of whisky.

"This is *my* mission, Mr. Churchill," Smythe said through clenched teeth. "Not yours. My brief is to gather information. Yours is to be a messenger. We don't need help from Scotland Yard and we certainly don't need help from amateurs."

Can you imagine that, my Dearest Cat? Me, an amateur? The Royal Navy ran the best intelligence operation in the war, bar none, and I daresay I had more than a little to do with that. Still, I knew what Smythe's answer would be. Unbeknownst to him, I had sent a cable earlier in the day to the P.M. asking him for more resources. The P.M. turned me down by return cable within two hours. "Proceed original plan. No departures. Repeat. No departures. Washington negotiations paramount. Stop."

Poor Ramsay doesn't understand. Our Navy is more important to Britain's survival than America's is to hers. The Americans simply don't want competition in the Pacific. To disarm when your former enemies are still nursing their grievances is folly. If only the Americans would forgive the Allied war debt, we could do something about the German grievances and start the healing process. Then we could truly look to disarmament.

My wise Cat already knows this, doesn't she? That's the true pity of being out of office. Not having a Prime Minister who takes my advice on important issues of state.

I think often of you & the kittens & hope you are all happy & well.
Always your loving husband,

W

26.

He Didn't See It Coming

Cleveland Heights
Tuesday, 13 August 1929
8:30 a.m.

Cockran woke up early and slipped silently out of bed. Closing the bedroom door behind him, he walked through the living room of the suite to the small kitchen where he put on a pot of coffee, scrambled two eggs and fried up some bacon from the provisions Hasim had left for him in the refrigerator. He set the table for two and walked back to the sitting room and carefully opened the door. Sheila was still fast asleep and snoring softly. He returned to the breakfast table and ate alone. He left a note for Sheila, telling her he had left for his appointment with the Westwoods, that the coffee was perked, the bacon warm in the oven, and fresh eggs were in the refrigerator. If she were still here, he would see her when he returned in a few hours.

8:45 a.m.

Halfway down the block from the Alcazar a black Buick sat idling. Tommy McBride pulled his fedora low over his face and slumped down in the passenger seat when he saw Cockran emerge and step into the green and black Auburn. He spoke out of the side of his mouth. "Follow him, Rory. Take him down at the first chance you get. The others will have finished their work by now."

McBride opened the door of the motor car and stepped out, closed it and stuck his head back inside the open window. "Be off with you. Timothy's waiting inside. He and I have some unfinished business with that woman at the warehouse last night. She may have seen too much."

The Westwoods' home was a two-story brick tudor mansion with a u-shaped gravel driveway in the front of the house where Cockran parked the Auburn. A privacy screen of evergreens shielded the mansion from passing cars. Several attempts at ringing the doorbell produced no response. Cockran followed a stone path around the side of the house to a large flagstone patio in the rear. Wooden chairs sat empty beside a brick grill with a view overlooking a small lake and a shingle-sided boathouse at the edge of their property.

Cockran walked up to one of the windows, protected from the morning sun, and looked inside. A small table for breakfast was set for two, a pot of tea in the middle of the table, and a silver toast rack beside it. Walking over to a screen door, he rapped on it sharply. Hearing no response, he opened the screen door and tried the handle to the rear door. It was unlocked. He entered into a kitchen and called out, "Hello! Anyone here? Mr. Westwood? Mrs. Westwood?"

Silence. Cockran walked across the tile kitchen floor and pushed open a swinging door which led to the dining room. The door opened only a foot until it was blocked by an obstruction. He pushed harder and squeezed through an eighteen-inch opening, sunlight streaming in from the windows to his right over the two bodies lying face down on the floor.

Mr. and Mrs. Westwood. Both gray-haired. Both clad in blue silk dressing gowns. Both with bullet holes behind their right ears, a large halo of blood spreading on the gold carpet. The man's left hand was outstretched as if he had been reaching for his wife. Cockran knelt down and felt in vain for a pulse on each body. He retraced his steps to the back door.

As Cockran stepped outside, a bullet from a silenced weapon thudded into the door jamb. He dropped to the ground as two more bullets ricocheted off the brick facade of the house. He scrambled for safety behind the brick grill at the far end of the patio, pulling his Webley from his shoulder holster. The shots were coming from the boathouse beside the small lake. He couldn't go forward. There was no cover that way but the brick grill and the corner of the house gave cover for a retreat to the front of the house. He would be vulnerable for a moment but it would take an excellent shot to bring him down. It was worth the risk. He cautiously peered around the corner of the grill and tensed for the dash. He fired two quick shots from the Webley, the echoes from his shots a booming contrast to the silenced weapon of his adversary, and sprinted for the front of the house. He heard the muffled pops from his adversary's weapon as he ran but they missed. Cockran reached the Auburn and leaped in. The engine roared to life and the motorcar accelerated onto South Park Blvd. as a final shot hit the rearview mirror on the passenger's side.

Cockran's mind raced as he sped down Lee Road, veered left at Fairmount Boulevard and headed back to the Alcazar. The bastard had done it again. First Devoy, and now an elderly husband and wife. McBride was good at that. Defenseless women and old people.

"Sheila," he called out as he opened the door, "I'm back." Cockran walked across the living room of the suite, pushed open the bedroom door and stared in shock. Sheila lay sprawled face down on the floor, the carpet beneath her head red with blood from a small hole behind her right ear, beside which lay the towel used to muffle the sound of the gunshot. Cockran felt for a pulse but didn't find one. Her face was bruised and she was clad in a skirt and blouse, a navy blue cashmere sweater on the bed, as if she had been interrupted right before finishing dressing.

He didn't he see it coming. Why? Sheila was dead. He had done nothing to protect her. The same way he failed Devoy. And Nora. He narrowed his eyes and stared blankly out the window at the Alcazar's courtyard below, his anger growing. When he started out, stopping the arms deal had been primary, getting McBride secondary. No more. He'd still do all he could to stop the arms deal but McBride was going to die. Or Cockran would die trying.

27.

To Avenge Her Death

Cleveland Heights
Tuesday, 13 August 1929
10:30 a.m.

Cockran told Hasim everything as they sat in the suite's living room. Beginning with Nora's and Devoy's murders and ending with the Westwoods and Sheila.

"I need your help, old friend. I can't stay here. If my enemies can buy the Feds, they can also buy the police in Cleveland. I must go to Chicago. That's where I'll find them and make them pay for what they did to Sheila."

Hasim nodded sympathetically. "You are correct. The services of call girls in Cleveland are more expensive than the police. What is it you wish me to do?"

"I need you to do two things. I must make one long distance telephone call, preferably from your private office and not from this room. It will only take a few minutes. Then, I'll take a taxi to Union Terminal. If you could wait until I leave to call the police, I'd appreciate it."

"No problem, my friend. You and I will return to my office by way of the service stairs. The maid will have cleaned all the rooms on this floor before noon. I will wait for her to discover the body and report it to me. Then I will notify the police." Hasim motioned towards the door. "We should leave now, before the maid arrives."

A few minutes later, Hasim opened the wall safe in his office, hidden behind the polished mahogany paneling and produced from inside it a bottle of Jameson's Irish whiskey. He poured the whiskey into two coffee cups already two-thirds full with the same sweet thick brew with which he had greeted Cockran two days earlier. Cockran raised an eyebrow and gave Hasim a quizzical glance. Hasim shrugged his shoulders. "It's the government's fault," he explained. "I never drank before Prohibition except on ceremonial occasions when I did not wish to offend my hosts. But when the authorities said that I couldn't drink at all, it became a matter of principle. We could both use a stiff drink right now," he said and raised his cup. "To Miss Greene. May she find eternal peace and salvation and may you take your revenge upon the evil ones who have committed this horrible crime. Now, my friend, what is the second thing you wish of me?"

"Thank you, Hasim. The other favor I have to ask will be more painful. Sheila's father knows I was here and knows that Sheila has met with me. I don't believe he knows she was with me inside the warehouse. She stayed in my suite last night because she didn't want her father to know that she had been in danger. What I can't take the time to do and what I need you to do is to personally tell Mr. Greene of his daughter's death; why I believe the IRA was responsible; and why I have gone to Chicago to avenge her death."

Cockran paused, coffee cup in hand and looked up at Hasim. "I know it's a lot to ask. Will you do this for me?"

"But of course I will, Bourke," Hasim said. "It is a sad duty but I feel an obligation myself as she was a guest in my establishment where she should have been safe from harm."

Cockran had the hotel switchboard track down Bill Donovan at his New York office. Cockran described the events of the night before, omitting only Sheila's name and the graphic details, focusing instead on Sean Russell and the dead Commerce Department agent.

"The devil, you say! The Commerce Department? My god, Bourke, that's at least four murders you've been close to. I'm a hell of a lawyer, but there's only so much I can do."

"What you can do," Cockran said, "is find out who that federal agent was and why he was out there last night. The arms were there, Colonel, and so was McBride."

Cockran looked up. Hasim was back, making urgent gestures of haste. "I've got to leave, Bill. I'll call you again when I get where I'm going," Cockran said and hung up..

"What is it, Hasim?"

"You must go! Quickly. The police are here. Someone must have called them."

"Were they looking for me," Cockran asked.

"Not by name. They asked who was registered in your room and I gave the name you used when you checked in. I also gave them a description which should draw suspicion away from you unless you lose six inches in height, gain fifty pounds and dye your hair black."

Cockran smiled. "I am once more in your debt, Hasim. Do you think it's safe for me to leave through the lobby and take a taxi?"

"There's no need to take that risk. My driver is waiting for you in the garage. He'll take you to the station. Here," he said, pointing to the corner, "take my private elevator."

"Thanks. Also, would you be so kind as to fetch from your safe those leather journals I left with you yesterday? They're part of this somehow and I need to study them some more."

Hasim did so and Cockran walked over to the corner where Hasim pressed a button and an entire section of wood paneling swung out to reveal behind it a small three-person Otis elevator. Hasim's bulk, however, would have made for uncomfortably close quarters had he and Cockran been joined by a third person. In the garage, Hasim embraced Cockran in a bear hug.

Twenty minutes later, Hasim's driver dropped Cockran off at Union Station beneath Terminal Tower with a half hour to spare. No one had appeared to be following them and he observed no one now as he purchased his ticket and started walking toward Track 18. On the way, he stepped into a phone booth, closed the door and placed a call to William Fitzgerald, a commodities trader in Chicago and a friend of John Devoy. Devoy's name overcame the trader's initial reluctance as did the name of Cockran's father whom Fitzgerald said he had met at the 1920 Democratic convention. Fitzgerald wasn't sure he had sufficient contacts at First Union Trust to find out as much as Cockran had learned in Cleveland but he promised to try his best. He also agreed to call in a marker with the alderman for the warehouse district and see what he could dig up on recent shipments received by bonded warehouses.

Sitting in his Pullman compartment, Cockran thought again of McBride. Calmly now. He looked at the Webley in its holster, propped against a pillow on the bed. He hadn't felt this way since his trip out west, seven years earlier, on the hunt for the unholy trinity. He had felt this way in the war. A quiet, deadly calm. Most men weren't nearly as bloodthirsty as former pacifists like his father believed them to be. At least not up close. It was true on both sides. Most of the dead and wounded in the Great War were hit by artillery fire and grenades, not by men who could look them in the eye when they shot them or hear their screams when a bayonet pierced their bellies. All the Apostles Michael Collins had recruited could do that.

So could Cockran. Not all men could. Cockran had been surprised to find that few soldiers in his unit ever fired their weapons in battle, barely ten per cent. After the war, he learned it was not uncommon. But it wasn't because those who wouldn't shoot were cowards. Maybe a few were but he had seen too many acts of courage and heroism from most of them to believe it. Cockran also discovered, somewhat to his surprise, that he had no qualms himself about killing other men—at long range with a rifle, short range with his .45 automatic, or a knife thrust into a sentry's kidney. Killing wasn't something he enjoyed, just something, given the situation, he knew he could do and did. He didn't know why. It didn't make him better. Just different. It was something most men didn't talk about.

28.

Another Hearst Publisher?

Chicago
Tuesday, 13 August 1929
7:30 p.m.

Bill Fitzgerald was a tall, red-faced, white-haired, blue-eyed Irishman in his late fifties, his face creased in a perpetual smile. Cockran sat with him in the dining room of the Yale Club. Fitzgerald wore a tailored gray chalk striped suit whose vest concealed a well-rounded stomach.

"You look just like a younger version of your father. The last time I saw him was at the Democrats' convention in 1920. Those were grand times. We had both parties lined up, I tell you. Self-determination for Ireland. I never saw John Devoy so mad as when Dev came in with his own plank. Split our delegation right down the middle. Not even your father's silver tongue could pull that one out. But enough about the old days, boyo. Let's get down to your business."

Fitzgerald described his efforts in detail but his contacts at First Union Trust had been unable to verify if checks had been drawn. All he found was the name on the account: Andrew Sinclair, the publisher of the *Chicago American*, another Hearst paper.

Cockran absorbed the detail and considered its significance. Another Hearst publisher? The hand of his old boss had turned up a second time. Well, not really his boss. He had never met Hearst personally. But regardless of who signed their weekly paychecks, every Hearst employee knew who he worked for. The Chief. Cockran couldn't conceive of how any publishers working for Hearst would dare to handle sums this large behind his back. First Westwood, the publisher of the Hearst paper in Cleveland, and now Hearst's publisher in Chicago. It couldn't be a coincidence, Cockran thought, and it wouldn't be the first war Hearst had helped drum up.

Cockran pushed the thought away. "What about warehouses? Any luck there?"

Fitzgerald shook his large head slowly from side to side. "No luck at all. There are just too many bonded warehouses in Chicago. Maybe ten years ago our intelligence would have been good enough but not today. Now, it's like searching for a needle in a haystack. Here," said Fitzgerald, handing Cockran a sheet of paper, "are five warehouses which meet the criteria you gave me. Bonded. Space leased within the last month. Shipments arriving daily. But there easily could be three or four times as many that I haven't been able to track down. I'm sorry."

Damn! Five warehouses. Too many to stake out. Maybe the Hearst publisher could help.

"Do you think you can arrange a meeting for me with Mr. Sinclair?"

Again, the large head moved sadly from side to side. "I'm a rich man, Bourke. But I'm just a trader and my money's far too new to mingle with the likes of Mr. Sinclair and his ilk. They have their own country clubs. We have ours. The Jews have theirs. We don't mix. Hell, boy, I wouldn't even be here at the Yale Club if I hadn't played football."

"That stuff only happened to me when I tried to date their Protestant daughters. Pop said it never happened to him and he married two of them."

"Ah, but your father was different. A natural aristocrat. Spoke French and Italian like a native. Traveled to Europe twice a year. A wiser man I never met. Not an average Mick like me."

"Thanks. I appreciate that." Cockran paused, touched, and not for the first time, that his father had meant so much to so many others. "Might you be able to acquire for me a Chicago police detective's shield for the use of an afternoon and identification to go with it?"

Fitzgerald grinned widely and took a sip of Irish whiskey from the coffee cup beside him. "Blessed be, Bourke, this is Chicago. For a price, anything is possible when it comes to the police or public officials. From the Mayor right on up to the highest-priced call girl on Lake Michigan's Gold Coast. A detective's badge falls somewhere in between. I'll have it delivered to your hotel."

Cockran reached inside his suit coat for his billfold. "How much will it be?"

Fitzgerald held up a pudgy, well-manicured hand. "Put that away. Your money's no good with me. 'Tis the least I can do to help you stop the bastards that killed John Devoy."

9:45 p.m.

"**Is** that you, Winston? This is Bourke," Cockran said loudly into the phone. "We must have a bad connection." Cockran was in his room at the Drake looking out at Michigan Avenue.

"No, dear boy, I can hear you clearly. It must be problems from your end."

Cockran smiled as the static broke up Churchill's voice. Churchill never had problems. It was always somebody else who did even if the Bell System in Chicago surely had more modern phones than the ones Bell shipped to Manitoba or wherever the hell Churchill was.

Cockran then told Churchill what he had learned both in Cleveland and Chicago about the bank accounts and the role of the two Hearst publishers in Cleveland and Chicago as well as the murder of the former. He further explained his inability to pinpoint a warehouse location in Chicago as he had been lucky enough to do in Cleveland. "I intend to start looking at those five warehouses after I visit this Sinclair, the Hearst publisher, tomorrow but I don't hold out much hope. There are just too many warehouses in Chicago."

Churchill's static-laden voice filled his ear. "Leave that to Smythe."

"What?" Cockran said. "I didn't catch that. Please say again."

"I said, leave it to Smythe. He and two of his men are in Chicago. They're staying at the Palmer House. Go see him tomorrow morning. Give him the information about the five warehouses. See what he can do. You concentrate on Mr. Sinclair. That looks far more promising."

Cockran next told Churchill about Sheila's death and what she overheard between McBride and Sean Russell. Blackthorn. The Collins journals. He was greeted by silence which extended for a good fifteen seconds.

"Winston. Are you still there?"

"Yes," Churchill responded. "I'm considering what to make of this new information."

Another fifteen seconds of silence and then Churchill spoke again.

"When you report to Smythe, tell him this as well. Maybe he will have some insight we don't."

Churchill paused a moment and then continued. "One other thing, Bourke. Keep to yourself what you've learned about the two publishers. Smythe doesn't need to know. He has what I would call a much more limited view of the scope of our mission. Call me after you've talked with Sinclair. It may be just what I need to persuade Ramsay to authorize a more robust interpretation of what I am permitted to do. Letting Smythe know as much as I do would not be helpful in persuading Ramsay to change his mind. The more I can learn on my own, the better my chances with the P.M."

29.

Blackthorn

Chicago
Tuesday, 14 August 1929
10:00 p.m.

The message had been waiting for McBride when he checked into his hotel after arriving from Cleveland. He placed the telephone call at once. It was short and cryptic. Like the earlier call in Cleveland, all the current IRA codes had been used correctly. But it was the voice which once again persuaded him. Many times that faceless voice had conveyed commands to him during the Civil War. Assassinations. Kidnappings. Bank robberies. Sometimes all three. Even the time they hijacked a mail truck right in the middle of Dublin. McBride knew him only as Blackthorn and had met with him in person on but a few occasions, those always at night, in the shadows. Like it was with the mail truck in Dublin when they intercepted almost all of the Collins' journals, all but the ones sent to Cockran's father. McBride would not have been able to recognize the man who steered him toward so much murder and mayhem had he passed him on the street. It was entirely in keeping with their relationship, therefore, that Blackthorn had scheduled their meeting here, in the middle of Grant Park, at 10:00 p.m.

McBride paused now, as directed, between two lamp posts which illuminated the path, lit a cigarette and proceeded on his way. Moments later, McBride was startled to feel the pressure of a hand grasp his right elbow. Whoever it was had moved as silently as the rest of the night.

"Welcome to America, Thomas," the hard Belfast-accented voice said. "Dev sends his regards. Are you making good use of our money?"

"Blackthorn!" McBride gasped.

Blackthorn smiled in the darkness, his face obscured by a fedora pulled low. The smile was all McBride could see. "I haven't heard that name in years but, yes, it will do nicely. Look straight ahead. The rules haven't changed."

McBride turned away so that his back was to Blackthorn. He'd never gotten a good look at the man in all the time he'd worked for him during the battle against the Brits and later the Free State. " And your answer about our money?" Blackthorn asked.

"Fine. Things are fine. No problems. A big shipment left Cleveland yesterday. The one from Chicago is being loaded now. After inspection, I'll authorize checks. Just like Cleveland."

"Fine. There's a good lad. And the other matter Dev asked you to look into?"

"You mean the journals…."

"The same," Blackthorn replied.

"I've had no luck with the journals. Not at the big house on Long Island or at his law school office. Nor his New York townhouse or the apartment in Cleveland. Nothing."

"Worse luck," Blackthorn replied. "Dev had such high hopes."

"I've never understood why they were so important."

"You don't have to. It's enough that I do. Traitors were among us back then and must be exposed." Blackthorn paused. "Are there any other places you could have looked?"

McBride shook his head.

"I see. Well, do not discount the possibility that Cockran may have the Collins journals with him. I approve now of your efforts to kill him. But, above all, you must find the journals."

McBride turned his head towards Blackthorn hoping to catch a better look at his face, but the man was nowhere in sight.

30.

Strictly Off The Record

Cockran disliked David Brooke-Smythe the moment he opened his mouth. His tone was clipped and condescending. Churchill might trust him but that didn't mean Cockran had to.

The hotel room in which they sat was small and cramped. It had no view. " Do you think this commodities trader you met with is a sound man?" Smythe asked.

"I never met him before today. But John Devoy said he was a man whom you could trust with your life. That's good enough for me."

"That's not good enough for me, Mr. Cockran. Not by half. Not when it comes from a man whom we had ordered shot on sight if we ever found him in the United Kingdom. For the life of me, I can't fathom how an old Fenian like John Devoy would turn on his old comrades and help the Free State against the IRA. Mr. Churchill may think he's a reliable source. He may even think the same of you. But Churchill's an amateur when it comes to operating like we do in the shadows, in the backwaters of the Empire. From Cairo to Dublin and now in Chicago."

Cockran didn't know why Smythe was trying to bait him. But two could play that game. "If I'm not mistaken, Mr. Smythe,

America is no longer part of your empire. Dublin still may be, but no more than Canberra or Ottawa. Words on paper. Isn't that what Michael Collins said?"

"That well may be, Mr. Cockran. I can't help thinking, however, that people of the caliber of the IRA are more reflective of the true character of the Irish people than your dead friend Collins. They killed Collins, didn't they? Snatched defeat from the jaws of victory, eh?" Smythe smiled and then his face grew somber. "Even your wife was killed by those brutes as I recall, God rest her soul. What does that say about the Irish?"

Cockran didn't reply.

"I'm just a member of His Majesty's Secret Service. I do what I'm told. So, if they tell me to go out and save the damned Irish Free State from their own kind, I'll do what I'm paid to do. But I can't help thinking how it would simplify things if Ireland were exposed as the true enemy she is. Your friend Mr. Churchill once knew that. Then he went soft."

Cockran narrowed his eyes but, again, he didn't reply.

"Don't misunderstand me, Mr. Cockran," Smythe replied smoothly. "I don't like any of the Irish, the IRA least of all. No offense intended."

Cockran didn't reply.

"I believe that concludes our business. Do you have anything more for me?"

"One more thing. Do you have any information on an IRA man named McBride?"

"McBride? No. Why do you ask?"

Because I intend to kill the bastard, Cockran thought. "McBride is leading the IRA team in the US. Someone overheard a conversation in Cleveland. McBride said he had a meeting set up here in Chicago at the direction of the Army Council. With someone named Blackthorn. If you find out anything about McBride's whereabouts, I'd appreciate your letting me know."

Smythe pulled a notepad from the inside pocket of his suit coat, opened it and began to write. "Blackthorn, you say the name was?

Can't say that it rings a bell, but I'll pass it on Thank you, Mr. Cockran. Every detail helps. I'll contact you if we learn anything."

Smythe rose and ushered Cockran to the door. "Look, Mr. Cockran. I meant what I said earlier. I'm a professional and I'm here to do my job. If my comments a few moments ago sounded harsh, I apologize. Most of the Irish are kind and peace-loving. Like your wife. Nora was a delightful young woman, so irreverent and full of life. Her death was a tragedy to all who knew her. Please accept my condolences for her as well as your father. He was a fine man."

"Thank you," Cockran said, unhappy to hear that voice once more speak of Nora.

2:00 p.m.

Cockran was ushered into the large wood-paneled office of Andrew Sinclair, publisher of the *Chicago American*, introducing himself as James O'Malley, a detective with the Chicago Police Department's Bunco Squad, briefly flashing his badge and ID which, in the event, had cost $750. The real Jimmy O'Malley was 62 and recovering from a heart attack.

"I appreciate your taking the time to see me today, Mr. Sinclair. 'Tis a major investigation that we have going, and we're managing to keep it out of the newspapers."

The publisher smiled. "I'm happy to help one of Chicago's finest, Detective. Especially someone whom my good friend, Chief Corcoran, speaks of so highly. Who are these criminals?"

Cockran was careful to maintain his composure at the reference to Corcoran. Fitzgerald had only arranged a bribe for the Bunco Squad captain and had made it clear that almost any copper in Al Capone's Chicago was for sale. But Police Chief Corcoran was not one of them.

"That's just it, sir, we don't know who they are. They are scam artists with a lot of money at their disposal. Their M.O. is to wire large sums of money into the bank accounts of wealthy Chicagoans. These people are then approached by the bunco artists and, if they're successful, they persuade the mark that they are investors from back

East who are using the bull market to drive up the price of a particular stock and then make a fortune selling it short. "

Cockran stopped, pretended to consult his notebook, and continued. "They claim they have to move quickly and they typically use the name of a big banker on Wall Street, whom the mark doesn't know, as the one who suggested utilizing the mark. Then they offer the mark the opportunity to participate in the scheme, typically promising a 500% return. But the brokerage house where the mark sends his money is only a front and the mark never sees the money again."

"Very interesting," said Sinclair. "But it's not for publication? Sounds like a good story."

"Oh, no, sir," said Cockran, "this is strictly off the record. My Captain said to promise that you would be the first to know once we make an arrest. But please, nothing until then."

"Very well. I gave you my word. But, again, what does this all have to do with me?"

"Well, the Chicago banks have been cooperating with us in this investigation and each week they send us a report of any unusually large deposits. Most of them, we can clear up with phone calls. But the really large deposits, we like to check out and warn people personally."

The publisher nodded his head. "I understand but I still don't see where I come in."

Cockran pulled out a sheet of paper from inside his suit coat and read from it. "Sir, we've been informed that you have an account at First Union Trust which received a wire transfer of over $1 million on Monday. It fits the M.O. of the scam artists and we've got to check it out. The reputation of the Chicago Police Department is bad enough. We'd be remiss if we didn't do everything we could to make sure a prominent citizen like yourself isn't swindled."

Sinclair laughed. "I appreciate your concern, Detective. And it is gratifying to know that some members of your department take their job seriously. But you don't have to worry about me. I'm not being swindled. I wasn't even aware that over $1 million had been transferred into that account I have at First Union. But I'm not surprised."

"Why is that?" Cockran asked.

"It's not my money. I'm only a trustee. The beneficiary of the account is my employer, Mr. Hearst. He uses that account, and others like it in various cities, for all the art treasures he is forever acquiring. He thinks the dealers would cheat him if they knew that he was the one doing the buying. I'm well off, mind you, but no one in Chicago is going to cheat me. Besides, I don't have any real control over the account. I never even look at the bank statements. I simply forward them every month to my co-trustee in New York. Hearst's investment banker."

"And who would that be?" Cockran asked.

Sinclair paused and frowned. "I'm not sure why that should be of concern to you, Detective, since neither I nor Mr. Hearst are in danger of being defrauded. But it's certainly no secret that Mr. Hearst's leading investment banking firm is Wainwright & Cromwell."

"So your co-trustee is..."

"Philip Cromwell, of course."

31.

I Have Ample Resources At Hand

Canadian Pacific Railway
Wednesday 14 August 1929
3:05 p.m.

Churchill picked up his fountain pen and thought back to yesterday's telephone conversation. He had been wrong about Cockran. Bourke was a good man. Reliable. His father's son. He took a sip of champagne and began to write.

Dearest Clemmie

I intended to begin this letter while we were still running along the north shores of Lake Superior, but we have been traveling so incessantly...

I had a long telephone conversation with our young American friend today. I won't bore you with all the details, but he is making remarkable progress in the small assignments I have delegated. He will soon be leaving for the West Coast...

I received your last letter and appreciate your tender concern for my wellbeing. But never fear. My safety is secure. I have ample resources at hand, and even more in reserve. All will be well.

Tender Love, my darling,
From your somewhat harassed
But ever devoted
W

Churchill put his cigar down and looked out across the Canadian prairie which stretched for miles. He thought ahead to his meeting with Herbert Hoover. It had been nearly fifteen years since that misunderstanding in London. Surely he wouldn't still remember. Would he?

32.

Winston Was Right

Mattie McGary was impatient. Sgt. Rankin was over thirty minutes late and all she could do was sit there in the elaborate lobby of the Drake Hotel with a tripod, a Speed Graflex, two 35 millimeters and two canvas bags. Mattie's bad mood was enhanced by an Extra edition of *The Chicago American* at her feet. The *Graf Zeppelin* had lifted off from Friedrichschafen at 3:00 a.m. that morning and passed over Berlin by noon, the occasion for the Extra edition.

CHEERING MULTITUDES FILL BERLIN
STREETS AS SHIP PASSES BY

LADY HAY RADIOS

Nine days to go, she thought, nine days to California if God and the prevailing winds were with them. The next four days, she knew, were the most critical for the *Graf*. On to Moscow, then across the vast emptiness of Siberia to Tokyo. The most dangerous part of the passage. Not for the first time did she envy Lady Hay-Drummond. She should have been the reporter on that ship. Winston had bloody well better be right about this story. Her godfather wouldn't steer her wrong, would he?

Mattie was wearing her trademark tailored khaki pants and a battered, photographer's vest over her white silk blouse, her hair covered by a canvas baseball cap. The Drake was hosting a charity affair that evening and the elegantly-gowned women and their tuxedoed escorts cast sidelong glances at her as if to say, whatever are you doing, my dear, mounting a safari in the middle of the Drake lobby?

That's it, Mattie thought, she'd waited long enough. She left word with the concierge for Rankin as to where he could find her and then slung the two bags over her shoulder, picked up the tripod and walked with long, athletic strides across the hotel lobby. Outside, the doorman hailed a taxi for her.

Mattie sat back in the taxi and relaxed. Action suited her so much better than waiting. She trusted the source of her information. The telegram from "H" had been quite specific. The street address for the warehouse along with explicit instructions to take her photographs of the weapons undetected. The letter of introduction she had from the New York corporation which owned the warehouse would not stand much scrutiny even though she really was doing a multipart photographic essay, "The Sinews of America", two parts of which had already appeared in *The World's Business*, the title of Hearst's pre-emptive strike in the monthly business magazine competition with that upstart, Henry Luce, and *Fortune*.

A large four-story warehouse loomed high above them to the left, the Chicago River to the right, the pavement still glistening from a recent shower. Lights blazed from the high windows on the warehouse's first two stories. Mattie moved quickly across the road and approached the glass door stenciled in black paint "Superintendent's Office". She tried the handle, but it was locked. A light was on so Mattie banged loudly on the door's window.

"Hello! Anyone there?"

After a few minutes of banging on the window without success, she heard a voice behind the door, "I'm coming, I'm coming, keep your shirt on!"

The door opened and a bulky figure in oil-stained overalls barred her way. Mattie pushed the door the rest of the way open and brushed past the man who had to stand aside to avoid a collision. Just what Mattie intended.

"Hey! You can't just walk in here like that."

"Of course I can, dear man. I'm late starting the photo shoot as it is."

"Nobody told me nothing about that."

"That's not my problem now, is it?" Mattie said sweetly. "Here, it's all been arranged," handing him the letter that would not bear close scrutiny.

"I'm Mattie McGary." she said, extending her hand.

The man took it, mumbled, "Pleased to meet ya," and continued reading the letter. Finally, he looked up and said, "Well, I guess it's okay. But you can't go near Bays 8 through 12 on the first floor. My boss made that clear to me. They got cops, foreigners and all kinds of stuff . My men can't even use the john there. They've got to go to the second floor."

"My, oh my," Mattie said. "That does sound serious. Don't you worry. The loo on the second floor will be fine. But show me where Bays 8 through 12 are so I can avoid them."

The illumination in the warehouse was poor, as if they were saving money on electricity. The ceilings were high, a good thirty feet, but the aisles were barely ten feet wide, one dangling light bulb for each aisle. The man pointed toward the police officer at the end of one aisle. "Right there. See? Where that cop is standing? That's where you ain't supposed to go."

"Fine," Mattie said, and pointed the other way. "How about I go over there?"

"Yeah, that's okay with me," he said as he headed off in the direction of his office.

Mattie moved toward the sound of activity in the distance and occasionally glanced up. Some of the crates here were stacked high enough that someone standing on the top crate could reach up and gain access to the latticework of the twelve inch wide wooden beams along the ceiling on which a person could walk.

Mattie arrived in the warehouse's far corner, Bays 24 through 28, and set up a tripod for the Speed Graflex. She started work to establish her presence in the area. After she had set the time exposure and taken several shots, she noticed no one seemed to be watching her to see that she stayed put. She moved the tripod to a new location and loaded a fresh plate in the Graflex. Then, she put six rolls of 35 millimeter film in her vest and headed toward the forbidden Bays 8 through 12. As she walked, she took the leather strap on the canvas camera bag hanging over her shoulder and moved the bag around until it was behind her, positioned between her shoulder blades, her arms free for climbing. Most of the crates in the huge warehouse were stacked two or three high but as she neared Bay 15, they were stacked four high and looked to be not more than six feet from the broad wooden beams high above her.

The crates were uniform, each one reinforced with wood slats forming a large X on the sides, affording her footholds as she slowly made her way to the top of the fourth crate. She reached up with her arms and easily grabbed the wooden beam above her. Hanging there, she swung her right leg upward and, in a moment, was stretched out lying face down across the beam. She felt safe enough up here until she looked down to the warehouse floor twenty-five feet beneath her.

Ignoring the queasy feeling in the pit of her stomach, she began to crawl forward on her hands and knees. Five minutes later, Mattie was in position between Bays 11 and 12. She carefully took the canvas camera bag from over her head placed it beside her. She sat there, legs dangling over the edge of the beam, opened the bag and pulled out her Leica. From within the bag she selected a telephoto lens and began taking a series of photographs. She watched the warehousemen as they stacked boxes on dollies for loading into the railcars, the names of the manufacturers clearly marked on their sides. Colt Firearms. Winchester. Marlin. Hercules Powder Company. Browning. My God, she thought, it was true. It was really happening. Machine guns, grenades. Artillery shells. Hearst was swell to let her do this. Winston was right. This was going to be one hell of a story.

After taking one roll of film, Mattie crept down to the rest of the bays and repeated the process. Four rolls of film in all. She had clear shots of the man in charge, a tall, good looking blond haired man who seemed to be directing all activity. She didn't have a good view of his face but the glimpses were enough. His movements were graceful, athletic, and he carried about him an air of command.

Moving on her hands and knees, Mattie crawled back to where she had placed her camera bag. She took out the last roll of film and put in a fresh one. She closed the camera's leather case and returned it to the canvas bag, fastening its straps and slinging it again over her shoulder and around her head so that it was once again positioned between her shoulder blades.

Mattie began to retrace her route. When she reached Bay 14, she froze, the sound of voices directly beneath her speaking German, a language she knew. They seemed to be on a break, smoking and occasionally laughing. She couldn't climb down here. She figured she would have to move over another three bays before she could climb down undetected. When she crossed the third aisle between the stacks of crates leading to Bay 17, however, she noticed the crates in that aisle and beyond were stacked only two high. That made it an 18 foot drop, clearly too far. She would have to do it here even though the crates were stacked three high, 12 feet below the beam, not six.

Damn, Mattie thought, why can't those Germans live up to their national character and start working again? You'd think they were Liverpool dockworkers. No, she decided, she couldn't go back. She would have to risk the 12 foot drop. She carefully pushed her legs over the side, the wood pressing against her waist, and eased herself back until she hung for a moment by her arms on the edge of the beam. She released her grip and attempted to land on the balls of her feet, her legs bent to absorb the impact. Her left foot hit the wood a bare fraction ahead of her right. The left foot hit squarely as she had planned but the right foot landed awkwardly, its side hitting first and severely twisting her ankle. The pain knifed through her right ankle as she suppressed a cry. Had they noticed? She lay there motionless. The voices had stopped. They must have heard her. She held her breath. Finally, they resumed talking.

Great, she thought, me with a bum ankle and Hans and Fritz won't get their lazy fannies back to work. She'd bet that grave-robbing Lady Hay didn't have problems like this on her airship. She pulled herself up to a sitting position and inspected her ankle. She unlaced the boot and pulled the sock off. She rubbed her ankle and then decided to test it, standing up and trying to put weight on her right foot but the pain was intense. She sat back down and pulled a first aid kit from her camera bag. She took a roll of adhesive tape and began crisis-crossing the tape under her foot and around her ankle. Then she slipped the boot back on and laced it tightly.

Mattie crawled over to the side of the crate and began her descent. Left foot first, inching its way along one side of the two wood braces which formed an X, until she reached the point where they joined together, no weight yet being placed on her right foot. She winced when she did so but the ankle held. She reached the top of the second crate and rested there on the horizontal brace at the top of the X. It happened moments later. She reached out with her right foot for the top of the first crate, leaning all her weight on her left foot. But when her right foot found the top of the first crate, it could no longer take her weight as it had done just a moment before. This is not going to be good she thought as she fell eight feet to the concrete floor below, landing on her back, a moment before her head also hit the floor and left her mind in darkness.

33.

Leave The Woman Here

Chicago
Wednesday, 14 August 1929
11:15 p.m.

Kurt von Sturm knelt beside the unconscious woman and felt for a pulse. Her hat had come off, leaving her red hair visible. She was exceptionally attractive.

"We found this camera around her neck, *Herr* von Sturm. I sent for you immediately."

"You did well, Bruno. This time. Did you check for identification?" Sturm asked.

"No, not yet. I immediately sent Franz to find you and then I took the film out of her camera," Bruno said, holding up an exposed roll of 35 millimeter film.

The woman seemed familiar, he thought, as he reached inside her vest looking for identification. Whatever she had been doing was not harmless. And she certainly had no business being this close to the bays where they were loading weapons.

Bruno and Franz had heard her fall. It must have been a good 18 feet to the top of the crates. If she had been up there, she could have easily seen everything. As he inspected the woman's press card he found in the left breast pocket of her vest, it identified her as Martha McGary, a correspondent for *The World's Business* and for the

International News Service, both of which Sturm knew were owned by Hearst.

Sturm wondered about the coincidence of a Hearst reporter being here tonight and taking photographs. Manhattan had been vague in responding to Sturm's concern about using the three Hearst art acquisition accounts to launder the IRA funds. He left the impression that Hearst knew nothing but, if that were true, why was a Hearst person here tonight? The world voyage of the *Graf Zeppelin* proved that Hearst was willing to buy news stories. Was he doing the same here? The inside story of an IRA arms deal? Had it been a mistake to use the Hearst accounts? He hoped, for Manhattan's sake, that it wouldn't prove to be a problem. In Sturm's experience, the Geneva Group showed little tolerance for mistakes. Neither did Kurt von Sturm.

In any event, working for Hearst was going to save this woman's life. They still had to use one more Hearst bank account and it would not do for a Hearst employee to wind up dead in this warehouse or even missing. After all, someone in the Hearst organization knew she had been here tonight. Good. Kurt von Sturm did not like to kill helpless women, especially one so beautiful.

Sturm stood up. "Here, Bruno," he said, handing over six more rolls of film. " Leave the woman here. Her pulse is strong. The boxcars are all loaded, are they not?"

"Yes, *Herr* von Sturm. They are locked and sealed."

Sturm looked up and saw the bulky figure of Tommy McBride approaching.

"Nice looking broad," McBride said.

"Keep your focus, *Herr* McBride," Sturm replied. "I want this woman followed until the shipment safely leaves Chicago. I want to know where she goes and who she sees. I don't believe she's from around here so she may be staying at a hotel. If so, search her room."

McBride smiled. "My pleasure. I'll see to her personally."

34.

She Needed A Drink

Chicago
Wednesday, 14 August 1929
11:40 p.m.

Mattie shook her head as the smelling salts took effect and the pain returned. She sat on the concrete floor, her back against one of the crates, her head supported by the hulking red-bearded figure of Robert Rankin.

"What the hell is going on, Rankin?"

"You appear to have fallen, Miss McGary."

"Tell me something I don't know," she said, rubbing her head and the back of her neck. "Damn, that hurts! Where the hell have you been? Why weren't you on time?"

"I'm sorry, Miss McGary. I was unavoidably detained by a task for Mr. Churchill"

Mattie sighed. "Fine." She froze. Something was wrong. She reached over her shoulder and knew. "My bag! Have you seen it?"

"I saw no bag."

"Help me look!" Mattie said, bracing herself on Rankin's shoulder, looking about her in all directions. "What about my other camera, the Graflex?"

Rankin shook his head. "I'm sorry, Miss McGary. All your cameras were destroyed. The plates. The tripod. Everything left in a pile." Rankin paused and then continued. "We really must be leaving.

You're in danger. There were two men around you when I came up and they ran off."

Mattie shook her head. "No, I don't think we're in danger. They took my two camera bags. If they wanted to kill me, they had every opportunity." *Wait a minute,* she thought. *Maybe they didn't get it after all.* Mattie routinely put the film she had shot in a deep pocket centered in the back of her vest, all four buttons of which were still securely fastened. As she had done when sitting on the girder, she undid two buttons and reached around with her right hand and groped deep into the vest's rear pocket, sighing with relief when her fingers identified all four rolls.

"You're right, Robert, let's get the hell out of here. I've got film I need to develop."

Once settled in the front seat of Rankin's motorcar, Mattie shivered and held herself as they headed back to the hotel. Once at the Drake, Rankin helped her from the car, her ankle throbbing with every step. She shivered once more and huddled close to the big Scot. She was still in pain. She needed a drink.

35.

Cockran and I Are Old Friends

Cockran had taken a long walk along the Lake Michigan shore after talking to Churchill and placing another call to Donovan who had agreed Churchill's plan stood little chance with the President. Worse, Cockran thought, he was no closer to finding Tommy McBride or the warehouse. Smythe had come up with nothing after checking out Fitzgerald's list of five likely candidates. That was what prompted Cockran's long walk. What to do next?

Cockran was a block away from the Drake when he saw a motor car pull up. Two people stepped out. A giant with red hair, red beard and five inches over six feet tall. A woman limped beside him, his huge arm around her back and under her shoulders for support. He only caught a fleeting glimpse, but Cockran was certain he had just seen Mattie McGary. What the hell was she doing in Chicago and how had she been hurt?

Cockran followed them into the hotel's lobby. The big man's attention was focused on McGary whose face was creased in pain. By the time they reached the desk clerk, Cockran was only ten feet behind and clearly saw the key from room 907 leave its box before it vanished inside the man's large hand. Had it really been less than a week since he had met her at the Dawsons' cocktail party? It seemed so long ago..

"Mattie!" Cockran said, his voice easily carrying over the sounds of the crowd.

Mattie turned and a bright smile emerged as she saw Cockran. "Bourke. How delightful to see you. Whatever are you doing in Chicago?" her lips softly brushing his cheek.

"You're hurt. What happened?"

Her smile vanished and her face darkened. "That's a long story and right now I need a drink. Will you join me in my suite?"

Before Cockran could answer, Mattie turned to the red-haired giant and gave him four spools of film. "Robert, be a dear and take this film up to my dark room. You know the floor."

Once in her suite, Mattie went into her bedroom while Cockran took his bags to his own room. When he returned, Mattie McGary was sitting on a sofa in the sitting room, her right ankle wrapped in a wet towel elevated on the coffee table in front of her. It was quite evident to Cockran that all she was wearing was one of the hotel's thick terry cloth robes and while her ankle was covered, the rest of her long and exceedingly attractive right leg was not.

Cockran fixed drinks for them from the bottle of Johnnie Walker Red on the sideboard.

Mattie took a long sip of hers, her face still troubled. "Thanks. So, I didn't expect to see you until California."

"California? I don't understand," Cockran replied.

"With Winston. You *are* meeting Winston in San Francisco, aren't you?"

"Perhaps. But how'd you know that? I still don't understand."

Mattie forced a laugh but it was not the same throaty laugh that had so captivated Cockran the first time they met. "You will. Just wait. I'm going to need more than one drink "

Mattie was wearing bright green enamel earrings which briefly caught the light as she leaned forward to place her drink on the low table in front of her, her terry cloth robe briefly gaping open. Cockran turned his head slowly away in what he hoped was a gentlemanly aversion of his eyes, but not so quickly as to deprive him of a clear glimpse of her freckled right breast. He could feel his pulse elevate at a distraction he didn't need. Before Cockran could ask a question, the red-haired giant returned and introductions were made and he learned that Rankin was one of Winston's body guards.

"Mr. Churchill didn't tell me that the two of you were old friends," Rankin said.

"Obviously, there are lots of things Winston doesn't tell a lot of people," Cockran said, "but it would appear we all have been enlisted by Winston to engage the IRA."

"Yes, but why are you here, sir? I was not informed you were to be in Chicago. Possibly in San Francisco, but even that was uncertain."

"My plans changed. There's something I need to do here," he said.

Cockran fixed more drinks and sat down in an arm chair placed at a right angle with the sofa on the side of Mattie which wouldn't distract him when she leaned forward for her drink.

"Since it looks like we're in this together against the IRA, let's fill each other in. I'll go first," he said and proceeded to give them the complete story from the time he left Mattie at the Essex House, the attack in Central Park, the meeting with Churchill in Montreal, the attack on the train from Montreal to New York, Devoy's death and the suspicions cast on Cockran, as well as the violent skirmish in Cleveland and the murder of Sheila and the Westwoods.

"So, that's about it," Cockran concluded, without mentioning his having jumped bail. "You talked about pooling resources. You have all that I know, what about you two?"

Mattie started to speak but Rankin interrupted. Cockran was surprised to see Mattie defer to the Scotland Yard Detective. "Mr. Cockran, I don't believe you've told us quite everything. What is it you need to do in Chicago? Does it perhaps involve an IRA man named McBride?

"He's the IRA team leader on the arms shipment. I assume you knew that. What's your point? If, in stopping the IRA arms deal, I come across Tommy McBride and he meets with a fatal accident, I'll shed no tears."

"And why is that, Mr. Cockran?" Rankin asked.

Cockran shook his head. "It doesn't concern you. It's none of your business." Revenge for Nora's murder was no one's business but his.

After a long moment of uncomfortable silence, Mattie abruptly stood up from the sofa, wrapped the robe tightly around her, and broke the somber mood. "Well, I, for one, am starved. You boys care to join me for an early breakfast?" as she limped to the phone and asked the operator for room service. "I like that about the Drake. Breakfast served 24 hours a day."

Rankin politely declined, saying that he needed to return to his hotel and get some sleep. Cockran was tempted. Breakfast was fine with him. He needed it. He enjoyed Mattie's company and, before Devoy's death, he had been looking forward to her next visit to New York.

"Sure, I'd like that," he said.

Upon hearing Cockran accept, Rankin amended his earlier answer and agreed to stay for coffee. Mattie ordered scrambled eggs, a rasher of bacon and hash browns with toast and marmalade for both of them, a pot of tea for her and coffee for Cockran and Rankin.

The two of them sat there across from each other over the room service cart which served as their table, Rankin sitting in a nearby armchair. Mattie raised her fork in the air after having speared a small bite of scrambled eggs and hash browns. "You know, Bourke," she said after she had finished the bite, pointing the empty fork at him, "you were right about one thing. Winston knows a lot which he doesn't tell others. I'm sure you've figured out that Winston asked me to meet you in New York. Anne agreed to help arrange it. Winston hadn't seen you in seven years. He said you and your father were his close friends but he wanted independent verification of whether I thought you were up to a 'small task', as he put it."

Cockran was annoyed at her and Winston's deception. "And how did I measure up?"

"I told him I found you to be attractive, obviously very fit, and reasonably mentally alert," she paused, smiled and then added, "for an American." Cockran smiled back as she continued. "But Winston never told me of the peril he's placed you in and he certainly had the opportunity to do so."

Mattie gestured towards Rankin. "I knew it would be dangerous because Rankin was supposed to be my bodyguard but Winston inexplicably had him doing something else when my cameras were smashed and stolen. Obviously, I can replace the cameras. It's the Chief's money, not mine but tonight could have turned out a lot worse than it did. Anyway, you've told me what you've been up to. It's only fair I do the same. Winston's people had a lead for me on where the weapons might be located here in Chicago. He asked me to check it out and obtain some photographic evidence. I took four rolls before I fell. Tomorrow, I'll go to the darkroom I've set up on the fourth floor, develop the film and deliver it to Winston in San Francisco."

Something she had said earlier had struck a chord with Cockran, but he couldn't quite put his finger on it. The reference to San Francisco jogged his memory. "You mentioned 'the Chief' replacing your cameras. You're referring to Hearst?"

"Yes. Why do you ask?"

"Because both the Cleveland and Chicago bank accounts where the wire transfers from New York were received are controlled by Hearst."

"That's impossible!" Mattie snapped. "Who are your sources?"

"They're good enough," Cockran replied. "I've seen the bank records."

"Have you told Winston?" she asked.

"Yes, earlier today. I wasn't certain until I talked directly with Andrew Sinclair, the publisher of *The Chicago American*. He's the one who told me that the account was maintained in his name for Hearst's acquisitions of art and antiquities. He told me Hearst had many accounts like this across the country, probably in every city where he owned a newspaper. That's when it fell into place. The Cleveland account was in the name of the retired publisher of the Hearst paper in Cleveland. I don't know if Hearst is directly involved. But there was a co-trustee on the Chicago account. Someone I know. Someone you've met."

"Who?" Mattie asked.

"Philip Cromwell. That evening at Anne Dawson's."

"Cromwell? That pompous ass? I don't understand," Mattie said. "I assumed Hearst had accounts like this. We did a story earlier this year on his acquisitions and he told me in an interview that he used middlemen to front his purchases. But he buys art, not weapons."

Mattie paused for a moment, learned forward and spooned some marmalade onto her toast. Her right leg was propped up on a stool beside the room service cart and in doing so, her robe fell away, exposing her right leg once again, this time with the curve of her hip clearly visible as well. Cockran caught a glimpse of this while she was preoccupied with the marmalade but he returned his eyes to her face once she sat back. Mattie didn't recover her leg. She looked at Cockran and said, "I wonder why Germans are involved. That's the angle I can't figure."

"Germans?" Cockran and Rankin said almost in unison.

"You never mentioned any Germans," Rankin said pointedly.

"I didn't?" Mattie said. "Are you quite certain?" Rankin nodded that he was and Mattie continued. "I apologize. I guess that hit I took to the head was more serious than it seemed." Mattie then relayed to the two of them, in more detail than she had previously told Rankin, what she had gone through prior to her fall and what the two Germans she heard only one bay over had been saying.

"They weren't far away. They must have heard me fall and then stole my camera bag."

Mattie turned to Rankin. "So, Robert, you're the professional. What's next? You have identifying numbers from the boxcars. I say we track down the destination of those railcars."

"I think we ought to be checking into Hearst's role in all this." Cockran said.

"That's ridiculous," Mattie said. "Hearst has nothing to do with this."

"I didn't say he did." Cockran replied. "But if someone is using his bank accounts without his permission or knowledge, I think he'd damn well like to know that. Look, I can appreciate your reluctance to snoop into your employer's business..."

"Nonsense," Mattie said, "that has nothing to do with it."

Rankin stood up. "It's late. We all need some sleep. I agree with both of you. I would be shocked if a man of Mr. Hearst's stature were involved in something like this. But it would appear someone close to him is. For the sake of his reputation, we need to check this out. Let's meet back here tomorrow morning in Miss McGary's suite at 9:30. Agreed?"

Both Mattie and Bourke nodded affirmatively as Rankin continued. "I could use your assistance, Mr. Cockran, in tracking down the destination of those four box cars. After she finishes developing her film, I believe it would be a good idea if Miss McGary would do some digging into the background of this Cromwell fellow."

As Rankin opened the door, he paused, turned his head back to Cockran. "By the way, I believe I know where this McBride fellow is staying. The Congress Hotel. I'll take you there tomorrow if you wish after we visit the rail dispatchers."

"Thanks." Cockran said, his pulse quickening at the thought of finding Tommy McBride.

2:00 a.m.

Rankin's hotel was only six blocks away. He decided to walk and started off down Michigan Avenue. The streets were deserted and a light mist was falling. Fifteen minutes later, Rankin was surprised, only two blocks from his hotel, to see two men approaching, the first he had seen since leaving the Drake. As Rankin approached within five feet of the pair, the taller of the two raised his hand and said in a clear English accent, "I say, old chap, would you possibly have a light?" Rankin was bone tired but he stopped and instinctively started patting his pockets, searching for his matches. The one behind him was good, really good, Rankin thought later. He never heard the man approach. Rankin had absolutely no warning when he was struck from behind. Rankin gasped in pain and the two men in front of him now joined the one behind in a barrage of punches and kicks. The big Scot was soon forced to his knees and then to his side.

The three attackers continued their kicks into Rankin's unprotected body. He knew he was on the verge of losing consciousness when the man to his front silently crumpled to the ground beside Rankin, his eyes wide open, dark blood flowing from a small hole between them. The kicks stopped and Rankin rolled onto his back and saw two more bodies there.

Before he lost consciousness, Rankin saw two men approach him wearing long dark coats, hats pulled low over their heads, each holding a silenced automatic pistol straight down at his side. Rankin heard the taller of the two men say, in what Rankin recognized was a Northwest Ireland accent, Donegal if he was not mistaken. "There's an alley two doors down where I can dump these fellas. And shouldn't you be getting the big one to hospital? He doesn't look too good." Rankin noticed as the man bent over to look at him that he had dark hair beneath the hat, bright blue eyes and a prominent nose which had been broken. Then, his world went black.

36.

You're Not An Angel

Chicago
Thursday, 15 August 1929
9:00 a.m.

Robert Bruce Rankin woke up and knew he was in heaven. Everything was white. The sheets. The bed. The walls. The angel beside him backlit by the sunlight.

"Good morning, Detective Sergeant. Nice to have you back with us."

Rankin was puzzled as he tried to clear his head. The angel had a mild upper-class Dublin accent with, he thought, faint echoes of an American accent. He thought he recognized her face from somewhere but he couldn't remember. But he had seen that face before. Large brown eyes, aquiline nose, high cheekbones. Yes, he knew that face.

The angel was seated beside him now, placing her hand behind his head, offering a sip of water. As she leaned closer, he noticed a green enamel pin on the collar of her white dress. A circular pin with a cross in the middle, on top the words "Royal Dublin Hospital", and underneath, "Volunteer". "You're not an angel," Rankin said.

She laughed, a high gentle sound that reminded him of Christmas bells. "No, I'm not."

"Where am I?"

"Chicago Mercy Hospital."

"How did I get here?"

"A good samaritan found you in the street and brought you here for comfort."

Rankin winced as he felt pain for the first time since awakening. He groaned.

"Can I get you anything?"

"Look at my chart. Tell me my condition."

"I don't need to do that," she said softly. "The doctors told me last night. You have three broken ribs, a deep bruise above your kidneys, your left wrist is badly swollen and you have a mild concussion. I woke you up every hour to make sure you didn't go into coma."

The door opened and a short, middle-aged nun in a black habit with white trim bustled in. "Well, how is our patient doing?" Before Rankin could respond, she answered her own question. "You seem to be getting some color back. My name is Sister Mary Ellen. Here, let me have your wrist," she said, grabbing his arm with one hand, her time piece in the other.

"Good for you," she said, "Not nearly so elevated a pulse. Here, open wide." Rankin obeyed as she took a thermometer from the stand, shook it down, and thrust it in his mouth.

"I'll be back in a few minutes," she said and smiled sweetly before scurrying out of the room, only to return five minutes later and liberate the thermometer from under Rankin's tongue. She frowned. "Not too good. Under 100 but just barely."

"How soon before I can leave?" Rankin asked.

"Not until the doctor says so," the nun replied. "But based on my experience, not until your temperature's back to normal and that swelling on your temple goes down."

Rankin picked up a white-framed mirror on the side table and winced at what he saw. The entire left side of his face from the forehead down to his jaw was swollen and discolored.

"I'll pop in after lunch, then," Sister Mary Ellen said, "and see how you're doing." Rankin put his fingers tentatively on his face and winced when he felt the pain.

The nurse left the room and the Dublin volunteer returned to the chair beside his bed. "What's your name," Rankin asked.

"Hush," she said, putting a finger to her lips. "We've no need for names, Detective Sergeant. There's no time. Are you feeling better?"

"A little," he allowed. "At least until I saw my mug in the mirror."

"I know from the identification in your wallet that you're with Scotland Yard and I conclude that you're here on official business. Am I correct?"

Rankin was wary. He didn't talk about official business to strangers. Not even Irish angels. Rankin stared at her for a moment and then said, "I'm sorry, Ma'am, but...."

She interrupted. "I understand. But I'll bet you're not investigating a robbery, are you?"

"Well, no."

"So that means you must be here preparing for the visit of an important British public figure. And since the Prime Minister is not due until October, it must be Mr. Churchill."

"As I said, Ma'am, I can't..."

The volunteer ignored him and continued, "Never mind. Let me ask you about an American. I am informed that you know one named Bourke Cockran. Correct?"

Rankin paused. How could she know about Cockran? He decided to say nothing but knew he hadn't kept the surprise from his face when Cockran's name was mentioned.

"Fine. I thought so. There's an urgent message I need you to deliver to both of them, in person. Not on a telephone, you understand? Tell Winston his life is in danger. Tell Cockran also. Be careful around open spaces with high buildings. Rifles. A cross-fire. Do you have that, Detective Sergeant?"

"Yes, ma'am, I do."

She leaned over and kissed Rankin on the forehead. "Now you, dear boy, should get some rest." She quickly stood up. "Winston's going to need all the help he can get."

37.

Mr. Capone Sends His Regards

Chicago
Thursday, 15 August 1929
2:00 p.m.

It was a wasted day, Cockran thought, as he sat in a taxi on his way to the Congress Hotel where he hoped to pick up the trail of Tommy McBride. His eyelids were heavy, the adrenaline that sustained him earlier in the day having slowly seeped from his body. Only the occasional jostling of the taxicab prevented him from falling asleep entirely.

The day had promised so much more at the outset, Cockran thought. He could hardly wait for it to begin. Rankin's unexpected offer the night before to lead him to McBride kept him awake for most of the night. But Rankin never showed up that morning and things went downhill after that. Cockran had been sorely tempted to spend the entire day staking out the Congress Hotel but he decided to visit the four rail dispatchers whose names Rankin had given him. They were of no help. A mid-day phone call to Donovan brought more bad news.

The NYPD had now brought in the FBI which in turn sent out an APB to all its regional offices. While no more arrest warrants were imminent, Cockran was now officially a suspect in Devoy's murder. Donovan argued with him to stop by the FBI's Chicago field office and clear everything up by answering a few questions but Cockran had refused. Finding a dead Commerce Department Agent lying next to Sean Russell's body in a warehouse full of IRA weapons did not increase his faith in federal agencies. Besides, Cockran was certain the FBI had inherited the dossier J. Edgar Hoover's General Intelligence Division had compiled on him after the war. As a reporter for Hearst, Cockran's 1919 expose of the 200,000 dossiers the GID had developed on "radical activists"—including Hearst himself—had not endeared him to Hoover or to the FBI's predecessor for whom he worked, the Bureau of Investigation. No FBI for now.

Donovan had discovered little else about Commerce Agent William Miller, aside from the fact that he once worked for the Inquiry. Agent Miller's file, however, was illuminating only for his complete lack of credentials of any sort. Before the Inquiry, Miller had never held anything more than the occasional odd job, and had not even graduated high school.

"If I didn't know any better," Donovan had said, "I would think that bozo was only hired muscle. But I didn't think the Inquiry went in for that sort of thing."

"Neither did I," Cockran replied.

Cockran knew he was being followed. The tail had picked him up when he left the Congress Hotel. He had flashed his police badge only to learn that McBride had checked out that morning. His luck was no better now than at any of the rail dispatchers he had visited earlier in the day. The contraband story and his police badge weren't working. Most of the people he talked to seemed incredulous that a Chicago police detective was actually investigating crime.

If there was contraband, one dispatcher had told him, Capone was behind it. "Neither you nor I," he told Cockran, "want to be involved in any of that. Trust me. It's a lot healthier."

The man following him had a light olive complexion with a trim mustache. He was tall, well-dressed, a gray fedora, double-breasted pin-striped suit, expensive tie and two-tone black and white shoes. He didn't look Irish or German for that matter, either. Cockran wasn't overly concerned. His tail was a big man but the street was crowded and Cockran was only three blocks from the Drake. Still, he had learned enough about the arts of surveillance through his time with MID during the war that he wanted to find out whether he had a team on him rather than one individual. Unfortunately, the street was too crowded for the usual ploy to work—stopping to look in a store window. The man had stopped too, and done the same thing, something he couldn't do if there were only a few people on the street.

Cockran tried Plan B. He came to a sudden stop, looked at his watch as if he had just remembered where he should be, shook his head in dismay, and started to cross the street. Once he reached the middle, he abruptly turned on his heel and walked directly back from where he had come, his eyes looking directly at his tail whom he had just burned. The tail kept on walking past him as if nothing had happened. Cockran would know if it was a team if there were another man on the other side of the street to take the place of the one he had burned. Upon reaching the sidewalk he turned and looked across the street, waiting to see if someone were reversing course. But there wasn't. Then he felt a large hand grasp him firmly by his left elbow.

"Mr. Capone sends his regards. Let's go get a cup of coffee. You're in no danger.... Not yet. I could have quietly killed you five different times in the last two blocks, if that's what we wanted. This is our town. We can pretty much do anything we want."

Cockran turned to face the man who had grabbed him. Up close, Cockran was surprised to see that the man was about the same age as him. "There's a coffee shop at the Drake and it's only a few blocks away. How would that be? We can talk on the way."

"Fine." Capone's man replied. "We know that's where you're staying, Detective O'Malley, Mr. Andrews or whatever your name is today? Tell you what, let's just stick with 'Cockran'."

Cockran registered surprise at the man knowing his name.

"Yes, Mr. Cockran, we know who you are. Room 1043 at the Drake. And you're wanted by the New York Police Department and the FBI in connection with a murder in New York."

"You're very well-informed, Mr...What did you say your name was?"

"I didn't and yes, we are well-informed. My name is Nitti, Frank Nitti. Look, Mr. Cockran, let me make it simple. You've been asking around, by our count, at four different railroad dispatch offices regarding contraband and rail shipments. Nothing like that happens in Chicago unless we know about it and we know nothing has happened. People pay us good money to see that bad things don't happen to them. Some of the railroads are our best customers. So, if you're planning something, I have one piece of advice for you. Don't.

"I suppose," Nitti continued conversationally, "that we could take you somewhere and, after a while, persuade you to tell us what you're up to but we're really quite busy with our regular operations. That's why I talked to Mr. Capone on his holiday in a Philadelphia jail and he decided I should tail you myself and give you this friendly advice. So, let me give you some final words to take with you. And they will be final if you don't take them. Leave Chicago. Now. Within twenty-four hours. Are we clear?"

"Yes," Cockran replied.

Nitti gave Cockran a pat on the back as if they were old friends. But his hand also came in contract with the Webley revolver in Cockran's shoulder holster. "Good. I'm glad to hear that. We won't be talking if we meet again and, if we do, just remember this. Our guns are bigger and we have more of them."

The man peeled off and Cockran walked up the steps to the Drake's entrance, the uniformed doorman holding the door open for him and tipping his cap.

38.

You Won't Be the First

Mattie was tired but her ankle was a lot better. It had been a busy morning. A trip to the *Chicago American* offices, Cockran's room, and the darkroom. The photos were even better than she had hoped. She hadn't eaten since 3 a.m. so she decided to return to her room and have lunch sent up. When Mattie turned the corner into her room's corridor, something didn't seem right. She couldn't quite place it. Then she realized. The maid was nowhere in sight yet she always cleaned this wing first thing in the afternoon and she never finished before 4 p.m.

Suspicious, she reached underneath her jacket and removed the Walther automatic pistol from her waistband in the small of her back. Holding it in her right hand and her key in the left, she pushed the door open and waited. She advanced carefully into the room, sensed movement to her right and felt the sharp blow of a pistol barrel on her wrist causing her Walther to drop harmlessly to the floor. A second later, a large arm was thrown around her chest and she felt the barrel of a pistol jammed painfully into her right side.

"Martha, my pretty little redhead. Wouldn't you be thinking that a pistol is not the friendliest way to be greeting a visitor?"

"You bastard! Who are you? What do you want?"

"Many things, Martha, my dear. But let's start with the four rolls of film you gave to that bearded man last night. You give them to me," he said as she felt large fingers close over and dig tightly into her right breast, "and won't I be giving you a good time in return?"

Mattie winced and struggled to free herself from his grasp but he only tightened his hold on her breast and pushed her into the middle of the room. Mattie struggled as he pushed her toward the door of the bedroom but he was moving her with frightening ease and literally threw her onto the bed. Flat on her back, she propped herself up on her elbows and looked into the face of a big man, six foot one , easily 220 pounds, she thought, mid-forties, curly gray hair, hard blue eyes, a belly bulging over his belt and a large, almost bulbous nose like W.C. Fields. He motioned at her with a pistol which had an ugly black silencer attached to its tip.

"The jacket and shirt. Take them off. First, you'll give me a little preview. Then, you'll give me the film. After that…well, I'm sure you can figure out what you'll give me next."

Mattie sat up and slowly took her jacket off, stalling for time. He waved his gun impatiently. "The top. Off with it. I know how they feel. Let's see how they look. I saw you with Cockran last night. The two of you have a little thing going, do you? You won't be the first woman of his I've had. His wife and I once had a little fling. Sexy bitch. Left her moaning for more I did. I'll do the same for you. All women end up enjoying what they can't avoid."

Mattie paused and slowly began to unfasten her buttons. He outweighed her by a lot. She needed a plan. The first button. Her Walther, in the other room, was no help.

The second button. Then it came to her. She smiled at the man and he actually grinned back. Men were stupid.

The third button. The spare development chemicals were in the new canvas bag beside her luggage. She pulled her blouse out of the waistband. He began unbuttoning his fly.

The fourth button. Yes, the acid bath, the final step in the developing process, would be a nasty surprise. She stood up from the bed. He didn't move. She knew exactly where his attention was focused and she planned to keep it there.

The fifth and last button. She did it slowly and provocatively, pushing her blouse aside, inviting him to look at her now uncovered breasts.

"T'is a lovely pair you have, my pretty. Now find me the photographs and the negatives."

"They're in the closet." Without waiting for an answer, Mattie moved toward the closet, making no effort to hold her blouse together, her breasts bobbing as she walked. Once there, she turned around to give him another view. "Bring me that chair. The shelf's too high to reach."

He kicked the chair over to her, his eyes barely leaving her. She picked it up and placed it just inside the closet door. He would have another distraction when she leaned over. She stepped up onto the chair and arched her back as she leaned toward the canvas bag on the top shelf. As she did, she could feel the fabric of her trousers pulled taut, outlining her backside.

"Beautiful ass, Martha. Just made for giving me a nice ride. It won't be long now. Don't tarry up there."

Damn right it won't be long now you bastard, Mattie thought, as she groped in the canvas bag. Her right hand found the familiar square bottle of the acid bath chemicals. She unscrewed it with her left and picked up blank photographic paper. Stepping down, she turned, her right hand clutching the unseen bottle tightly to her waist, her left hand holding the paper. She thrust the photographic paper at him, making sure her hand did not obstruct his view of her breasts which were bobbing once more. He reached for the papers almost absent mindedly, his eyes never leaving the target she intended. He never saw her right arm sweep up in a wide arc, splashing the contents of the bottle directly in his face. He howled in pain, brought his hands to his face, dropping his gun on the floor as he sank to his knees, crying, "My eyes! My eyes!"

Mattie never wore high heels, except on formal occasions. She'd photographed enough industrial sites that one minor accident had been enough to persuade her to take a grizzled old foreman's advice that she invest in several pairs of steel-capped workman's boots. They turned out to be so comfortable, once she had broken them in, that she wore them everywhere except on those rare occasions when she dressed up. Unfortunately for her intruder, she wasn't dressed up now and, as he knelt there in front of her, head on the floor, hands clutching his face, she stepped behind him and delivered a vicious steel-toed kick between his legs. The man froze, sucking for wind and curled into a fetal position, the pain in his eyes eclipsed by the new agony in his groin.

Mattie moved quickly. The acid bath would not inflict permanent damage and she wasn't sure how long her kick would keep him down. She picked up his pistol and tucked it into the waistband of her trousers in the small of her back and sprinted out of the bedroom. Her shoulder purse and Walther were laying on the floor by the suite's entrance. She stooped, picked them up, and opened the door. Every second counted. She didn't refasten her buttons. That would come later. She sprinted down the hall towards the fire stairs. An elderly couple exited their room and stared in wide-eyed astonishment as she ran past them, shouting back over her shoulder, "There's a man after me! Call the house detective! Call the police!"

Mattie reached the fire stairs and pushed the door open with one motion and lunged inside. She took the stairs two at a time, not pausing to catch her breath until she reached the fourth floor. She stood still and listened. There were no sounds of pursuit. She stuck the Walther into the front of her waistband. With the other weapon at her back, it was a snug fit. She then buttoned her blouse, leaving the tails out, concealing both weapons. She ran her hands through her hair, took a deep breath, and walked out into the hall. Moments later, she was back at her darkroom and pushed the key into the lock. She gave a sigh of relief as she went into the room and closed and locked the door behind her.

39.

How Long Have You Known Mattie?

Chicago
Thursday, 15 August 1929
4:45 p.m.

Cockran opened the door to his room and froze at the scene before him. His bag was open, clothes flung from drawers and papers strewn everywhere. Cockran had started the process of repairing when the phone rang.

"Yes?"

"Bourke!" Mattie exclaimed. "Thank God you're back. Someone broke into my room! "

"Yours too? I've had the same on this end." He paused, eyeing a green enamel earring on the floor. "What were they were looking for?" he asked, still staring at the earring.

"The film, of course, but it was down in my darkroom."

Suddenly, Cockran remembered exactly where he had seen that green enamel earring before. A laugh, the flash of a breast, a green earring in contrast to her crimson hair.

"What were they looking for in your room?" Mattie asked. His mind raced. Why had she been in his room? Who was she working for? "Hello? Cockran? Are you still there?"

"I'm not sure," he lied. "Maybe they thought you left the film with me."

"Oh."

The silence was building. Cockran couldn't think. "Look, stay there. I'll be right over."

He placed the receiver down and picked up the earring. It was Mattie's, no question. Then it occurred to him that he had never verified with Churchill that Mattie or Rankin were who they said they were. Rankin could have lied to him about McBride to get him out of the hotel so Mattie could search his room for the journals. Who knew what her real agenda was?

Cockran quickly picked the phone back up and had the switchboard place a call to Churchill who confirmed that he had indeed enlisted both Rankin and Mattie's help. Cockran paused. How should he broach the subject of Mattie's duplicity?

"Winston, how long have you known Mattie?"

"All her life, my boy," Churchill replied. "She's my godchild."

"But Mattie works for Hearst. Don't you think she may have conflicting loyalties?"

"Not to worry, Bourke. I trust her as I do you."

"You didn't trust me enough," Cockran replied, "to tell me about Mattie. Or Rankin."

Churchill took the rebuke in silence, so Cockran continued. "It's less a question of trusting Mattie than of trusting her employer. Remember when you covered the Cuban rebellion which Hearst and his papers soon turned into the Spanish-American War? Hearst may have opposed American involvement in the Great War but he has considerable experience in fomenting little wars. Not to mention twisting the English Lion's tail."

"Theoretically, there may be some merit in what you say," Churchill replied, "but the possibility is remote. After all, Hearst has offered me a contract of $2,000 an article to write for him. Still, let me ponder these new developments and digest them. Much has happened that you don't know. Much I must think about. I'll ring you back later."

40.

The Plot Thickens

Banff, Canada
Thursday, 15 August 1929
5:30 p.m.

Winston Churchill put down his champagne flute and looked up at the Canadian Rockies surrounding the hotel terrace where he had just finished editing the typescript of a newspaper article he had dictated the night before. A broad-brimmed hat protected his fair, pink face from the glare of the evening sun as he unscrewed the cap of his fountain pen.

Dearest Clemmie,

The plot thickens, as Mr. Doyle would say. As I expected, Smythe and his men made absolutely no progress in Chicago in locating the weapons, a feat my people had no difficulty performing in Cleveland or Chicago. Imagine the expression on his face when I told him my own agents in Chicago were able not only to trace the money being used to buy the weapons but they also have photographs, hard evidence, of the weapons being loaded. Consequently, I will be well fortified for my encounter with President Hoover in California.

My darling Cat, your faithful Pig is safe and secure and all will be well.

Your loving husband,
W.

Canadian Pacific Railway
11:00 p.m.

The windows outside the train were pitch black as it rumbled through the dark Canadian night, the peaks of the Canadian Rockies soaring unseen above them, stars the only illumination as the train emerged from the second of the two tunnels through Kicking Horn Pass, each of which had a 270 degree turn inside the mountain. Churchill pushed his chair back from the table in the center of the private railcar's dining section. Across from him were his younger brother, Jack, and Inspector Walter Thompson of Scotland Yard, Churchill's longtime personal body guard.

"Inspector," Churchill said, taking a sip of brandy, "we shall soon be in America. Do you still have those important documents I gave you?"

Thompson frowned. "The letters from your physician and the British Ambassador?"

"Good fellow, Tommy, good fellow. Exactly what I meant. Guard them with your life. As we leave civilization, it will be our only defense against the savages."

"Excuse me, sir," Thompson said, "but do you really believe those letters will persuade the Americans to allow you to bring alcohol into their country for 'medicinal purposes'?"

Churchill frowned. "Why ever not? The Americans may be savages but surely they would not dare to endanger my health."

"Are you quite sure," his brother Jack said, looking up from his newspaper, "that we can persuade the American authorities that you need champagne for medicinal purposes?"

"Of course, we can," Churchill replied. "It has long been established by medical science that a single glass of champagne imparts a feeling of exhilaration. The nerves are braced, the imagination is agreeably stirred, the wits become more nimble. Now, mind you, a bottle produces a contrary effect but I learned quite early in my army days never to overindulge. As I've told you on more than one occasion, Jack, I have taken more out of alcohol than it has taken out of me."

41.

You've Been Swell and I Haven't

Chicago
Thursday, 15 August 1929
10:30 p.m.

It was time to get out of Dodge. Rankin had disappeared but Churchill hadn't seemed concerned. Cockran had struck out trying to find where the railcars that Rankin had identified were headed. Al Capone's gang wanted him out of town. And, if you believed her, someone who looked and sounded a lot like Tommy McBride had ambushed Mattie in her hotel room.

After what happened to Sheila Greene, however, he wasn't taking any chances. He had changed their rooms and bribed the desk clerk to alter their names on the registration forms. He also left a message for Sergeant Rankin in a sealed envelope telling him their new room numbers.

Cockran had originally intended to visit four more rail dispatch offices tomorrow. But given Frank Nitti's threat, he would not do so. Besides, he was running into the same pattern Hasim had encountered in Ohio. At Cockran's request, Hasim had used all of his contacts, both legitimate and not, but he had come up empty handed as to where the Cleveland arms shipment had gone after Cincinnati. Cincinnati, the Queen City, was a gateway to the south, much like St. Louis. Wherever these weapons were being shipped wasn't by direct route nor was it on a single rail line. It was as if the IRA were sweeping up their tracks behind them.

Mattie was taking a shower and Cockran had ordered room service for both of them.

"Food's here," Cockran shouted through the closed door as he heard her turn off the shower and briefly imagined what she would look like as she toweled herself off. Moments later Mattie emerged wearing trim khaki slacks and a white silk blouse, the top two buttons unfastened. Her feet were bare and she ran her fingers through her damp red hair.

"Dinner. How lovely. You are such a dear," kissing him on the cheek.

"How do you suppose McBride knew your room or that you had the photographs?"

Mattie carefully sliced a small bite from her rare steak and chewed thoughtfully as she listened to Cockran's question. "He saw us embrace in the lobby the other night and he saw me give the rolls of film to Rankin". Mattie hadn't told him about the sexual side of her encounter with McBride. There was no need for him to know McBride had intended to rape her or that baring her breasts had been necessary to distract him. The same went for his leering reference to Cockran's wife. What was that all about? She knew from Anne Dawson that Cockran's wife had been killed during the Irish Civil War in 1922 but nothing more. She couldn't imagine any woman married to Cockran having an affair with someone like McBride so she wondered if he had been the man who killed her. If so, he may well have raped her as well. She wondered if Cockran knew. She guessed that he didn't. From her knowledge of the Irish police, the naked condition of a female murder victim would not make its way into any report. The Church wouldn't approve. She shook her head to clear the image and changed the subject.

"Tell me more about Frank Nitti. He sounds even more scary than McBride."

Cockran shook his head. "A different kind of scary. Thanks to prohibition, he's pretty well off. Polite, well mannered, well dressed and, I have no doubt, deadly. But without the government, he'd have to go straight or become a petty thief." Cockran said.

"The government?" Mattie asked.

"When governments prohibit people from having things they want 'for their own good,' the market will supply that need at an artificially increased price," Cockran said and smiled. "It's made them rich men and I wouldn't be at all surprised if Al Capone and Frank Nitti were the largest financial backers of the Women's Christian Temperance Union."

"So the police can't enforce Prohibition?" Mattie asked.

"Far too many police are paid to look the other way. As long as the gangsters play the game by the rules, the police won't care."

"Rules? Gangsters play by rules?"

"The successful ones do. Rule number one is never kill civilians. It's bad for customer relations. Rule number two is don't kill any cops. It's bad for business."

"So what's next?" Mattie asked.

"I'm going to San Francisco to find McBride. If I have time after that, I'll see what I can do about tracking down any IRA arms being assembled there."

"I should go with you," Mattie said. "but I'm concerned that we haven't heard from Sergeant Rankin all day. Maybe I should wait to make sure he is safe."

Cockran shook his head. "I don't think you should."

"Why?"

"I spoke with Winston while you were showering." Cockran said, "He said we weren't to worry about Rankin. He wants both of us out of town. He believes you're in danger and so do I."

Mattie frowned, wrinkling her nose in distaste. "What's his point? So I'm in danger. He knew I was going into that warehouse last night. As if that weren't dangerous?"

"With Rankin not around to protect you, Winston wants you with him."

"Why?"

"He wants you and the film in his possession as quickly as possible. And he wants me to stay with you at all times. For your safety, he said."

Mattie felt the color rise in her face. "Like bloody hell you will!" she snapped. "Rankin was no bargain as a guardian and you're no better. You don't even have a bloody weapon."

"Actually," Cockran began, "I do."

Mattie cut him off with a withering look. "Having one and using it are two different things entirely, aren't they, Mr. Cockran? It didn't help that poor girl in Cleveland, did it?"

She could see Cockran was stung by the reference to Sheila and she instantly regretted it.

Mattie put down her silver and smiled at Cockran. "I apologize, Bourke. It's not you. All my life, I've had men for bosses who wanted to protect me. But I can take care of myself. Let me show you," she said and reached behind her to pull out her Walther PPK.

She smiled. "I didn't have this with me at the warehouse but I have ever since."

"Not that it did you much good today," Cockran replied. "Your boots and developing fluid seem to have been more formidable weapons," he continued, a small grin on his face.

"*Touche*," Mattie said and smiled in return. She liked a man who fought back and she liked this man very much. She looked at her wristwatch. "My goodness, 11:00 p.m." She stifled a yawn and stretched her arms above her head, her breasts straining the silk fabric, her nipples visibly erect. "I'm going to tuck in. Where shall we meet for breakfast?"

Make your move, Cockran, Mattie thought, but he seemed preoccupied because all he said was, "Whatever suits you is fine with me."

"8:30 in my suite. The same order as today okay with you?"

Cockran nodded and she bent over and kissed him on the forehead, her right breast pressing into his left shoulder. "Thanks. You've been swell and I haven't."

42.

Was She Losing Her Touch?

Chicago
Friday, 16 August 1929
7:00 a.m.

Was she losing her touch? Mattie McGary wondered as she sat up in bed, wide-awake at 7:00 a.m., and tossed the covers aside. What did Cockran need? An engraved invitation?

When Mattie was covering the uprisings in the French colonial empire, especially Morocco, she learned French and was struck by the word *aventure* which could mean either "adventure" or "love affair". To Mattie, the dual meaning was serendipitous because her field assignments, when she was lucky, had been accompanied by a new love affair on several occasions. But not recently, she reflected with a sigh. The last time was six months ago in Paris where she spent a week in bed with Ted Hudson, a gorgeous blond American MID agent, an old boyfriend with whom she had enjoyed an off-and-on affair, mostly off, since 1924. She hadn't really wanted to resume the affair but she needed someone to rub in the face of her last lover, an artist and former French Legionaire who had cheated on her. Ted had been happy to oblige. The payback having Andre see her together with Hudson in all their old haunts was delicious, the obligatory sex with Ted less so.

Mattie sighed again. The promise of her summer *aventure* was melting. Mattie had expected better. After all, Anne Dawson had warned her of Cockran's reputation on the Gold Coast and had said it affectionately because she clearly liked Cockran, maybe even loved him a little. But, as a happily married woman, she confessed, she wasn't his type. Cockran, she had confided to Mattie, was drawn to *unhappily* married women, the more attractive and intelligent, the better. Mattie was still single but, at the advanced age of 29, she believed her experience ought to count for something, certainly as much as any young Gold Coast matron. But so far luck had not been with her. And Mattie knew it was better to be lucky than good.

No, things didn't look promising with Cockran. And that would make it more difficult to learn what she needed to know. Her people had heard of the Collins' journals and wanted her to search his room for them, especially any references to "Thorpe" or "Blackthorn". But his room had already been ransacked by the time she arrived, having bribed the maid $5 to let her in. The journals were nowhere to be found. She didn't like searching his room but it had to be done.

Mattie looked at her wristwatch. 7:30. She had left a wake-up call for eight but her thoughts had brought her mind awake. She got out of bed, walked naked to the bathroom, and turned on the shower. Maybe she would have a better chance with Cockran on the train.

She stepped out of the shower ten minutes later and was toweling herself off when she heard a rapping on the door. Cockran's early, she thought, so she started to put on a robe. She stopped. Might she have her chance right now with just a towel? Definitely, she thought, just the towel. She looked in the mirror and held the towel up with one arm across her breasts. Good, she thought, and walked to the door, leaving the chain on and opening it with her left hand to look into the bruised face of Robert Rankin, his left arm in a sling.

"Whoops! Robert! Where've you been? What happened to your face? Hang on, I just stepped out of the shower." She closed the door, undid the chain and turned the knob. When she reached the safety of the bedroom, she shouted "it's okay to come in."

A moment later, wrapped snugly in a terrycloth robe, she listened to Rankin's story. When he finished telling her about the Royal Dublin Hospital volunteer, she smiled. You could add

Detective Sergeant Robert Bruce Rankin to the list of those Winston didn't tell everything.

"I think we should take the assassination threat seriously, Robert. I'll call Winston now."

"But Miss McGary, the woman was quite emphatic. No telephones."

"You're such a boy scout, Rankin," Mattie said. "I'll talk in code. Winston will know what I mean. She placed the call but, in the event, the hotel operator at Churchill's hotel in Banff Springs told her that the Churchill party's train had left yesterday evening.

"Robert, call Bourke. He's in room 943. Tell him to come on over as soon as he can. I've got breakfast coming at 8:30 for the two of us. Call room service for yourself."

Inside her bedroom, Mattie dropped her robe and began to dress. No seducing Cockran this morning, she thought, but the train to California was still ahead of them. Time would tell.

8:30 a.m.

Cockran was skeptical. "It can't be McBride and his men. I know his reputation. He couldn't handle a rifle if his life depended on it. It's not his style. Shooting old men and women is all he's good for. Close range. Back of the head. I also can't imagine why the IRA would have a second squad here in America just for Winston. It doesn't make sense."

"It's not a chance we can take," Mattie responded. "We need to warn Winston. It will be difficult to reach him before California as we will be on the train. We can make a phone call at one of the stops, but if he's not in his hotel room at Vancouver when we call, we'll miss him."

"A telegram?" asked Cockran.

"Possibly. But we've got to be careful. I think I have a code that could convey an element of danger to him but I could do it much more easily if he could hear my voice."

Mattie stood up. "I'll think about a telegram. Meanwhile, let's plan our day."

"Miss McGary...Mattie," Rankin said, "I think you and Mr. Cockran should assume you are under surveillance. We should be especially careful in booking our train passages."

"I don't have that much experience evading surveillance. How about you, Bourke?"

Cockran grinned. "I've had training but you couldn't tell it from Central Park and yesterday with Nitti. Do you have any pointers for us, Detective Sergeant?"

"Yes," said Mattie, "how do you propose the three of us getting to California without being noticed?"

As they discussed various methods of deceiving whoever was after them, it quickly became apparent that Rankin had no better ideas. It would do no good to lose any tail at the hotel because Union Station and the Northwestern Terminal would be staked out as well.

"So we won't go to the train stations," said Cockran. "We make them think that but we head in the opposite direction."

"I don't understand," said Mattie.

"It's simple. Rankin here goes down to the Drake's concierge. His size makes him unmistakable and the arm in the sling more so. He orders three train tickets, the two of you to San Francisco and me back to New York. They'll find out. We know they have inside contacts here at the hotel. Otherwise they couldn't have gotten access to our rooms."

Mattie visibly stiffened at this but managed to ask, "What does that accomplish?"

"It means that once they slip a bribe to the concierge, they'll be waiting for us at one of the train stations. But we won't be going there. We'll be on our way to St. Paul."

"St. Paul?" Rankin and Mattie said together.

"Yes. Northwest Airlines and the Great Northern have a special arrangement. I saw it in the *Tribune* yesterday. We can take a flight from Meigs Field this afternoon and catch a train this evening from St. Paul to San Francisco via Spokane, which arrives Monday evening. Rankin can catch a direct train to San Francisco which will get him there earlier."

"So how will we get these tickets?" asked Mattie.

"I have a friend. Fitzgerald, the commodities trader who got us the bank account information. Once I give him a call, he'll arrange for tickets and have them delivered here."

Mattie was skeptical. "But even if they won't be staking out Meigs Field, won't we have to lose anyone who tries to follow us from the hotel?"

"Not if it works as I anticipate," said Cockran. "I should be able to persuade my trader friend to let me borrow his chauffeur for an hour and meet us at the Drake's service entrance."

"Well, Mr. Cockran," said Mattie, "you seem to have thought of everything. Are you sure you haven't done this sort of thing before?"

"Not recently," Cockran said. "But I was in counterintelligence in MID during and after the war. Then in Ireland, I had to evade British agents in setting up some of my interviews. Look, let's get to it. Robert, you go downstairs, order the tickets for tomorrow afternoon for all three of us, the two of you to San Francisco and me to New York. Then get some rest. I'll arrange the details for the other tickets. We'll meet back here at noon."

9:30 a.m.

Mattie looked both ways and saw no one following her as she entered the Western Union office. She stood at the long table along one side of the office and filled out the yellow telegraph form: H— TRAVEL PLANS CHANGED. STOP. MISSION IN DANGER. STOP. ARRIVE SF 6:25 P.M. MONDAY VIA PORTLAND.—M. She took it over to the counter, paid the cashier, and waited five minutes until the telegram had been sent and she received a confirming copy. She was bothered by the threat to Churchill. That was unexpected. Not what they had anticipated. Not at all. Things were slipping out of control.

Mattie left the Western Union office and headed back to the Drake. The morning was bright and clear and she was enjoying herself as she contemplated the prospect of flying to St. Paul followed by a long train journey with Cockran. She stopped short, however, and did a double take when she passed a diner on the corner where, bold as brass, she saw the hulking figure of Tommy McBride, his ample posterior almost swallowing the shiny red stool on which he rested. He was talking in an animated fashion, between huge forkfuls of food, to a thin-faced man beside him with greasy hair, a receding chin and a long jagged scar on the side of his face.

Mattie was less than a block from the Drake and she hesitated. Should she risk going back to the hotel and alerting Cockran or should she look for a phone booth? Her question was answered when, at that moment, she spotted across the street a familiar bell-shaped emblem, prominently displayed on the outside of a wood and glass structure. Not waiting for the light, she dodged traffic as she crossed the street and entered the phone booth. Her taped ankle was holding up fine. With her back to the diner, she dialed the Drake and asked for Cockran's room and didn't notice the two men swivel on their stools as the big man grinned and gave his scar-faced companion the thumbs up sign.

43.

Halt! Federal Agents! Hands Up!

Chicago
Friday, 17 August 1929
9:30 a.m.

Mattie waited outside the phone booth for Cockran to arrive, careful to keep the structure between her and the diner across the street as McBride and his companion lingered over their coffee. When McBride turned his face to talk to the man beside him, Mattie could see bright red splotches on his face. Good, she thought. She hoped it felt as bad as it looked.

She sighed with relief when, five minutes after her telephone call, Cockran and Sergeant Rankin arrived. She had on a battered canvas baseball cap to hide her red hair. Cockran was intense and focused. He quickly outlined the rudiments of running a three-man surveillance team, two behind the suspects on either side of the street and one of them in front, forming an isosceles triangle. They would switch positions when either man turned so that at least one and usually two of them would keep the two targets in sight.

Mattie had never seen this side of Cockran before and she liked it. The man clearly was obsessed with getting McBride. The three of them dutifully fell into a surveillance triangle when McBride and his companion, a man with a jagged scar on his cheek, emerged from the diner and headed south, Rankin on point and Mattie and Cockran in the trailing positions. McBride and Scarface turned left or right several times as they walked, leading Mattie to believe they knew they were being followed. But the triangle held and Cockran was on the point when the two men turned right and headed down a dark side street. For a brief moment, until Mattie and Rankin reached the intersection, Cockran and the two men were out of their sight.

Mattie was on the near side of the street and Rankin on the far side when they reached the intersection and turned right. Mattie stopped and gasped and turned toward Rankin, a look of fear in her eyes. Cockran and the two men were nowhere to be seen.

Rankin broke into a sprint, wordlessly passing Mattie who ran after him. She saw him reach his right hand inside his jacket where she assumed he kept his service revolver. Mattie started to do the same for her Walther automatic centered in the small of her back but she settled for shifting it to the front when she saw Rankin had not unholstered his weapon.

Mattie could hear the low rumble from the idling engine of a motorcar as they reached the entrance to a narrow alley between two apparently deserted four story warehouses.

"Halt! Federal agents! Hands up!"

Mattie and Rankin stopped and stared at two men in grey suits and dark ties, each holding a gold badge in his left hand and a .38 revolver in his right. McBride and Scarface stood behind them, broad grins on their faces. Cockran was still nowhere in sight.

Mattie and Rankin slowly lifted their hands in the air and one federal agent carefully frisked them and relieved them of their weapons while the other kept his .38 revolver trained on them. Then he cuffed their hands behind them as McBride walked up to Mattie.

"You bitch!" McBride said as he slapped her in the face with the full force of his open palm, the sharp crack echoing in the otherwise silent alley. He caught the other side of her face and twice slapped her again until she could no longer keep back her tears. Her face was on fire but she didn't cry out. She wasn't going to give him the satisfaction. "You're going to pay for this, you bitch," pointing to his face with his left hand.

"Put them in the car, boys," McBride said and the two federal agents quickly moved to obey his orders. Pushed into the long motorcar, Mattie was startled to see Cockran slumped on the floor of the back seat, hands behind him, blood trickling from the corner of his mouth, quite unconscious. Down at the end of the alley, Mattie could see a warehouse and a long metal door slowly rolling up as the motorcar moved toward it, McBride and his companion on the running board on either side, the two federal agents in the front seat. Once inside the warehouse, they pulled a groggy Cockran from the back seat and McBride slapped his face several times until his eyes opened and he was able to stumble forward under his own power.

All three hostages were lined up with their backs against the brick wall. The two federal agents had drawn their revolvers and McBride's companion, Scarface, was holding a Thompson submachine gun with one hand, the barrel pointing down.

This was not going to turn out well, Mattie thought. She flinched as she heard the explosive sound of automatic weapons chewing up the bricks twenty feet in front of her, fragments of brick and stone flying up in the air. She opened her eyes and saw three silhouettes in the open garage door. Her eyes adjusted and she could see the three men more clearly now. The two men on the flanks held Thompson .45 caliber submachine guns, gripping them with both hands, smoke trickling from the barrels. They were wide, olive-skinned men with thick necks, dressed in brown suits, fedoras pulled low. The man in the middle was tall, slender and olive-skinned also. His suit was beige and he was wearing two-tone brown and white wing-tipped oxfords. He was casually holding a pair of beige calfskin gloves in his right hand.

"Hold it right there, boys," the man in the middle said in a low, menacing tone of voice.

44.

Mr. Capone Is A Peaceful Man

The automatic weapons fire had instantly brought Cockran to full alert, adrenalin flowing as he recognized the familiar figure of Frank Nitti. As he regained his senses, Cockran had been mentally kicking himself for walking into McBride's trap. He wondered briefly if Mattie had set him up but quickly discarded the thought. No, he had done this all by himself, his mind focused on revenge instead of stopping the IRA, an obsession about to get them killed.

"We're federal officers and you're interfering with an official investigation," the senior of the two men said. He was balding and his ample belly matched McBride's.

"You're feds, are you?" Nitti said with a smile. "Let me see some identification."

Both agents slowly extended both badges to Nitti, who inspected them closely.

"Commerce Department? Since when did they start giving out guns and badges?"

"I can explain," the balding agent said, but Nitti cut him off.

"I don't want your explanations. I can see what's going on here. My employer, Mr. Capone, is a peaceful man. He deplores violence and murder in his territory. Mr. Cockran is behaving as instructed.

He is attempting to leave town and you are impeding his efforts. As he is under our protection, we cannot have that. My employer was unfairly blamed for what is called 'the St. Valentine's Day Massacre' and I fear he would be blamed for what was about to happen here. This is our town and we can't have anarchy on the streets now, can we?"

"I don't know who you are," the bald agent "but this is a federal matter."

Nitti spoke softly. "That is your problem, my friend, not mine."

"What's my problem?" the agent demanded.

"The fact that you don't know who I am," Nitti's voice a bare whisper now.

The Commerce Department agent laughed. "I don't need to know who you are. Take your two goombahs and get your greasy wop ass out of here. *Capisce?*"

"*Capisco,*" Frank Nitti whispered as he pulled a revolver from a shoulder holster inside his coat and, in one fluid motion, swung its barrel up until it touched the balding agent's forehead. He pulled the trigger at the same time, blowing out the back of the man's head, bone, blood and brain tissue flying into the face of the second federal agent.

Nitti turned to Cockran. Replacing his revolver, he shrugged and placed his hands out palms up and said in a casual tone of voice as if he were ordering a cocktail in a speakeasy, "Explaining three bodies would be difficult. One more in Lake Michigan is no problem."

Nitti turned to McBride and the surviving federal agent. "Take the bracelets off my friends' hands," Nitti said pleasantly. "Now!" Nitti barked when the two hesitated.

A white-faced McBride and the agent quickly unlocked the handcuffs. Nitti gestured for Cockran and the other two to enter the back seat of his maroon Cadillac. "All of your bags are in the trunk, Mr. Cockran," Nitti said. "I took the liberty of having them packed. I don't want the three of you to miss your plane," he said as he closed the Cadillac's door with a firm thunk.

Nitti motioned for Cockran to lower the rear window. "I appreciate your courtesy in leaving so quickly after our conversation.

Don't worry about your airplane's departure. I'll place a phone call in a few minutes and make sure it doesn't leave without you." With that, Nitti walked up to the driver, slapped his hand on top of the Cadillac and the big car moved forward.

45.

Your Virtue Is Safe With Me

Chicago
Meigs Field
Friday, 16 August 1929
12:45 p.m.

Nitti obviously had influence, Cockran thought, as the long maroon motor car pulled up at a gate leading directly onto the airfield. His man, Angelo, who looked as if he moonlighted as a bouncer, approached the gate and spoke a few words to the attendant who promptly swung it open. The chauffeur got back into the motorcar and said over his shoulder, "I'll take you directly out to the plane. In case you didn't notice, there was a black Packard that tried to follow us from the warehouse but we gave him the slip a couple miles back." Cockran hadn't noticed.

The Cadillac rolled slowly across the tarmac and pulled up parallel to the airplane. The 12:55 p.m. Northwest flight Chicago to St. Paul was a Ford Trimotor, its corrugated metal fuselage catching the glint of the early afternoon sun, its nose high in the air, its three heavy-duty Ford engines still idle. Inside the plane was an aisle with single wicker seats on either side, each with its own window. The air hostess assisted Rankin to a seat near the front cabin and led Cockran and Mattie to the two seats side by side in the rear of the cabin, as Cockran had requested.

"The Fords are fairly noisy once we're in the air," he told Mattie, "But back here at least, we have a better chance of carrying on a reasonable conversation without shouting."

Other passengers were boarding now and the air hostess seated them and began passing out pillows and blankets. The cabin seated twenty-two, but it was barely half full. There were four empty seats between Mattie and Bourke and the other passengers. The Ford engines roared to life, the cabin shaking from the vibration as the plane slowly moved forward onto the runway. Minutes later, they were airborne. When the plane had reached its cruising altitude of 3,000 feet on its nearly two-hour journey to St. Paul, the air hostess began serving hot tea, coffee and fruit juice in heavy crockery mugs, followed by sandwiches. At cruising speed, conversation was possible. Two or three nights alone with Mattie McGary was an appealing prospect to Cockran, complicated only by the troubling prospect of how or whether to confront her with the green earring. There had to be an innocent explanation. He hoped there was.

"Fitzgerald promised to follow up on the freight cars and telegraph any information he finds to the Fairmont in San Francisco," he told her. "Several of his bigger clients are high-level executives with some of the railroads. He thinks he'll have better luck tracking the freight cars."

Mattie nodded and took a small bite of her sandwich. "I found out more about our friend Philip Dru Cromwell. Did you know his father had been a partner at the Morgan Bank?"

"No, I didn't. I'm surprised. From what I heard of him when he was in government service, he wasn't the kind of guy to keep that sort of thing to himself. I wonder why he did."

"Embarrassment. His father committed suicide in the panic of '07. Jumped from a hotel window. The Sherry-Netherland. Took his mistress with him too. Lots of big headlines."

"What about his connection with Hearst?" Cockran asked. "You still touchy about that?"

"Come on, Cockran, I apologized for that once. Hearst is a great boss. He's very loyal to his people. All he expects is loyalty in return."

"So what about Hearst and Cromwell?"

"You understand I couldn't be too open about what I was looking for but, as far as I can tell, Cromwell was named Hearst's lead investment guy four years ago. Since then, he's become indispensable. I mean, he's no Joe Willicombe," she said, referring to Hearst's well-known right-hand man. "He has nothing to do with the publishing empire, but Hearst apparently trusts him implicitly with everything else involving money. It's Cromwell's primary job to make sure that the Chief's investments provide all the money he wants when he decides to go shopping. Cromwell is responsible for making sure Hearst has sufficient cash at any point to indulge any whim. And in today's economy and the stock market, he's been able to do that."

"So you don't think Hearst is involved?" Cockran asked. Mattie was glib, too glib.

"No, I don't," Mattie replied, "but it doesn't make it any easier that Cromwell seems to be using the Chief's personal acquisition accounts. Nothing is closer to his heart and there is nothing he is more sensitive about. I can't raise it with him until we're face to face."

After a while, they both grew silent, the strain of continuing to talk over the noise of the engines requiring too much effort. When the plane landed in St. Paul, Cockran seized the opportunity to raise the subject he had been avoiding since Chicago.

"Mattie, I didn't want to mention this earlier but there's a problem with our tickets."

"Problem? What problem?"

"Well, it seems there weren't two Pullman compartments left on tonight's train. All they had was a double compartment."

"So? What's the problem?"

"Well, I mean..."

Mattie laughed. "Mr. Cockran, I believe you're blushing. Are you afraid of heights? And you think I'll want the bottom bunk? Or maybe you snore? I'll bet that's it," Mattie said.

"I don't think so," Cockran replied.

"Don't worry, then, Cockran. Your virtue is safe with me."

46.

Aquinas Explained

Cockran and Mattie shared a taxi with Rankin whose direct train for San Francisco left thirty minutes before theirs. They saw Rankin off, and Cockran carried Mattie's suitcase as they walked from Track 5 to Track 7 for the Great Northern's Empire Builder No. 1.

The Empire Builder sat there waiting, the steam from the engine hissing softly. Once inside their compartment, Cockran ordered sandwiches and coffee from the Pullman porter. Once the food arrived, they sat across from each other on soft leather couches, a table between them while Mattie pulled out her notes on Cromwell.

"I know you're suspicious of the Chief" Mattie said, "but you really shouldn't be."

"Why's that?"

"Well," Mattie replied, tilting her coffee cup at him, "if Hearst had wanted to supply guns to the IRA, he wouldn't have waited this long to do it. And he wouldn't have needed to use someone else's money. Three million dollars is really not that much to Hearst. If he wanted to do something like that, he could have done it back in 1920 or 1921 before Ireland was free. Hearst never really forgave us Brits for dragging America into the Great War and tweaking the Lion's tail over Ireland would have been just his style. But not now. It doesn't make sense. But then again, Cromwell doesn't make sense either. He is the epitome of your East Coast Establishment, a rich investment banker. Why would he be involved in IRA gun running?"

Cockran had no answer either but his suspicions of Hearst—and Mattie—were not allayed. In the early evening, Cockran made them cocktails. When they finished their drinks, they headed for the dining car. In ten minutes a table for two opened up. Cockran looked across the crisp white linen covering the table, a small brass lamp providing illumination, as Mattie gave her dinner order to the white-jacketed Negro waiter. Cockran was struck again by the red hair framing her freckled face, her large green eyes drawing attention to her high cheekbones.

"A penny for your thoughts, Bourke, but this gentleman is waiting for your order," Mattie said. Cockran grinned sheepishly. How could he be so attracted to someone he didn't trust?

They talked of many things over dinner. Many pleasant, some not. Her two older brothers and her fiancé, all of whom had been killed in the war. Mattie probed gently about Cockran's wife but he would only say she was an innocent casualty of the Irish Civil War.

Mattie talked about her childhood, growing up in Scotland in her family's big country house outside of Inverness and the smaller place across from the Isle of Skye. Hiking in the Highlands in the summer. Closing up their parents' big house in September and returning with the servants to their house on Eaton Square for the Season. The society balls her mother loved to attend, the sparkling dinner parties she loved to give.

Mattie said she liked best those seven years when her father served in Parliament because he would have to travel to Inverness or Edinburgh from London almost once a month and would frequently take Mattie with him. "Father always reserved separate compartments for us but he let me stay in his compartment reading until it was time to go to bed. Even though there was an upper bunk in his compartment, he would never let me spend the night. Sent me off to my own compartment. I didn't like it and that's why I don't mind sharing a compartment even though I mostly travel alone. Overnight trains remind me of happier times."

Cockran raised an eyebrow. "Mostly alone?"

Mattie took a sip of her coffee and smiled. "Mostly. Let's go back to our compartment."

They reached their compartment. The porter had turned down the two beds, a top and bottom bunk. The bottle of scotch was still on the table. "A nightcap?" Cockran asked.

"Sure," Mattie replied, picking up her glass and handing it to him. The two of them sat on the leather bench side by side, taking occasional sips. Mattie had turned off all but one lamp so that the compartment was deeply cast in shadow.

Mattie had taken his hand and they sat there saying nothing for a good ten minutes before Cockran spoke. "Why are you doing this for Winston? Risking your life. Being attacked by an Irish thug. Is it all for a story?"

Mattie did not respond immediately but continued to look out at the dark beyond the window, the occasional light of a farm house in the distance. "The story is part of it. I wouldn't be doing it otherwise. A girl's got to make a living, you know. But there's more. Winston's part of it, too. I've known him since I was a child. He and Father were new MPs together. They first met when they gave speeches on the same night at the Free Trade Hall in Manchester. Winston was a Tory then, Father a Liberal but they were both Free Traders. Winston is a very warm, kind and loyal person. He inspires a similar response in his friends."

She squeezed his hand and snuggled closer, pulling his arm around her shoulder. "The fact that some of my best friends are Irish plays a part as well. Not the Anglo-Irish, or even my relatives, but Catholics. Professionals like you. Lawyers, writers, artists. Catholics all. I was in Dublin, you know, covering the Treaty ratification. I couldn't believe the hypocrisy, the vanity, the sheer jealousy of the Treaty opponents. My editor made me leave before the Civil War really started, but I've kept in touch with my Irish friends over the years and..." Mattie paused and took a sip of whisky, "when Winston asked for my help on his assignment from Ramsay, I was flattered. I like adventures and a good story so I agreed."

"Do your editors know what you are doing?" Cockran asked.

Mattie smiled and cocked her head at him. She really was beautiful, Cockran thought. "Not exactly. Hearst knows I'm working on a story on weapons manufacturers, the 'Merchants of Death' angle. It has a long deadline and it provides good cover for what I am doing now. Cromwell was on my list long before I met him at Anne Dawson's. Who knows? Maybe Winston really can persuade President Hoover to have federal authorities intervene."

Cockran shook his head. "The world doesn't work the way Winston thinks it does. Not in America, anyway. There is nothing illegal in what the IRA are doing. 'The business of America is business' is what Coolidge said, and Hoover is no different. The only way Hoover will have the federal authorities take any action against the IRA is if he finds they're bootlegging whiskey to raise money to buy arms. Even then, he'll only go after the whiskey."

"Let me ask you the same question," Mattie said. "Why are you doing this for Winston, especially when you have a book deadline? They shot at you in Cleveland. You're the prime suspect in Devoy's murder. And Al Capone threw you out of Chicago."

"I'm not doing it for Winston. Confirming there really was an IRA operation being mounted and tracing where the money went was all Winston asked and that was what I did."

Mattie waited but Cockran said no more. "So why are you doing it?"

Cockran paused and turned his head towards her, looking out the window again at Mattie's profile and the darkness beyond. "I told you in Chicago. A good friend was killed because of what I did for Winston. John Devoy knew how to stop all this. And they killed him."

"Who," asked Mattie, "the IRA?"

"Yes. The same man who attacked you yesterday and killed that girl in Cleveland."

"Who was that? McBride? He was the one who killed your wife, wasn't he?"

Cockran nodded, wondering briefly how she knew it was McBride who killed Nora. It wasn't from him. "You've made a nasty enemy with that one. He won't soon forget you."

Mattie compressed her lips tightly and said softly "Good. I don't want him to forget. I'm not going to. I want him to remember me every time he looks in the mirror."

Cockran didn't know how she got him started or how it all came out but Mattie's questions after that were so persistent and her tone so empathetic, her green eyes locked on his, that he began talking about something he had never shared with anyone. Not his father, his son, his mother-in-law, step-mother, Donovan, or even John Devoy. His conversations with Nora. How much he loved her. How he couldn't bear to disappoint her. By the time Cockran finished, they had drained the rest of the bottle of Johnnie Walker Red and only Mattie's gentle hand on his arm in restraint stopped him from cracking open a new bottle. "No, Bourke, let's go to sleep. You're absolutely right. Your Nora was a wonderful as well as an uncommonly wise woman. I wish I had known her. You're wrong about one thing though," Mattie said.

"What's that?"

"Nora wouldn't think that they were venial sins, let alone mortal ones, for you to have killed the three IRA moneymen. And she wouldn't have thought your failure to confess would keep the two of you from spending eternity together."

"Why do you say that? I think I know Nora a little better than you."

"Perhaps. Tell me this, Cockran. Are you a believer? I usually don't ask personal questions like that. But even allowing for how much you've drank, you've trusted me enough to tell me about three men you killed in cold blood. So I don't think I'm prying too deeply."

Cockran slowly shook his head. "No, I don't suppose you are. And, no I'm not."

"Did Nora know that?" Mattie asked, the train swaying as it rounded a curve.

Cockran felt a grin spread across his face. "Sure. She only made me go to Mass with her when we were back home in Galway. She said she didn't want her parents knowing she was sleeping with a heathen. She made me promise that all of our children would be raised in the faith. Paddy and his grandmother go to Mass every Sunday. I don't. Christmas and Easter is all. I guess she knows now that her daughter was sleeping with a heathen. But what's your point?"

"Well, I'm not much of a believer myself but certainly more than you. I don't want to believe in a God who would look benignly on the war that took my brothers and my fiancé Eric from me. But I did study comparative religion at university in Edinburgh so I know precisely how a practicing Catholic like Nora would view your killing those three men."

Cockran poured himself a glass of water. His head was clearing.. "Go on."

"I've read more than one book by Thomas Aquinas and I know what he wrote about the just war, which obviously is more than you've done. Especially if you're afraid Nora thinks you won't be spending eternity together because you killed them. I hope you do spend eternity with Nora. But if you don't, it'll be because of some other mortal sin you don't confess."

"I'm not certain I understand."

Mattie sighed. "I'm not surprised. Let me give you an example. If you were a sniper and you had in your sights an unarmed medical corps man attending to a soldier who had tried to kill you just the day before, would you shoot either him or the wounded soldier?"

"No to both. You don't shoot wounded and you don't shoot unarmed medics."

"Good answer. Nora still has a fighting chance of seeing you in heaven. Same scenario except you've got in your sights a two-man team on an artillery field piece. Both are unarmed. One loads and unloads shells while the other pulls the lanyard. Would you shoot them?"

"Of course. Both of them are complicit in placing the lives of my men in jeopardy."

"Correct again. Aquinas would agree with you. I'll bet Nora

would also. Even though the gun loader is not firing the weapon, he makes it possible for the shell to explode and kill the other side's soldiers. So what makes the IRA moneymen any different? They're only a short step removed from the soldier loading the field piece. They're the ones who are buying the shells and field guns that permit that gun crew to fire on your buddies. Michael Collins knew that and he knew that civilians as well as his soldiers were going to die as a consequence. That's why he had you take them out. No good Catholic girl like Nora who went to university like she did and studied Aquinas like she must have could possibly come to any different conclusion. If your father had sent you to the Marist Brothers in Paris where he was educated, I daresay that would have saved you years of thinking you were not living up to Nora's expectations."

Mattie stood up and yawned. "Now, if you'll excuse me, I'm going to the loo and change. That's enough theology for tonight. I'll wrestle you for the lower bunk when I'm back."

Cockran walked down the corridor to the men's washroom, changed into a pair of navy blue thin cotton pajamas, and returned to their compartment more quickly than Mattie. Then he stretched out on the lower bunk, his hands behind his head, not quite believing what had just happened. St. Thomas Aquinas explained. She knew more about Aquinas than he did but that didn't mean he trusted her. Not until he could figure out her game. But she might well be right about how Nora would feel. If he had a chance alone to think about it, he might well buy it. But he wasn't going to do it now. It was late and he was beat. Both Aquinas and his suspicions could take a rest until tomorrow. Green earring or not, he still liked Mattie McGary. A lot.

47.

Better To Be Lucky Than Good

The Empire Builder
Saturday, 17 August, 1929
12:15 a.m.

S well, McGary, you did it again, Mattie thought as she walked down the corridor. No better aphrodisiac when talking to a man than discussing theology—Thomas Aquinas no less—as interpreted by the dead wife he still loved. At this rate, she would never get Cockran into bed.

Mattie returned to their compartment a few moments later, carrying her clothes stacked in a neat pile and still wearing the cotton slippers she had put on when they returned from dinner. Her emerald green silk robe, knotted tightly at her waist, reached almost to her ankles. She knew it accentuated her figure and it should be clear, even to Cockran, it was all she was wearing, save for her diaphragm. Right, she thought, as if she had ever needed that with him before.

When she opened the compartment door and stepped inside, Cockran was already on the lower berth. "So you've accepted my invitation to wrestle, have you?" Mattie asked.

"No, we Americans are much more civilized than you Scots. I flipped a coin. You lost. "

"I lost?" Mattie asked.

Cockran nodded. "Yep. Fair and square. I called 'heads' and heads it was. Here, want to see the coin?" he said, handing her a gold dollar coin.

Mattie leaned down towards Cockran, placing her hands on the upper bunk, intentionally giving Cockran a better view of what was beneath the silk robe. Not as complete a view as she gave him early Thursday morning, with her foot wrapped in ice, but inviting nonetheless.

"You know what I think, Cockran? You're an only child and you didn't have any siblings to wrestle with growing up, like I did with my brothers. So you're afraid you'll lose to a girl. You're soft, Cockran. And probably ticklish, too. That was always my secret weapon with my brothers. Are you ticklish?" she asked.

"Not that I know of...." Cockran replied.

Mattie pushed herself back from the top bunk, looked down at Cockran and said, "You know, there's only one way to find out." Then, without any warning, she leaped at Cockran landing with both of her forearms on his chest, momentarily knocking the breath from him. Her knees straddled his waist and the fact that she was wearing nothing underneath should have been obvious to the most insensitive man. She moved her strong hands just below his rib cage and discovered that Cockran was indeed ticklish. Extremely. Cockran roared with helpless laughter, thrashing his legs up and down, unsuccessfully trying to stymie her assault.

"I knew it! You big sissy!" said Mattie. "You Americans are all talk."

Cockran was finally able to grab each of her arms, just above the elbow and stop her tickling, both of them laughing and out of breath. In pulling her arms away from his abdomen, her robe, which had loosened in the struggle, gaped open so that Cockran found himself suddenly face to face, not six inches away, from the same right breast she had shown him in the hotel room, its pink nipple erect and inviting. His mouth opened in surprise.

"Freckles?"

"Yes, she has freckles. Here, want a closer look?" she asked, pushing its nipple into his open mouth. He responded appropriately with his tongue until she felt a tingle between her legs and she drew back, exposing her other breast.

"I have two," she said, "and they're very jealous if one receives more attention."

Cockran smiled. "We wouldn't want that to happen, now, would we?"

"No, we wouldn't," she replied, moving her other breast slowly forward into his still open mouth, like an airship snuggling up to its mooring mast, gasping as she felt her body react and grow slippery inside, knowing she was ready for him much sooner than she expected.

Mattie had an unvarying routine in taking a new lover. She always liked to be on top for the first time. Like she was now. She thought it helped to set the right tone from the beginning. Besides, with her in control, it was the one way she could ensure, with an unfamiliar lover, that when they were finished, she would be as satisfied as he was. She thought it only fair and no one had ever objected. Neither did Cockran.

His pajamas and her robe were soon on the compartment floor. She straddled his waist, raised her hips directly above him and reached behind her to move him into position between her legs. "Oh my," she said and thought this was definitely going to be good.

It was. Afterwards, Mattie lay stretched out on top of a softly snoring Cockran, her head on his chest, her robe and his pajamas still on the compartment floor below. Oh yes, she thought, that was so much more than she had been expecting. Nothing average about that boy. Wasn't she the lucky one? She smiled. It really was better to be lucky than good. And barely ten minutes ago, she reflected wickedly, no one would have suggested she was being good. She smiled again and snuggled in, pulling the blanket up over them both. And so, she thought, another *aventure* begins. He had been well worth the wait. She wondered briefly if it would lead anywhere and decided that, for the moment, it really didn't matter. She was already looking forward to tomorrow night.

48.

A Message To Hearst?

Miles City, Montana
Saturday, 17 August 1929
7:30 a.m.

Cockran awoke before Mattie. They were arranged like spoons, Mattie in front, Cockran behind, both comfortably fitting into the small lower bunk. He carefully slipped out and replaced the covers over her naked body. He checked his briefcase where he kept the journals. It was undisturbed. He searched for his pajamas, placed them in the suitcase and dressed for the day.

When the train stopped at 7:30 in Miles City, Montana for ten minutes, Cockran debarked and attempted to place a phone call to Churchill's hotel in Vancouver. There was no answer.

Mattie was still sleeping when Cockran returned to their compartment with two steaming mugs of coffee from the dining car. He placed a saucer on top of hers to keep it warm and sat down to leaf through the leather portfolio of her photographs which she had promised to show him earlier, before their tickling match. The ones she was most proud of. "No death or destruction," she had explained. Cockran was impressed. The composition, the contrasts, the angular lines. Striking images all. Mines. Skyscrapers. Assembly lines. Steel mills. Warehouses. Romanticized but timeless. Cockran had just placed the last photograph down when he saw it. A copy of a telegram. He knew gentlemen didn't read other people's mail but

Mattie had invited him to look at her photographs and she must have known that the telegram copy was in there. It was probably nothing, he told himself, as he pulled it out of the pocket, unfolded it and saw the message advising "H" of their new route to California via Spokane and Portland and the cryptic message "Travel plans changed. Mission in danger." First she had searched his room. Now this. Why was she sending this message to Hearst? Cockran understood their plans had changed but what mission was she talking about and how did Hearst fit in?

Cockran still hoped for innocent explanations, both for the telegram and her search of his hotel room but whether she could be trusted or not really didn't matter. Sleeping with her had been a mistake. Enjoyable to be sure but still a mistake. Once they had stopped the IRA and he had put Tommy McBride in the ground, he and Mattie were finished. He knew now he couldn't safely see her just a few times each year. If nothing else, their talk last night had proven to him he could seriously fall for this woman. She was that special. He wasn't going to let that happen. Under normal circumstances, it would be time to break it off. And if the two of them weren't up to their necks in this IRA business, that's exactly what he would do right now. Before it went any further. He didn't think he was a cad now but that's exactly what he would become if he didn't do something soon. Except he couldn't. Not now. He had to stop the IRA first and, if he were lucky, find McBride. Like it or not, Mattie was a part of that but, once it was over, he would end things between them as gently as possible. Would that make him a cad? He thought not but others might very well think so and there was nothing he could do about it.

Part III

California, 1929

I am very much obliged to you for your kind cables and invitation. I look forward greatly to my visit to you in California... We must discuss the future of the world, even if we cannot decide it.

Winston Churchill to William Randolph Hearst,
29 July 1929

Hoover does not run away from his troubles. He feels competent to solve them, and acts in most cases with a promptness and decision which have not been seen in the White House since Mr. Wilson's early days.

The New Republic
June, 1929

49.

Whose Side Was Mattie On?

Oakland, California
Monday, 19 August 1929
6:30 a.m.

A summer thunderstorm was raging outside the windows of their Pullman compartment as the Empire Builder pulled into Union Station on the eastern shore of San Francisco Bay. The building was all stone with two sprawling three-story wings radiating out from a central clock tower over twice as high.

Grateful for the size of his tip, the Pullman porter carried both Bourke and Mattie's suitcases into the shelter of the slate roof's overhang before returning with a large umbrella to escort them to their bags. Cockran was wearing his trench coat now and Mattie a dark green oilcloth hooded slicker which, from its weathered appearance, had seen much duty in the field. Cockran put his equally battered briefcase, which had once belonged to his father, beside the two suitcases. "You find a red cap to take our bags," he said, "while I rustle us up a taxi."

Having secured a taxi, Cockran made his way back to the middle of the terminal where he found an elderly Negro redcap standing guard over his suitcase and briefcase. "What happened to the lady's bag?"

"The lady went off with two friends, sir," the redcap said. "She said that she'd meet you at the hotel."

Cockran was puzzled. Friends? Maybe some of Hearst's people had met her. Or possibly Winston had sent someone. But why would she leave without him? What was so urgent that she couldn't wait a few minutes and explain? Something didn't add up

"Which way did they go?"

"That way, Sir. Toward the ferry," the redcap replied, pointing in the opposite direction.

"What did the friends look like?" Cockran asked.

"They were both tall and blond, Sir. They spoke English with a foreign accent and then the lady began speaking in a foreign language and so did they. Sounded like German to me, Sir."

German? What the hell?! Alarmed, Cockran shouted over his shoulder to the redcap to guard his bags as he headed toward the exit and sprinted for the ferry. He made it just in time to see the Southern Pacific ferry pull away and head for San Francisco across the choppy bay. Barely twenty yards away but it could have been a hundred yards for all the good it did him. And right there at the stern, calmly standing between two blond-haired men, he could see Mattie McGary under no apparent duress as she turned from one man to the other, talking to each as if they were old friends.

Cockran's shoulders slumped as he walked slowly over to the taxi stands which waited patiently for debarking ferry passengers. He didn't know what to think. Germans? What the hell was going on? Whose side was Mattie on?

50.

Jack Manion

San Francisco
Monday, 19 August 1929
1:30 p.m.

Cockran had to assume the worst even though his last glimpse of Mattie talking easily and animatedly to the two blond Germans in the bow of the Oakland Ferry belied that notion. She certainly didn't look like a kidnapped woman. Besides, what the hell could he do about it even if she were? Go to the San Francisco police? And tell them what exactly? "I skipped bond on an arrest warrant in New York in connection with a homicide investigation and now my girlfriend—well, not exactly my girlfriend, but a woman I've slept with twice—is missing, possibly kidnapped. Can you help me?" Right. They would help him. To a one-way ticket for Manhattan once a burly NYPD homicide detective arrived to escort him back.

Once he had checked into his room at the Fairmont Hotel, where Sergeant Rankin was also staying, Cockran called the Scotland Yard detective but no one picked up the phone. He left a terse message with the hotel operator. "Urgent, call me re: M. Room 815. BC". Cockran next arranged a meeting for 6:00 p.m. that evening at his hotel with John Devoy's San Francisco contact, Jack Manion, who hadn't been home when he called. His wife promised to get the message to him. Finally, Cockran placed a long-distance call to Bill Donovan in New York where it was still the middle of the afternoon and told him about Mattie.

"Those boys play rough," Donovan said. "You could use some official help. You should have let me arrange for you to see the FBI in Chicago. They could have cleared you. Then you'd be in a position to go to the authorities in San Francisco to report the kidnapping. There's no way you can do it now."

"Why's that?" Cockran asked.

"Whoever you pissed off has more power than I thought." Donovan replied. "Someone did an end run on me and the NYPD issued another warrant for your arrest this afternoon."

"What's the charge?"

"John Devoy's murder. Keep lying low or you'll be facing extradition to New York."

This was not good but he had to play it out. Cockran knew from combat that rest could be a weapon so he decided to take a short nap. He left a wake-up call for 5:30 p.m. but an insistent knocking on his door woke him earlier. The clock on the nightstand read 4:30 p.m. Shaking away the cobwebs, he shouted, "Hold on, I'm coming." It couldn't be Manion yet. Who was it?

He walked over to the closet, retrieved the Webley revolver and carefully opened the door to see the grimy face of a street urchin with shiny black hair and bold blue eyes.

"Good afternoon, Sir," he said, pressing an envelope at him. "A gentleman paid me to deliver this to you," the boy said, handing Cockran an envelope with his name and room number.

"How much did the gentleman pay you?" Cockran asked.

"Fifty cents, Sir."

"Wait right here," Cockran said. "And I'll pay you also."

Cockran was back in a moment holding a silver dollar in his hands while watching the urchin's eyes grow wide. "It's yours if you describe the gentleman who gave you this envelope."

The boy was more than happy to oblige. Tall, dark hair, blue eyes and broken nose. It fit to a tee the good Samaritan who had killed Sean Russell and the Commerce Department agent that night in Cleveland. Cockran thanked the boy, gave him the silver dollar and closed the door.

The message inside the envelope was terse and written in the same Spenserian script which had characterized his father's handwriting.

Mr. Cockran, the IRA have taken Miss McGary. The map shows where. Please help her. A friend.

First the Germans and now the IRA? The second sheet of the message was a map. Dunsmuir, California, the McCloud River, Mount Shasta and William Randolph Hearst's country estate "Wyntoon" were all clearly marked. As was the rail line running north from San Francisco with the written note alongside the rail line "SF to Dunsmuir equals three hours ten minutes."

Cockran's instincts had been correct in assuming the worst but how did these Germans fit in with the IRA? He placed a call to the concierge who promptly got back to him. The first train to Dunsmuir left from Union Terminal at 10:00 the next morning. Cockran promptly purchased two tickets hoping that, when he talked to Rankin, he could persuade him to help rescue Mattie.

Cockran sat down and stared out the window at San Francisco Bay. The Concierge had confirmed that Wyntoon was William Randolph Hearst's northern California country home. Which only proved to Cockran that Hearst was in this conspiracy up to his neck. That bastard was up to his old tricks. Cockran had always been skeptical of his father's claim that Hearst had delivered the Spanish-American war. But he was a skeptic no more. Still, if Hearst was financing all this, why would he have the IRA kidnap his own reporter? Something didn't add up.

6:00 p.m.

There was a loud knock on his door. Cockran rose, peered through the peephole and saw the large, broad-shouldered frame of a tall, ruddy faced man in his early fifties with a full head of brown hair on its way to gray. "Bourke Cockran?" the man asked when the door opened.

Cockran nodded. The man put out a big right hand. "Jack Manion. Pleased to meet you."

Cockran invited Manion in and offered him a drink. He accepted and Cockran mixed a new drink and freshened his own. He turned to face a drawn .38 caliber police revolver.

"OK, Cockran, tell me exactly what kind of relationship you had with John Devoy?"

"He was my friend. But the operative tense here is 'was'. Devoy's dead. Murdered."

"I know Devoy's dead," Manion responded. "I also know there's a warrant out for your arrest in New York for his murder. I talked to Johnny Greene in Cleveland. He's not a happy man and he's not too fond of you. His daughter's been killed. Was she a friend of yours too? If so, your friends seem to have acquired an unhealthy habit of turning up dead. Can you give me one good reason why I shouldn't toss you in jail right now until someone from New York or Cleveland can come fetch you?" he said, bringing out a leather case which he flipped open with a practiced motion to reveal a San Francisco Police Department captain's badge.

"Can I set these drinks down?"

"Very carefully," Manion replied. "Then take a seat on the couch over there."

Cockran gave Manion his drink and then placed his own on the coffee table in front of the couch. Manion kept his revolver still pointed squarely at Cockran's chest.

"Go on. Explain yourself. Start at the beginning. I've got plenty of time."

I don't have much time. A woman's been kidnapped and I need your help to find her."

"Talk first, Cockran. Help later. *If* I believe you."

Cockran paused and took a deep breath as he began to retell the story. "It starts back in Ireland," Cockran said. Fifteen minutes later, Cockran had brought the story up to Devoy's discovery of the missing funds. He paused, took a sip from the glass beside him, and twenty minutes later had brought his story up to where he had started—Mattie's kidnapping.

Manion returned his revolver to its shoulder holster and put his hands on his knees. "I believe you, Cockran. John called me the day before he was killed. He told me you were a man to be trusted. My boys in the Chinatown Squad knew I was friends with Devoy and when notice of that murder warrant came in this afternoon, they showed it to me. That's when I checked with a colleague in New York to see who was in charge of the Devoy murder investigation and what his reputation was. Brendan Rooney is his name. You know him?"

Cockran shook his head.

"He's a bad copper," Manion replied. "Anyone can buy him. That's the bad news for you. The good news is he has no loyalty to those who buy his services. So if you have friends in New York who are big enough, the word is he can be scared off.."

Manion finished his drink and walked towards the sideboard to refill, taking Cockran's proffered glass as well. "Tell me how I can help with this woman who was kidnapped."

"I'm not sure." Cockran said, "If she's near Dunsmuir, it's a three hour train ride."

Manion grinned. "For starters, we don't need to travel by train. We can fly there. And," he said, sweeping his arm over the living room of Cockran's suite, "for the price of one night in this grand hotel, I can provide three, maybe four, good solid men. Honest, underpaid policemen from my Chinatown Squad are always looking for legitimate off-duty work. If you throw in a bottle of Jameson's, you'll have friends for life to boot."

There was a knock on the door. Cockran walked across the room and checked through the peephole to see Robert Rankin. Cockran invited the Scotland Yard man in and introduced him to

Manion. The two Celts hit it off at once, their police work a common bond.

Cockran quickly filled Rankin in on their plans to rescue Mattie including Manion's suggestion that they charter a plane to do so. They would need heavier weapons than their police revolvers but flying in could be passed off as a hunting trip. It would take them ninety minutes flying time compared to a train trip taking twice as long. Also, if there were any unpleasantness involved in rescuing Mattie, they could leave at a time of their own choosing.

"I'd dearly like to go with you lads," Rankin said. "But my first duty is to see to Mr. Churchill's safety and there is still much to do here. He arrives tomorrow."

"Who's your liaison with the Police Department?" Manion asked.

Cockran saw Rankin wrinkle his forehead at what was obviously for him a foreign question. "Liaison? From my limited experience with American police departments, primarily Chicago, it did not occur to me to seek out their assistance."

"San Francisco is not Chicago, I assure you, Detective Sergeant," Manion replied. "We don't have our hands out. We are pleased to provide additional security for visiting dignitaries."

Manion produced a fountain pen and picked up a blank sheet of paper on which he wrote a note. "Here, take this to Central Police Headquarters first thing tomorrow morning. Ask for Detective O'Connor and give him this. He'll provide all the help you need. Then, if you think you have matters well in hand, meet us at Mills Field tomorrow morning at 7:00 a.m."

After Rankin left, Cockran ordered two thick steaks from room service. As they ate, they had a clear view over the Union Pacific Club to Grace Cathedral beyond, its front and spire illuminated with floodlights, while Cockran listened to Manion's stories. Since March of 1921, Manion had been the head of the San Francisco Police Department's Chinatown Squad. Chinatown was a city unto itself and Manion's first assignment had been to target the tongs who used hired assassins to control and skim profits from the gambling, narcotics and prostitution enterprises that flourished there. The tongs also took protection money from legitimate businesses operated by intimidated Chinatown merchants and Manion had stopped them cold.

As a consequence, many of the merchants considered Manion to be the unelected Mayor of Chinatown. His squad consisted of twelve men who worked around the clock in three shifts of four men each. They had their own network of informers and the thought that any search or seizure could be unreasonable never crossed their minds. The tongs feared them. The Chinatown merchants thought they were guardian angels who allowed them to live the American Dream.

After dinner, Manion got down to business on the IRA arms shipment. "I've had no luck, Bourke, in learning about the account into which the funds were transferred at the Crocker Bank. Compared to Cleveland or Chicago, San Francisco is a clean town."

"I understand," Cockran said. "But what about the..."

"The warehouse? That's different. I know all about the warehouse. I have it under surveillance as we speak. It's not even in San Francisco. It's across the bay, in Oakland."

"Oakland? Why Oakland?" Cockran asked.

"Oakland, I am sorry to say, has a more unsavory reputation than the City. Still, our police departments work fairly well together and the honest cops know each other. There are just a lot fewer of them in Oakland. Within thirty-six hours of your phone call from Chicago, I had the warehouse identified. It's stacked to the rafters with weapons and ammunition."

"Have you found out where the weapons will be shipped?" Cockran asked.

"No, we haven't tried yet." Manion replied. "New shipments are arriving every day. But with the information you received from Fitzgerald in Chicago, I'll have my men making the rounds of train dispatchers. We have good sources there. It shouldn't be a problem to find out where the arms will be shipped next."

51.

Take The Folders, Leave The Money

T he Fokker Trimotor glistened in the morning sun, its fuselage painted a bright royal blue. Cockran turned to Jack Manion. "How have you managed to hire this aircraft? Who owns it?"

"Hearst."

They had been walking away from the plane and Cockran stopped in his tracks. "Hearst? Like in William Randolph Hearst who owns the property where they're holding Mattie?"

Manion smiled. "The same. Sort of a nice symmetry, wouldn't you say?"

"Are you entirely certain this is wise?" Cockran asked.

"T'is not a problem. The pilot's an old friend. To Pat, we're just a small hunting party going up for a day trip to Mt. Shasta. He's flown Hearst there a couple times. Besides, it's the largest private plane in the area. We'll need it to accommodate the three of us and my three men who will be joining us soon. Relax, Bourke. You're not in Chicago any more."

The aircraft cabin was crowded. The Fokker Trimotor FV II was built for the rich and carried six normal-sized people. But two of the three officers from Manion's Chinatown Squad were not small, both six feet tall or more and well over two hundred pounds. One of them had his hunting jacket unbuttoned with his shoulder holster visible.

Cockran was certain from the bulges in the coats of the other two that they were similarly armed. As was he, the Webley snug in its hoster inside his leather flight jacket. Their rifles had been stowed in the luggage compartment at the rear of the plane as well as, when the pilot's attention had been distracted, a Thompson submachine gun.

Within eighty-five minutes, the small Trimotor was banking for its approach to the grassy airfield, a ten-minute drive from the small California mining town of Dunsmuir. Once they landed, Manion picked up the keys to a battered 1925 four-door Dodge sedan from the airfield attendant. While the pilot made arrangements for refueling, Manion's chief assistant, Ed Kelley supervised the loading of weapons and ammunition into the Dodge's large trunk. Manion drove with Cockran and Rankin beside him in the front seat, Kelley and the others in the back.

They headed east along Highway 89 which ran beside the McCloud River. They stopped a few miles down the road at a roadside picnic table overlooking a scenic gorge, the second, Manion told them, of the three waterfalls they would pass along the white water river before it snaked its way through the Hearst property. Below them, the river was gray with volcanic ash, the residue of volcanic eruptions in 1914 and 1915 of nearby Lassen Peak, a 10,457 foot plug dome volcano.

Manion spread the map out on the picnic table and laid out their plan of attack. "No sense our trying a frontal assault on the gate. They'll have a telephone to the house for sure. But there is dense forest on either side of the road which leads into the property. I'm thinking we can take our automobile in as far as three or four miles and then make it the rest of the way on foot."

Manion folded the map and the six men climbed back in the Dodge. Above them, the sun was shining in a cloudless sky and the mountain air was crisp. Ten miles down Route 89, Manion turned right onto a gravel road, the Seiberling tires crunching the surface beneath, a mute witness to the tall forest of spruce, pine and Douglas fir and two large signs flanking either side of road. PRIVATE PROPERTY. NO TRESPASSING. VIOLATORS WILL BE PROSECUTED.

Four miles into the forest, Manion brought the vehicle to a halt and pulled off to the left into a clearing where the trees were smaller. He carefully backed the vehicle through the thicket of trees until it would not have been visible to a casual eye from a passing motor car.

A hard half-hour's hike uphill brought them to the top of a ridge. The sound of the river was much louder and they could glimpse the shimmer of sun shining off the white water below. The trek down the ridge was accomplished more easily. Once there, the roar of the ash-laden water accompanied their hike until Manion spotted a large rock slide, a place where he believed they could ford to the other bank. Manion pulled out the map again and motioned to Kelley to join him.

"Eddie, we're less than half a mile from the River House. It's the main guest house. I'm not partial to splitting up our forces until we have to, but if we can gain the element of surprise with a flanking movement on whoever's guarding the bridge and come at them from both sides, then it's worth a shot. It looks a lot tougher going on the other side of the river, but we can't pass up this chance to come at them from behind. I'll leave the map with you."

In the event, Manion, Cockran and Rankin made better time than expected. Fording the river had not proved difficult, the rock slide affording them good purchase save a slippery foothold or two. It was nearly impassable along the edge of the river so they headed up a heavily forested ridge until they reached the top. Once there, they traversed the spine of the ridge more easily. They made quick time and were situated behind the Manor House shortly before noon, with several Douglas firs and only one hundred yards of open ground standing between them and the house. Manion took out a pair of army surplus field binoculars and surveyed the scene.

Manion raised his binoculars again. "Hello, what have we here? Take a look, Detective Sergeant," he said, handing the binoculars to Rankin. "The hedge in front of the patio. If I'm not mistaken, there's a body there. Certainly a strange place for a nap."

Rankin agreed and handed the binoculars to Cockran. "See what you think, sir."

Cockran took the binoculars, searched for the patio hedge and found it, two legs sticking out from behind the hedge. He handed the field glasses back to Manion. "What does it mean?"

"It means we go find out. Check your weapons. Chamber a round. I'll take point."

They proceeded cautiously across the lawn, weapons drawn. Cockran reached the body first. The man wasn't taking a nap, several bullet wounds in his chest were proof of that. Cockran checked for a pulse. There was none, but rigor mortis had not set in. It might have been one of the two blond haired men Cockran had seen with Mattie on the ferry but he couldn't be certain.

Manion and Rankin joined Cockran and the two detectives examined the body. "Dead about four hours I'd say" Rankin said in a low voice. "Look at the color."

Manion nodded his agreement and then motioned them toward the front of the mansion and its main entrance enclosed within a round stone turret, a conical slate roof rising to a point above it. Once there, Manion signaled Ed Kelly's team to cross the bridge and join them. Then he grasped the hanging iron handle and turned. The door silently swung open. They stepped inside through the turret into a large, two-story antechamber at the end of which was a large formal staircase framed by three large leaded glass windows on the first landing which framed a stunning view of Lassen Peak.

Three bodies were sprawled at the foot of the staircase and a fourth at the top. Like the body outside, rigor mortis had not set in. Again, Cockran recognized none of them.

They quietly moved upstairs, alert for any sign of the enemy but the only sounds were their own soft footfalls. The second floor had four bedrooms opening out onto a balcony that ran along three sides of the foyer below, two in the rear and two in front. Both rear bedrooms had the same view of Lassen Peak as the top of the landing. The first three bedrooms yielded no result. In the right front bedroom, they found their sixth and final body. It was sprawled on the floor, face down, barely a foot away from a chair on which sat a leather shoulder holster and beside it, a .38 caliber revolver with five of its six bullets still unfired. The corpse had greasy black hair and a jagged scar across a receding chin. The automatic weapon which had been used to effect downstairs obviously had been used on this man as well. He had been shot in the back, four entrance wounds going diagonally from the right side of his waist up to his left shoulder. A *coup de grace* had been fired directly into the back of his head.

Manion went to the fireplace and placed his hand on the burned wood sitting in the grate. They were warm to his touch. "This one's been dead as long as the others.But the wood's not yet cold. Even if these fellows have been dead between four to six hours, whoever did this didn't leave that long ago. After four hours, even if this started as a roaring fire, these ashes would be stone cold. When we get back downstairs, I'll have Kelley check the other fireplaces."

Cockran's attention was not focused on the fireplace but rather on the head of the four-poster bed. He walked to the side of the bed away from the fireplace and saw something white in the corner, bunched in a ball. He stooped to pick it up and recognized at once that it was one of Mattie's white blouses. It still carried the scent of her perfume and several buttons were missing. Beside it on the floor was one of Mattie's brassieres along with a torn pair of her silk step-ins as if someone—an eager lover?—had ripped them off. He recognized both from their two nights together on the train. He looked over at the corpse and then back to her undergarments. The mystery of Mattie McGary just kept on growing. What in hell had happened? Why were Mattie's clothes here? What had Mattie been doing in this room? Who killed that man? And where in the hell was Mattie? He motioned Rankin over and showed him the clothes. "This shirt is hers. She was wearing it yesterday." Rankin didn't need to know Cockran recognized her more intimate apparel as well.

Rankin inspected the garment. "Aye, it certainly appears to be Miss McGary's.

"Who do you suppose did this?' Cockran asked. "Smythe and his men?"

Rankin frowned. "Smythe and his men don't have automatic weapons."

"My tip was good. Someone had Mattie here. The IRA is as good a guess as any."

I agree.", Rankin said, "While I conduct a thorough search of the main house to see if I can find any clues as to Miss McGary's whereabouts, perhaps you and Inspector Manion could do the same with the rest of the buildings."

"Good, " Manion said. "I'll also file a missing person's report as soon as we're back in the city. We'll get her photograph from *The Examiner* and her face soon will be all over California.

"Meanwhile," Manion said to Ed Kelley, "send the other two up the road and have them fetch the automobile and bring it back down here. By then, we should have finished our search."

Manion stooped down and picked up the Thompson submachine gun. "Have the boys take this with them in case they encounter any of our adversaries."

Cockran and Manion split up to search the other buildings on the grounds leaving Rankin behind to search the main house. Forty five minutes later, they had returned and taken a seat in the front foyer when they heard Rankin cry out. Each man rose from his seat and moved quickly towards the door where they were met by Rankin. "In the Billiard Room. I've found a safe!"

When Cockran entered the room, he saw a section of the paneling on the wall, adjacent to the fireplace, open on internal hinges.

"It's ingenious," said Rankin, "but I've seen it before. The craftsmanship makes it difficult to detect," he said, closing the panel where, to Cockran's eye, it was almost invisible.

"How do you open it?" Cockran asked.

"Simple. In the upper right-hand corner," Rankin said, pushing in the panel less than half an inch. There followed a click and the panel swung open to reveal a substantial wall safe.

"How about the safe?" Cockran asked..

"Not to worry, sir, I've already opened it. It's a model I'm familiar with. Made in England where it's very popular among the criminal class because of the ease of entry. Some safes have tumblers so silent you need a stethoscope. Not this one," Rankin said, as he pulled the handle down and opened the safe, revealing stacks of U.S. currency inside. Cockran noted denominations of twenty, fifty and one hundred dollar bills.

"They appear to be an efficient, well-organized operation,"

Rankin said, as he reached in and pulled out three accordion files, "Purchases", "Warehouses", and "Shipping".

Cockran took the files to the billiard table and spread them out. The detail was astonishing. For the first time, Cockran began to believe Churchill's plan might succeed. The carbon copies of the purchase orders were all meticulously cataloged in alphabetical order, all COD, each in its own manila file. Ditto the bills of lading at the bonded warehouses. The contents of the accordion folder labeled "Shipping" told Cockran at a glance what he had spent two futile days in Chicago attempting to find out about the railroads used to move the arms and ammunition from the Chicago warehouse. Nestled in the back of the accordion folder was another slim manila file bearing the heading "*SS San Pedro,* Venezuela" and a shipping date for next Wednesday, August 27, from Long Beach harbor.

The final file was unmarked but inside were carbon copies on letterhead of the U.S. Commerce Department's Office of the Inspector General. Each sheet contained a detailed, single-spaced typewritten report on Cockran's activities in Cleveland and Chicago. At the bottom of each sheet was a list of names to whom the report had been distributed. The name "P.D. Cromwell" was checked with a red pencil on each sheet.

Damn! Cockran was elated. Hearst's money man! Hearst's mansion. All the proof he needed. Hearst was behind this! But the mystery of whose side Mattie was on was not becoming more clear. Cockran raised his head from the file as he heard a horn sound outside.

"Let's go. Take the folders. Leave the money." Manion said. "It's too late for them to change anything now."

52.

They're Together Now

The Fokker returned Cockran to San Francisco at 5:00 p.m. The Churchill caravan had pulled into San Francisco earlier that day and messages from Winston awaited both Cockran and Rankin at the front desk of the Fairmont. Cockran was to meet Churchill that evening at the Union Pacific Club where he was giving an address. Rankin didn't disclose the contents of his message and had refolded the sheet of paper and stuck it in his pocket.

Once in his room, Cockran showered and changed into a suit. There was a knock on the door but before he could reach the door, a large manila envelope was pushed under it. He opened it and pulled out a single sheet of paper. Thank God, he thought, Manion was as good as his word. The sheet had Mattie's photo above which in bold, black letters was a single word "MISSING" with a physical description of Mattie; that she was a British citizen who worked for the Hearst papers; and that anyone with information as to her whereabouts should contact either Manion of the SFPD or Rankin of Scotland Yard.

Cockran was still concerned about Mattie as he walked up the steps of the Union Pacific Club and through the entrance while a liveried light-skinned Negro doorman held open the polished brass door. While something was being done to publicize her disapperance, her being held by the IRA at Wyntoon was baffling if she and Hearst were in this together. He asked at the desk for Mr. Churchill and was directed down a long marble hallway to the library.

Cockran entered the library and was confronted by a tall, middle-aged man with a military bearing, dark hair, graying at the temples, and a mustache. "May I help you, sir?"

"I was directed here. I'm looking for Mr. Churchill," Cockran replied.

"And you would be?"

Cockran identified himself. He could see the man relax.

"Ah yes, Mr. Cockran. Mr. Churchill's expecting you. I'm Inspector Walter Thompson, Scotland Yard," he said, extending a hand, which Cockran grasped.

"A pleasure to meet you, Inspector. Sergeant Rankin has spoken frequently of you."

"Has he now? How is Robert feeling? I understand he had a spot of trouble in Chicago."

"He did at that," Cockran allowed. "But he seems to have recovered nicely."

"Mr. Churchill is over there in the far corner, away from the window, going over the notes for his speech. We're taking Sergeant Rankin's warning about gunmen quite seriously."

They shook hands again and Cockran walked over to Churchill who was sitting in a red leather chair, half-moon spectacles perched on his nose, reviewing typewritten notes for his speech. Engrossed in his reading, Churchill did not look up until Cockran spoke.

"Hello, Winston. You're looking far better than last we met."

Churchill looked up, a broad smile on his face, and placed his reading glasses in the inside pocket of the coat to his three-piece navy chalk-striped suit. He rose from his chair with surprising quickness for a man his age, grasping Cockran's right hand in both of his.

"Bourke, my dear boy! How good to see you. I was so sorry to hear about Mattie. I have Smythe and his men looking into the information about her that Sergeant Rankin gave us today. Don't worry, Bourke. She's quite a resourceful young woman. All will be well."

Damn! Cockran thought. That meant the Brits *hadn't* rescued Mattie. But then who was behind the killings at Wyntoon? And where was Mattie? To Churchill he said, "I'd like to help find Mattie. I wasn't that impressed with Smythe when I met him in Chicago."

"I don't think that would be advisable, Bourke. Leave it to the professionals." Churchill said. "Let's move on. I don't have much time before my speech. Rankin tells me you made significant progress today. Pray fill me in later on this Cromwell fellow and his ties to Hearst."

Cockran stiffened. "No, Winston," he said. "If you still want me working on your report for the President, then I'm going to be involved in the search for Mattie."

Churchill smiled. "Of course, dear boy. Smythe is not our only resource. Trust Rankin. He will be our liaison with the police until Mattie is safely returned to us. Robert is doing something for me right now but he'll be back before my speech is over. Why don't you talk to him then?"

Cockran reluctantly agreed that Winston was right. He had to trust Manion and Rankin. Yet, for the last seven years, trust had not been part of his vocabulary. He nodded, sat down in a red leather armchair and began to unfasten the straps of his briefcase.

"The one thing we don't have, Winston, is access to banking records in San Francisco. We know the money went to the Crocker Bank but, unlike Cleveland and Chicago, we can't identify the account. We have everything else. The warehouse in Oakland and the Venezuelan ship in Long Beach on which the arms and munitions will be shipped next week."

Cockran paused while a waiter brought in an iced bucket on a silver service and poured champagne. "Even if you persuade Hoover, however, what can he do in such a short time? You won't see him until tomorrow. Orders can't go out until Thursday. Friday is next and the government here doesn't do any more work on weekends than you do in England."

Churchill reached over and patted Cockran on the arm, a twinkle in his eye. "You'd be surprised at how quickly a motivated government can accomplish something. Government regulates so much since the war. All it takes is imagination. In England, I daresay we could take a team of Board of Health Inspectors aboard the vessel and quickly discover a stowaway with symptoms of smallpox. That ship would be in quarantine for the next ninety days."

"That's because your Board of Health is part of the national government," Cockran said. "Here, it's the state or local government and they don't have to pay attention to the President."

Churchill frowned. "I know that, Bourke. I'm a student of American history and I know what you say is accurate in theory. But, in practice? I daresay any local functionary would find it most difficult to say 'no' to his President. And your President is nothing if not a resourceful man. I trust Mr. Hoover to do the right thing. Don't worry. All will be well."

Cockran shook his head. Hadn't he been listening in Montreal when Cockran patiently explained the American political scene to him? Apparently not. Winston had always been, in Cockran's experience, far more fond of talking than listening. So he changed the subject.

"Did Rankin tell you about the warning in Chicago? The attempt on your life?"

Churchill waved his hand. "Pay it no regard. Robert and Tommy have taken a few extra precautions. It's nothing new. They all make threats. I've been the target of Bolsheviks, Arabs, Turks, Irish, Muslims and Hindus alike." He leaned closer. "On extended journeys I always take my old Mauser with me. I'm still a crack shot. Haven't lost my touch, you know."

Churchill picked up the sheets of paper beside him. "I will be leaving for San Simeon immediately after my speech. President Hoover will be arriving there in time to greet the *Graf Zeppelin*. I want you there for my briefing of the President. You're an eye witness to much of this. The fact that you're the son of a prominent politician will give your views added weight."

Cockran didn't think so. Moreover he didn't think of his father as a politician. Rather, he had been an extraordinarily successful lawyer who, from time to time, would heed the call from Tammany Hall to stand for Congress when they needed to run a *bona fide* statesman. His father had been a seven-term congressman who had never served more than two consecutive terms because he wouldn't take orders from Tammany Hall. As *Time* magazine had written in his obituary, "Fearless, magnificent, king of orators, his public career lasted for 40 stormy years. He quarreled numberless times with Tammany leaders, over whom he towered majestically."

He believed his father would have towered majestically over Hoover as well. But he knew Hoover wouldn't see it that way. A self-made millionaire—and a Protestant—he would look down his nose at the son of someone he saw as an Irish Catholic Tammany Hall hack despite the fact his legal skills allowed his son to grow up in the lap of luxury on Long Island's Gold Coast.

"Winston, I don't think..." Cockran began to respond, but Churchill cut him off.

"Don't decide hastily. We will talk further after my speech."

"Winston, I really think you should look at the Collins' journals. Several attempts have been made to steal them. Perhaps you can see in them what I cannot."

"I doubt that very much," Churchill replied. "Michael and I had very few secrets from each other. We each knew who our enemies were. But now, I really must turn back to my speech. Mind now. Pay attention. I daresay you'll recognize my conclusion." He smiled. "I understand this club doesn't admit Jews. Did you know I resigned from the Reform Club because it had a similar policy? In light of the recent violence against Jews in Palestine by the Arabs, who better than these narrow-minded Americans to hear my views on the Jews?" He took a sip of champagne and picked up his pen.

7:00 p.m.

The overflow crowd was jammed into the Club's main dining room, a large, high-ceilinged room with windows on three sides looking out over the city. Bankers, lawyers, businessmen, stock brokers, financiers. The cream of San Francisco's business community, most of them in black tie, their ladies in long gowns. Cockran excused himself from his table and watched Churchill's speech from the back of the room.

It was vintage Churchill and he was in good form, alternately smiling, scowling, a self-deprecating comment here, a flash of wit there. Cockran could tell Winston was ready to conclude. "The vastly outnumbered Jews have done no harm to the Arabs of Palestine. On the contrary, they have brought them nothing but good gifts, more wealth, more trade, more civilization, new sources of revenue, more employment, a higher rate of wages, larger cultivated areas, a better water supply—in a word, the fruits of reason and modern science. There is no country of which it can more be truly said than of Palestine 'that the Earth is a generous mother and will provide for all her children if they will cultivate her soil in justice and in peace'."

Prolonged applause greeted the end of Churchill's speech and Cockran had a catch in his throat at Churchill once more using his father's "the Earth is a generous mother" quote. He patiently waited while dozens of people gathered around Churchill, eager for a private word with the former Chancellor of the Exchequer and, many thought, a future prime minister.

The crowd around Churchill had thinned considerably when Churchill caught Cockran's eye and beckoned him forward. As he made it to Churchill's side, Churchill said, "Ah yes, Sergeant. I saw your signal to me from back there. Do you have a message for me?"

Catching on to the charade, Cockran played along. "Yes, sir, I do."

Churchill turned back to the group around him. "Excuse me for a moment. Sergeant Cockran is one of my minders. He's with Scotland Yard. I won't be a moment." Churchill reached out expansively with his arm and and drew him from the group, just out of earshot.

"Just lean close, Bourke, and pretend to whisper something in my ear."

Churchill turned and walked back to the group. "I'm so sorry, ladies and gentlemen, but I'm reminded I have an interview with the press at my hotel in ten minutes. I must depart now lest I reinforce my well-known reputation for tardiness. I will still be a few moments late but especially with journalists, since I am one myself, I always like to give them a sporting chance to get away."

The well-wishers around Churchill chuckled appreciatively.

Inspector Thompson, Sergeant Rankin and two San Francisco plain clothes police officers formed a moving diamond around Churchill and Cockran, the Scotland Yard detectives were in the front and rear, while the two San Francisco police were on either side.

Churchill and Cockran talked as they walked down the long marble hallway towards the entrance. "Have you considered my request to join me with the President?"

"Winston, it's not a good idea. I'm not involved in politics and I don't know if my father ever met Hoover. But the President will have heard the name Bourke Cockran. That will recall to him first of Tammany Hall and next of Al Smith. It was an especially ugly campaign last fall. Full of vicious, anti-Catholic propaganda which, in my opinion, Hoover did nothing to stop. He gave pious lip service to it. It can't be a good idea to remind him of all that."

"Let me understand," Churchill said. "You believe your presence will remind the President of his recent election victory? And this will somehow color his view towards me?"

"Something like that," Cockran replied. He hesitated before continuing. "And I did write an editorial page column for *The New York American* which accused Hoover of not doing enough to discourage the anti-Catholic campaign being waged by his supporters on his behalf."

Churchill chuckled. "I wouldn't worry about that if I were you. We politicians have a thick skin. It's not as if we read everything people write about us."

They were ten feet from the entrance and Churchill stopped and guided Cockran over to the side. "Stopping this arms shipment is critical to the Free State's future. The sheer size of the shipment, if it makes its way to the IRA, could destabilize Ireland for a generation. As for Mattie, I know you are concerned about her but I am quite optimistic, so please don't worry."

Cockran interrupted. "You're not the one who was with her when she was kidnapped. You made me responsible for her safety. I failed. I've got to find her. I'm certain the IRA is behind it."

Churchill ignored the comment and continued. "I know you want to have a go at this McBride fellow. I understand completely. But I want you to be cautious. Don't let your emotions take over. Michael Collins told me at your dear wife's funeral that he was sending you on a mission to America precisely because he feared you would disregard your own safety in seeking revenge. I don't know what your mission was but I concurred with Michael's thinking at that time. You must believe me. If I had known that any of the people connected with your wife's death were playing a role in this matter, I would never have involved you."

Churchill paused and took a cigar out of the inside breast pocket of his suit coat and lit it. "I understand your feelings about Mattie. If we haven't located her or heard from her by tomorrow, I absolve you of any obligation to join me at San Simeon. The safety of my god-daughter is more important. I will also leave Rankin behind specifically to make certain that everything is done to locate her."

Churchill paused. "Now, please forgive me but I must return to the library."

With a puff of smoke from his cigar and his cane tapping the marble floor in time with his steps, Cockran watched the receding back of Winston Churchill as he headed in the direction of the library where they met before his speech.

8:45 p.m.

Churchill walked into the library. A tall, strikingly attractive woman with dark brown hair was standing in the far corner, her regal profile looking out the window at the street below. There were five other men scattered around the room in overstuffed leather chairs, a few with frowns on their faces as they occasionally glanced in her direction. Churchill vaguely recalled being told that women were only allowed in certain areas of the Club but the woman appeared unbothered by the disapproving stares. He walked over to the woman and spoke in a low voice. "My dear. How good to see you. I am pleased my message reached you."

The woman turned and warmly embraced Churchill. "Winston, darling."

"Did you have a pleasant journey from Chicago?" Churchill asked.

"Fine. Quite pleasant. The service was excellent."

"How are the others?" Churchill asked.

"They're all fine. They're together now," the woman replied.

"Excellent," said Churchill. "Excellent. We have much to talk about, you and I, but now is neither the time nor the place. Why don't you come see me around 10:00 p.m.? The Fairmont. We can have a quiet late supper. Just the two of us. We won't be disturbed."

53.

Unfinished Business

San Francisco
Tuesday, 20 August 1929
9:00 p.m.

Cockran left the Fairmont elevator, walked to his room and pulled out his key. As he opened the door, he heard the shower running. He stopped, carefully closed the door with his left hand and pulled his Webley from his shoulder holster with his right. He quietly opened the door again and stepped inside, the revolver sweeping the room. It was empty. But the bathroom door was closed. The shower had stopped. Cockran walked softly over to the bathroom door and threw it forcefully open. The terrycloth robed figure inside was startled by the noise and turned to face an equally surprised Cockran. "Mattie! It's you! You're safe!"

Mattie McGary had been showering in Cockran's room for half an hour mentally going over one more time all that had happened during her visit to Wyntoon. The unexpected journey north with the attentive and solicitous Germans had taken most of the day arriving at their destination when the sun was low on the horizon. She was astonished to see they were at Wyntoon. Hearst had never invited her there but she had known exactly where she was. Hearst had several photographs of the manor house at Wyntoon in the large office he still maintained at the *San Francisco Examiner*. Being at

Wyntoon had given her a much better understanding of the forces at play behind the scenes.

But if she had been surprised to be arriving at Wyntoon, she had not been surprised by most of what had happened after that. In fact, by then, she was more or less expecting it. But those were things she had no intention of sharing with Cockran. He had no need to know and a lot could still go wrong. Telling him some of the truth was one thing. That came with the territory. But telling the whole truth? No, that wasn't an option. Still, she wasn't sure just what to say.

Mattie had just doffed a terrycloth robe and was towel-drying her hair when the bathroom door flew open and she found herself face to face with a large Webley revolver. Cockran!

"My, oh my," Mattie said, as she let the towel fall to the floor, her wet red hair glistening in the steamy room. Mattie still didn't know what, if anything, to tell Cockran about Wyntoon. And right now, it didn't matter. She wanted to put Wyntoon behind her and focus on the future. And she knew just how to do it . "What a large weapon you have, Mr. Cockran," she said as she slowly untied the belt on her robe. Then she shrugged the robe off her shoulders and it fell to the floor, pooling around her ankles. "As you can see, I'm not armed."

She smiled and walked toward him as he lowered the revolver "You seem surprised to see me. You were expecting to find some other naked woman in your bathroom, Cockran?"

Cockran stammered, "No.... I mean, you're safe. What happened?"

She had reached him now and put her arms around his neck and gave him a long lingering kiss which Cockran returned, his hands beginning to explore her body. A full thirty seconds later, she pulled away, looked up at him and said, "We can talk about all that later. You and I have some unfinished business."

Cockran smiled. "We do?"

In response, Mattie grabbed him by his shoulders, turned him around and pushed him into the bedroom, reaching up as she did so to pull the shoulder holster back over his arms, letting it drop on the floor beside her. "Yes, we certainly do."

They had reached the bed by now. Mattie walked around him, pulled down the covers, and bent slowly over at the waist as she did so, a pose she held far longer than necessary to arrange pillows. It was a practiced move for Mattie, designed for first time lovers but one she had not been able to employ for Cockran in the confines of a Pullman compartment. She looked back over her shoulder to see Cockran eyes focused exactly where she wanted. Good.

Mattie slowly straightened up and turned to face him. "Staring at my ass, Cockran? I think a Pullman compartment is not the best venue for us to learn whether you're as good on top as you are underneath." she said, putting her arms around him. "Want to find out?"

Cockran did and Mattie stepped back and watched as his boxer shorts hit the floor. Oh my, she thought. The train really had been too dark to fully appreciate his body as her eyes feasted on her first good look at her new and gloriously naked lover. It was obvious no foreplay was going to be needed for him, she thought, as she reached out for him.

One hour later, they lay in each other's arms, back to front, Cockran's left arm across her breasts, a cool breeze from the open window beginning to dry the perspiration covering both their bodies. Mattie sighed . Cockran had been more than good and she was lucky. He was much better on top than underneath. She had been right. It had been *exactly* what she needed.

It was a good thing, Mattie thought, that they were in an expensive hotel suite with solid plaster walls rather than the thin partitions of a Pullman compartment. When she was being shown a good time—and tonight had been so much more than a good time—she was not shy, or quiet, about expressing her enthusiasm.

"Even nicer than the train. Thank you."

"You're welcome. I could say the pleasure was all mine, but I don't think that's true."

Mattie laughed. "You got that right, McGee."

"So, tell me about it. What happened yesterday morning?"

Mattie sighed. She didn't want to lie to this man. There were things she had withheld from him but she hadn't lied. She wasn't going to start now.

"I apologize for leaving so abruptly without telling you where I was going. But it all arose so suddenly. There were things I had to do and I did them. Now I'm back. And I'm glad I am. You made me one happy girl," Mattie said. There. She had said it and it was the literal truth. The operative word was "had". Any woman in her position would have done the same.

But Cockran wasn't buying it. "Who were those two blond men with you on the ferry?"

Nice guys, considering, but it was difficult to sound firm when you were naked so Mattie ignored his question, rose from the bed and walked to the bathroom where she wrapped herself in a terrycloth robe. Returning to the bedroom, she began to make herself a scotch and water as she gathered her thoughts.

"Can I fix you a drink?" she asked.

"No thanks. Will you answer my question?"

Mattie paused before answering. "No, I won't. Who I was with, where I went and what I did doesn't concern you. Please, Bourke, leave it at that. You don't need to know."

"But Mattie..." Cockran began but she cut him off.

"Leave it alone, Cockran. I don't want to talk about it."

Later, with Mattie asleep beside him, Cockran was wide awake and puzzled. Why wouldn't she even tell him she had been at Wyntoon, let alone at one point naked in that bedroom? Had she actually been in the room when that man had been killed? Had he been her lover? What exactly was her game? Had she really been the IRA's captive as the anonymous note suggested? But if so and now that she was free, why not admit it? Until he knew the answers, he wasn't about to disclose to Mattie what he had learned at Wyntoon about Hearst and Cromwell. He would let Churchill sort it out. Whose side was Mattie on?

Cockran got up from the bed. Mattie stirred briefly, then snuggled back in as he reluctantly pulled the covers higher over her body. He loved her body but he hated being a pawn in someone else's game. Not being able to see the entire chessboard. Not knowing where the other pieces were or what moves came next.

Cockran put on a terrycloth robe. That's the problem, he thought. Few people were content to be pawns, moved about at the will of another. Even if they were in someone else's game, they were always starting up their own. Games within games. Churchill probably knew that, expected it and didn't care. He wondered if Mick Collins had thought about it the same way.

But what was Mattie's game? Where did she fit in? Who was she working for? Hearst? More than likely. Wyntoon certainly showed he and Cromwell were in this IRA arms deal up to their ears. But what were their motives? Hearst at least would be bashing the Brits and selling more papers if another civil war broke out in Ireland. Cromwell? Hell, he probably owned stock in most of the arms and munitions makers in the US.

Mattie's motives still nagged. Why had she seduced him? He had no illusions about his attractiveness to the fairer sex. Once he had sworn off single women, the young Gold Coast matrons he dated were as much interested in revenge on their husbands as they were in him. Yet Mattie attracted him like no other woman since Nora. And, like Nora, she had seduced him, the only two women who had ever done so. This in itself was suspicious. Flattering but suspicious because it was usually Cockran making the first move.

But what if he was wrong? What if she really was working for Churchill and not Hearst? And what if she was beginning to care for him? Part of him hoped that she was but he was conflicted. He had avoided commitment for so long because he didn't want to break any more hearts. But Mattie was different. He'd never felt this way about the others. That was what the speech was for—to let them down as gently as possible. Could he do that with Mattie? He didn't know. And if she were playing him for a sucker, that would hurt too.

Cockran pondered the immediate future. He had no plan on how to uncover Mattie's true loyalties. And he had no better plan than Churchill's to stop the IRA. But he had a plan for McBride. Oh, yes. He knew exactly what he was going to do when he found Tommy McBride.

54.

Giraffes!

En Route to San Simeon
Wednesday, 21 August 1929
9:30 a.m.

The morning sun was bright and the sky was deep blue and cloudless. Mattie and Bourke had risen early and caught the Southern Pacific's 6:30 a.m. train to Los Angeles. They were scheduled to arrive early in the afternoon at the small seaside town of San Luis Obispo, the train station nearest to San Simeon. Hearst would have a car waiting for them.

Cockran couldn't concentrate on what lay ahead in San Simeon—Churchill and the meeting with the President. His mind kept wandering back to Tommy McBride. Jack Manion's men had staked out the warehouse in Oakland for the past two days with no sign of him. So Cockran would give Churchill the information he had found at Wyntoon. He would even meet with the President today if that is what Churchill still wanted him to do. He hoped he was wrong about Hearst and Mattie but, if not, he and Winston were heading straight into the lion's den.

11:30 a.m.

Giraffes! Cockran couldn't believe it. Hearst really did have giraffes! Mattie had warned him, but he thought by now that he could tell when she was pulling his leg. Deception? Well, that was different. Three giraffes, their long necks extended upward, were nibbling the tender leaves near the top of the low lying trees.

"I'll be damned!" Cockran said, turning to Mattie, "you weren't kidding, were you?"

They were sitting in the back of William Randolph Hearst's large Buick convertible which had met them at the train station in San Luis Obispo. The sky was still cloudless, but a steady breeze off the ocean ruffled their hair as they headed back up the Pacific Coast Highway to the tiny fishing village of San Simeon, forty-three miles to the north. They drove through the village, San Simeon Bay on their left, and turned right onto a wide, carefully laid gravel road leading to the hill beyond, *La Cuesta Encantada*, The Enchanted Hill, rising in the distance. At the base of the hill they passed an airfield where a Fokker Trimotor had just landed. Cockran could see from the identification that it wasn't the same plane, but it was the twin of the one he and Jack Manion had chartered for the flight to Wyntoon. At the far end of the field was an airship mooring mast.

Further along the road they passed on the left the headquarters for the cattle ranch which Hearst maintained on the property. A few miles further, they came to a ten-foot high wire fence. They passed through special double pull gates designed to allow automobiles and people entrance to the enclosure without affording the wild animals inside a chance to escape, with only one gate opening at a time. The enclosure covered several square miles and, as the road continued to wind upward, Cockran saw in the space of only fifteen minutes not only the giraffes but six bison, four zebras, four llamas, a yak, three cassowaries, two emus and many more gazelles and antelopes. Finally, they came upon a herd of kangaroos blocking their path, sitting in the middle of the road. The Buick crunched to a halt on the gravel and the chauffeur sounded the horn. The kangaroos were unimpressed but, gradually, they moved off the road.

They had been climbing steadily higher and at each switchback, Cockran could see the blue of the Pacific in the distance. They made the final turn and saw looming in front of them the twin bell towers of *La Casa Grande*, a Spanish style mission cathedral sitting squarely on top of *La Cuesta Encantada*. Below it were spread out three substantial but smaller guest houses in the same California Spanish style. *Casa Del Sol*, located to face into the setting sun, *Casa Del Monte*, to the north and closer to the mountains beyond, and *Casa Del Mar*, to the south and facing the sea. Gardens, marble pathways and terraces crawled down from *La Casa Grande* to the smaller houses overlooking an outdoor pool which seemed large enough to sail a small boat in. Cockran had never seen anything like this in his life, not even the grand mansions near his father's house on Long Island.

Mattie was looking at him and smiling. "Wait until you see the zoo."

"Zoo?" Cockran asked. "You mean he has more wild animals than the ones we saw?"

Mattie laughed. "You bet. The last time I was here there were four lions, two pumas, two chimpanzees, mountain lions, cheetahs, leopards. Not to mention the elephants."

When the Buick pulled up in front of *La Casa Grande*, Hearst and Churchill were outside waiting at the foot of a broad marble staircase. Hearst was a big bear of a man who looked much younger than his 66 years. His shoulders were slightly slumped forward, a shock of gray hair falling over the forehead of his large head. He was easily six inches taller than the smaller Churchill, who had apparently taken an even earlier train than Cockran and Mattie. Though the temperature was in the low eighties, both men wore light-colored vested summer suits.

Mattie was first out of the convertible and warmly gave a hug and a kiss on the cheek to Hearst who awkwardly returned the embrace. Mattie turned and did the same to Churchill.

"Chief, meet Bourke Cockran. You and his father were once in Congress together."

"Yes, we were," said Hearst, in a surprisingly high-pitched voice for such a large man. "A fine fellow, your father. Marvelous speaker. Occasionally prone to exaggeration. I don't really think I represented 'every incitement to murder' or 'every encouragement to riot' as he claimed when I campaigned for mayor of New York. But that was all long ago. 1905, actually. He made up for it the year after. Supported me for governor. Your father was quite a man but, whatever his other faults, he was an even better judge of journalistic talent. I personally edited your articles on the GID dossiers. They're still some of my favorites."

Cockran was surprised to learn he had been hired in 1919 despite Hearst's total recall of his father's 1905 speech and flattered that Hearst would remember his stories from ten years ago.

"Thank you, sir," Cockran said. "I liked them, too."

"Please," said Hearst, "call me W.R. You were in Europe for us after that, weren't you? I'm sorry you left. It wasn't the money, was it? I've never lost good people because of that."

"No, sir, it was personal. It wasn't the money."

"Good, good. I'm pleased you could join us. We have more guests than usual this weekend because of the *Graf Zeppelin*, but if you need anything, don't hesitate to ask."

Hearst turned to Churchill. "Winston, I believe Mr. Cockran is staying with you in *Casa Del Sol.* Would you be so kind as to show him to his rooms? I am certain his bags will be there by now. Come, Mattie," he said, turning back to her and extending his arm. "We have a lot of catching up to do. And there are some photographs you mailed me which we must go over."

The sun was directly overhead. Churchill and Cockran walked slowly back the guest house where Churchill and his entourage were lodged. A pleasant breeze was blowing and they were soon inside the house's cool exterior.

A table had been set up for them in the cool shade of the covered terrace of the large, two-story structure, looking out through three arches toward the Pacific. "Our host has a big evening planned for us." Churchill said. "They have been in wireless contact with the *Graf Zeppelin*. It will arrive in San Francisco this afternoon and in San Simeon before dusk."

Churchill guided Cockran out to the terrace. "The real celebration is tomorrow's luncheon to which Hearst has invited the press and any number of additional guests. More importantly for you and me, President Hoover will arrive today at 4:00 p.m."

Churchill had ordered a simple lunch for the two of them, a grilled veal chop, asparagus and a bottle of claret, the latter an indication of the high regard in which Hearst held his English guests, as the house rules, otherwise strictly enforced, prohibited the consumption of alcoholic beverages in rooms or anywhere else except in the Great Hall and Refectory in *La Casa Grande.*

"We never had an opportunity in San Francisco to discuss the adventure you and Rankin had this week," Churchill said. "Give me all the details. Robert can be a little close-mouthed."

Churchill's eyes sparkled as Cockran told him of the invasion of Wyntoon by San Francisco's Chinatown Squad and Cockran as well as the damning records they had secured.

"Who is this Cromwell fellow?" Churchill asked.

Cockran explained what Mattie learned about Cromwell and his connections with Hearst. He reminded Churchill of the position Cromwell had when they both worked for the same American agency in the war and its aftermath, careful not to actually name the top-secret Inquiry to a foreign statesman.

"Ah, yes, your Inquiry," Churchill said, grinning broadly as he placed his claret glass back on the table. "A spy like you, eh my boy?"

Cockran shook his head in mock dismay. So much for top-secrets. "You know better, Winston, far more than I, the difference between spies and intelligence." Cockran rose from his chair, walked over to the center archway and looked into the distance. "I'm still not persuaded that Hearst has nothing to do with this." He recounted for Churchill the telegram he had found from Mattie alerting Hearst to their new route of travel and Mattie's refusal to tell him where she had gone or what she had done after their arrival.

"How did they know to be waiting for the train from Spokane if it wasn't Hearst?" Cockran asked. "Trains from the east and the north arrive in Oakland. You and I were the only ones to know about our coming from the north and the only ones I told were Rankin and Mattie."

Churchill joined Cockran in the archway. "So you continue to suspect Mattie?"

"Yes and no. I know she had to be the one who tipped Hearst off but I don't want to believe she's really involved. But it's difficult to know what happened at Wyntoon, especially if she won't admit to having been there when I know damn well she was."

"I think you are making too much out of too little. Hearst has nothing to gain and much to lose being mixed up in a dirty business like this," Churchill said. "But, in any event, it really doesn't matter, does it? You have done a splendid job, Bourke. In a few hours the President will be here and I feel certain he will do the right thing, Hearst or no Hearst."

Churchill turned away from the archway, walked back to the table and drained the last of the claret from his glass. "Now, if you'll excuse me, Mr. Hearst has invited me to watch a tennis match and I must have my afternoon nap before then." He pulled a watch from his pocket and opened it. "Please come to my chambers at 6:00 p.m. and we will rehearse our little presentation for the President. Also, bring those Collins journals with you. I'll look them over after we've talked to Mr Hoover."

55.

The Great Engineer

San Simeon
Wednesday, 21 August 1929
3:00 p.m.

"A golden future lies ahead for America," Churchill said, as he sat with William Randolph Hearst watching a spirited tennis match between Mattie and Bourke on one team and Hearst's mistress, Marion Davies, and Churchill's son, Randolph, on the other. Out of deference to their host, others watching kept a distance from Hearst and Churchill as they talked.

"Your stock market is a marvel. Since I've come to North America, my investments have increased in value by nearly 20 per cent. Everywhere I have been in America, that is all people talk about. It is astonishing. The housemaid who makes your bed is a stockholder on margin. The chauffeur, the train conductor, the waiter, all have their open accounts."

Churchill paused and looked at Hearst. "Who is your investment man? A fellow named Cromwell, I believe?"

"More or less," Hearst replied. "I don't pay that sort of stuff much attention. I never invest on margin. Cromwell is here though and should be joining us for dinner once the airship arrives, maybe earlier if the President is on time."

Mattie and Bourke had won the first set and accepted a challenge for a rematch.

"So tell me, W.R., what are your views on the Young Plan?"

"It's better than the Dawes Plan which, in turn, was better than the reparations called for at Versailles. But why do Americans have to keep coming up with 'plans' for reducing German reparations? We had no business getting involved and pulling your bacon from the fire in the first place. If we keep pouring money into Germany, we're going to have a stake in their success and our economy will be tied to Europe. I don't like that."

Hearst paused and shouted, "Well struck!" after Marion had hit a return down the line and beyond Mattie's reach. "I tell you what else I don't like," Hearst continued, "are these disarmament treaties. Americans should never allow others to limit their freedom to do what they think necessary. No country should. There can be no peace in Europe unless France and Germany are friends. So long as the United States continues to insist that the Allies, especially Great Britain, repay their loans, France will keep bleeding Germany; America will keep investing in Germany; and the investment bankers will be the only ones making money."

"It is a shame, W.R., that more Americans are not as farsighted as you."

Hearst laughed. "It's easy, Winston, is it not, to find wisdom in those who agree with you? But I'll bet there's something on which we don't agree."

"Pray, tell me more. I'm already in your employ but I shall do my best to be objective."

"There will be another European war within ten years. The French population continues to decline while Germany's increases. Unless France reconciles with Germany, war will come."

Churchill took a sip of champagne. "I quite agree, W.R., but where do we disagree?"

"When, not if, war comes to Europe again and Great Britain takes sides, you will implore America to come to your aid. And I will resist. This time, the American people will be with me."

"Why is that?" Churchill inquired.

"The Merchants of Death. The munitions makers. Americans know about them now and, for those who don't, I will tell them. I have more newspapers now than I did then. The circulation for my magazines is four times what it was fifteen years ago. My newsreels are in more theaters. And radio stations, Winston. Radio stations. My goal, in the next five years, is to own a radio station in every city where I have a newspaper."

"A five year plan, W.R.? Surely you, of all people, are not imitating the Bolsheviks?"

Hearst smiled and took a sip from a tall glass of lemonade. "Actually, Winston, my time table is three years, not five. If I had said three, you would have seen through my plan."

"Plan?" Churchill said, and then he caught himself. "Oh, I see. The 1932 elections."

"I'm a Democrat, Winston, a free-trader like yourself. It's why I didn't support Al Smith. 1932 will be my last chance. I'll be 69 years old then. But I'm in excellent health and I'll have more money than any other potential candidate."

"Interesting," Churchill said. "So you don't think Governor Smith will be a candidate?"

"Oh, he'll be a candidate, all right. But the party will never nominate a Catholic again. Not for a generation. They can't afford to lose the South, not if they hope to carry the country."

Churchill nodded. "What about the new governor in New York? Roosevelt, I believe his name is. Assistant Secretary of the Navy during the war. Related to the former president?"

"A different branch of the family but they are cousins. Frank is a nice man but he has to be reelected first. He barely won last year and the Republicans are sure to put up a strong challenger. I'll be meeting with Frank next month. I've never thought him a man of strong principle but I need to look him in the eye. Find out what deals he's cut with Tammany."

The tennis match had ended with Marion and Randolph having avenged their earlier defeat. The four younger people gathered around Hearst and Churchill and a fresh pitcher of lemonade which had appeared moments before the set ended. Churchill had noticed that, their animated conversation notwithstanding, Hearst had been watching the tennis match during their talk, knew the score and had ordered lemonade once Marion's team was serving for the set.

Churchill watched as Marion came over, her perspiring face glistening in the sun, and bent over and gave Hearst a hug. "We won, Pops! Did you see us?"

"Yes, I did, my dear. Your backhand in game seven to Mattie was the turning point."

"You *were* watching!" she squealed. "I love you. You're the best, Pops," and gave him another hug. Churchill hoped he was maintaining a benign expression. Hearst had invited Churchill to a large dinner party in New York in late October being given by his wife, Millicent, as if it were the most natural thing in the world for him to be the guest of Hearst and his mistress here in San Simeon and Hearst and his wife in New York.

"The President will be here at 4:00 p.m.," Hearst said, "and tea will be served at 4:30 p.m. in the Great Hall, if you would care to join us, Mattie, Mr. Cockran?" he said, nodding to each in turn. "Dinner will be at 8 o'clock as usual unless the *Graf Zeppelin* is delayed."

4:30 p.m.

Herbert Hoover seemed stiff, Cockran thought, as the President picked up his tea cup from the long, low table in front of the chintz-covered sofa on which he sat. He wore a light colored summer suit but the high celluloid collar which encased his thick neck looked decidedly uncomfortable. Cockran had met only two American Presidents. His father had been a close friend and adviser to both. He met Grover Cleveland in 1904 when Cockran, Sr. had returned to Congress after an eight-year hiatus. Theodore Roosevelt had come to dinner at their Sands Point home in 1910. Both men had seemed far more comfortable in their own skins and more self-assured than the prosperous-looking, well-fed man sitting in front of him.

They were in the eighty-foot long Assembly Room which had an elaborate twenty-foot high coffered ceiling. The sofa faced away from the room's dominating element, a sixteen-foot high French Renaissance mantle. Covering the entire wall to the left of the fireplace was a seventeenth-century Brussels tapestry by Rubens.

Elaborate oriental rugs were everywhere.

Ten people were seated in a large semicircle around the sofa, Churchill and Hearst in matching armchairs immediately to the left and right of the President. Philip Cromwell sat next to Hoover on the sofa and was the only person to whom Hoover had shown any sign of animation, grasping Cromwell's hand in both of his, thanking him warmly for his support during the last election. Marion Davies and three of her Hollywood friends were in the other chairs, along with a quiet young German businessman, Kurt von Sturm, whose employer, a Cromwell client, was arriving shortly on the *Graf Zeppelin*. Sturm was almost too good looking, Cockran thought, with piercing blue eyes and longish blond hair for a German, swept back from his forehead. He noticed Sturm occasionally staring at Mattie. To his surprise, it bothered him. There was something in the way he looked at her that he didn't like.

Cockran also had not been surprised at the coolness displayed by Hoover to Hearst. The Hearst papers had all endorsed Hoover in the last election but Hearst had supported Secretary of Treasury Andrew Mellon for the Republican nomination. He had only supported Hoover in the fall because of his antipathy to Al Smith and Tammany Hall. The Chief himself, however, had written several editorials denouncing the anti-Catholic attacks made by Hoover supporters on Al Smith in the South and Midwest. Hoover, the hypocrite, had piously asserted on one occasion—and one occasion only—that religion should not be an issue in the campaign. He had hoped that no one would vote for him because he was a Quaker and that no one would vote for his opponent because he was a Catholic. Cockran had been disgusted. Pontius Pilate had sounded more sincere in washing his hands of Christ before turning him over to the bloodthirsty mob.

Mattie had warned Cockran that Hoover would still remember his war-time arrest by Churchill's British Naval Intelligence. She had proved to be correct as the President had not greeted Churchill like the close war-time and post-war colleagues Churchill had professed them to be. Hoover limited himself to a curt "Good day to you as well, Mr. Churchill" in response to Winston's effusive greetings at how delighted he was to see again his old comrade in arms. The only mistake that Cockran could see that Winston had made then was in not keeping the plump bastard in jail a few more days. Cockran had seen pictures of Hoover during the war and a week of bread and water rations would have done him a world of good, then as now.

Cockran had noted Cromwell's surprise at his and Mattie's presence but the man had hidden it well, greeting them both cordially. If he knew anything about Cockran and the raid on Wyntoon, he gave no indication. It gave Cockran pause, seeing Cromwell beside the President, talking as if they were old friends, knowing that he was sufficiently well connected not only to put federal agents on Cockran's tail, but to be copied on their reports as well. Hoover had been Secretary of Commerce for eight years. Coincidence? Cockran didn't believe in coincidence.

Hoover's voice broke into Cockran's thoughts. "I do believe we have the opportunity to secure peace and prosperity for this generation and many generations to come."

"What role do you believe the Kellogg-Briand Pact will play in achieving this?" Hearst asked, referring to the treaty negotiated by the Coolidge administration's Secretary of State, Frank Kellogg where all the major nations had renounced war as an instrument of policy.

Cockran was impressed. Hearst was sharp. It was a good journalist's question.

Hoover pursed his lips until it looked to Bourke as if he were sucking a lemon, and then carefully responded, "It will be useful in theory, but I am looking for more practical results. Ships not being built by the United States and Japan. Or, in the case of Great Britain," Hoover said, nodding in Churchill's direction, "ships being decommissioned. Practical steps. Judge us by practical steps. Will our country, will the world, be a more peaceful and prosperous place three or seven years from now? I will be content to have my reputation judged by history on the basis of the answer to that question."

Mattie's friends in the White House press office were right, Cockran thought. Hoover really believed his press clippings. That he was the Great Engineer. Would Churchill allow himself to be provoked? Churchill, however, remained quiet while Hearst continued to probe.

"Wouldn't you think a more logical target for disarmament would be a strict limit on the size of standing armies? Or forbidding the development of long-range bombing aircraft?"

"Well...," Hoover said, "that is an admirable goal as well. But everyone knows that the naval arms race between England and Germany was one of the prime causes of the last war."

"Oh really?" Hearst said. "And here I thought the causes of the war were the secret treaties which obligated the great powers to come to the aid of lesser nations and the huge standing armies which made it possible for them to do so. Russia and France coming to the aid of Serbia and Germany the same with Austria-Hungary. If millions of men had not been under arms and ready to march, perhaps diplomacy might have had a chance to work."

Hearst paused and took a sip of tea, the cup looking small in his large hand. "Perhaps I missed the news. Winston, was there a large naval battle between you and Germany off the coast of Serbia which led to the Great War. You were, as I recall, First Lord of the Admiralty?"

Cockran kept his courtroom face on, showing no emotion but, inside, he was having one hell of a good time. Hoover knew he was being made fun of by a man who could buy and sell the self-made millionaire from Palo Alto, California many times over and who would still be the most powerful press baron in America when Herbert Hoover was an ex-president. If Hearst really were funding the IRA arms deal in order to sell newspapers, Cockran thought, he must be confident that he has Hoover in a box from which he can't escape.

Fortunately for Hoover, Marion Davies and her three Hollywood friends didn't know much history and so laughter had not greeted Hearst's question. Cockran assumed their German guest was not that fluent in English. But Cromwell frowned at Churchill's straight-faced reply.

"I most certainly was, W.R. My proudest accomplishment in

public life was that when war came, the fleet was ready. But, alas, it was ready in Scotland, at Scapa Flow, and was nowhere near the Balkans. We possibly had a few destroyers nearby in the Mediterranean."

Cockran watched with admiration as Marion Davies then smoothly inserted herself into the conversation and steered it away from politics to motion pictures, asking the President about his favorite films and Cockran soon discovered that the German, von Sturm, was quite fluent in English and still stealing covert glances at Mattie. Thirty minutes later, the servants had taken away the tea service and Cockran saw Churchill approach the President and Hearst.

"W.R., if I might impose on your hospitality. The Prime Minister has given me a private message to deliver to the President and I wonder if, for a few moments before dinner tonight, you could provide us a room where we might talk undisturbed?" Without waiting for a reply, Churchill turned to Hoover. "Would that be convenient, Mr. President?"

Hoover paused, wary, and said, "I suppose so. This won't take long, will it?"

"No, Mr. President, just a few moments of your time. But it is a most important message and on a subject close to your heart."

"Of course, Winston, Mr. President," Hearst said. "I would be pleased to do so. My private library on the third floor will be at your disposal. James will direct you to the appropriate elevator."

56.

Geneva Doesn't Tolerate Mistakes

The Neptune Pool
San Simeon
Wednesday, 21 August, 1929
5:30 p.m.

Kurt von Sturm stood in the shade of the portico beside the elaborately tiled, near-Olympic-size Neptune pool, looking out at the Pacific Ocean over a mile away.

"Will the escape of the McGary woman adversely affect the shipment or the final payment to the Irish?" Cromwell asked.

"No, as to the latter question. As for the former, it's too late to worry about Miss McGary. But we are depending more than ever on the quality of the men you have provided as security for our warehouse in Long Beach. I lost four good men in the British raid at Wyntoon. I underestimated the strength they could muster at the point of attack. Would it be possible to double the number of men you have assigned to Long Beach?"

Cromwell removed the cigar from his mouth and pointed it at Sturm. "Don't worry, Kurt, it won't be a problem. We have plenty of good men we can call upon. And more where they came from. Trust me. They're all ex-Army. I'd stake my life on these men."

"I do worry, Philip. The Geneva Group pays me well to worry. They don't tolerate mistakes. I've made a few on this assignment. I don't intend for there to be any more."

"Trust me, Kurt. There won't be. By the way, did you notice the President's attitude toward Churchill? He was telling me earlier today that he and the President were old friends from the war. Sure didn't look like that to me."

57.

There Is Nothing I Can Do

The Gothic Study
San Simeon
Wednesday, 21 August 1929
7:15 p.m.

Churchill seemed surprised. That was obvious to Cockran as they sat in Hearst's private library, an enormous room called the Gothic Study with a long wooden table presided over by a portrait of a younger Hearst at the far end of the room. Bookcases lined the walls and light from the early evening sun filled the room through clerestory windows. No one but Hearst and Marion Davies were allowed on this floor. Hoover and Churchill would not be disturbed.

The two statesmen sat in comfortable leather chairs at the opposite end of the study from Hearst's portrait. The chairs were placed side by side at slightly less than a ninety-degree angle. Cockran and Mattie were sitting in a matched pair ten feet away. A single Secret Service agent stood halfway down the room, out of earshot, his silent figure as immobile as the floor lamp.

Cockran had earlier observed with interest Hoover's frosty but correct reception of Churchill. Now, with no one present but Churchill's entourage and the Secret Service, Hoover was almost rude, his body language showing visible impatience. Not that Cockran hadn't seen Churchill produce that effect when he was dominating a conversation with a monologue. But now, Churchill was on his best behavior, reporting that the Prime Minister would be most grateful to the President for granting a few moments alone with his personal emissary.

Churchill got right to the point. "Less than a month ago, British Intelligence received reports that the terrorist Irish Republican Army planned a massive arms purchase in the United States involving millions of dollars. His Majesty's Government consulted with the leaders of the Irish Free State and both of our governments agreed to ask the aid of the United States. While the Prime Minister and I represent different parties in Parliament, we are of a single mind in helping our fellow Commonwealth member. When he learned I was traveling to the United States, the Prime Minister asked me to personally convey this request to you."

Hoover nodded and squinted his eyes until they were narrow slits in his large, puffy face. "What proof do you have of this, Mr. Churchill? Surely you should understand that the United States cannot concern itself every time the natives are restless in a corner of the British Empire."

Cockran stiffened at the President's slur on the Irish. The man was a complete bigot. He was tempted to reply but stayed silent, listening as Churchill measured his words. "With all respect, Mr. President, the Irish Free State is a full member of the British Commonwealth and its location, far from being remote, makes it of vital concern to Great Britain's national security. As for proof, my young colleagues here, Miss McGary and Mr. Cockran, have personally observed the weapons being assembled at three separate locations in the United States. Mattie, Bourke," Churchill said, gesturing to them, "would you be so kind as to tell the President what you have seen and show him the documents you have managed to obtain?"

Cockran went first, detailing what he observed in Cleveland, passing over to the President copies of the Cleveland bills of lading he had obtained from the safe at Wyntoon, leaving Hoover with the impression that he had obtained them at the warehouse itself.

"How did you obtain access to this warehouse in Cleveland? Through the help of a union leader? A Teamster, I believe?" Hoover asked. "But you didn't have the owner's consent?"

Cockran had had enough. He was not a patient man. Still, he made it a point in front of judges to always respond politely and respectfully to their questions, however stupid. But this guy wasn't a judge. He was a damn engineer who had been elected to only one public office in his life. When it came to the law, Hoover couldn't find his ass with both hands.

"I disagree, Mr. President. The key to the warehouse was delivered to me through an agent of the owner. I had every legal right to be there." Not to mention the fact that an agent from your old Commerce Department was in the company of a known IRA terrorist.

"So you say, Mr. Cockran. So you say," Hoover replied. "But my sources of information indicate the owner of the warehouse was not aware you had been given a key."

Cockran wondered how the hell did Hoover have any "sources" on something he just heard for the first time? "The person who gave me the key was an employee of the owner, the night watchman, who clearly had authority to do so."

"Be that as it may…" Hoover began but an impatient Cockran cut him off.

"No, Mr. President, it is a fact. Before you accuse a person of trespass, you need to consult a lawyer, someone who knows more than you apparently do about the law of libel."

The President's face grew red but he said nothing and Churchill promptly intervened, diverting Hoover's attention from his large Irish adversary to the far more appealing Mattie McGary. Unfortunately, it didn't work. Hoover had to do something to reclaim his manhood and Mattie turned out to be a surprisingly easy victim after she told her story.

"So you had the warehouse owner's permission to be there?" the President asked.

"Yes, sir."

"Did he know you were going to be crawling over the tops of crates and walking along the ceiling beams as you described?"

"Well, he knew I was going to be taking photographs all over the warehouse."

"Yes, but you took these photographs surreptitiously so you knew it was impermissable?"

"Well, not exactly, but...."

Cockran was suspicious. He had never seen Mattie so defensive, so tentative. It's almost as if she were trying to be unpersuasive, he thought. Then Churchill intervened.

"Mr. President, the IRA are a ruthless gang of terrorists. You can't always play by the Marquis of Queensberry's rules with people like this when they are planning more mayhem for a peace-loving people like the Irish."

Hoover let the barest traces of a smile form on his pursed lips. "It remains to be seen, does it not, Mr. Churchill, just how peace-loving the Irish are and whether their race has the capacity for self-government? Ireland isn't Canada. Or even Australia."

Cockran was angry now and strained to control himself. His knuckles were almost white as his hands tightly gripped the chair's soft leather arms. He leaned forward as if to speak, but Churchill had already seen the effect Hoover's words had produced and Cockran was grateful Churchill had quickly responded before Cockran could say something he might regret. "I respectfully disagree, Mr. President. The Free State is every bit as much a respected member of the Commonwealth as other great nations such as Canada, Australia and South Africa. Moreover, the Irish diaspora has contributed hundreds upon hundreds of thousands of immigrants, not only to these Commonwealth nations, but to your own country."

"I'm aware of that, Mr. Churchill, but most of those who have accomplished anything beyond increasing our birth rate were of Scotch-Irish descent. No offense intended, Mr. Cockran, merely a factual observation," Hoover said, glancing in Cockran's direction. "What I find disturbing, Mr. Churchill, is that seven years after you British, perhaps unwisely, gave southern Ireland her freedom, they have still not managed to eradicate terrorism. Even more disturbing and ominous for their long-term chances of establishing a democratic government is that some of the more prominent opposition leaders, including this de Valera fellow, as late as last year were making public statements claiming that the rebels were morally and legally entitled to take power by force. I also believe he threatened an invasion of the North."

"You seem well-briefed, Mr. President, but all nations have their growing pains," Churchill replied. "It took eleven years after America declared independence to establish your constitution. But let us return to the purpose of the Prime Minister's request. Bourke, pray detail for the President what you observed in San Francisco."

Cockran started to speak but Hoover held up his hand. "What you observed in San Francisco, Mr. Cockran, was comparable to what you observed in Cleveland?"

"Yes, sir."

"And the bills of lading you possess indicate that the weapons and ammunition have been sold and title no longer resides in the manufacturers?"

"Yes, sir."

"You are a law professor, I believe? At Columbia?"

"Yes, sir."

"As you know, my background is in construction and engineering. Unfortunately, my Attorney General did not accompany me on this trip. Would you be so kind as to advise me what federal laws you believe have been violated by these arms purchases?"

Damn! Cockran thought. Hoover *had* been well briefed. But how did he know to even ask his lawyers? Had that bastard Cromwell poisoned the well? Was Cromwell Hoover's "source" for Cleveland? Hoover had identified the same weak point that Cockran had made to Churchill. There were no federal laws being violated and there was no upside to claiming the violation of nonexistent laws. Instead, he appealed to the President's better nature, even though it was obvious that the man didn't have one.

"There are no laws which have been violated *per se*, Mr. President. But surely the Commerce Department, acting together with the State Department and local authorities, could find some pretext to detain the shipment from leaving port in Los Angeles until after you have had an opportunity to review the implications of these shipments for American foreign policy."

Hoover's eyes narrowed again and his lips pursed. "I am perfectly aware of what the Commerce Department may do. The problem, Mr. Cockran, and you, too, Mr. Churchill, is that you are too late. Title has passed. Whoever purchased those weapons owns them. They have rights which our Constitution protects and the government may do nothing to hinder them in the exercise of those rights, which includes shipping them out of the country."

Hoover paused, filled his pipe with tobacco, and lit it. "Mr. Cockran, as you concede, there are no laws that have been broken in connection with these weapon purchases about which the British Government is so concerned. I daresay, however, we do have laws on the books with respect to both Americans and foreign nationals rendering assistance on American soil to a foreign intelligence service, even a former ally like Great Britain."

Cockran briefly wondered if the IRA had paid off the President the same way Al Capone bought aldermen in Chicago. No, Cockran reflected, Hoover probably hadn't been bought. But that still left him no better than a common thug who thought that because he had power, he could threaten to use it whenever it pleased him to do so. A typical politician.

Hoover shifted in his chair and looked directly at Churchill. "What your government should have done, Mr. Churchill, was to approach our government immediately, through proper channels, specifically, your ambassador in Washington, to Mr. Stimson, our Secretary of State. At that point, something could have been done. Had I approved, the Commerce Department could have issued an advisory bulletin to all weapons manufacturers in the country asking them to refrain from selling arms destined for Ireland. They would not have been obligated to honor the request, mind you. Nevertheless, the Commerce Department plays a critical role in facilitating U.S. exports and I have no doubt that few would have ignored our request."

Hoover raised his hands palms up in resignation. "But now? Now, there is nothing I can do. Please convey to your Prime Minister, Mr. Churchill, my sincere regret that I was not able to be of assistance and that I very much look forward to his visit in the fall."

With that, Hoover quickly rose from his chair before Churchill had a chance to do the same. The Secret Service agent opened the door for the President. When the door closed, Churchill turned to Cockran with a laugh and a twinkle in his eye. "Well, how do you think it went, my boy? He never once mentioned the unpleasant episode of his arrest during the war. That's a good sign, wouldn't you say?" Churchill laughed again. "I fear we may have to find another way to foil the IRA than depending on the U.S. authorities. Join me for breakfast tomorrow and we'll explore our options."

Cockran wondered, and not for the first time, exactly what Winston had in mind. It's not as if he hadn't been told to expect an outcome like this.

7:00 p.m

The elevator door closed in front of the President and his two Secret Service agents. "Do you boys know who that was?" Hoover asked with a chuckle.

"No, sir," they responded in unison.

"Winston Churchill. He was Britain's last Chancellor of the Exchequer. But during the war, he was in charge of their navy." The President laughed. "Tried to have me arrested for espionage in 1915 because I was feeding starving children in Belgium. Can you imagine that?"

"No, sir."

"At the time, neither could I. I have many close friends in England. No one in his party really trusts Churchill. He's only out for himself. He changed parties twice. They call him an adventurer, a half-breed American. Do you know why?"

"No, sir."

The President laughed again. "His mother was an American. Fine looking woman but a genuine round-heeled tramp. I'm told she had multiple affairs including one with King Edward before the war. I heard another was with that Cockran fellow's father. A real Irish blowhard he was. After her husband, Lord Randolph, died, she twice married men half her age. Some say Lord Randolph died of syphylis and wasn't even the sire of Winston's younger brother."

The elevator door opened and the President walked out into the Great Hall.

"Breeding will always tell, I suppose," Hoover remarked to no one in particular, as his two agents were now scanning either side of the room. "I never could stand that man. I can't believe Ramsay MacDonald showed such poor judgment in sending him as an emissary."

Hoover let out another short laugh. "Not that I would have lifted a finger to help the Irish. I didn't need the Catholic vote last year anyway."

As the entourage reached the door, Hearst's butler approached. "Excuse me, Mr. President," the butler said, "but Mr. Hearst asked me to tell you that there's been a change in plans. High winds have prevented the *Graf Zeppelin* from landing here on the grounds. The ship has advised us that weather reports for tomorrow do not offer a brighter prospect. As a consequence, they have determined to fly on to Los Angeles and moor there tomorrow morning. Mr. Hearst asked me to tell you that he has reserved the Hollywood Roosevelt Hotel for a luncheon reception for the crew of the *Graf Zeppelin* on Friday. A train will be leaving tomorrow evening for Los Angeles and he would be pleased if you would join him in his private railcar for the journey."

The President nodded. "Thank Mr. Hearst for his kind invitation which I accept. Tell him I look forward to seeing him at dinner tonight."

58.

The Shadow of the *Graf Zeppelin*

Los Angeles
Thursday, 22 August 1929
8:30 a.m.

The giant airship slowly turned into the wind, the morning sun flashing off its silvery skin, until it was heading directly west toward the mooring mast where Kurt von Sturm patiently waited along with the forty men of the ground crew. Behind them, fifty yards away, a crowd numbering in the thousands lined the airport fence.

The shadow of the *Graf Zeppelin* now reached the men gathered at the base of the mooring mast, which had been turned until it was directly in position to receive the airship's nose cone. Once the nose cone was locked in place, the mooring mast was designed to swing in an arc of three hundred sixty degrees so that if the winds shifted, the zeppelin's long fuselage would turn with the wind. At a signal from the landing master, the ground crew fanned out, twenty men each, on either side of the airship's shadow. The airship was now barely one hundred feet above them and, as if on cue, landing lines appeared on either side of the ship, dropping down to the men below, each of whom grasped a line and, muscles straining with the effort, slowly walked the giant airship the last few yards to the mooring mast.

A prolonged cheer arose from the crowd when the connection was finally secure and the *Graf Zeppelin*, for the first time in its illustrious career, made landfall on the California coast.

Kurt von Sturm was the first man up the stairs to the door of the *Graf Zeppelin* once the stewards had put the steps in place. He gave a crisp military salute to the Captain, Ernst Lehman, who returned the salute with a smile and grasped Sturm's hand in his own. They had been together in the war, Sturm serving as executive officer on Lehman's airship, the last before Sturm received his own command.

"What a pleasure to see you, Kurt. It seems a lifetime since we dropped you off in Lakehurst. Yet it was less than three weeks ago. You have been keeping out of trouble?"

"Me? Trouble?" Kurt laughed. "I'm on holiday, Ernst."

Lehman stood aside and beckoned for Sturm to enter, which he did. He turned left and walked down the airship's familiar narrow corridor to the Grand Salon. As he entered the salon, he saw Zurich and Berlin in the right-hand corner lingering over the remains of their breakfast.

Sturm greeted them both and sat down. A white-coated steward silently appeared at his right hand and offered coffee which Sturm accepted. At Zurich's direction, Sturm presented a complete report. Legal title to the arms and munitions would officially pass to Geneva's nominees when McBride delivered the bonded warehouse receipts and the releases on the Swiss accounts to Sturm in exchange for the gold bearer bonds in Zurich's cabin in the airship.

"Were there any unforeseen problems?" Zurich inquired.

"More than I would have preferred. But none that were insurmountable."

"What were the nature of these problems?" Berlin ventured.

Zurich cut him off. "*Herr* von Sturm can cover that with us later."

"I have made one change in plans" Sturm said. "I have accepted Manhattan's offer to provide security at the warehouse. While it didn't endanger the shipment, there was a fire fight in northern California at the Hearst mansion, with what I believe were British Intelligence agents. Six men were killed. Four of ours, two of the Irish. With myself, that leaves only six good men to guard the weapons for the next four days until they are safely on board a cargo ship headed for a South American port where they will be broken down into more manageable shipments, less easily detected by the British or the Free State."

"You lost four men, Kurt?" Zurich said. That is more than a minor problem."

Sturm nodded, accepting the rebuke. "I did not mean to minimize the difficulties we encountered. But the battle at the Hearst mansion was isolated. The shipments were not endangered. The assembly in Oakland went off perfectly. Unlike Cleveland and Chicago, there were no intruders in the warehouse. We captured one of the opposition and learned from her all we needed to know. Unfortunately, after we secured that information, I should have pulled my men out and left the Irish behind to finish up the dirty work. To my regret, I didn't."

Sturm shook his head in resignation. "Ten good men, good Germans, would have been more than enough to provide security at the waterfront warehouse. We need the Americans but I can't place my faith in men whom I have never met. Nor will I place trust in those who have not earned it. Once I have the bonded warehouse receipts and McBride has the bonds, I will order the Irish to stay away completely. Manhattan has promised me fourteen more men. If they are good men, it will bring our numbers back up to what I originally considered was necessary."

Sturm's expression was quiet and determined as he looked across the table at the two older men. "The question is, are they competent men? Are they good enough?"

Zurich's eyes narrowed. "For Manhattan's sake, they had better be."

With that, Zurich rose from the table and beckoned Sturm to follow. Inside Zurich's cabin, he closed the door, locked it behind them, and walked over to the upholstered bench along the wall which converted at night into a comfortable bunk. He undid the straps and opened the leather valise, showing the contents to Sturm. "Four million dollars U.S. in gold bearer bonds from America, Great Britain, Italy and Switzerland. Nothing from Germany."

59.

My Final Word

Casa del Mar Terrace
San Simeon
Thursday, 22 August 1929
9:00 a.m.

The first rays of sun were beginning to rise over the mountains behind them as Churchill, Cockran, Rankin, Mattie and David Brooke-Smythe sat around a glass-topped table on the terrace in front of *Casa del Sol*. Before them was a full English breakfast of poached eggs, roasted tomatoes, a rasher of bacon, toast and marmalade.

Mattie was uncharacteristically silent and Cockran was still disappointed at how she acted the evening before with the President. Hoover had handled her easily and she had folded like an accordion.

Cockran was also disappointed that Churchill had not shown more dismay at President Hoover's flat refusal the evening before to lift even a single finger of his pudgy right hand to extend assistance to the democratically-elected government of a peaceful European nation. It's not as if, Cockran thought, that there were a lot of those left. He had been writing about the decline of European democracies ever since he took his position at the law school. Mussolini in Italy was only the first. In the ten years after the war, liberal democracies with market economies were becoming an endangered species. European countries which had ousted their kings were turning away from democracy in favor of authoritarian dictatorships. Italy in 1922 had soon been followed by Bulgaria, Spain, Turkey, Albania, Poland, Portugal, Lithuania and, earlier this year, a coup in Yugoslavia. Could Hoover really be ignorant of this? Or indifferent?

Churchill, to his credit, had been doing his best in the past thirty minutes to save Ireland's freedom from a return to the gun. "I am quite disappointed in you, David," he said to Smythe. "You must be capable of doing better than this. With far less resources at their disposal, Cockran and Rankin have had far more success. Without them to locate the IRA warehouses, we would have had no idea of the enormous scope of the weapons being purchased."

Churchill paused, took a sip from his weak scotch and water and lit a new cigar before continuing. "Equally important, thanks to them, we now know where the entire weapons consignment is being stored and when it will be shipped. The very least you can do, the very least, is to take your ten men and mount a commando raid on that warehouse in Long Beach."

Smythe had been attempting to get in a word edgewise for the latter half of Churchill's monologue but to no effect. Cockran had watched as Smythe's complexion grew from pink at the beginning to beet red before he was finally able to respond.

"That is entirely out of the question, Mr. Churchill. My men and I have no authority, I repeat, no authority, to use firearms on this trip except in self-defense."

"I daresay you and your men will have ample opportunity to employ your weapons in self-defense if you mount a raid on that warehouse tonight." Churchill replied. "In the process of defending yourself as you conduct what I would label an 'inspection in force', who knows what sort of accidents might happen with all those weapons and ammunition lying about?"

"I am not as clever as you, Mr. Churchill. I do not believe in creatively interpreting what are otherwise perfectly clear orders and I take them from the Prime Minister, not you. My men and I will leave this morning for Los Angeles. We will wait there until after the reception for the *Graf Zeppelin* in the event President Hoover reconsiders his decision. But if he does not, my men and I shall return to England."

Smythe paused, took a slice of toast from the silver rack in front of him, and started to apply butter and marmalade. "In the interim, I will send two of my men, and two men only, to this warehouse in Long Beach where Sergeant Rankin and Mr. Cockran indicate the weapons shipment is now located. As per my brief, I will report promptly to you any of their findings so that you in turn may convey them to the President. With luck, I will have this for you by the end of the day or by tomorrow morning at the latest." Smythe rose from the table, placed a white linen napkin carefully on his plate. "And that, Mr. Churchill, is my final word on the matter."

"Does that happen often, Winston? Someone saying 'no' to you?" Cockran asked as he watched the retreating back of David Brooke-Smythe.

Churchill chuckled. "Other than Clemmie? Usually not. We politicians have a tendency to compromise and find common ground without being so absolute. Military types like Smythe live in a much less nuanced world. More black and white."

"It might be just as well, Winston," Cockran said. "I'm not sure an inspection in force is one of your better ideas. A small group, possibly only me, Rankin and perhaps Inspector Thompson, would be all we need to gain entry; set a few explosive devices; and leave."

Churchill shook his head. "A tempting suggestion but I cannot agree. Both Thompson and Rankin are Scotland Yard. I cannot have them engaged in actions of that kind."

"Excuse me, Winston? Didn't you just ask Smythe to do the same thing?"

"Not the same thing at all, my boy. Not at all. Smythe is an intelligence agent. They get themselves involved in all sorts of activities that police officers simply cannot consider."

"What about Rankin accompanying me in our effort to rescue Mattie?"

"Point taken. That was a much closer call. Clemmie and I are quite fond of Mattie and kidnapping is a crime here as well as in Great Britain. Purchasing arms to accomplish a revolution in a peaceful country is, as President Hoover pointedly reminded us, not a crime in the United States. More importantly, Rankin was accompanied on that occasion by fellow police officers who were attempting to rescue the kidnap victim, no matter how far outside their jurisdiction they happened to be. Still, Inspector Thompson and I have had a long talk on this with Sergeant Rankin and, as a consequence, we do not believe he would make the same decision today."

Churchill put down his cigar and took a sip from the scotch and water. "Besides, I didn't expect Smythe to agree to what I suggested. I simply wanted to give him a plausible scenario from my standpoint. A sporting chance, as it were, to do the right thing. That he passed up such an opportunity is no surprise to me."

Cockran nodded and Churchill, having the floor, did not relinquish it. "Robert, I think it's time we asked our most recent guests to join us. Be a good fellow and go with Mattie to bring them in. But you need not return yourself. We have matters to discuss which are not meant for your tender ears."

Rankin smiled broadly. "Ah, yes. Maybe now Mr. Cockran will believe me about the angel I saw in Chicago."

60.

The Apostles

The sun was higher in the sky now and Cockran shaded his eyes for a better view of a group of four people approaching, one of them the unmistakable shambling figure of William Randolph Hearst looming a head taller than Mattie and the other two.

"I believe no introductions are necessary?" Mattie asked.

They weren't. "Hazel! Joe!" Cockran cried as he rose to embrace the two newcomers whom he had last seen seven years before. Hazel Lavery and Joe O'Reilly.

Tall and strikingly attractive with soft brown hair and a long aquiline nose, Hazel was the American-born wife of the prominent Anglo-Irish painter, Sir John Lavery and her portrait adorned the Irish Free State's bank notes. Cockran had last seen Hazel on the day of Nora's funeral. The same was true of her companion, Joe O'Reilly. Small, dark-haired and sharp-featured, O'Reilly had been Michael Collins' principal assistant. He was with Collins in Dublin when the Big Fella gave Cockran a Webley revolver and a list with three names.

At Hearst's instructions, a larger table was brought over to accommodate all six of them.

"You're a long way from home, Hazel," Cockran said after accepting a glass of champagne from a hovering servant. "What are you doing here?"

"We knew what the IRA was up to. Winston asked us and we agreed to help."

Cockran knew he looked as confused as he sounded, " Who is 'we'? I don't understand."

"Well, for starters, it's Joe's man, Bobby Sullivan, who killed those two men in Cleveland and who saved Sergeant Rankin in Chicago. Not to mention Bobby and all of the other Apostles saving Mattie's skin from the IRA at Mr. Hearst's place up north," Hazel said.

"Apostles?" Cockran asked. "You mean Mick Collins' old squad?"

"Actually, yes. It's still the Big Fella's squad," Hazel said, "Some have left and a few more were added from time to time at Kevin's suggestion. But basically the same."

"Kevin?" Cockran asked.

"O'Higgins. The Free State's Minister of Justice. Continuing the Apostles was his idea. Kevin knew a regular police force would not be enough to protect the Free State, especially since he was determined to emulate English bobbies and have our police entirely unarmed. At first he ran the squad out of contingent funds from the Ministry of Justice. After 1925, that all dried up and he came to me to see if I could raise the money from my friends. Which I did. Wealthy friends are useful. When Kevin was killed by the IRA two years ago, my husband John and I decided that we had raised enough capital to establish a foundation whose income could fund operations of the Apostles indefinitely. Our investments in America did very well."

"So who's in charge now?" Cockran asked.

"That would be me," O'Reilly said. "It hasn't been easy. I wasn't used to being the one who makes decisions. The British may have given us our country back, but they didn't give us much experience in running it. The Big Fella would have changed all that. Wasn't it himself who was always saying, 'I didn't go risking my life time and again only so Dev would be free to lecture us from on high that the people have no right to be wrong.' And wouldn't he have booted us in the backside if we hadn't done all we could to keep the freedom he won for us?"

Cockran was still trying to put all the pieces together. "When did you first get wind of the IRA arms deal, Joe?" Cockran asked.

"The beginning of the summer. The Apostles have their own informants within the IRA. Once we heard about new arms being bought, we started making our plans to come to America. When Mr. Churchill called Hazel, we saw no reason not to honor his request to help."

"I'm not sure I understand quite how Mr. Hearst fits into all this," Cockran said.

"It's easy enough," Hearst said. "I'm a newspaper man and Mattie is one of my best reporters. She told me what she and Winston hoped to accomplish. It sounded like a good story. The Merchants of Death angle. It's too easy to outfit an army in America if you have the money. The arms makers fall all over themselves. I still hold them responsible for the Great War and someday, with Mattie's help, I'll nail them for it." Hearst paused and took another sip of lemonade. "Your contribution, Mr. Cockran, was an unexpected bonus."

"And that was?"

"Serving up Philip Cromwell's head to me on a platter. I had no idea he was using my bank accounts to launder the money. We'll have to hush that up but otherwise Cromwell fits the role of a Merchant of Death perfectly. Without men like him, governments couldn't wage wars."

"You still look puzzled, Bourke," Mattie said.

Cockran stood up and pulled Mattie aside, excusing themselves from the rest of the group. "If Hearst isn't behind this, why'd you send a telegram in Chicago to him telling him of our travel plans to California?"

Mattie arched her eyebrows. "Looking through my things after taking advantage of me?"

Cockran felt the color begin to rise in his cheeks. "It's not as if you hadn't already done the same thing. How about that emerald earring, the one I found in my hotel room?"

Now it was Mattie's turn to blush. *"Touché,"* she said. " I'm sorry. Hazel said Joe wanted to see the Collins journals. Anyway, the telegram wasn't to Mr. Hearst, it was to 'H'—Hazel."

"Ah," Cockran said. "My mistake. But how did you manage to leave your bra and panties behind at Wyntoon?"

Mattie blushed again. "How did you know *that?"*

"I got a tip the IRA had you there so Rankin and I and a few others mounted a raid to rescue you."

Mattie hesitated and tears began to form in her eyes. She took a deep breath and exhaled. "I didn't tell you about Wyntoon because I didn't want you to know McBride tried to rape me. First in Chicago and at then at Wyntoon along with one of his men. And I would have been raped if not for the Apostles. You have enough reasons to hate McBride for killing Nora. You don't need me giving you extra baggage. But I didn't want to lie to you either. So, if I told you nothing, it wouldn't be a lie. Lies aren't a good basis for a friendship. I like you Cockran. A lot." she said "and I want us to be friends."

Cockran made no reply but simply took her in his arms. She liked him but she didn't know him that well. One more evil act by McBride against someone he cared for was not "extra baggage" in the sense that Mattie meant it. When the time came for killing, he believed he would do so as coldly and unemotionally as he had back in 1922 and before that in the war. He saw Joe O'Reilly standing ten yards away, keeping a distance but clearly wanting to approach. Cockran motioned him over.

"Bourke, I'm sorry that we didn't let you know the Apostles were involved. We didn't know how you felt about us. If you held a grudge, Mr. Churchill believed we couldn't risk losing your help.

"What grudge could I possibly hold against the Apostles, Joe?"

"Mick promised to avenge your wife's death and we never delivered. That promise was important to Mick. He sent out the order to the Squad the same day. But with the war and then Mick being killed himself...." O'Reilly shrugged his shoulders. "By the time we won the war, McBride had skipped the country and we didn't know where he went. Bobby Sullivan—he was there that night the Big Fella and I met you at McDaid's—he felt the worst of any of us because Mick had given him the primary responsibility for McBride. Bobby said the two of you had a lot in common, but he wouldn't say why. He was the first one I called when we heard what was going down with McBride and the IRA arms deal in America and he rounded up everyone else while Hazel and I made the travel arrangements."

"Don't worry about it, Joe." Cockran said. "You and the Apostles did your best. I can't quarrel with that." Cockran paused, wondering if he should bring up the mysterious message which had led him and Jack Manion to Wyntoon. "Uh, Joe. The same day your boys rescued Mattie, I received an unsigned note, complete with a map, telling me Mattie was being held at Wyntoon by the IRA. Know anything about that?"

O'Reilly looked embarrassed. "I do. It was Bobby Sullivan. He's more or less been your guardian angel ever since New York. Once we learned that the IRA had taken Mattie, Bobby was hot to go after her but our mission was the arms shipment. So, I told him no, not until I cleared it with Hazel. Bobby was furious. Called me a coward." O'Reilly paused, a wistful look in his eyes. "He never would have said that to the Big Fella. Anyway, Hazel gave the okay within an hour. Bobby was fit to be tied while we waited so that's when he sent the message."

O'Reilly grinned. "Once Hazel gave the okay, Bobby was fine. Took me aside and apologized. Said he knew I wasn't a coward. I'm glad Hazel approved the rescue. No one in their right mind ever wants to be on the wrong side of Bobby Sullivan."

"Now that we know where the arms are being shipped from, what do the Apostles plan to do next?" Cockran asked.

O'Reilly grinned again. "We're going to Los Angeles. Long Beach actually. Wouldn't you be thinking we've got ourselves a warehouse to blow up?"

Cockran nodded. Of course. Like any man, the Irish Free State had a right to defend itself. If a government wouldn't protect you from violence, you had a right to do so yourself. His father would have preferred a law suit but, for Cockran, that point had been passed in their last session with Hoover. If the U.S. Government was going to do nothing, the Irish Free State had a right to act. The bastards were going to pay. Michael Collins had taught him that.

61.

Take a Look, Irishman

Los Angeles, California
Thursday, 22 August 1929
4:00 p.m.

The Bradbury Building was located on the southwest corner of Third Street and Broadway. Six stories tall, it had a large central atrium in the building's interior around which offices were located. Twin open-grill elevators were located on either side of the lobby and gave their passengers an open view as they slowly rose. Sturm and McBride took the left elevator to the sixth floor and walked down an interior corridor to room 610. The top half of the opaque glass door contained the legend in gold letters, "P.D.C. Investments, Inc."

Sturm produced a key and opened the door. The office consisted of a single room with a beat-up wooden desk, two side chairs, a swivel chair behind the desk, and two file cabinets. In the right-hand corner of the room was a large square safe. Cromwell had made the room available, explaining that one of his investment companies owned the building.

Sturm went over to the safe, knelt in front of it, and spun the dial combination. He opened the large door and pulled out the large leather valise which Zurich had given him that morning on the *Graf Zeppelin*. He placed it on the desk, undid the straps and opened it.

"Take a look, Irishman. Exactly $4 million in gold bearer bonds. $2.5 million are in dollar denominations and $500,000 each in English pounds, Italian lira and Swiss francs. Yesterday's *Wall Street*

Journal is inside so you can compare the exchange rates."

Sturm handed McBride the page with the exchange rates and sat down on one of the side chairs. Thirty minutes later, McBride had filled four pages of a paper pad with notes, conversions of the lira, pound and Swiss franc into dollars. Sturm had not expected him to be so meticulous. Or so apt at mathematics without an adding machine.

McBride surprised him again when, after counting the bonds, he placed a phone call to the Hotel Cecil and gave directions for three of his men to meet him at the Bradbury Building, instructing them all to be armed. McBride's men arrived twenty minutes later. "Would you be needing to have this fine leather satchel returned to you, Mr. von Sturm?" he asked.

"Consider it a gift, *Herr* McBride. A small gesture of gratitude for all your work."

Immediately after McBride closed the door and Sturm heard his footsteps receding down the hallway, he placed a phone call. "He's on his way down now. Follow him and report back"

Malibu, California
6:10 p.m.

A stiff breeze moved the early evening clouds overhead and, across the highway, the beach was lightly populated, a few surfers still catching waves. Sturm was wearing sun glasses but the man with him at the table outside the roadside diner was not, squinting against the glare. "I followed them, *Herr* von Sturm. They passed the branches of at least four banks on the way." Bruno Kordt said. "They went directly to Union Station and placed the bag in a storage locker."

Sturm laughed. "I suppose that was because the Irishman couldn't find a mattress large enough to hide it under. What was the locker number?"

"Number 44."

"And you have someone watching it now?"

"Yes, *Herr* von Sturm. We'll know if it's moved."

62.

The Odds Are Against Us

San Simeon Airfield
Thursday, 22 August 1929
6:30 p.m.

B ourke Cockran and Joe O'Reilly climbed into Hearst's royal blue Fokker Trimotor, and turned left into the passenger cabin. There were six wicker arm chairs in two groupings, three in front and three in the back. Each set had one chair facing the other two for ease of conversation. Cockran and O'Reilly settled into a pair in the front which faced forward as the aircraft's motors idled on the airstrip outside the village of San Simeon. "Tell me about the threat to Churchill, Joe," Cockran said.

"Hazel tipped Sgt. Rankin off when he was in hospital in Chicago. But we think the danger's over," O'Reilly answered. "It was to happen today during the reception at San Simeon for the *Graf Zeppelin*. Once the airship went to Los Angeles, we're told it was called off

"Who was behind it?"

"The IRA, of course," O'Reilly said. "Who else would you be expecting?"

"But why Churchill? And how did you find out about it?"

"We don't know why. Mr. Churchill may know but he's not saying anything. As to how we knew, don't you suppose the Big Fella would be kicking my arse from one side of Dublin to the other if we didn't have one of our own inside the IRA team here in America?"

"So it was your man inside the IRA who also tipped you off to the arms buy?"

"No, that was someone else," O'Reilly said. "We're just doing what Mick said from the very beginning. No one ever beats us at the intelligence game again, boys. No one."

Los Angeles Metropolitan Airport
Van Nuys, California
9:15 p.m.

The Apostles were all waiting at the airfield when the Fokker landed. O'Reilly introduced Cockran to Michael Collins' old squad. Only two faces were familiar. In contrast, they all knew who Cockran was and they came over to shake his hand, express regrets for his wife's death and promise, to a man, that McBride would get what was coming to him.

"Have you boys found us a place to stay?" O'Reilly asked.

"'Tis a fine place we found, Joe," one of his men responded. "On the beach. A small house. No more than a twenty-minute drive from the warehouse."

Once at the beach house, O'Reilly spread out on the kitchen table the architect's plans for the warehouse which Hearst had secured for them. The windows were open and the sound and smell of the ocean drifted in, the breeze assisting the efforts of an electric fan. "The odds are against us, boys," O'Reilly said. "Seamus tells me they've added ten more men in the last twenty-four hours. They've increased their perimeter guards from four to eight. Inside, six other men are constantly patrolling. But it's a big warehouse so they can't be everywhere at once." O'Reilly pointed to the back entrance. "This is where we're going in."

O'Reilly turned to the man beside him, Bobby Sullivan, a tall man, late twenties, close-cropped dark brown hair, cold blue eyes and a prize fighter's crooked nose. Cockran remembered him from that night in Dublin at McDaid's. He had been just a kid. But the eyes were as cold and blue tonight as they had been then.

"Bobby, you and three of the squad will take out the perimeter guards," O'Reilly said. They change shifts at midnight. Use knives if you can, silenced weapons if you must."

O'Reilly turned to Cockran. "Patrick and Seamus are ordnance specialists. I've been advised by someone with a military background that these four places would be optimum locations for the dynamite. Do you agree?" Cockran smiled at the oblique reference to advice Churchill had given eagerly the day before, no doubt wishing he could be with them tonight.

Like Bobby Sullivan, Patrick also looked to be in his late twenties, a full head of light brown hair. Skinny as a rail and nearly six feet tall. In contrast, Seamus was barely out of his teens, a babyface with red hair and blue eyes who probably had to beat the girls off with a stick.

"If what you're trying to do is collapse the roof, that may be all you need," Seamus replied in an oddly high-pitched voice, "but I'm thinking it's not the roof we're out to destroy but the weapons. We need to place charges where the ammunition and powder are, not the main supports for the roof. So what do we know, Joe, about where the ammunition is stored?"

"We haven't been able to find that out. We know there are artillery shells and mortar rounds at the left front of the building, fifty caliber machine gun belts by the rear door."

"Right, then,"Seamus said. "Those are the two main places. They're far enough apart at opposite ends of the building. Explosions there should create a fire of a sufficiently large proportion to reach any ammunition in the middle as well. Patrick and I will place the charges in the rear first. Then I'll do the artillery shells and mortar rounds myself and set a ten-minute fuse. That should give Patrick time to pick a third spot in the center of the warehouse with no more than a seven-minute fuse. We'll leave only a two- or a three-minute fuse on the .50 caliber ammunition. I'll set it off as we leave the building. The explosions ought to be nearly simultaneous. Make sure you get word to our man about these steel plates we'll be needing."

63.

Thought You Could Use Some Help

Long Beach, California
Friday, 23 August 1929
1:30 a.m.

The sky was cloudless with no moon as two long, dark-colored motorcars pulled to a halt in a deserted side street three blocks away from Pier Three and the warehouse which serviced it. The Apostles disembarked, each wearing a long, dark coat, some with soft hats, others with short-billed caps pulled low on their foreheads. Inside their coats, suspended from a leather strap with a catch release, were Mauser submachine pistols with sound suppressors.

Bobby Sullivan pulled a silenced automatic pistol from his pocket. It looked like a Colt .45 to Cockran. He turned in a practiced motion and shot out the single street lamp still burning on the block. Cockran stood next to O'Reilly and Sullivan as the other men gathered around.

"The game is on, boys. Let's synchronize our watches," O'Reilly said. "Bobby, you and your men will have fifteen minutes to take out the eight perimeter guards. No slip ups. Cockran and I and the rest of Team Two will hole up in the deserted shop just down this alley. After Team One has taken out the guards, Bobby will position one of his men adjacent to the spot where the sleeping quarters for the ten off-duty men are located. Make sure your man is no more than ten yards away. As soon as he hears a shot fired, your man goes right up to the window. It will be open for ventilation. He drops two hand grenades in the open window and then heads to the back of the building to cover our exit."

O'Reilly looked at the luminous dial of his wristwatch. "It's 1:41. At 1:56, Team Two will move and we'll be taking Seamus and Patrick with us."

Fifteen minutes was an eternity to Cockran. He assumed most of O'Reilly's men had not been in the Great War. The minutes before you went over the top were the worst. You had time to think. Too much time. Fortunately, it hadn't been that way for Cockran the last time he was in combat. It had happened spontaneously. Boys were missing in no-man's land and Wild Bill Donovan was going after them. Who was coming along? You had no time to think. You grabbed your weapon and headed out after the old man who was leading from the front. Tonight, Donovan wasn't there. O'Reilly and Bobby Sullivan were the ones leading from the front. And Cockran had time to think. About Nora. About Paddy. About Mattie, too. And, yes, about Tommy McBride. In the war, he gave no thought to the men he might kill. Tonight was different. McBride should be inside and if he was, Cockran would find him. And kill him.

Fifteen minutes later, Cockran and the rest of the Apostles in Team Two were crouched behind trash bins less than eighty feet from the rear door on the south side of the warehouse which faced the water on its western side leading out to Pier Three. They looked at the light over the door to the warehouse—Bobby's signal—and saw that it was still on.

"This doesn't look good, Bourke," O'Reilly whispered. "But we can't wait. After we've been inside the warehouse fifteen minutes, Bobby will set up a diversion in the front with unsilenced weapons. When the other man in Bobby's team hears that, the grenades go in the window. Or sooner if we're forced to fire first." O'Reilly turned to the short, fair-complexioned, blue-eyed man beside him, a cloth cap pulled over his forehead, "Seamus, take out the light."

Seamus did and the team moved forward, three of them along either side of the alley. Cockran and O'Reilly were on the left-hand side and, as they reached the intersection with the street, they knelt behind two trash barrels in the cover cast by their shadows. Cockran looked down and saw he was kneeling on the outstretched left arm of a body hidden in the barrel's shadow. The man's wrist was still warm and Cockran instinctively reached out with his left hand to check for a pulse in the carotid artery. He pulled his hand back, covered with the sticky blood from the large gaping wound in the man's neck. Bobby Sullivan had been here.

Cockran patted O'Reilly on the shoulder and mouthed the words "one down" and held up a single finger. O'Reilly nodded and looked across the narrow alley at the other three Apostles and gave them the same signal. One of them held up two fingers and Cockran could see the work boot on a second body across the alley from him.

Thirty seconds later, Team Two was inside the warehouse, the rear door on the south side unlocked as promised. Cockran watched as Seamus and Patrick located the .50 caliber ammo and placed four taped dynamite bundles in the middle of four crates which were stacked two high. The dynamite was on top of the second stack of crates and would not be observed from the warehouse floor. The grease-smeared fuse was run between the crates with barely two inches extending out into the aisle blending in with the dark cement floor. Also as promised, two large metal plates were laying on the floor and the two men lifted them to the top of the crates and placed them in an inverted "V" over the dynamite. It wasn't much but the two plates would direct some of the blast down into the crates. Five minutes had elapsed since they entered the warehouse.

Taking on the most dangerous part of the operation for himself, O'Reilly then headed toward the west side of the warehouse with Patrick while Cockran stayed behind to cover Seamus as he placed his charges. Again, the charges were put on top of the crates and, again, two metal plates left there by the Apostles' inside man were laying nearby. Cockran helped Seamus move them both atop the bundles of dynamite. He had a big grin on his face. The kid was actually enjoying this. Eight minutes had elapsed and once he lit the fuse, they would have ten minutes to exit the building.

Seamus finished placing his empty satchel behind one of the warehouse girders when they were spotted. "Stop right there!" a dark-clothed figure shouted.

Cockran turned and fired a short burst from his silenced machine pistol at the man twenty feet away illuminated by the golden glow of the cone of light above him. The man crumpled where he stood but not before squeezing off two shots from a revolver. Seamus lit the first fuse.

"Get to the back! Quickly!" Cockran said. "Light the other fuse. I'll cover you."

Just then, grenade explosions in the sleeping quarters rocked the warehouse. Cockran turned toward the sound just as another man came running around the corner of the next aisle. Reflexively, Cockran cut him down with another short burst. Without the grenade blast, he never would have seen the man coming. Like riding a bicycle, he thought, comforted by the timely return of his muscle memory and not a little bit of luck.

Cockran heard a short burst of gun fire from the rear of the warehouse. Seamus! he thought and began to run.

Kurt von Sturm was not accustomed to waiting for a fight. He preferred to take the offensive like he had done that night in Wittmundhaven, killing the Allied sentries and destroying the naval zeppelins. After the raid on Wyntoon which had liberated the McGary woman and cut his forces in half, he had been depending on the ex-Army types Cromwell had supplied to provide a static, perimeter defense. He wasn't impressed. He almost would have preferred McBride and his men to these incompetent Americans. How they managed to defeat the Imperial German Army he would never know. He didn't believe any of that racist nonsense about the Jews stabbing Germany in the back but someone had to have done it for these American clowns to have prevailed. Sturm thought the Social Democrats and the Communists were far more obvious candidates than the Jews.

Would there be an attack tonight? Sturm didn't know but, if it did, his six men were ready for a counter-strike with two hunter-killer teams of three Germans each.

Bruno Kordt silently approached. "Two of the Americans have

failed to report in."

Sturm nodded to his chief aide. "Assume it's the enemy. Move out with your team."

He watched as Bruno gave hand signals to two other men, armed like him with Schmeiser machine pistols, and they moved swiftly toward the west front of the warehouse. He heard the faint sound of automatic weapons fire from the front and, using his own hand signals, directed his two men to the rear, with Sturm taking the point. They had advanced no more than twenty yards when he heard the blast of several grenades shake the building, coming from the area of the sleeping quarters. He understood immediately what it meant and shook his head in admiration. His adversaries were good while Cromwell's mercenaries were incompetent. Any advantage the defenders had in numbers had just been neutralized, the only consolation being that none of his own men had died in the blast.

Sturm moved on, rounded a corner and saw a red-haired man kneeling by a two-high stack of crates. The man stood up and Sturm sent four quick rounds thumping into the man's chest before he could unsling his weapon from over his shoulder. The impact knocked the man on to his back and, as Sturm approached, he could see it was only a young boy who had yet to begin shaving. The lad never had a chance Sturm thought as the boy lay shuddering on the floor. "Jesus, it hurts! Mother of God..." but he never finished the sentence as Sturm shot him once in the forehead at point blank range. In the silence which followed, he heard a sizzling sound. A fuse! Lit and already retreating between the crates. He tried to reach the fuse and put it out but it was too far in. He looked up at the crates. Ammunition. Sturm shook his head again. It was over. That wouldn't be the only fuse. It was time to pull his men out. No need for them to die along with the incompetent Americans. He heard rapidly approaching foot steps and signaled for his two men to head for the exits. They would make their separate ways to the safe house.

Sturm stepped into the shadows as a figure ran past him and stopped to kneel beside the dead boy, uselessly taking his pulse. Cockran! His back was to Sturm who could have easily cut him down. But Sturm didn't. The mission here was no longer of primary importance to Sturm.There were other matters to attend to now. Besides, the lawyer had proved to be a formidable adversary. Sturm was not sentimental but he took no pleasure in killing. Unnecessarily shooting a man in the back was not honorable. And Kurt von Sturm was an honorable man. He silently headed for an exit.

Cockran passed the crates where the first charge had been placed. Seamus had already been there as the two inches of the fuse that had been sticking out into the aisle were no longer visible but he could see its glow in the darkness. They had less than five minutes.

Cockran stopped, inserted another clip in his machine pistol and turned the corner. Seamus lay sprawled in the middle of the intersection of two aisles, his machine pistol still clasped in his outstretched hand, a massive halo of blood surrounding his head. Cockran knelt by Seamus and felt for a pulse but he was gone. Damn! The kid was so young and, moments ago, had been so happy.

The clip in Seamus' machine pistol was full so Cockran slung the weapon by its strap over his shoulder. He headed for the rear and the sound of the guns where two Apostles, the rear guard, were down as well. Besides him, that left only O'Reilly and Patrick inside the warehouse. Cockran turned another corner and, twenty yards away, O'Reilly and Patrick were pinned down by at least four men with revolvers. Damn! None of them were McBride! He saw that O'Reilly and Patrick would not reach the rear exit without exposing themselves. He looked at his watch. Focus! Forget about McBride! Four minutes left.

Cockran ran up the aisle to his right and hoisted himself on top of the first level of crates and then a second. He placed Seamus' machine pistol beside him and could see all four shooters, two of them trying to outflank O'Reilly and Patrick. Cockran emptied his entire clip and cut both men down. O'Reilly gave him a thumbs-up and Cockran again looked at his watch. Three minutes.

Cockran's body jerked as a shot rang out and he felt a searing pain in his left shoulder. Instinctively, he rolled off the crate's edge dropping five feet to the crate below. He landed on his wounded shoulder, his weapon falling to the floor. The pain was intense. If he blacked out, he was dead. He heard the faint wail of sirens and glanced at his watch. Two minutes.

Cockran was on his back looking up when he saw a man appear at the edge of the crate from which he had just fallen. Was it McBride? He couldn't tell. The man held a .38 caliber pistol, his arm fully extended. As Cockran watched helplessly, the man's body jerked with the impact of three bullets in the chest and he tumbled forward, bouncing once beside Cockran, then onto the floor five feet below.

Cockran looked in the direction of the shots and saw Bobby Sullivan standing ten feet away. Smiling. "Thought you could use some help," he said, tucking into his pants one of the two Colt .45s he had been holding.

Cockran winced again when he felt a strong arm grab his leg and pull his body roughly across the top of the crate. He stared at a dark-clothed figure, his face smeared in grease but unable to conceal the unmistakable reddish blond beard of Robert Rankin who threw Cockran over his shoulder as if he were no more trouble than a fifty-pound sack of potatoes. He looked at his watch for the last time. One minute.

They reached the rear door in less than thirty seconds where Cockran saw Jack Manion and the diminutive Ed Kelley, both in dark clothes like Rankin, each blazing away with a pair of long-barreled .38 caliber revolvers like a Mutt and Jeff version of Tom Mix. Under their covering fire, O'Reilly helped a wounded Patrick out the door while Manion and Rankin bundled three more Apostles into a canvas-topped Cadillac, the sounds of the police sirens unmistakable.

"What about Team One?" O'Reilly asked. "Are they all right?"

"Sullivan told me they lost one man." Rankin replied.

"I lost my bloody watch Pat," O'Reilly said. "How much time till it all goes up?"

"Any second now, Joe. Less than a minute for sure."

O'Reilly reached out and touched Manion who was standing on the car's running board beside Rankin. "Jack! Get us the hell out of here! Fast! This whole place will blow any second."

"You heard the man, Kevin," Manion roared. "Let's see that lead foot of yours!"

The Cadillac responded with a surge of power and, within one block, was approaching fifty miles per hour when the sky lit up behind them, followed almost immediately by the ear-splitting sound of the explosion and the concussive blast which shook the sedan and the passengers inside. By the time Cockran could turn around and look back through the small oval of the rear window, they were three blocks away and the flames seemed five stories high and growing, fed by more explosions as they sped away.

7:30 a.m.

Manion and three other members of the Chinatown Squad had taken Cockran, O'Reilly and the rest of the Apostles back to the beach house. They had lost four men in the raid. Silently dealing with their grief the Irish way, no one spoke. The wakes would come later. The whitewashed kitchen was set up as a temporary infirmary for the wounded. Water was boiling on the stove, the counters were cleared and sheets were torn into bandages.

Rankin had cleaned and dressed Cockran's wound, telling him no bones were broken and he would be sore but if he kept it clean, there shouldn't be a problem. Cockran had slept fitfully for a few hours and woke to the sound of the surf and the smell of coffee from the kitchen.

Cockran rose and pulled on the same pants he had worn the night before. He could barely move his left arm. Shirtless and barefoot, he walked into the kitchen to find Rankin, Manion and Sullivan seated around the kitchen table, each holding a steaming mug of coffee.

"Top o' the morning to you, Bourke," Manion said. "Believe it or not, this wild-eyed giant here makes a fairly passable pot of coffee for a Scot. Can I pour you one?"

While Cockran sat down at the scarred pine kitchen table and accepted a cup of coffee, Rankin fashioned a sling for Cockran's left arm from a pillow case and a safety pin..

"So how are you feeling, Bourke?" Manion asked. "You passed out in the motorcar."

"A little light-headed," Cockran replied. "I was shot once before. In the war. My leg, not my shoulder. Woke up in a field hospital feeling much the same way I do now. I hope I recover more quickly. I was on crutches for a month and the wound was infected."

"That's why you should see a physician." Rankin said. "The house doctor at the Roosevelt Hotel in Hollywood. Miss McGary should be here momentarily to take you there."

"I remember hearing police sirens. Did we have any problem with them?"

Manion laughed. "Police in Southern California are a joke. They make the boys in Oakland almost look honest by comparison. If any of them had stopped us — and they didn't — a ten dollar bill would have gotten us a motorcycle escort to wherever we wanted to go."

Cockran noticed a look of concern flash on Rankin's face.

"Inspector Thompson and Smythe met yesterday evening with Chief Davis of the LAPD about additional security for the zeppelin reception today. Can they be trusted?" Rankin asked.

Manion laughed again. "You can trust 'Two-Gun' Ed Davis to sell himself to the highest bidder. But Mr. Churchill ought to be safe enough."

Cockran nodded. "I wasn't in much shape last night to thank you two. You guys came to our rescue like the cavalry. How did you end up there?"

The big Scot sat down in a chair opposite Cockran and beside Manion. "If it's all the same to you, Mr. Cockran, I would prefer that Mr. Churchill not be told of my involvement last night. Once I told Mattie how the two of us plus Captain Manion and his Chinatown Squad had almost rescued her at Wyntoon, she persuaded me to call Captain Manion to see if his boys wanted to have another go at the IRA. Then she had Mr. Hearst lend another plane and fly the four of them down here. Miss McGary wanted to come herself but, for her safety, I refused."

"I heard you talking about me," Mattie McGary said as she pushed in the screen door from the back porch and walked in, a bundle of newspapers under her arm. "No one, and certainly not you, was going to keep me away from the story I've been working on all summer."

She stopped short and gasped when she saw Cockran. "Bourke! What happened? Are you all right?" she said as she rushed to his side, a look of concern on her face.

Cockran started to respond, "Well, I've felt better..."

Mattie cut him off and turned on Rankin. "For God's sake, Rankin, you were supposed to keep him safe!"

"I'm sorry, Miss McGary, but someone had already shot him by the time I found him."

"Ease up, Mattie," Cockran said. "Sullivan and Rankin saved my life. If you hadn't asked him to get Jack and the other Chinatown boys to help, I wouldn't be here."

"I'm sorry, Robert, I apologize," Mattie said as she leaned over and kissed Cockran on the forehead. "Is it bad, Bourke?" she asked, taking his hand in hers.

"It hurts like hell, but Robert says it's not a serious wound. He's arranged for a doctor to visit me at the hotel at 11." Cockran pointed to the newspaper she was holding under her arm. "So why the papers? What's the latest news?" He asked.

"Here," she said, dropping three copies of the early edition of the Los Angeles *Herald-Examiner* on the kitchen table. "See for yourselves. You boys made the front page."

Cockran and Rankin picked up a copy of the paper with the large black headline, "Long Beach Inferno", below which were two large photographs of a blazing building outlined against the dark night sky. Below the fold was a small headline, "South American Arms Shipment Destroyed". Below that, "Exclusive *Examiner* Photographs Inside". The byline and photo credits were both Martha McGary. Even if she used a telephoto lens, Cockran thought, she could have been killed or seriously wounded when that place went up.

Meanwhile, Mattie sat down on the floor beside Cockran's chair, possessively wrapping her arm around his leg. It felt good to have her beside him. He felt a pang of regret. McBride likely had been killed in the blast. He had wanted to see the bastard die but, if he was dead, it was all over. He had to keep his promise to himself and return to Manhattan. Without Mattie. He didn't want to end it so soon but he wasn't going to hurt her by letting it go on any longer.

Rankin put the paper down. "Miss McGary, you assured me that you would stay away from the warehouse. It wasn't safe for you to be there."

"Then you're twice the fool I thought you were if you believed me for a minute."

"Where did you get the South American reference?" Cockran asked.

"Because that's all the police know and all they are saying right now. The ship's manifest which shows weapons to be loaded Monday indicates their destination was Ecuador."

"What about Cromwell? The IRA? The real story?" Cockran asked.

"Don't worry. That will come tomorrow or the day after. The Chief is saving that surprise for himself. He wants to show Cromwell the story personally before it goes to press."

While Mattie had been talking, Bobby Sullivan joined the group in the kitchen.

"Did anyone escape?" Cockran asked. "Were all those inside killed?"

"The police think so, but they can't be sure," Mattie answered.

Bobby Sullivan looked up from the newspaper and spoke for the first time. "None of the remaining IRA men were killed last night. They were all pulled out before we got there. O'Reilly received a call from our man on the inside before I went to bed this morning."

Cockran stared at Sullivan, his eyes narrowing, his lips compressed.

Sullivan answered Cockran's unspoken question. "Yes. McBride is still alive." Then he smiled. "Tommy's the last one and doesn't he deserve to die even more than Sean or Timothy?"

"Timothy?" Cockran asked, mentally recoiling at a smile that really wasn't a smile.

"Cronin. One of McBride's men. Nasty scar on his jaw. I killed him at Wyntoon." Sullivan replied. "A mate of Sean Russell whom I killed in Cleveland. They both had it coming."

Cockran's eyes narrowed as he felt Mattie tighten her grip on his arm. They had stopped the IRA cold. The arms deal was dead. It was time Tommy McBride ended up the same way.

64.

Two Gun Ed Davis

Hollywood
Friday, 23 August 1929
9:30 a.m.

Tommy McBride looked across the street at the Pig 'N' Whistle, a restaurant and soda fountain less than three blocks from the Hollywood Roosevelt Hotel. Rolled into a tube and clutched in his right hand was the front section of *The Herald-Examiner*. The IRA couldn't blame him, McBride thought. It wasn't his fault the German had not done his job. If Tommy and his men had been there, things certainly would have been different. No one could blame him.

McBride entered the restaurant. He had been surprised at the locale because it meant that at last he was going to put a face to the voice of the man he knew only as Blackthorn. A soda fountain ran along the left side of the room. Booths lined the right-hand side, a mirror above them reflecting the black and white tile on the walls. A man at the back waved a hand in greeting. He was alone in the last booth, enjoying an American breakfast of scrambled eggs, hash browns and a rasher of bacon, a small pot of tea his only concession to his British heritage. McBride slipped into the seat opposite, surprised at the older man's cheerful demeanor.

"Good morning, Thomas. Can I order you some breakfast? I was perfectly famished."

The voice was unmistakably Blackthorn's. After the waiter had taken his order, McBride slapped the paper down on the table between them. "I don't see what's so good about it. We just lost our best chance in seven years to rid ourselves of those Free State bastards," he said, "or weren't you aware ?"

Blackthorn smiled. "I'm aware of it, Thomas, all too aware. I expected far more efficiency from our German allies." He said and took a sip of tea. "But it is the Germans' loss, not ours." He arched his eyebrows. "You did receive the bearer bonds from the German yesterday, didn't you?" McBride nodded. "And you have put them in a secure place?"

"Of course," McBride snapped. "You take me for an idiot?"

"Naturally not, Thomas. But pray tell me where you have secured our assets?"

McBride explained and was taken aback at the vehemence of Blackthorn's response. "A locker?! In a train station? I may have misjudged you, Thomas. You may be daft indeed."

McBride objected. "The banks were closed. I had to put the money somewhere until they opened today."

Blackthorn sighed. "I suppose so, Thomas, but really now, a train station locker? Never mind. Your new mission is more important. The British agents with Churchill were responsible for destroying the arms shipment so your other mission—to kill him today—is of paramount importance."

Blackthorn reached inside his suit coat, pulled out a sheet of paper and unfolded it, moving the remnants of his breakfast out of the way as he began to explain.

McBride frowned when Blackthorn had finished. "Wait a second. You seem to have it all planned. But this new plan is more risky than the one you showed me in Chicago. That one involved rifles from long range at Hearst's castle. This new plan involves hand guns at close range. What if something goes wrong? How will I get the bonds to the bank?"

"Not to worry, my good man." Blackthorn replied. "I will secure the bonds for you and deposit them in the Wells Fargo Bank today. That is where you were to take the money?"

"Well, yes, but..."

"No buts, Thomas. Now, if you would be so kind as to pass the key to the train station locker over to me. I will arrange for everything."

McBride hesitated. "I don't know....I was told to put it in the bank myself. My orders from Dev were to keep the money under lock and key at all times until I did that."

"But you received those instructions — and I can attest to their accuracy — before your second mission was conceived. Your first mission was a failure, Thomas, even if the fault was not directly yours. You must not fail a second time and I am affording you the opportunity to salvage something from your first mission. You are vital to the success of the second mission. My role in that is almost over. I will personally attend to securing the bonds and make certain we salvage something from your first failure. You have my word on that."

The waiter arrived with McBride's breakfast and Blackthorn pulled a time piece from the watch pocket in his trousers and looked at it. "I must leave now, Thomas. Be of good cheer. It's not often in life that one is given a new chance to make amends so quickly. And you know, Thomas, that it was a grave error in judgment on your part to obey the German's orders to pull your men away from the warehouse last night? The Army Council will be looking for scapegoats. It's just as Dev always says: 'There must be scapegoats.' Trust me on this, Thomas, no one will dare make a scapegoat of the man who killed Winston Churchill."

Blackthorn rose and placed his hand on McBride's shoulder. "Your other three men, however, are a different story. In light of their being absent last night from the warehouse, you obviously have no choice but to conduct a field court martial and sentence them to death."

McBride blinked. He had been worried that Blackthorn would blame him for last night but now he was throwing him a life preserver. He craned his neck to look up at Blackthorn. "When in hell are we going to have time for a bloody court martial?"

"We just did, Thomas," Blackthorn said, patting his shoulder. "We just did. I'm on my way now on your behalf to arrange for the sentence to be carried out. By the time the morning is over, there will be no witnesses left to the fact that you were out drinking when the largest arms shipment in the history of the IRA was destroyed. And now, if I could trouble you for the key?"

Reluctantly, McBride fished in the right-hand pocket of his trousers and handed the key to Blackthorn. He stared straight ahead and watched Blackthorn's reflection in the mirror as he walked out the front door of the Pig 'N' Whistle and stepped into the back seat of a black and white automobile. Not to worry, McBride thought. Not to worry. Winston bloody Churchill was a dead man. Everything would turn out all right after all.

10:15 a.m.

Blackthorn settled down in the back seat of the automobile bearing the markings of the Los Angeles Police Department, a small American flag and a gold badge on the front bumper announcing it was the personal vehicle of the Chief of Police. Blackthorn extended his hand, recalling the first time he had met Ed Davis.

"How're you doing?" Davis had said on that occasion. "I'm Ed Davis, the Chief of Police hereabouts. But you can call me 'Two Gun,'" he had said, pulling back the lapels of his navy blue serge suit to proudly reveal a pair of pearl-handled .38 caliber police special revolvers nestled in twin holsters, one under each armpit.

Blackthorn looked now into the narrow squinting eyes and bright red face of his companion who pulled a crisp white handkerchief from the breast pocket of his suit and patted the perspiration on his bald forehead, across which were plastered several strands of brown hair, combed up and over from the fringe of hair above his ears.

"Thank you, Chief, for taking time out of your busy schedule to meet with me again." Blackthorn pulled a plain white envelope from inside his coat and handed it to Davis. "In the envelope, Chief, are the names of three individuals and the rooms they presently occupy at the Hotel Cecil. My employer is certain that these three men are the ones responsible for the destruction of the warehouse last night in Long Beach. I presume you're aware of that?"

"You bet I am, Mr. Brooke," Davis replied. "That sure was some blow out."

"Well, yes it was. My employer is disturbed. He had clients in South America who had paid good money and were expecting to receive weapons in return. My employer believes one of his rivals was responsible. He refused to cut the rival in for what I believe you Americans would refer to as a "piece of the action" and he believes this is the method his adversary has chosen to teach him a lesson. Unfortunately, my employer is an old-fashioned sort. He believes in 'an eye for an eye.' To begin with, that would be the three men at the Hotel Cecil." Blackthorn smiled. "There will be others, of course, including the adversary himself. But that need not concern you or your fine organization here in Los Angeles, as my employer's adversary maintains his primary residence back East."

"Happy to help, Mr. Brooke. Happy to help. We don't like riff raff in L.A. Ah....I believe the agreed price for this service I am to render your employer was...?"

"Ten thousand dollars U.S. in small unmarked currency," Blackthorn said, handing him a second envelope. "I believe you'll find everything in order."

Davis opened the envelope and quickly thumbed through the bills with a practiced eye before depositing them inside the blue serge suit coat. "Three prisoners shot while trying to escape. Now tell me again about this reception for the zeppelin. All you want is for one of my men to stumble and fall? And for that you're willing to pony up another five Gs? I don't get it."

"It's personal, Chief. You don't have to get it. My employer has gambling interests all along the east coast and well into Canada. You may have read that Mr. Churchill recently completed a tour of Canada. Unfortunately, that tour included certain private, by-invitation-only, gambling establishments operated by my employer in Montreal and Toronto where Mr. Churchill gambled heavily at *Chemin de Fer* and lost. As I believe you Americans would say, his bank draft 'bounced' and he has refused all of my employer's entreaties that he honor his debt."

Blackthorn watched the light of recognition dawn in the police chief's beady eyes. Gambling was as illegal in the United States as alcohol and just as prevalent. Once in Los Angeles, Blackthorn had quickly found out that a string of gambling ships anchored just outside the three-mile limit were under the personal protection of Two-Gun Ed Davis who was paid well by the ships' owners to tip them off before any federal raids. Accordingly, Blackthorn had carefully chosen the gambling debt cover story to explain why Blackthorn's employer only wanted to teach Churchill "a little lesson". No one would be hurt.

"Boy, I sure wouldn't want to get on the wrong side of your employer, Mr. Brooke. He sounds like a hard man."

Blackthorn smiled as he handed the third envelope over to Davis. "He's a firm man, Chief. But fair. Firm but fair. Now, if you'll be so kind as to have your man drop me off at the Hollywood Roosevelt Hotel, I have business to attend to."

"Sure thing, Mr. Brooke," Davis said. "Ralph, the Roosevelt Hotel and step on it. A pleasure doing business with you, Mr. Brooke. Look me up again next time you're in L.A. We like to be real friendly to our visitors here in Southern California. 'To protect and serve' is our motto. With the emphasis on service, if you get my drift."

The police car pulled up in front of the Hollywood Roosevelt and Blackthorn briefly grasped the extended sweaty palm of Two-Gun Ed Davis. "I understand, Chief. I do indeed."

65.

Churchill's in Danger!

Hollywood, California
Friday, 23 August 1929
1:30 p.m.

A genial smile spread across the features of Herbert Hoover's bland, broad face. "And so it gives me great pleasure to introduce Dr. Hugo Eckener, the designer of this great airship who has so kindly interrupted his historic voyage to be with us today."

The crowd in the Hollywood Roosevelt's Blossom Ballroom burst into sustained applause. Kurt von Sturm rose to his feet to join in the celebration along with the other zeppelin officers at whose table he sat. Sturm was impressed with the hotel's architecture. He could see why Hearst chose it as a venue. On the outside, it had the same Spanish-Moorish design as *La Casa Grande* at San Simeon. Occupying a prime three-acre site on Hollywood Boulevard, the hotel complex contained four buildings and three hundred thirty-five guest rooms around an interior courtyard, adjacent to which was an Olympic-size swimming pool. He and the zeppelin officers had entered through a two-story high Spanish colonial lobby with tall potted palms alongside Moorish arches. A sweeping marble staircase at one end of the lobby led up to the Blossom Ballroom, also done in a Mediterranean style, parquet floor, and mirrors galore.

Sturm had briefly considered canceling his appearance at the luncheon after the disaster at Long Beach last night because there was still much to do, the destruction of the arms notwithstanding. But it had been the airship's captain, Ernst Lehman himself, who had invited Kurt and it would have been a sign of disrespect to have disappointed his father's old friend. He didn't often think of his father or even talk about him to anyone. Watching your father die in the flaming coffin of a zeppelin was not something to share. Had he lived, it might well have been Peter Strasser, not Ernst Lehman, as captain of this magnificent ship on its epic voyage. Once Germany reclaimed her greatness, Sturm thought, and passenger zeppelins became reality, then he would reclaim both his name and his dream to again command an airship. But greatness for Germany came before loyalty to the Geneva Group. Sturm knew what he had to do. He had always known.

Sturm looked over at the next table where Cockran and Mattie McGary were seated. He took note of the sling on the man's arm. Apparently one of Cromwell's incompetent Americans hadn't been as compassionate as Sturm. McGary had been there as well and entirely too close as her photographs proved. She was a brave and beautiful woman. He noticed the casual way her hand rested on Cockran's forearm. He envied Cockran. Maybe he should have killed him last night after all. He noticed a silver locket on a thin silver necklace around her neck, the same locket he had seen on a bracelet on her wrist two days earlier durng the tea with President Hoover. He wondered if it were a recent gift from Cockran as she had not been wearing it that night at the Chicago warehouse.

Sturm by now had recalled where he had seen Mattie before. In Munich, six years earlier, at the residence of Ernst "Putzi" Hanfstaengl, the foreign press chief of the little-known National Socialist Workers Party. It had been the day before what was now called the Beer Hall Putsch. Her silvery gown had been cut low in the back as well as the front, her décolletage as daring between her breasts as it was on each side. He had tried in vain to be introduced to Mattie but Putzi's hand was on her ass and he set his sights instead on Hanfstaengl's statuesque blonde wife who was only too happy to oblige. But he had occasion two days later to recall the stunning journalist when he saw *The London Daily Mirror*'s front page coverage of the *putsch* over McGary's by-line with a photograph taken in the middle of the action, a shaken Adolf Hitler fleeing the scene, stepping over the bodies of his less fortunate followers. Sturm's usual prey were married women. McGary wore no wedding ring but she was someone for whom he indeed would make an exception. He would do his best to bed her should they ever meet again. And, if past were prologue, his best was very good indeed.

Dr. Hugo Eckener, his thinning grey hair cropped close, eyes blinking behind wire-rimmed spectacles, acknowledged the crowd's applause with an embarrassed wave of his hand. "Allow me to pay tribute at this time to the valuable support from the United States Navy Department. I am also grateful to President Hoover for his kind words which coincide with my own view that the era of great adventure is not over. But, above all, we salute Mr. Hearst whose financial support has allowed us to show that airship travel is as safe as ocean liners."

Eckener paused and wiped the perspiration from his forehead and his eyes. Or was it a tear? Sturm couldn't tell. "Something similar to what inspired Magellan must also have been in our blood when the idea of flying around the world in an airship occurred to us. Our plan developed the thought that this great trial of the airship, by which the public would judge it, would give a definite proof of the craft's usefulness under any weather conditions."

Eckener paused again and this time Sturm could see it was indeed a tear at which he was dabbing. "Due to its light construction and the vulnerability inherent in its large size, the *Graf Zeppelin* can thrive and exist only in an atmosphere of unclouded peace. It is like one of those opalescent butterflies which fascinate as they flutter in the summer sunshine but seek a sheltered corner whenever a storm blows up. Often, when people greet it so enthusiastically, I have felt as if they were seeing in it a sign and symbol of the universal dream of lasting peace."

Sturm was the first to his feet, catching Eckener's eye and raising his glass in a silent toast to his father's old mentor. That Germany had to have her revenge for the Treaty of Versailles went without saying. But there was more than one way to accomplish that. Doing so with technology like Dr. Eckener's "Dream Machine" was one way. And now that there would be no IRA *coup d'état*, Sturm knew the plundering of Poland by Weimar Germany and the Soviet Union would not take place as planned. But Sturm didn't mind. As he had told Philip Cromwell when they arrived on the *Graf Zeppelin* barely two weeks earlier, he had conceived the mission to America and the IRA *coup d'état* as a back-up plan. Sturm smiled. Careful men always kept more than one contingency plan in reserve. And Kurt von Sturm was a careful man.

2:30 p.m.

The crowd burst into applause again and rose to its feet. Cockran sat directly in front of the dais at a table with Robert Rankin, Inspector Thompson, David Brooke-Smythe, Churchill's brother Jack, and their two sons. Churchill was seated on the dais next to Hearst. President Hoover was on the other side of the podium. His left arm still in a sling, Cockran was not able to join in the applause which greeted Hugo Eckener upon the conclusion of his remarks. He watched as Hearst, Hoover and, finally, Churchill, shook the German airship pioneer's hand. One Secret Service agent was guiding Hoover behind the podium and off the platform. They were met by six more Secret Service agents who formed a protective barrier around him and guided Hoover through double swinging doors into the kitchen.

As soon as the President and the Secret Service entered the kitchen, Inspector Thompson and Rankin joined Churchill on the dais along with two detectives from the LAPD. Thompson whispered in Churchill's ear and Rankin guided him by the elbow off the platform.

The LAPD had been adamant that the kitchen was the safest means of egress. The police had said specifically that they didn't want the President leaving through the front lobby, a journey that would have required him to descend an elaborate marble staircase to the hotel's lobby. To his credit, Hoover had been reluctant to leave through the kitchen, primarily on the grounds that it wasn't dignified.

But that had all changed at the security meeting between the LAPD and the Secret Service, which Thompson, Rankin and Smythe had attended on behalf of Churchill. Smythe had spoken up in support of the LAPD's position, Rankin later told Cockran, based on the IRA's threat to Churchill's life. That had been enough to persuade the Secret Service and Scotland Yard as well, notwithstanding Churchill's views to the contrary.

As had been done in San Francisco, Rankin and Inspector Thompson, along with the two LAPD detectives, formed a moving diamond around Churchill. Rankin was at the diamond's top and Thompson at the back while the two detectives flanked Churchill on either side. Smythe was right behind Thompson followed by Cockran, Mattie, Jack Churchill and the Churchill sons.

What came next happened quickly but, as with the fire fight at the warehouse, Cockran remembered it all later as if it were being played in slow motion. The kitchen was a nightmare in white, a buzz and noise emanating from the genuine enthusiasm shown by the kitchen staff at the President's passage. One of the Secret Service agents behind the President was as tall as Rankin and Cockran could see him at the far end of the aisle at least a hundred feet away.

The white-uniformed kitchen help lined the ten-feet wide aisle but maintained a respectful distance, leaving the aisle free. The tall Secret Service agent had just left the room when the LAPD detective on Churchill's right tripped and fell heavily into a large refrigeration unit. The eyes of Churchill's body guards all turned toward the fallen detective but Cockran was the first to see Tommy McBride enter the aisle, his right arm extended, holding a revolver.

"Look out! There's a gun!" Cockran shouted but McBride was too fast and fired twice, both shots hitting Churchill in the back. Then, another waiter in white coat emerged from the left and began firing. The noise level of the shots in the confined space of the kitchen was ear splitting and Cockran watched Smythe draw his weapon and add to the noise level by firing several shots in the general direction of Tommy McBride.

By this time, Rankin had thrown his large body over the stricken Churchill, providing an effective shield against further harm.

Inspector Thompson had pulled out his weapon as well but, unlike Smythe, had not fired it.

Smythe continued firing and Cockran watched, in disbelief, as he shot Rankin squarely in the back. The impact of the bullet rolled Rankin partly off of Churchill's body and Smythe shot again, hitting the now exposed Churchill with a third shot in his back. With the shot at Rankin, Cockran had taken the sling off his left arm and moved quickly forward. He was almost on top of Smythe when the man's shot hit Churchill. Before Smythe could fire again, Cockran slammed into Smythe's back, grabbed his right wrist, and jerked it sharply upward, the man's next shot firing up into the ceiling, away from Churchill and Rankin.

The pain in his left shoulder shot through him as Cockran wrestled a protesting Smythe to the ground. "You fool! Let me up! Churchill's in danger!"

"Not any more," Cockran said softly. "Not any more."

Cockran's knee was firmly in the middle of Smythe's back and, having relieved him of his weapon, Cockran looked around. Blood was everywhere, a vivid contrast to the white kitchen uniforms. The second gunman was dead. Four or five other kitchen staff were down as well, all having been hit by wild shots or ricochets. Tommy McBride didn't have a scratch on him, as he stood there between two LAPD detectives, his hands handcuffed behind him.

Cockran lifted Smythe to his feet but ignored the demand that he return Smythe's weapon. Instead, Cockran handed it to Inspector Thompson. "This man was firing wildly, endangering the lives of others. Winston and Robert, how badly hurt are they?"

"I'll bloody well be fine as soon as this giant Scot allows me up." Churchill growled.

"Sorry, sir," Rankin responded, unfolding his long frame and standing up.

Churchill stood up, dusted himself off and turned to Inspector Thompson. "Tommy, you were right. I apologize," Churchill said, as he shook Thompson's hand. "I thought these bloody bulletproof vests were as unnecessary as they were uncomfortable."

Cockran heard Smythe's voice raised in anger behind him and he turned to see Smythe and two of his men engaged in an argument with the LAPD detectives over who was to take custody of McBride. Cockran motioned for Inspector Thompson to join him.

"See here, my good man," Smythe said. "The attack took place on American soil but it was a Member of Parliament against whom the assault was directed. I'm with British intelligence and I must insist that you turn this man over to us for interrogation."

"Well, I suppose I don't see any harm," the American detective began to say.

Cockran watched Thompson put a hand on Smythe's shoulder, "David, you've done enough damage. You and your men return to your rooms. We will discuss this all later."

Smythe started to protest, but Thompson turned away from him and flashed his badge at the detective. "Scotland Yard. Inspector Thompson and Detective Sergeant Rankin. We are in charge of Mr. Churchill's security. Would you mind terribly if we questioned this man for a few moments? You're welcome to join us. We'll be in room 412."

"Gee, you're Scotland Yard? Well, of course, Inspector, be my guest. I'll tell my captain where you are as soon as he arrives."

66.

No Loose Ends

Los Angeles
Friday, 23 August 1929
4:00 p.m.

The *Graf Zeppelin* floated gently inside the large circle, the mooring mast at its center, the afternoon sun highlighting its shimmering silver skin. Within the great ship, its crew were all busily engaged in pre-lift off operations. The ship's passengers were gathered in the airport departure lounge, the bus to take them out to the airship idling quietly in front of the lounge.

Not all of the passengers waited expectantly in the lounge for departure. Two of them were already on board, seated at a table in the ship's salon, talking quietly with a third man. It had been fifteen minutes since Ernst Lehman had sent word to the first officer that all pre-flight preparations had been completed. But the ship would not depart and the remaining passengers would continue cooling their heels until these men had finished.

"Nothing can be salvaged?" Zurich asked.

"Nothing. A complete loss," Kurt von Sturm replied.

"But how could this happen? Who is responsible?"

"We assume it was British intelligence, the same crew that was at Wyntoon. But the American Cockran was with them."

"How many men did we lose?"

"I only lost two. The rest were supplied by Manhattan."

"And the Irish?" Zurich inquired.

Sturm shook his head. "Sadly, none. They weren't even there. I sent them away. For the first time in this mission when something went wrong, the Irish weren't responsible."

Zurich picked up a crystal snifter of brandy in front of him, swirled its contents, and inhaled the fumes. "Two mistakes. First was Wyntoon. And now this. Can Geneva afford to give him any more opportunities to fail?"

"I don't understand," Berlin said. "Who do you mean?"

Zurich replaced the snifter on the crisp white linen tablecloth and replied in a soft voice that caused the other man to lean forward to hear. "I think we all know who I mean."

The white-haired banker then turned to Sturm. "Kurt, would either the disaster at Wyntoon or last night have occurred had there been competent security provided?"

"No, sir," Sturm replied. "Both locations were eminently defendable."

"If the decision were yours, my young friend, would you afford Manhattan the opportunity to make a third mistake?"

No, Sturm thought, but he knew the question was rhetorical. "That is not for me to say."

"But you agree with me that Manhattan has failed?"

"Yes, Manhattan has failed," Sturm replied.

A white-coated waiter silently entered and began to remove the empty glasses in front of the trio. Zurich turned his head to the waiter. "Tell Captain Lehman we need only ten minutes."

"Very good, sir."

"Now, Kurt," Zurich said, turning back to Sturm, "the money. What about the money?"

"I cabled our executive secretary today that I had the releases. In a few hours, the double signature accounts will be closed, the funds transferred, all traces of their existence removed. De Valera can do nothing about it. If he complains to the authorities, the bank's hands are clean. They will tell them it must have been a swindle. Foreigners in Switzerland are so easily fooled."

"And the bearer bonds delivered to McBride?" Zurich asked.

"Where is he now? Where is the money?"

"I don't know. He was staying at the Hotel Cecil."

"Find him. Find our money. I want it back."

"As you wish," Sturm said. "And Manhattan?"

Zurich paused a moment before responding. "I leave that to your judgment. But no loose ends. Tie them up."

Sturm's exit from the airship acted as a signal. Fifteen minutes later, the passengers were all on board and the ground crew was walking the great ship back from the mooring mast. Minutes later, he heard the booming voice of Ernst Lehman as it carried over the tarmac. "Up ship!"

Sturm watched as the ground crew released their hold on the landing lines and the airship slowly began to rise, its Maybach engines driving it forward, the afternoon sun still sparkling over its silvery skin. Sturm thought of his father and the legendary name in airship circles which he had been forced to temporarily abandon. He smiled. He would take care of the loose ends as Zurich had ordered but his day was coming. Germany's day was coming. His success here in California had been everything he had hoped. Once he had attended to those loose ends, he could return to the fatherland. If things unfolded there as he had every reason to expect, he knew that one day he would reclaim the name of Kurt von Strasser; his beloved Germany once more would be a great nation; and his father would be proud. Of that, he was certain. Germany's revenge was that close to being within his grasp. Failure was not an option.

67.

I'll Survive the Embarrassment

Santa Monica
Friday, 23 August 1929
7:00 p.m.

Mattie McGary watched from the open drawing room window as Philip Cromwell's chauffeur-driven LaSalle pulled up in front of Marion Davies' mansion by the sea. He was in black tie and ignored his blonde companion sitting silently beside him and filling out a silvery gown, low cut in the front and undoubtedly the back as well. Mattie had a dress like that.

The Ocean House, as it was called, was located on Beach Palisades Road in Santa Monica. Owned by Marion Davies and built by Hearst, it was a white, Georgian style three-story U-shaped structure, its broad front facing the Pacific Ocean, a towering, palm tree-topped cliff to the rear of the house. At 110 rooms, it was the largest beach house in California. Its fifty-five bedroom suites looked out on the Pacific through eighteen two-story high Ionic columns. Beside the house was a one hundred ten foot long fresh water swimming pool, lined with marble and spanned by a Venetian-style bridge in the middle. Nearby were over a thousand lockers for guests. When it came to his mistress—whom he loved dearly—Hearst spared no expense.

"He's here, Chief," Mattie said over her shoulder as she watched the unfolding scene.

Cromwell's chauffeur held the door open and boldly stared at the blonde's nearly exposed breasts as she and Cromwell stepped out of the LaSalle and walked across the gravel path to the mansion's entrance where another servant opened the door. "Good evening, sir."

Mattie hurried to the drawing room door, not wanting to miss any of the drama. She peeked out carefully. Sure enough, the self-assured Cromwell handed his hat to the butler without stopping, and proceeded in the opposite direction from Mattie down the black marble hallway toward the wood-paneled dining room and the adjacent reception room where cocktails were being served. Cromwell had been in those rooms many times before but, Mattie thought, never again, you pompous bastard. You almost got my new boyfriend killed.

"Excuse me, sir," the butler said. "Mr. Hearst asked that you join him in the drawing room." Cromwell stopped and looked back. Mattie could see a frown on his face. He told his companion to proceed without him and he turned to follow the butler who said, "This way, sir."

Mattie hurried into position as the butler opened both doors to the drawing room and stood aside while Cromwell walked in. "Mr. Cromwell is here, sir," the butler announced.

Mattie saw Cromwell frown again when he saw her beside Hearst. She was wearing a high-necked, backless green silk gown, champagne flute in one hand, the other casually resting on Hearst's shoulder.

Hearst turned and greeted Cromwell warmly in his high-pitched voice. "Philip. How good to see you. Mattie and I are working on the first edition for Monday's Herald-Examiner. Galleys are on the table. I think you'll find them interesting."

Cromwell walked over to the wide mahogany trestle table upon which were spread out a montage of photographs. There were a series of photographs of last night's fire at the Long Beach warehouse. Below that were a series of photographs which were obviously the interior of a warehouse including several telephoto lens close-ups of weapons being loaded into a boxcar. Underneath the warehouse photos were ones of Cromwell himself, several in white tie and tails, taken at a charity ball in New York last spring. Others were of Cromwell in hunting attire, riding to the hounds.

Then, at the far end of the table, Cromwell saw the galley of the front page whose headline in bold black type said it all. "Merchant of Death." In smaller type below that: "Wall Street Financier Exposed." Below that, in smaller type, "Mastermind Under Federal Investigation for Mail and Wire Fraud."

Mattie saw the blood drain from his face. He turned on Hearst, fury in his voice. "You can't do this. Publish this libel and my lawyers will sue you for every penny you're worth."

"Don't be tiresome, Philip. I have lawyers too. You're forgetting one important fact."

"What's that?"

"I buy ink by the barrel. While your lawyers are busy filing papers in court, my newspapers across the country will be demanding, on a daily basis, your indictment for mail and wire fraud. There's bound to be a U.S. Attorney somewhere in the country eager to use your scalp as a political stepping stone. In fact, I bet there'll be a lot more than one."

"You wouldn't dare. Those were your bank accounts. I'll swear it was all your idea."

Hearst chuckled. "I think the papers Mr. Cockran found at Wyntoon ought to persuade the authorities you're lying, if it ever gets that far. But I don't see that it needs to go that far. I'm a reasonable man, Philip, and while I'll sell a lot of newspapers with this "Merchant Of Death" story and your subsequent prosecution," Hearst said, gesturing to the galley on the library table, "it won't make up for how much you cheated me during the past five years."

Hearst gestured toward one of the leather armchairs that sat in the corner of the oak-paneled room. "Have a seat, Philip. We have much to discuss.

"I made a mistake in hiring you, Philip," Hearst said. "I realize that now. Nevertheless, as with all the people who work for me in critical positions, I keep careful track of their financial situation. You have been no exception. I've had my accountant reviewing in the past few days all of your transactions on my behalf since 1924. There is, he believes, at least $10 million unaccounted for. Here," Hearst said, handing him a manila folder that was laying on the small table between them, "are his findings. Check them out. I believe you'll find it all in order."

Cromwell opened the folder and quickly scanned its contents. He tossed the folder back on the table between them. "Your accountant's crazy. I've only taken the commissions we agreed upon. They're nowhere near $10 million. Look, W.R., you can hire lawyers. I can hire lawyers. But in the end, it won't get us anywhere. Tell me what you want."

Hearst gave Cromwell a genial smile. "My money back. That's all. Plus a small penalty, naturally. What I believe the lawyers call 'punitive damages.'"

"How much?"

"Here," Hearst said, "is a detailed, itemized financial statement for you through the market's close today. Underneath it is a document I've had my lawyers draw up between us."

Hearst had shown Mattie all the documents earlier. She was surprised that Hearst could so easily accumulate so much knowledge about Cromwell's holdings. Even the numbered account he held at a bank in Switzerland. She waited while Cromwell picked up the settlement agreement and release that Hearst's lawyers drafted. The "Whereas" clauses alone ran for four pages, documenting not only his thefts from Hearst but the role he played allowing Hearst's art accounts to be used to launder IRA funds for arms purchases. She smiled. The Chief was taking everything! Stocks, bonds, real estate. Cromwell would have almost nothing left.

Cromwell looked up at Hearst. "I won't do it. I can't do it. You don't understand...."

Hearst wasn't smiling now. "I understand, Philip, only too well that you tried to cheat me and now you're going to pay. Actually, I think I'm treating you quite well. Your country place in Long Island. Your town house on Park Avenue. The stocks you hold on margin. They're all yours to keep. If you're as good as everyone says you are, you'll be back on top in no time."

Hearst lifted his bulky frame from the chair and walked over to a writing desk, picked up a fountain pen, unscrewed its cap as he walked back toward Cromwell, and thrust it at him. "Your last chance, Philip. Sign the papers now or this story runs," he said, gesturing to the black headlines and the silent scream they carried of the end of Cromwell's life as he knew it.

"I'll survive the embarrassment," Hearst said. "I don't think you will."

"You don't understand. I've worked my whole life to escape the shadow of my father's scandal. This will leave me less than he had when he leaped..." Cromwell paused and caught himself. "When he died. Do you know how long it took me to do that? To have a net worth higher than his? 1920! You're crazy! You expect me to throw that all away?"

"Yes," Hearst replied, holding out a pen. "Sign."

Reluctantly, a sullen Cromwell took the proffered pen from Hearst. The scratching sound of the thick nib when it moved across the heavy paper was deafening as Philip Dru Cromwell IV left his name behind on five separate pages of the twenty-page document, the only evidence of the last twenty-two years of his life, his net worth now less than his father's in 1907. Hearst had made it clear to Mattie that such had been his intent in determining his "punitive damages".

Cromwell rose from his chair and folded his copy of the long legal document in half and then in half again. He stuffed it inside his dinner jacket. Suddenly, he appeared to have difficulty breathing, even though Mattie could feel the breeze from the Pacific Ocean.

"Are you quite all right, Philip?" Hearst asked, concerned. "Should I call for a doctor?"

"No, I'll be fine," Cromwell muttered. "I'll show myself out."

"As you prefer, Philip," Hearst replied. "Do have a pleasant evening."

Hearst turned to Mattie and extended his arm. "Shall we go into to dinner, my dear? I believe I may even join you in a cocktail. Or possibly two. A celebration is certainly in order. And in our absence, I'm certain that Marion has already exceeded her quota for the night.

Hearst paused for a moment and then continued. "I do love her so much, you know, and I worry about how much she drinks. You two are nearly the same age. You don't suppose you could talk to her about it? She might take it better from a contemporary."

Mattie leaned up and kissed the older man on his cheek. "Chief, I love you and all you've done for me and my career." She stopped and laughed. "But I'm a Scot; I drink too much myself; and you don't pay me enough to do something as dangerous as carrying a message to one of the two women in your life. Don't worry about Marion. She is one tough cookie, a hell of an actress and an even better businesswoman. Just keep finding her juicy parts. If you ever see her drinking affect her acting, then tell her so. I don't think she'll take it badly. She loves you too and you'll never meet a more loyal person."

Hearst bent over and kissed Mattie on the forehead. "Except perhaps you, my dear. Now let's go celebrate before Winston drinks all my champagne. The man's capacity is astonishing."

9:00 p.m.

The peroxide blonde whimpered silently in the corner of the large rear compartment of the LaSalle, lights from passing street lamps highlighting the silver satin of her evening dress and a single quivering naked breast which had erupted from the plunging neckline when Cromwell had forcibly grabbed her bare shoulders and thrust her hard into the padded leather door.

"Daphne! If you mention one more time that I made you leave Hearst's dinner party when you were seated next to Douglas Fairbanks, I'll rip the rest of that goddam dress off and let you out right here! Then you can walk home naked or fuck the first taxi driver who'll give you a ride. Either one shouldn't be a new experience for you. Now shut up and let me think."

Once away from Hearst, Cromwell's confidence returned. Hearst couldn't do this to him. Cromwell knew too much about Hearst's empire and his political plans. There had to be a way to turn this around, he thought. There *must* be a way. Cromwell mentally sifted through the important people he knew in Washington; the ones who owed him favors. It was no use. He knew publishers, but none were as big as Hearst. He knew politicians, but none who could touch Hearst. He knew the goddamn President, for Christ's sake, but Hoover had nothing to give that Hearst wanted. Most of Hearst's wealth was tied up in land and the natural resources under it. California, Mexico, South America, England. Everything else was tied up in his publishing empire. Newspapers, magazines, radio stations, newsreels. Hearst didn't need access to markets abroad or protection from foreign competition at home. Hearst was untouchable.

But wait, he thought, maybe not. Cromwell was a member, still the only American member, of the Geneva Institute for Industrial and Scientific Progress. That was it. The Geneva Group! That was the answer. Hearst had many interests abroad. Potentially vulnerable interests if the proper authorities could be influenced. Or, if necessary, eliminated and replaced. The last ten years had not been wasted! Hearst would be no match for Geneva. Equally important, Kurt von Sturm and three of his men were still in Los Angeles. They also were staying at the Hollywood Roosevelt. Sturm had told him after the zeppelin reception that he and his men were not leaving Southern California until later in the week. His men wanted to meet movie stars.

Excellent! Cromwell felt much better. He had a plan. It was a good plan. He felt in control now. Back in charge. It was his game again. He knew from broad hints Zurich had dropped in their conversations that Kurt von Sturm was an assassin as well as the Geneva Group's executive director. And an assassin was exactly what he needed. If Sturm did not think that this was an operation which Geneva would approve, then Cromwell would commission it personally. Sturm was in his thirties. What man his age could say no to $1 million? Maybe he should arrange to see Sturm tonight. If Hearst could be killed in the next 24 hours, perhaps Sturm could even recover Hearst's copy of the agreement. If Sturm could do that for him, it would certainly be worth more than $1 million. Yes, he would see Sturm tonight.

Cromwell looked over at Daphne. She was no longer whimpering, breathing evenly and deeply through her open mouth, asleep from too much alcohol, her breast still exposed. She looked sexy. Just as soon as he was finished with her, he would see Kurt von Sturm.

Cromwell liked being in control. Back in his suite at the Hollywood Roosevelt, he fortified that feeling with the blonde starlet. Daphne had forgiven his earlier violence when he dropped the names of several Hollywood producer clients of his to whom he promised an introduction and placed a $500 bill within her gown's plunging neckline. After that, she had been content to let him do whatever he liked. As if he gave her or any woman a choice.

Daphne was naked now and kneeling before him. Cromwell stood looming over her, one big hand holding her blonde hair tight, the other fondling a breast as he jerked her head forward and back, forcing her to take him inside her mouth again and again until at last she brought him to a finish. Cromwell pushed her away and Daphne stood up, coughing and gasping for breath. "Go clean yourself up," Cromwell said, slapping her squarely on her bare bottom, watching his red handprint slowly fade as she walked away.

Cromwell was wearing a white terrycloth robe with the monogram of the Hollywood Roosevelt. He tied it loosely around his waist and retrieved the snifter of brandy from the night table. He picked up his latest personal financial statement, the one that no longer accurately represented his wealth after that pirate Hearst had finished blackmailing him. He picked up the telephone and had the switchboard connect him to Sturm's room but after ten long rings, the operator returned to tell him what was fucking obvious. Room 737 wasn't answering. Damn!

Cromwell slammed the receiver down, walked into the sitting room and refilled his glass, his back to the French doors leading to a small balcony. The doors were open. He was momentarily puzzled. He could not recall opening them. He walked over to the doors and, feeling the gentle breeze of the warm night, walked outside and rested his hand on the waist-high balcony. It was a cloudless night, the stars a vivid contrast to the black of the sky, the lights of

Hollywood stretched out before him. It would all be his once more. Yes, all he had to do was find Kurt von Sturm and he would be back. Where he belonged. In control.

"Beautiful night, is it not, Manhattan?"

The voice startled Cromwell and he attempted to keep his hands steady as he turned, but the rolling contents of the crystal snifter gave him away. Kurt von Sturm was off to his left, sitting in a chair at the end of the suite's balcony, some twenty feet away.

"Von Sturm. I didn't know you were there," Cromwell said as he turned to face Sturm. "But why are you here? What...what do you want?" Cromwell stammered.

"Your resignation," Sturm responded, holding up a copy of the Hearst agreement. "Interesting document I found on the desk in the sitting room."

"You can't be serious! You don't have the authority. I demand to see Zurich or Berlin. "

Cromwell watched as Sturm got up from the chair and moved behind him towards the French doors, placing himself between Cromwell and any exit from the balcony.

"I'm afraid that's quite out of the question. The Hearst agreement speaks for itself."

"Wait! You don't understand! I have a job for you. I need you to kill someone for me. I can make you a very wealthy man. Very wealthy."

Sturm laughed. "I don't think so, Manhattan. That's the trouble with you Americans. You assume everyone else thinks as you do. That money is as important to them as it is to you. The world doesn't work that way. Some things are more important than money. Maybe one day America will learn that. Just as you are about to learn it tonight."

"But...where's Daphne?" Cromwell asked, his voice breaking.

"I gave her a small gratuity and asked her to give us some privacy. She seemed most eager to leave." Sturm smiled. It was not a pleasant smile. "We are quite alone, Manhattan. Trust me, this won't take long." he said, pulling a Luger from his jacket and casually screwing a sound suppressor into its barrel.

Cromwell panicked. "Oh my God!" he said and dashed for the door, but Sturm was too quick for him and hit him a glancing blow to the head with the Luger's butt which stunned him and knocked him to the ground. Cromwell almost lost consciousness but he could feel Sturm above him. Then he felt Sturm lifting him by his armpits and pulling him over to the balcony. The loosely tied terrycloth robe opened and he could feel a breeze on his naked body beneath. His dazed mind couldn't quite grasp what was happening until he felt Sturm's strong hands fold him face first over the balcony railing. His mind was clearing now and he realized what Sturm was doing. Too late, much too late, he started to resist. He felt Sturm grasp his kneecaps and lift him up and over the balcony and out into space. Cromwell was wide awake now and flailed his arms helplessly as a scream erupted from his throat and he felt the robe slip off as he fell, his body twisting in mid-flight so that he could see the green concrete around the hotel pool rushing up to greet him. Cromwell flailed his arms and legs, trying to reach the water. He didn't.

Sturm heard the sickening sound of Cromwell's skull hitting the concrete and looked down at the naked body sprawled face down ten stories below. A pool of blood was spreading around his head. He knew, from years of similar experience, that he had only minutes left to leave Cromwell's suite. He went to the desk in the sitting room and scrawled, in a practiced hand identical to Cromwell's, a last message from Philip Dru Cromwell IV on a thick sheet of cream-colored Hollywood Roosevelt stationery: "*I leave to rejoin my father. He will understand what I have had to do.*"

68.

I Was Only Following Orders

Hollywood
Saturday, 24 August 1929
8:30 a.m.

The sling was back on Cockran's left arm and he could feel the pain through the four aspirin he had taken thirty minutes earlier. The hotel's physician had warned him sternly not to engage in any more strenuous physical activity. As a result, he had spent a chaste night in bed with Mattie, sleeping soundly. A room service breakfast was spread out before them.

"Did you read *The Examiner* this morning?" Mattie asked with a broad smile.

"Yes, I did," Cockran replied. "I appreciate my name not being mentioned. Until Donovan can clear that warrant up in New York, I'd just as soon not draw attention to myself."

"No, not that story. The one on page four. About Philip Cromwell."

"What about Cromwell?"

"Here, look for yourself," Mattie said, handing him the paper. "He jumped off a tenth floor balcony. Like father, like son, I'd say, except the story won't play as big as his father's death. The attempted assassination of a prominent British statesman tends to push other stories off the front page. Plus, he didn't take a naked blonde mistress over the side with him."

"You saw him last night," Cockran said. "Did Cromwell appear suicidal to you?"

"Not especially," Mattie replied. "Cromwell didn't look happy. But not suicidal."

"It's a pity that Hearst was too embarrassed by the use of his art accounts to run that "Merchant of Death" story." Cockran paused and then grinned. "Are you certain Hearst had nothing to do with the arms deal? Cromwell's death certainly looks suspicious....."

Cockran ducked as Mattie threw a piece of toast at him. "Give it a rest, Cockran! I can always arrange for a story in the *Examiner* letting the NYPD know exactly where to find you. Besides, with Cromwell dead, the Chief says we'll run the story."

There was a knock on the door. Motioning him to stay seated, Mattie rose and walked over to the door and opened it to admit Robert Rankin. Mattie ordered another pot of tea from room service and the three of them took seats around the glass-topped coffee table.

"Did you have any luck with McBride?" Mattie asked. "I'm surprised the Los Angeles Police allowed you and Inspector Thompson to take him away for questioning."

"They were happy to do it," Rankin replied. "They don't need a confession to convict him of attempted murder. They have plenty of witnesses. When they heard the other crimes about which we had suspicions, they told us to take as much time as we needed."

"So have you learned anything?" Mattie asked.

"Alas, no. Inspector Thompson and I were not successful in learning anything new."

Cockran narrowed his eyes as he felt a wave of cold displeasure. Noticing this, Rankin added, "My sentiments exactly. That's why last night around midnight we called Mr. O'Reilly and asked him if he and his associates would like a go at McBride."

"I'm surprised that Scotland Yard would turn a prisoner over to civilians."

Rankin took a sip of tea from the porcelain cup. "They weren't civilians, sir. One of Mr. O'Reilly's men is a part-time constable. Somewhere in the west of Ireland. Between Galway and Donegal. A small village, I believe. He even had a badge. Quite official looking."

Mattie laughed. "And I thought you were such a boy scout. Have we learned anything?"

"I believe so. That's why I came up here. I just heard from Mr. O'Reilly. He said that McBride had a number of things to tell us which we would find most interesting."

McBride's eyes were nearly swollen shut. The shades of the fifth floor room in the hotel were closed against the morning sun. McBride was sitting on a straight-backed chair, his ankles tied to each front leg, his hands bound firmly behind his back. His face was beginning to bruise and dried blood was congealed on his lower lip. Cockran inwardly winced when he saw the unmistakable mark of cigarette burns on McBride's upper torso, his flabby whiteness a vivid contrast to his flushed red face. McBride had been tortured.

Good, Cockran thought, as he watched Bobby Sullivan remove the gag from McBride, grab him by the hair and yank his head back.

"Tell them, Tommy! Tell us your story again."

"It wasn't my fault. I swear it! There was a war on. I was only following orders," McBride said through swollen lips. "That's all it ever was. Just following orders."

"There's no fucking war on now, McBride," Sullivan said as he cuffed him on the side of the head. "No excuses! Just tell us what happened. Tell us about John Devoy."

McBride nodded. "It was me who killed him. Blackthorn told me to do it. Said that Devoy was a threat to our mission. I tried to talk him out of it. I told him that burning the newspaper offices was enough. He wouldn't listen to me. He made me do it."

"Come on, McBride," Sullivan said. "Mr. Cockran here might believe your confession was coerced. Tell him the details. Tell him when you did it. Tell him how."

McBride did as he was told. The time, the place, the method of execution.

"There's a good lad," Sullivan said as he turned to Cockran and handed him a document. "Here's an affidavit we had a stenographer type up for McBride to sign confessing to the murder of John

Devoy. In case you need it to clear yourself in New York."

Cockran thanked him, folded the document and placed it in his coat pocket.

Sullivan turned back to McBride. "Now the other part. Tell us about Nora Cockran."

Sullivan stopped and turned to Mattie. "Miss, you might not want to stay for this next part."

Mattie looked at Cockran, an unspoken question in her eyes. Cockran nodded a silent assent. "Thank you, Mr. Sullivan," she said. "You are very kind, but I'll stay."

"It wasn't my idea," McBride protested. "It was all Blackthorn's idea on that too."

"Who is Blackthorn?" Sullivan asked. "Mr. Cockran needs to know."

"It's like I told you. He was one of our British informers during our fight with you Free Staters. He was someone Dev told me we could trust. Blackthorn was the one who gave us all the information for which banks to rob and when. That's how we came to rob the bank in Galway. He told me we had to send a message; make an example; let the Free Staters know the gloves were off. That even their women weren't safe. He gave us a list."

Cockran was sorry he didn't have his revolver with him as he listened to McBride.

"The bank was easy. We could have knocked it over at any time. But Blackthorn had his men following Cockran's wife. Waiting for her to come to town. They knew she did her banking there. It was them who pointed her out to me. We were to take her hostage. She was at the top of the list. I swear I never laid eyes on her before then. It was nothing personal, only business. But we were only following Blackthorn's orders. It wasn't our plan to kill her. If she hadn't been on Blackthorn's list, nothing would have happened to her."

Cockran didn't know the two other Apostles in the room very well. They were both armed but he couldn't be sure they would lend him their weapons. Sullivan might. He had been brutal enough. O'Reilly, whose back was to Cockran as Sullivan continued questioning McBride, might do it for him as well. Cockran had heard all he needed to know. Perhaps he had time to slip back to his room and retrieve his own revolver before they finished.

"Tell them about Mr. Churchill. Why did you try and kill him yesterday?" O'Reilly asked, taking over from Sullivan.

"Blackthorn set that up, too. Not that I needed an excuse to kill Churchill, but it was an IRA operation all the way. Blackthorn knew all the codes. The same ones Dev gave me. I had my orders."

No, Cockran decided, he couldn't leave now. He had to know. "Who is Blackthorn? What's his name?" Cockran asked.

O'Reilly turned away from McBride to face Cockran. "Don't worry about that, Bourke. It's right there in Mick's journals, the ones the Big Fellow instructed me to ship to your father if he were ever killed. If you knew his code, if you read them right, it's obvious. Mr. Churchill gave them to me yesterday to read. He told me he had a good idea of who it was but he wanted to see if I came to the same conclusion. I'm to meet him for breakfast this morning and compare notes."

"Who? Tell me!"

"David Brooke-Smythe. One of the men we didn't get on Bloody Sunday. The Big Fellow always thought someone had tipped him off."

"Where is Smythe now?" Cockran asked Robert Rankin.

"Under arrest and handcuffed to his bed. Two of O'Reilly's men are standing guard outside. I did that as soon as Joe told me. If I'm wrong, Mr. Churchill can apologize but I'm taking no chances."

"Does Winston know about this?" Mattie asked.

"No, miss," Rankin replied. "Inspector Thompson told me not to wake him. Told me Mr. Churchill can be quite cross when wakened early."

"I don't care how cross he's going to be," Mattie said. "He's going to be even more upset if we don't wake him. I'll go do it," she said as she began to make her way out of the room.

Cockran watched as Mattie headed to the door. O'Reilly was facing him now so he quietly moved up behind Bobby Sullivan as the door closed behind Mattie. Sullivan must have sensed his presence, however, because he placed his hand firmly on one of his two Colt

.45s as he turned to face Cockran and, wordlessly, took it from his waistband and handed him the weapon butt first.

Cockran nodded, took the weapon and said "I think the rest of you ought to leave now."

O'Reilly turned away from McBride, shrugged his shoulders and nodded to Sullivan in a signal to leave. Cockran turned back to McBride and didn't hear the door open behind him. He felt a gentle touch on his arm. Mattie was back, whispering in his ear. "You don't want to do this, Bourke. You really don't. Remember Aquinas. You don't execute prisoners no matter what they've done. Not like this. Nora wouldn't approve. You know that."

He knew that, he thought, but he cocked the automatic anyway. Then he stopped.

"Let me have it, Bourke," Mattie said, grasping his arm tightly. "You know what Nora would want. Give me the gun."

Slowly, Cockran uncocked the trigger, handed the .45 to Mattie and turned without a word and left the room.

"Take the damn thing, Bobby," Mattie said, handing the gun back to Sullivan, "before I shoot the bastard myself. I always thought Aquinas was full of crap."

69.

Now We Have A Hostage

Hollywood
Saturday, 24 August 1929
10:00 a.m.

Mattie waited impatiently for the elevator to arrive and take her up to Churchill's suite. Cockran had been more important, however, and her instincts had been correct. She had persuaded him for now but he needed more work. It wasn't over for him. Not while McBride was alive. Or Smythe. She turned left on leaving the elevator and headed down the long corridor. Smythe's room was the first one on the left. Number 910. She noted in passing that there was no one on guard as Rankin had told her. She thought briefly of knocking on the door but decided it was more important to advise Churchill of the new developments. She proceeded down the corridor and stopped twenty feet later when she noticed a smear of blood on a door marked "Linens". She carefully opened the door and gasped at what she saw. Two bodies on top of each other, each wrapped in blood-soaked sheets. She stepped into the linen closet and looked at the two bodies, recognizing them both as colleagues of Joe O'Reilly. She knelt to check for pulses she knew weren't there. Both bodies were still warm to the touch. What to do? Continue to Churchill's suite? Find Robert Rankin or Inspector Thompson? Before she could turn, a large hand was clamped over her mouth and another arm was wrapped around her middle. The last thing she saw was the handle of a large revolver as it began its descent toward her head.

Mattie slowly regained consciousness. Damn it! Not again! Her hands and feet were tightly bound, her mouth was gagged and her head hurt like hell. Wyntoon had confirmed what she already knew. She couldn't bear being in a situation where others were in control. For a brief moment she thought that maybe she ought to be more careful in the future. But that wasn't going to help now. She changed her mind when she heard Smythe's voice from the next room. She decided to make no noise to alert her captors that she was conscious. She would be careful.

"You did the right thing, Geoffrey," she heard Smythe say. "Killing her wouldn't have helped. Now we have a hostage and that may buy us more time. Has the air charter company returned my call?"

"Not yet, sir."

Mattie heard a telephone ring and Smythe's clipped voice as he answered it. "Yes? This is Mr. Brooke. Right. I wish to confirm that the aircraft I have chartered for 6:00 p.m. is ready. Good. Please advise the pilot to be prepared to depart as soon as my party and I arrive. We may be there sooner than 6:00 p.m. Excellent. Now, if you would be so kind as to give me directions to your airfield from the rail station in San Fernando? My party will be leaving from there."

"Everything is arranged, Geoffrey," Smythe said when he hung up the phone. "Give us five minutes, then create your diversion. After that, join us on the afternoon train to San Francisco. We will leave it at its first stop and head back to the airfield. If Scotland Yard has half a brain, they'll check with the concierge and find out that I purchased two Pullman compartments on that train. They'll be so busy congratulating themselves on their cleverness that, by the time they get around to having the authorities stop the train, the rest of us will have already landed in San Diego and booked passage on the night train to St. Louis. We'll see you again, Geoffrey, when we've finally returned to civilization—each of us, I might add, one million American dollars richer."

Mattie heard someone move into the room from the outer chamber. She kept her eyes closed until she felt the cool splash of water thrown into her face. Though already alert, she feigned grogginess as she opened her eyes.

"Geoffrey, remove the bindings from her ankles," she heard Smythe say.

Soon she was sitting upright on the bed, her hands still bound in front of her. Smythe was standing directly over her holding a silenced automatic pistol. "Miss McGary, I regret you have seen fit to interfere in my affairs. Nevertheless, you may be useful. You will accompany us to the train station. If you cry out at any time, I will shoot you on the spot. Are we clear?"

Mattie nodded her head in acquiescence and felt the gag being removed from her mouth. Smythe lifted her to her feet and guided her by her elbow to the next room.

"My men will be on either side of you. I will be directly behind you with my weapon pointed squarely at your spine," he said and placed an overcoat over his arm concealing the weapon. "I'll only have time for one shot but if it does not kill you, it will certainly cripple you."

Mattie watched as Smythe carefully propped an envelope on the writing desk beside the telephone addressed to "Inspector Walter G. Thompson, Scotland Yard". Mattie's hands were then untied and she was given a towel to dry her face before they led her out of the room and down the corridor to the elevator.

As they walked through the lobby to the entrance, Mattie noticed the elegant profile of Hazel Lavery talking to the concierge, the shorter figure of Joe O'Reilly standing beside her. Heeding Smythe's warning, she said nothing. Smythe's men did not know either of them but Mattie had taken care, on Winston's instructions, to point out Smythe to Hazel at the zeppelin luncheon. It was a long shot, but it was her only hope. That somehow Hazel saw her leave.

70.

Take Care of McBride

Hollywood
Saturday, 24 August, 1929
11:00 a.m.

The faint echo of gun shots came as a surprise to McBride. He was pleased to see that, judging by the blank expressions of panic that washed over his captors, they had been surprised as well. The bearded Scot left the room quickly with one of the Apostles and met that bloody Cockran just outside the door. Just minutes ago, he thought he was a dead man—and at the hands of that arrogant, self-righteous American traitor. But he should have known. The dumb bastard didn't have the balls. No wonder it had been so easy for him to roger his sexy wife. A real man would never have let that happen. Tommy thought he might get out of this jam yet.

The door cracked open and McBride saw the head of his sole guard peek in through the opening in the doorway. He was just a kid. They made brief eye contact, long enough for the kid to shoot him a nasty look, when the kid's body suddenly lurched with a loud crack. A second shot followed, exploding the kid's skull and sending his body crumpling into the room. The door pushed all the way open, and filling the frame of the doorway was the figure of a well-dressed man who looked vaguely familiar.

"Who the fuck are you?" McBride mumbled through the blood-soaked rag in his mouth.

"Now, now, Tommy. Is that any way to greet your liberator?" the man said. Moving to the chair, he flipped out a sizable knife and cut McBride's bonds. Before McBride had a chance to take the rag from his mouth , the man yanked it out for him. "Shut up and get moving," he said. "This is all the help you get. Make your own way to that godforsaken bog you call home."

With that, the man left and disappeared down the hall. Tommy McBride did the same.

11:15 a.m.

Churchill had been safe so Cockran, Rankin and Sullivan quickly searched the nearby room of David Brooke Smythe—Blackthorn—and discovered nothing but severed bindings, a blood stained carpet and a note addressed to Inspector Walter Thompson:

> *I return to England. You had no authority whatsoever to place me under arrest. You are in this country purely in a private capacity as a body guard for Mr. Churchill. MI-6 has complete authority over the operation of British agents abroad and I was specifically placed in charge of this mission by the Prime Minister himself. I will stress in my report to my superiors in no uncertain terms that you deliberately interfered with my mission.*
>
> *I am particularly offended that you would order my arrest solely on the word of an Irish assassin whom you would not let my men and me interrogate. Notwithstanding that he had almost successfully carried out the assassination of the man whom you were allegedly guarding.*
>
> *My agents and I are leaving as previously arranged. Do not compound your mistakes by attempting to interfere. I am authorized by my superiors to use deadly force if I deem it necessary to the success of my mission. I so deemed it necessary with respect to those incompetent Irishmen you left to guard me. I shall not hesitate to do so again if the need arises.*
>
> *Miss McGary has kindly consented to accompany us on our journey and to bear witness to your incompetence and malfeasance.*
>
> *David Brooke-Smythe*

Cockran's heart sank when he heard two more sharp reports from the floor below. Damn it! He knew immediately what had happened. The initial shots were meant to lure them away from

McBride and Cockran had fallen for it. Sullivan was already half-way down the hallway, running towards the stairwell when Cockran moved into action after him, dropping Smythe's note on the floor.

"Robert, keep Winston safe!" he shouted back over his shoulder as he sprinted after Sullivan. He arrived at McBride's room three steps behind Sullivan to find a dead body and an empty chair. Cockran couldn't believe what was happening. McBride was just another decoy put in play by Smythe. But it didn't change the fact that Nora's murderer was free. McBride was hurt. Badly. His torture and beating made him easy prey. Now, having escaped the custody and protection of Scotland Yard, Cockran had all the pretense he needed to kill him when he found him. Smythe had Mattie but McBride was his for the taking. McBride or Smythe? Who to seek?

Cockran caught up with Rankin back in Churchill's suite.

"Mrs. Lavery and Mr. O'Reilly saw Smythe and another man entering a taxi with Mattie," Rankin said. "I made a few inquiries and learned from the concierge that Smythe purchased some tickets on a morning train to San Francisco."

"When does it leave?" Cockran asked as O'Reilly and Bobby Sullivan entered the room.

"There are two trains. One is the Coast Line. The other the San Joaquin Valley. Both are Southern Pacific. One leaves at 11:15; the other at 11:45."

Two weeks ago, Cockran might have hesitated, so deep was his desire to avenge Nora by killing McBride. He had learned a lot since then. From many brave people who all had proved him wrong. He knew whom he could depend upon. He knew what Nora would want.

"Joe," he said, "You and Bobby keep the Big Fella's promise. Take care of McBride. I'm going to San Francisco after Mattie and Smythe. I can't be sure which train Mattie is on so I'm going to the airport and hire an airplane from Hearst or someone else. I've got to be there before either of those trains."

O'Reilly looked him straight in the eye and simply nodded. As he headed to the door, Cockran realized that Bobby Sullivan was no longer there.

71.

The Rules Of The Railroad

North of Hollywood
Saturday, 24 August 1929
11:45 a.m.

Mattie McGary's hands had been tied again as she sat in the Pullman compartment, staring out the window, deliberately avoiding the gaze of her guard, whom she knew only as Geoffrey. Outside, the sun was shining brightly, the train gathering speed as it passed through the golden brown countryside moving north through the Hollywood hills toward San Fernando. She knew that Smythe and his men would be leaving the train at San Fernando so she hadn't believed Smythe's assurances that he would release her unharmed in San Francisco.

Mattie tensed when she heard a sharp rapping on the door, followed by the muffled voice of a conductor. "Tickets, please."

"Try the next compartment," Geoffrey replied. "My mate has them for both of us."

Mattie breathed a sigh of relief. She had been seriously contemplating seeking the conductor's help. It was a long shot, but if she shouted and at the same time attempted a sideways kick at Geoffrey's head...no, it wouldn't have worked. They would find her body sooner than if she did nothing because the conductor's absence would have been noted. But she would be no less dead. The conductor, too.

It would be another thirty minutes before they reached San Fernando. If she could make it to the door and into the corridor, they might not shoot her. Another rapping on the door. "'Tis the conductor, sir. And aren't I needing to see your tickets? The gentleman next door says that you have them."

"Well, I don't. So just bugger off," Geoffrey replied.

"Sir, I must insist. If I must, I'll unlock the door myself. 'Tis the rules of the railroad."

Geoffrey rose reluctantly to his feet, walked two paces to the door and turned the knob. The door burst open with considerable force, slamming into Geoffrey's face causing him to stumble and fall awkwardly back onto the compartment.

Mattie watched as Bobby Sullivan, dressed in a conductor's uniform, stepped into the compartment, closed the door with his left hand, raised and extended his right hand, in which he held a silenced Colt .45 automatic. Geoffrey attempted to struggle to this feet while reaching inside his jacket for his own weapon but he was far too slow as Sullivan fired two muffled shots, both of which found their target in the middle of Geoffrey's forehead.

"Bobby! How'd you get here?"

"No time for that," Sullivan replied. "Let's get you out of here first. We can talk later."

Sullivan carefully laid the .45 down on the bench beside Mattie and pulled a pocket knife from his jacket, opened the blade and cut her bonds. He picked up the .45 and, holding it at his side, opened the compartment door, stuck his head out and looked up and down the corridor. He motioned over his shoulder to Mattie with a nod of his head. She came over to stand beside him. She noticed the DO NOT DISTURB sign on the inside of the compartment door and slipped it off the knob. Following Sullivan into the corridor, she put the sign on the compartment's handle.

Moments later, they were seated in Sullivan's own compartment, two cars down.

"Smythe and the other man may try to search the train once they find their companion dead," Sullivan said. "but the odds are they won't want to draw that much attention to themselves. It cost me a hundred quid to rent the conductor's spare uniform. It's not a particularly good fit," pointing to the cuffs of his pants which were several inches short.

Mattie smiled. "Thanks for rescuing me again. So you saw me back at the hotel?"

Sullivan shook his head. "Not me. Joe and Mrs. Lavery. They saw you leave with Smythe and two of his men and knew he was up to no good."

"Look, Bobby, we've got to get off the train as soon as possible. I must call Winston. Scotland Yard undoubtedly assumes Smythe is on his way to San Francisco. I heard him say he secured tickets through the hotel concierge. But they're not going there. He and the other man are getting off the train in San Fernando and flying down to San Diego."

"They won't be going anywhere," Sullivan said. "Leave them to me. I know all about Blackthorn. McBride was first on my list but I'm flexible when it comes to scum like him."

Mattie shivered as Sullivan's cold blue eyes stared into hers. He was the single most cold and frightening man she had ever met. Smythe and even McBride paled in comparison.

"You wait here. Keep the compartment locked. This won't take long."

Mattie sat there for a good five minutes before Sullivan tapped softly on her door.

"There's only one man in Smythe's compartment and he's as dead as the one I killed.".

"Good. You got him. Was it Smythe?"

"T'was not Smythe. Nor was it me who shot him. He was dead before I arrived."

"Where's Smythe?"

"In the club car. With a tall gin and tonic in his hand and a leather valise at his side. The club car is too crowded for me to have a clear shot. Not while he's seated."

"Then we've got to get off the train now," Mattie said, "so I can call Winston. Our first stop is San Fernando but we can't wait that long."

Sullivan nodded. "I agree, but how do you propose stopping before San Fernando?"

Mattie grinned. "Can't you persuade your friend, the conductor, to stop at one of the smaller stations before we reach San Fernando?"

Sullivan nodded. "I'll try me best," he said and picked up a pile of clothes neatly folded on the seat. "I'll go down to the loo and change my clothes and return the conductor's uniform."

Sullivan returned a few minutes later with a large floral print dress and veiled hat..

"What's this?" Mattie asked.

"Our ticket off the train. The conductor's wife is traveling on the train to visit her sister. The only safe way to stop the train before San Fernando is for a medical emergency. Put this dress on and stick a pillow underneath. He'll tell the engineer a pregnant passenger has gone into labor."

Mattie nodded, grabbed the dress, slipped it over her head and put the pillow in place. "So the conductor is doing all this for an extra hundred pounds?" Mattie asked.

Sullivan smiled. "Actually, it's only dollars. He thinks you're traveling with your parents and that we want to elope. 'Tis amazing how romantic conductors can be."

12:05 p.m.

The train stopped for no more than two minutes at Burbank and Sullivan stood at the station's window and watched the train depart as Mattie placed a telephone call to Churchill..

"Winston? Mattie. I'm free. No, he didn't let me go. It was Bobby Sullivan. Two of Smythe's men are dead. No, I'm fine. Listen, Smythe is not going to San Francisco. It was a ruse. Yes. He's chartered a plane at the airport in Van Nuys. He'll be there within the hour. One more thing. I overhead Smythe say they would each be a million dollars richer. And three million dollars is exactly what was transferred from the IRA accounts in New York."

72.

You Really Don't Know? She Never Told You?

Los Angeles Metropolitan Airport
Van Nuys, California
Saturday, 24 August, 1929
12:30 p.m.

Cockran was sitting in a wicker arm chair inside Hearst's royal blue Fokker Trimotor, its engines idling, when he saw a young man run up in front of the plane, waving his hands, a piece of paper clutched in his right hand. The pilots cut the engines and a moment later, Cockran heard a knock on the cabin door. He opened the door and the young man hurried up the stairs.

"Mr. Cockran? I have an urgent message for you," he said, pressing the paper into Cockran's hands. Cockran unfolded the paper and looked at the message:

> *Mattie safe. Smythe on way to Van Nuys airfield. Has chartered an aircraft for San Diego. May have the IRA $3 million. Stop him.*
> *W.*

Thank God she's safe, Cockran thought as he refolded the paper and then knocked on the door to the plane's cockpit.

"Yes, sir?" said the co-pilot who stuck his head out the door.

"A slight change in plans. How much would you charge for a charter to San Diego?"

When told such a short flight would be less than $100, Cockran doubled that and told them the new plan. The pilot would go back to the airfield manager's office and file a new flight plan for San Diego. The co-pilot would seek out the pilot for Smythe's charter and offer him twice the amount Smythe was paying if he could develop a fuel line problem and turn the charter over to them. Cockran then phoned Churchill who in turn consulted with Inspector Thompson. Thompson agreed to contact the San Diego Police Department and have three squad cars meet the plane upon arrival. They discussed attempting the same thing at the Van Nuys airfield but Inspector Thompson vetoed it. He told Churchill there was something about the LAPD that he didn't trust. Jack Manion, however, had assured him the San Diego police were trustworthy.

Their respective missions accomplished, Cockran huddled with the two pilots in the air field's reception area and filled them in on what awaited them in San Diego. "I'll wait in the galley to the right of the entry door. Make certain Smythe is seated with his back to me. If I can get the drop on him during take-off, I will. But I won't take any unnecessary chances. Once we arrive in San Diego and he sees the police cars, he'll know the game is up."

Cockran was comfortably seated in the Fokker's galley for barely five minutes before he heard the two pilots and Smythe enter the aircraft. To the right inside the plane's entryway was the galley. To the left was the main cabin with six slip-covered wicker seats arranged in two conversational groupings. There was barely enough space to squeeze between the two groupings to make it to the three seats in the front. Cramped luxury but large windows lined both sides of the cabin in a long strip giving the interior an airy feel.

"This way, sir. Mind your head. Have a seat and strap yourself in. We'll be off soon."

There were no straps or seats in the galley and Cockran wedged himself into one corner and braced his feet against the bulkhead for take off. The engines would be at their maximum RPM during the take off and the climb to what the pilots had told him would be their

2,000 feet cruising altitude to San Diego. He hadn't told the pilots but Cockran had no intention of waiting for the San Diego police. Smythe would be armed and his best chance to slip into the passenger compartment undetected and take him unawares was during the take off. If Smythe resisted, as Cockran hoped he would, he'd kill the bastard.

The Trimotor was gathering speed now and the noise from the three engines was deafening. When he felt the craft lift off, he carefully let himself out of the galley and walked up the sloping floor to the doorway leading to the passenger cabin, the Webley in his right hand. Smythe was seated in the front grouping on the left with his back to Cockran who weaved through the three seats in the rear grouping to Smith's chair.

In one motion, Cockran wrapped his left arm around Smythe's neck and pressed the Webley revolver firmly against his side. "Remove your weapon. Place it on the floor. Don't even twitch or I'll blow a hole in your back."

Smythe reached inside his Saville Row lounge suit and carefully removed a Walther PPK automatic and dropped it to the floor beside his chair with a soft thump. Cockran directed him to move to the back of the compartment into the single forward-facing seat in the left rear corner of the plane. Cockran then picked up Smythe's weapon and moved to the two rear-facing seats diagonally across from Smythe, barely four feet away. With his weapon secured and Smythe in the rear of the airplane, Cockran now had a clear field of fire to shoot him without danger to the pilots. Which was his plan. But first came questions. A lot of them.

By now, the Trimotor had reached its cruising altitude and conversation was possible.

"Where is the $3 million you took from the IRA?"

Smythe's eyes narrowed. "How did you find out about that?" he said and paused, "Ah yes, that Scottish bitch. She must have overheard us. No matter. I don't know how she did it but she managed to kill my man who was guarding her. It saved me the trouble of doing it myself." He laughed. It was dry and mirthless. "Do thank her for me."

Smythe seemed unperturbed and casually draped one knee over the other as if he were sitting in a club having drinks with a friend. "Do you mind if I smoke?" he asked.

"No," Cockran said, "but move slowly."

Smythe pulled a flat silver cigarette case from inside his gray flannel suit coat and took out a cigarette, replaced the cigarette case, and lit up with a matching cigarette lighter.

"So what about the money?" Cockran asked.

"Ah, yes. The money. It was four million, not three and I'm afraid, old chap, that I haven't the foggiest idea. It certainly wasn't where I expected it to be."

"Where was that?"

"In a locker. At Union Station in Los Angeles. Where that idiot Irishman said he left it."

"You mean McBride?"

Smythe laughed. "Yes, how careless of me. There are so many Irishmen who are idiots, I can understand your confusion. But yes, McBride."

"Why would McBride have any money left? Didn't he spend it all purchasing the arms?"

Smythe took a puff from his cigarette and coolly blew the smoke into the air. "For having been such a problem, Mr. Cockran, you are remarkably ill-informed. Of course McBride spent all the money. To make it seem as if the IRA were buying the weapons itself. But it was all front money to be repaid as soon as the arms were purchased and safely on their way."

Cockran was confused. "Repaid? By whom?"

"The German," Smythe said.

"What was his name?"

"I don't know. McBride and de Valera only called him 'the German'."

"Who was supplying the money? Who was behind all this?"

"I don't think McBride knew. He only knew it was arriving on the zeppelin."

"Why would Germans want to do that?" Cockran asked.

"I don't know and I don't care," Smythe said. "The Germans are no threat to us now. Certainly less of a threat than Churchill, damn his eyes!" Smythe said with sudden vehemence.

"Why kill Churchill? What do you have against him?" Cockran asked.

Smythe's eyes narrowed and his face contorted in rage as he drew one last time on the cigarette and then stubbed it out with his heel on the floor beneath him. "Because that bloody half-breed American is responsible for giving Ireland away to the bloody Papists."

"I don't understand," Cockran said. "If you hate the Irish so much, why did you help McBride? Why didn't you carry out your mission and help Churchill stop the arms deal?"

Smythe laughed again. "That's exactly why de Valera tipped me. He thought I *would* help stop it. What a pompous fool! I very much wanted the IRA to get all the weapons it could."

"De Valera opposed it? And you wanted to help the IRA? I don't understand."

"Well, you should," Smythe snapped. "De Valera was born here, wasn't he? Makes him a bloody American, doesn't it? He did it for the money. Isn't that the only thing you Americans care about? De Valera told me that the Germans offered him a million dollar commission if he would let the $3 million he raised in America be used to purchase the arms. He told me that once the arms were seized, it would discredit the IRA forever in Ireland and free him from relying on their suport. And then he would use the $4 million to buy his way into power. He wants to buy a bloody newspaper, he does."

Smythe laughed again. "The bastard had the IRA kill Michael Collins and now he wants to double cross them and buy an election victory. Serve the bloody Irish right to elect that black-hearted coward."

"But that doesn't explain why you wanted the arms deal to succeed. Why help the IRA?"

"The same reason I didn't stop the assassinations Collins planned for Bloody Sunday even though de Valera warned me. We needed something spectacular to persuade Lloyd George to take the gloves off. Having ten of our best agents killed at once was a small price to pay."

"But why an arms deal now?" Cockran asked. "Bloody Sunday was eight years ago. The Treaty was seven. The Free State is part of the Commonwealth."

"That it may be," Smythe said, "but it damn well shouldn't be. When de Valera came to me, hoping to discredit the IRA, the bastard gave me a chance I thought was gone forever."

"I don't understand," Cockran said.

"Then you're a bloody fool," Smythe said. "Because if the IRA takes over the South, a war with Ulster is inevitable. Only something like that could ever force Britain to reoccupy Ireland and put those Fenian bastards in camps along with their women and children where they belong. Just like we did with the Boers."

Cockran had heard enough. He knew Smythe was playing for time, looking for an advantage but Cockran had learned almost all he needed to know. "My wife Nora?" Cockran asked, his voice barely audible. "Why did you do it? Why was she on your list? Why?"

Without asking permission, Smythe slowly reached inside his suit coat and pulled out the silver case and lit another cigarette. "To teach you a lesson." Cockran kept the revolver trained on the man's chest but Smythe ignored it and coolly blew smoke into the air. "Oh, I know you right well, you bloody American bastard. You're the one who kept carrying messages between Churchill and Collins. I read all about it in the field reports. I know you right well enough. If anyone but Churchill were in charge back then, we would have sent the army back in. Collins made a fool of him and England. You're as much responsible for that as anyone."

"Why not have *me* killed, then?" Cockran asked.

"No one cares about a dead American." Smythe said with a laugh. "Besides, you had already done your damage carrying those bloody messages between Churchill and Collins."

"But why have my wife killed? Why put her on the list you gave McBride?"

"Kill your wife? Are you daft? I would never do that. That's not why she was on the list."

Cockran was confused. "But, why....?"

Smythe laughed. "You don't know? You really don't know? She never told you?"

"Told me what?"

"I courted your wife for almost a year, you bloody idiot! I was in love with her and my leave was cancelled the weekend I was going to pop the question. It was another month before I could make it back to Dublin and, by then, you had come into the picture. Bloody rich American, you were and Nora told me she was in love with you. And your money as well, I'd wager."

Cockran was astonished. Nora and Brooke-Smythe? He knew she once had been involved with a British officer who had a "double-barreled" name—much to the annoyance of her parents— but she had never volunteered who the man was, only that he could be sweet to her but was too often a "pompous prig" to others, especially her friends. He also knew she had broken things off after they met but he knew none of the details, let alone the man's name. My God, he thought. She had been seeing David Brooke-Smythe! "So irreverent and full of life...her death a tragedy to those who knew her" was what the bastard had said to him in Chicago. It had bothered him to hear the Brit speak of Nora but it had gone right over his head. It never occurred to him that Smyth actually knew Nora. Not that he needed another reason to kill the man code-named Blackthorn.

"But if you loved her, why was she on a list that led to her being killed?"

Smythe laughed again. "Pay attention you bloody fool! I told you she wasn't on a list to be killed. Don't you bloody Papists ever read the Bible? The Book of Deuteronomy. Chapter 20, Verses 10 to 18. When you conquer a city, it says, 'You shall put all its males to the sword but the women and everything else in the city—all its spoil— you shall take as booty and you shall enjoy the spoil of your enemies which the Lord your God has given you.'"

Oh my God, Cockran realized with horror. "You mean...."

"Exactly. She wasn't to be killed. She was the spoil of war to be *enjoyed.* Your wife was on a list to be *shagged* by McBride, not shot,"

Smythe said, a leer on his face. "His men were to take their turn with her as well. The same with other wives and daughters of Free State supporters who needed to be taught a lesson. Make them realize they can't keep their own women's honor safe without the British Army. Your wife's honor certainly wasn't."

Smythe laughed once more through hate-filled eyes as Cockran struggled to process what the man was saying. "Stripped her bare and gave it to her good, I've heard. How does it feel to know that a low-life scum like McBride was the last man to sample the bliss of being inside your wife's lovely body? A blessing she died, wouldn't you agree? You know how the Irish love to gossip. The shame would have killed her if the IRA hadn't. Spot of good luck for you too, eh? Spared you from hearing his lads down at the pub swap stories over a pint about just how much your wife enjoyed McBride's shag, didn't it?

"Thomas did that with me, you know. Boasted that he bulled her from behind and left her moaning for more. Did her right in front of all his lads. What a sight that must have been, eh?"

Smythe exhaled smoke through his nose, his eyes never breaking contact. Cockran knew the British agent was only goading him into letting down his guard but he couldn't keep his rising fury under control. He had thought he would be cold and merciless like he had been in San Francisco. But he would settle for merciless.

"Not surprising, that. At least not to me. I mean McBride rogering her on all fours. Our Nora always liked it best from behind, don't you think? She did with me."

The Englishman's icy blue eyes never left Cockran whose finger tightened on the trigger. Nora in bed with Smythe? Smythe had to be lying but it didn't matter.

Smythe paused, a smile on his face now, but hate still in his eyes and matched by Cockran's own. "I chastised him, of course, when I learned your wife had been killed. A pity that. I understand his men were disappointed because it happened before they had taken their turn with her. Then I heard she went after them with a knife, cut two of them up pretty bad. And for what? A little harmless slap and tickle? I daresay that girl enjoyed a jolly romp in the sack as much as any man."

"Well, with such a savage display of ingratitude," Smythe said, waving his hand dismissively, the cigarette still between his fingers, "who could blame the lads when she forced them to act in self-defense? Besides, she made her choice when she married you. Protecting her virtue should have been *your* concern. It certainly wasn't mine. After all, what did one more dead Irish whore with a stranger's seed cooling in her belly matter to me?"

Cockran's trigger finger tensed, his mind filled with fury at the monster in front of him but Smythe flicked his burning cigarette directly at Cockran's face causing him to flinch as he fired. The gunshot was like thunder in the small cabin and Cockran knew the shot had missed. Smythe was on top of Cockran before he could fire a second time. Smythe slammed Cockran back into the seats and he lost hold of the Webley. The revolver fell between the two front facing wicker chairs and Smythe spun around to retrieve it. Just then, the co-pilot opened the cockpit door to see what had happened. Cockran dove at Smythe as his back was momentarily turned and the two men tumbled forward over the wicker seats, slamming into the co-pilot with full force and driving him back into the cockpit.

The aircraft lurched to the left in a steep bank, throwing Cockran hard into the cabin wall. He looked up and saw Smythe reaching for his own pistol. The pilot regained control of the plane and brought it back to an even keel and, as he did so, Cockran launched himself at Smythe, the force of their two bodies collapsing the backs of two wicker seats. Cockran grabbed Smythe's wrist and squeezed with all his strength, pressing his thumbs tightly into the man's wrist until he dropped the automatic. Then he swung his arm and slammed his left elbow down into Smythe's exposed neck.

Smythe let out a choking cry and Cockran moved to seize his advantage, picking Smythe up by his legs and shoving his entire body back through the passenger cabin doorway into the aircraft's cramped entry way. Smythe crashed into the side of the plane and the impact caused the aircraft's entrance door to fly open. Smythe, framed by the aircraft's open door, quickly regained his balance and reached down to a now-exposed ankle holster. Ignoring the rush of air from the outside, Cockran saw the Webley on the floor three feet away and dove back into the main cabin as Smythe fired and missed. Cockran scrambled on the floor for the Webley and, without standing up, fired two shots directly through the right rear wicker seat and the thin plywood behind it. Smythe cried out and Cockran cautiously returned to the entrance lobby.

Smythe was slumped on the floor, bleeding profusely. The small pistol from his ankle holster lay uselessly beside him. Both shots had torn into Smythe's right shoulder. His left hand clutched his wounded shoulder and his back was braced against the side of open door frame. Cockran kicked the pistol away from Smythe's reach. He knew he could safely close the aircraft's door, bind Smythe's shoulder and turn him over to the authorities when they landed. He also knew, as a lawyer, that Smythe's confession would never stand up in any court, American, English or Irish. The same for McBride's confession tortured from him by Bobby Sullivan. He had known all that from the moment Smythe stepped into the plane.

His rage abating, Cockran coldly confirmed his original decision. To make the bastard suffer. Nora once had been defenseless too, just as Smythe was now. He deserved the same mercy shown to her. He raised the Webley and fired a third shot, shattering Smythe's knee cap, pleased to hear him cry out in pain, tears flowing from his tightly closed eyes as he moved his left hand from his shoulder to clutch his ruined knee. A fitting punishment, Cockran thought, for someone in bed with the IRA. He waited patiently for a long thirty seconds until the other man opened his eyes. He wanted Smythe to see what came next. The hatred still blazed in the Englishman's eyes and now matched by Cockran's own as he braced himself with his left hand on the top of the door frame, his right hand on the side.

"Know your Bible, do you? How about 'an eye for an eye'?" Cockran shouted, making himself heard above the engines' noise. "Remember that you heartless bastard because vengeance is *mine* and not the Lord's!" he said as he kicked Smythe squarely in the chest.

Smythe screamed "No!" and reached with his left hand to grip the door frame just as Cockran kicked him again and saw in his now wide but still hate-filled eyes the knowledge that he was going to die as the impact of the second kick caused his left hand to slip off the door frame and then he was gone, the sky swallowing him up. Cockran held on tight, leaned out the door and watched. It was a long, slow fall.

73.

You've Got Some Good Points

Santa Monica
Saturday, 24 August 1929
9:00 p.m.

Cockran's father had been right. He had his revenge—or the bigger part of it—but it was all he had. He had felt empty after killing Smythe, missing Nora more than he had in years. Was there a chance for something more? He hadn't thought so before tonight but now perhaps there was. His arm was around Mattie as she snuggled close. They were sitting in a wicker love seat on the terrace in Marion Davies' seaside mansion, torch lights on either side and a breeze in their faces as they looked at the last fading glow of a Pacific sunset. Churchill sat in a wicker chair beside them, a large brandy in one hand, a cigar in the other, talking to Rankin.

Cockran had sat silently beside Mattie for the last ten minutes while the others talked, replaying in his mind their conversation an hour before when both were walking along the beach alone. He hadn't told her what he had learned from Smythe about all they had done to Nora nor her prior relationship with Smythe. His mind could barely process the thought. Had Nora actually been to bed with Smythe? He thought not but didn't discount the possibility entirely because she had been seeing him for nearly a year. For a good Irish Catholic girl, Nora had been remarkably free-spirited, a true woman of the post-war era. Like Mattie, a dedicated suffragette. With Smythe dead and McBride in custody, he had as much closure as he was going to get for Nora's death. Now, it was time to move on. Without Mattie. He was growing too fond of her. And, worse, she of him. It was time for the speech, time to stop being a cad. If he waited, it would only hurt her more.

Mattie had been silent as they walked, holding hands while he talked. He stared straight ahead, occasionally glancing down and noticing that her eyes were glistening, several tears streaming down her cheek. He had stopped and looked at her face for the first time. "You're one of a kind, Mattie, but Nora would always come between us and you deserve so much more than that. You need someone who will love only you because you are a woman who deserves to be loved."

Mattie laughed. That same laugh which had so captivated him only two short weeks ago, the laugh which had stolen his heart. Then she spoke. "No."

"No? What do you mean?" Cockran asked, confused. "You *are* a woman who…"

"Of course I am," she said, "but I'm also a big girl who makes up her own mind. I don't need a man to do that for me. We've only known each other two weeks and that's not long enough for me even if it is for you. Which I don't believe for a minute. Listen, I've not made up my mind about you. You've got some good points, mind you, including that cute birthmark on your ass. Plus you make me laugh and you're not half-bad in bed either, but we need more time to discover each other's flaws. I have a few but if you're like most men, you have many. So I intend to get to know you better before I make up my mind. When I do, I'll let you know."

Cockran was momentarily speechless. This had *never* happened before. True, he had never fallen so hard so fast for any woman before except Nora but he had lots of practice at this.

Mattie turned and took both of his hands in hers. "Cockran, I may be falling in love with you. I wouldn't have slept with you if I didn't think it were possible. I'm not that kind of girl. At least not any more," she said and Cockran thought she may have blushed but it was dark.

"Look, I'm 29 years old. Almost an old maid. I know you care for me because you were willling to risk your life to rescue me at Wyntoon. Whether you think you could love me doesn't matter right now. Eventually it will and if I fall in love with you but you don't with me, I'll move on and we'll still be friends. We're not at that point yet. When—or if—we are, I'll let you know that, too."

Cockran had shaken his head in disbelief. Had he lost his touch? It had been nearly three years since he broke it off with the Vanderbilt girl. But Cockran had not given in easily and he tried again. "I don't want to see you hurt. My feelings for Nora ..." but Mattie cut him off again.

"Give it a rest, Cockran. It's not going to work. I'm not going away until I've made up my mind about you. And when I do, Nora is not going to come between us. I know she'll always be the love of your life and I don't care. It's one of the things which makes you interesting. And special. As long as you keep Aquinas in mind, the two of you will spend eternity together. But make no mistake, you can love more than one person and I don't care if I'm second best."

Mattie paused and dropped one of his hands. "Let's keep walking," she said. "Bourke, you're not the only one who lost their first love. If the flaws we discover in each other aren't enough to keep us apart, then having the rest of our lives together is no small thing and your Nora will no more come between us than my fiancé Eric will. Even though we never married, Eric was my first, right before he left for the third Battle of Ypres ..." Mattie said, pausing and trying, unsuccessfully, to hold back more tears. She took off the necklace around her neck and handed it to him. "Open the locket" she said and he did.

Inside were small photographs of a striking young man whose dark curls could rival Byron and a young and very beautiful Mattie McGary whose long auburn locks were a match for her lover. A perfect couple. "Eric?" Cockran had asked.

Mattie nodded. "Eric Seale. I was only 17, too young to be officially engaged so he gave me this locket in early August, 1917. He died less than a month later at Passchendaele. I wore it every day for at least three years after he died but then I put it away. I'm not sure why. One of the things I first found so endearing about you, your reputation with married women notwithstanding, was that you still wore your wedding ring. I've always kept Eric's locket with me and after you and I were reunited, so to speak, in San Francisco, I decided it was time to start wearing his locket again to remind me that we've both lost our first loves and that life is fragile and nothing is guaranteed. Open the other side of the locket."

Cockran did and saw a folded packet of heavy bond paper. He unfolded the paper and saw a tracing that read "Lt. Eric R. Seale".

"It's from the Menin Gate Memorial at Ypres", Mattie had said. "Eric has no grave. Neither do 54,895 other British and Commonwealth soldiers whose bodies were never found when the battle was over. Their names are inscribed on the inside of the Gate. A military ceremony is still held there every night in their memory." Mattie said, tears again streaming down her face.

Cockran had taken Mattie in his arms and held her tightly, stroking her hair. They walked and talked for a long while after that, but Mattie was a stubborn woman and Cockran eventually came to the conclusion that she was not going to change her mind unless he lied to her and told her he had no feelings for her. But that would be a lie and Cockran couldn't do it. He couldn't lie to her. He was still his father's son in many ways. He had stopped and taken her hands in his. " I may have fallen in love with you as well. I don't know. It's been a long time."

"Good. That's settled then," Mattie had said. "We'll have lots of time to find out each other's bad points and I think we're going to have a good time doing it." She looked up at him with a smile. "You *will* keep shagging me silly, won't you? That *is* one of your better points

9:15 p.m.

In response to Churchill's question which interrupted his reverie, Cockran took a sip of scotch and recounted the series of admissions Smythe had made to him in the Trimotor's cabin. "Tell me, Winston," he asked, "Were you aware of Smythe's involvement? And if so, when?"

Churchill smiled and blew smoke from his cigar into the breeze. "I suspected Smythe ever since I was at the Colonial Office in '22. But we were out of power too soon after General Collins' death for me to do anything. Intelligence is a dirty business and Smythe was dirtier than most. I am surprised to hear that he had advance warning of Bloody Sunday and did nothing. But I'm not surprised to learn that he was collaborating with the IRA in the Irish Civil War. There are zealots in the North just as there are in the South, and the Free State is their common enemy. Smythe was one of them but I am afraid there are more where he came from."

Cockran squeezed Mattie's arm. "I know I was taking a chance with Smythe but I couldn't see him meekly surrendering in San Diego. I should have just shot him in the back when I had the chance and not endangered other people."

"No, Bourke, you did the right thing," Churchill said, his voice a low growl. "Shooting someone in the back is something no one should do unless they have no other choice."

"Mr. Churchill's right," Robert Rankin added. "That's why Mattie wouldn't leave you alone with McBride who certainly deserved to be shot in the back."

Cockran took a sip of scotch. "McBride. You know, ever since McGary here was captured," Cockran said, squeezing Mattie's shoulder once again, "—what is it dear, the third time in the last week?—I haven't given that bastard much thought. Where is he now? After the Apostles re-captured him, did you finally turn him over to the LAPD?"

"No," Rankin said. "I fear he has escaped once more."

Cockran jerked upright, moving his arm off Mattie's shoulder and slamming the crystal tumbler of scotch down on the table in front of him. "Escaped? When? How?" he asked, the anger in his voice barely contained, pain shooting through his left shoulder as his body tensed. With Smythe dead and McBride in custody, he had thought he was through with revenge.

Rankin nervously took a sip of water. "I guess I'm the one responsible, sir. Once Miss McGary was brought back to the hotel, Mr. O'Reilly told me there were a number of crimes McBride was wanted for back in Ireland, not the least of which was your wife's death. But there was all that paperwork involved in getting our Foreign Office to waive extradition for the attempt on Mr. Churchill's life, not to mention dealing with the LAPD who seemed to have their hands out for a bribe whenever you turned around. So Mr. O'Reilly asked me if they couldn't just take him. Just like we had let them question him. I told Mr. O'Reilly that interrogation was one thing but custody was something else entirely. I simply didn't have the authority to let him do that and I was certain Inspector Thompson did not either. And then Mr. O'Reilly asked me what would happen if McBride somehow escaped and made his way back to Ireland and trial? Would that pose any problems? I told him that my primary job was to provide security for Mr. Churchill. So I couldn't do much about what happened to an escaped prisoner, now could I?"

Cockran let out a long sigh and sank back into the wicker loveseat and felt Mattie put her arm around him. "So McBride has 'escaped' and O'Reilly is taking him back to Ireland?"

"Perhaps, but I can't be certain," Rankin said.

"Why is that?" Cockran asked.

Churchill interrupted. "I think I can explain. O'Reilly and the other four men with him have lost six of their comrades on this trip to America. As a consequence, they did not appear to be in a good frame of mind, notwithstanding their success at the warehouse two nights ago. Before the Free State, you know, many of them, possibly including Mr. O'Reilly, were members of that secret society known as the Irish Republican Brotherhood. There are trials and then there are secret trials. I advised Robert not to inquire too closely into what kind of trial Mr. O'Reilly had in mind."

Churchill took a puff on his cigar and laid it carefully in the ashtray beside him, then took a sip of brandy. He reached inside his coat and pulled out two envelopes. "By the way," he said to Cockran, "Mr. O'Reilly asked me to give you these. Something about settling old debts. He said you'd understand. Open this one first."

Cockran took the envelope which had his full name on it, W. Bourke Cockran, Jr. Inside was a handwritten note:

Bourke,

    I've never forgotten the promise Mick made that rainy night in Dublin on the day you buried your Nora. He reminded me of it when he left on his last trip to Cork. He made me pledge to honour it if he couldn't. All the Apostles tried, Bobby Sullivan more than most. But we failed. Fortune has blessed us with a second chance. So don't you be worrying. We won't fail again. By the time we're done, the Big Fella will have kept his word to his last Apostle.

Joe

Cockran passed the note to Mattie and opened the second envelope. Mattie's head was on his shoulder as he unfolded the single sheet of paper inside, its contents illuminated by the two torches flaming above them:

Mr. Cockran,

    I regret things didn't turn out the other day as you and I had wanted. While it's a poor substitute, you might wish to join the rest of us on a small fishing trip I have planned in San Diego. I'll make sure we wait at least four days before we go ahead without you. We will be staying at the Harborside Hotel. Please come. You won't be disappointed.

Respectfully,
Robert Sullivan

Cockran, blinking back tears, looked up and passed the second note to Mattie, then turned to the others. "Thank you, Winston. Robert. I understand. You did the right thing. The Apostles have waited a long time for this. The Big Fella would've been pleased. So am I."

Cockran placed his hand on Mattie's shoulder and said in a mock Irish brogue. "And could you be sparing my company for a day of fishing with Bobby and Joe and the rest of the lads?"

"Go to it, Cockran," Mattie said, leaning close and kissing him on his cheek. "But remember. It's their play not yours," she whispered in his ear. "He's no longer a threat. Look but don't touch. Remember your Aquinas. You've got a date with Nora that I don't want you to miss."

Cockran smiled and whispered back. "Aquinas? Oh, yes, I remember him. Didn't we discuss him the same night you promised my virtue was safe with you?"

Cockran winced in silence as Mattie brought the heel of her sandal sharply down on his instep.

74.

Top Of The Morning To You, Tommy

San Diego, California
Sunday, 25 August 1929
8:00 a.m.

His bonds were getting looser. McBride had been in a dingy hotel on the waterfront for the past three days and two nights. They kept him bound and gagged but he was otherwise alone in the room. They fed him only once a day but they had stopped torturing him and he was gradually recovering his strength.

The last two times they retied him, he had tensed the muscles in his wrists and forearms. If he worked at it, he thought he could be free in a few hours. His captors, five in number, had rooms on either side of him as well as the one O'Reilly stayed in across the hall. He assumed there was a guard in front of his room at all times, but he couldn't be sure. All he knew was that every morning, the housekeeper asked if she should make up the beds and there was always a man there to respond, "Not today, sweet. Our mate has a terrible hangover once again."

This morning, McBride was surprised when he heard a timid knock on the door, a key being inserted, and then the door opened. A middle-aged woman wearing a threadbare housekeeper's dress entered, a bundle of linens on her arm.

"Excuse me," she said, and started to back out. McBride motioned her over with his head, shouting through the gag, "Please help me."

The woman, with flecks of gray in her hair and apprehension filling her round brown face, carefully approached and untied McBride's gag.

"Thank you, sister. And isn't it a good deed you've done for me this fine morning?"

8:05 a.m.

Joe O'Reilly cleared his throat with a little cough, gaining the others' attention. "The trial is over. We need to move on to the sentencing. Protocol calls for a firing squad. Somehow, I don't believe that would be meeting with the American authorities' approval. As the presiding officer of the court which convicted him, I'm open to suggestions."

O'Reilly nodded as Dermot raised his hand. "Let's do him like he did John Devoy. Flat on the floor and stick a bullet in his ear." O'Reilly noticed several men silently nod approval.

Hugh O'Donnell quickly spoke up. "A bullet in the brain is too clean and quick for the likes of Tommy McBride. I say we stick a pole up his arse till it comes out his mouth and then roast him slowly over a bonfire on the beach."

O'Reilly laughed along with his men. "And wouldn't you be thinking that McBride has that waiting for him in eternity anyway? The local fathers wouldn't approve a bonfire that big."

Even before the trial, knowing that a firing squad was not feasible, O'Reilly had been giving thought as to how Tommy McBride should die. The problem was, Joe really wasn't a killer. He had been Mick's assistant, not an Apostle. That is why O'Higgins had put him in charge when he reconstituted the Squad. "You're a bright lad, Joe," Kevin had said. "You were always at the Big Fella's side. You had to have learned something even if, like me, you didn't shoot anyone." But he hadn't learned enough, O'Reilly thought, to come up with a suitable death for Tommy McBride.

O'Reilly had heard the Big Fella promise Cockran that McBride's death would not be easy. But what the hell did Mick mean by that?

O'Reilly didn't know. He wished he did.

O'Reilly looked over at Bobby Sullivan, who was sitting wordlessly in the corner, his face expressionless. He hadn't forgotten that Bobby had been the first one to offer Cockran a weapon back in Los Angeles after McBride had confessed to killing Cockran's wife.

"Bobby, would you be having any suggestions?"

"Aye, I would. Thanks for asking. I've got ideas both as to how. And who. Let's discuss the 'who' first. Because if I can't persuade you that I'm the one to do it, you can all go to hell and figure out your own way. Agreed?"

The other men murmured and O'Reilly said, "Go ahead, we'll hear you out."

"I have an older sister named Mary. She lives alone now in Dublin. Waits tables at Bewley's. But when she was married, she still lived in Donegal. There was a bank robbery. She was taken hostage by Tommy McBride and his gang. Raped by all of them. Thank the Lord, we got her back but she was never the same. The doctor said she must have been barely four weeks pregnant when it happened but, after McBride and his boys finished with her, she lost the child a month later and couldn't have more. Donegal Town is not a large place. Everyone knew what happened to her. Her husband was Joe Flaherty. The craven bastard told me he couldn't bear all the whispering behind their backs. Said it was always worse for the man when it happened to his woman. Imagine! *He* couldn't bear it! What did he think Mary was going through? So they moved to Dublin and within six months her husband left her and moved to America. Bought himself an annulment. Claimed they never lived as man and wife. That's one of the reasons I signed up for this mission, Joe. I won't be traveling back with you boys. Not before I make a little side trip to Detroit to pay my respects to my former brother-in-law."

O'Reilly watched as Bobby Sullivan smiled for the first time in a long while. A cold smile. He knew all the Apostles were killers, but he never wanted that smile directed at him.

"Tommy McBride is an unexpected bonus and wouldn't I be kicking myself if I passed up the chance to take care of him as well? So, is it agreed? Am I his executioner?"

O'Reilly looked at the other three. "All those in favor, raise your right hand."

Four hands shot into the air as one and O'Reilly said "It's unanimous. Now, tell us how."

Bobby smiled again, a smile that made you glad you weren't his former brother-in-law.

"And would you be up for some fishing with an old sailor I met the other day from Donegal?

8:15 a.m.

Tommy McBride looked down at the unconscious housekeeper. The dumb biddy had said she was going to tell her hotel manager about the poor man kept bound in his room. He had grabbed her from behind and choked her until she passed out. She was breathing evenly now but she would stay silent for a while. From the laughter through the thin walls, he thought they were all in the next room. Soon, a guard would be reposted outside his room. Fortunately for him, they had not taken his wallet. He didn't expect there were taxis in this part of town but if he could steal a motorcar and make his way to the train station, he was home free.

McBride checked his appearance in the cracked mirror. He winced. The ugly red blotches on his face were almost gone but one of his eyes was still half closed. He looked like he had come out on the short end of a bar room brawl. On the waterfront, he just might fit in.

McBride quietly opened the door and cautiously peered out, looking both ways. He quietly closed the door behind him and walked softly down the hall. When he reached the exit door and opened it, he abandoned all caution, tearing down the steps two at a time. He went from the third floor to the first in less than thirty seconds. Slightly out of breath, he paused to regain his composure before stepping out into the dingy, threadbare lobby.

"Your key, sir?" the desk clerk said as McBride walked to the hotel's front entrance.

"My friends are still upstairs. I left the key with them. They'll be down soon."

Five steps later and McBride was free. The skies outside were overcast and a light drizzle was falling. McBride turned up the collar of his shirt, pulled his soft cap lower and began his search for a motorcar. His search was soon rewarded. One block away from the waterfront, he found a beat-up Model A pick-up truck parked just off the street in a dimly-lit alley.

In the rain, no one else was around. The truck driver was doubtless inside the small bar one door down. The only establishment which showed any signs of life. McBride was pleased. Luck was with him. Maybe the keys would even be in the truck. It didn't matter. Crossing the ignition wires would pose no problem. McBride had done it before.

The truck's engine coughed to life and McBride eased in the clutch and moved the truck slowly forward. McBride was ten feet from the alley's end when a large black Chevrolet pulled to a halt, blocking the alley. His eyes widened in fear when the driver's door opened and a man stepped out, a silenced automatic pistol in his right hand. He remembered well those cold blue eyes, that hard face, that broken nose. McBride knew that even if that merciless bastard were cutting his heart out, his expression would never change. He didn't know why he believed that. He just knew he was lucky to be alive after the same man had caught him escaping. He also knew he never wanted to be alone in the same room with him again. Ever.

His hands frozen to the wheel, McBride watched as he walked up to the truck.

"Top of the morning to you, Tommy," he said in a flat, neutral tone. "We missed you. We had a special treat planned. Keep your hands in plain sight and step down from the truck."

McBride did so and then it happened. He hadn't believed it possible. The man smiled. McBride shivered. He couldn't explain why but he wanted him to stop smiling.

75.

I Wasn't At No Bloody Trial

Pacific Ocean off San Diego
Sunday, 25 August 1929
11:00 a.m.

Tommy McBride awoke with a splitting headache. He shook his head to clear the cobwebs but it only made his headache worse. His arms were bound behind him. His feet were tied as well. He was wearing some kind of life preserver. It was bulky and the collar kept him from resting his head against the wall. As his thoughts began to clear, he could see he was below decks in some kind of boat. His senses returning, he noticed that it reeked of fish.

The hold of the boat was dimly lit through several grimy portholes. He heard a noise and then a hatch opened, sunlight streamed in and one of the bloody Free Staters came down the ladder. He severed the bonds around his ankles and roughly pushed him up the ladder. It was a glorious day. A high blue sky, temperature in the high-seventies, a light breeze at ten to fifteen miles per hour. McBride squinted, adjusting his eyesight to bright sunlight. McBride could see he was on a fishing trawler that had endured many years of hard service.

The other four members of Michael Collins' old Squad were assembled at the stern of the vessel. Joe O'Reilly and his captor from that morning were standing near the stern of the boat talking to two others McBride didn't know. The other two men were reaching into a bucket tossing large chunks of raw meat over the side of the boat. The man behind him pushed McBride roughly forward, bringing him to a halt.

O'Reilly spoke first. "Tommy McBride, you have been tried and found guilty in a court martial convened by the Irish Republican Brotherhood for the murder of John Devoy."

"What trial?" McBride asked. "I wasn't at no bloody trial."

"The prisoner will remain silent while sentence is passed or I will have you gagged," O'Reilly said in a quiet voice. "You have also been tried and found guilty for the rape and murder of Nora Cockran, the wife of a member of the Squad."

"Go on, you're joking. When was that bastard ever a member of your murder gang?"

McBride's headache intensified as a big fist reached around from behind him and cuffed him hard on the side of his head. "That's your last warning, boyo." Bobby Sullivan said.

O'Reilly resumed speaking. "Finally, you have been tried and convicted for the rape of Mary Flaherty, the sister of a member of the Squad."

"Who the fuck would she be? I can't be responsible for every Irish lass who drops her knickers and invites me inside. Besides, it's not rape if they enjoy it and I'll bet she did. I know I brought Cockran's whore off and I'll wager I did the same with Mary whatshername."

McBride howled as he felt a searing pain in his right thigh. He looked down at a thin metal rod protruding from the middle of his leg attached to a thin filament. He looked up to see the man with a broken nose smiling at him. In agony, he watched while the man calmly placed another spear into the front of a long pistol-like device.

"The sentence, Joe, the sentence. Let's hear it. I've got work to do," the man said.

"The sentence for each crime is death in the manner chosen by the designated executioner which, in your case, Tommy, is Bobby Sullivan."

McBride chilled. It couldn't be. It just couldn't be. Yet, he thought through the pain, he dimly remembered that the bank manager in Donegal had been named Michael Sullivan, a prominent Free State supporter. They had robbed his bank two weeks after the job in Galway. Mrs Flaherty, the bank manager's newly wed daughter, was the second woman on Blackthorn's list and McBride's second Free State spoil, his first shag after the Cockran woman. Once he had taken his turn with her, he had urged the others on, telling them with a laugh, "Have at her, boys. There's plenty of room left in the banker's daughter. Her treasure vault is wide open to take more deposits." McBride felt his bladder release once it dawned on him that Mary Flaherty's maiden name was Sullivan, the same name as the cold-eyed, spear gun-wielding Apostle in front of him.

"Move him to the edge," Sullivan directed. "Make sure his wrists are secured."

The trawler had slowed to five knots and McBride could hear Bobby Sullivan clearly. "I've been doing some reading in the last few days, Tommy. About the fish in these waters. There's tuna, dolphin, swordfish. Even sharks. People are afraid of sharks, you know that, Tommy? They think sharks attack humans. But that's really not true. Sharks only feed on other fish. They never sleep. They don't attack humans as a rule unless they mistake you for a fish. Or, possibly, if you're bleeding from a wound."

McBride chilled again and looked down at the growing red stain on his pant leg..

"I've also read," Sullivan continued, "that a shark attack is relatively painless."

Sullivan smiled. "And wouldn't you want to be knowing why? It seems that the first chunk they take out of you, your system goes into shock, and you're numb after that. But I also read that this doesn't always happen if your system has suffered an injury before the shark attack. In that event, your system is already dealing with the initial injury so that any more damage simply intensifies the pain."

McBride watched in horror as he saw the face of Bourke Cockran appear beside Bobby Sullivan who turned and offered the spear gun to him. My god, no! McBride thought.

"Thanks, Bobby," Cockran said quietly, "but this is your show. Anything I'd do would be too quick and painless. Besides, Joe told me about your sister. You go ahead."

Sullivan nodded and, with no further warning, fired the spear gun once more. McBride screamed in agony again as the spear point ripped into the tender area where his groin merged into the top of his right thigh. More blood spurted.

"It's time to go shark hunting, boys," Sullivan said. "Toss him over the side. I think he's bleeding enough now but get more raw meat out of the storage locker and toss it overboard with him, just in case."

McBride pleaded with the others to shoot him; to let him die now. Cockran turned his back. The only reply was Bobby Sullivan's cold voice, "You lived like an animal, McBride. Now die like one. Do it, boys."

The water was surprisingly warm, McBride thought as he landed on his back, sunk beneath the surface and bobbed back up. Once he did, the collar of the life preserver cushioned his head and kept it tilted at an angle out of the water. He watched as the trawler slowly turned and headed back toward the distant shore. He shouted for them to stop; to come back. To let him die like a man. But, in only ten minutes, the trawler was a distant speck on the horizon and Tommy McBride was alone. The last two human faces he saw were Bobby Sullivan and Bourke Cockran standing at the trawler's stern, both men staring at him with open, cold and expressionless eyes.

McBride floated on his back in the placid sea. The salt water coming in contact with the wounds from his dual impalement increased his pain. With his hands tied behind him, he could do nothing; he was helpless; all he could do was float there, bleed and wait. It seemed like forever since they had left him. The sun beat down on him and his lips were parched and cracked. Once, he blacked out, only to awaken with a start, fresh pain reminding him where he was.

McBride was surprised he never saw the shark's fin. Instead, he was startled when he felt a bump, and then another. The third time wasn't a bump. It was a bite, but much more than a bite. A large, flesh-rending tear which ripped away a good portion of his upper leg. Sullivan had been right. His system didn't shut down with shock.

And the pain, which he thought he couldn't bear before, only intensified as a second shark joined the first.

No one heard him scream.

3:30 p.m.

Cockran stood at the boat's stern looking back. The sun was lower in the sky. Sullivan had walked away and the other men kept their distance, sensing his need to be alone. It was over, he thought, at last it was over. Perhaps the healing could begin again. Without the infection of McBride and Smythe beneath, the scar tissue this time should be stronger. He thought of his father who had lost two young wives. The second, Cockran's mother, had died giving birth to him. But his father had loved the son whose birth caused her death, even though his heart had been broken. Eventually his heart healed and twelve years later he married Anne Ide, a good woman, the wife who had finally outlived him. Nora was gone only seven years now. He had his revenge at last. But more importantly, he now realized, he had time for Mattie to decide if his good points outweighed the bad. With revenge out of the way, he had time to accomplish something more with Mattie. He had his father's example to follow.

For the first time in a long time, Cockran felt light-hearted. It was only three more weeks until Paddy came home. He couldn't wait. They had sand castles to build. He hoped Mattie would be there with them. A Scot should know all about castles.

76.

He Didn't Finish The Scone

Dublin, Ireland
Friday, 27 September 1929
8:30 a.m.

A tall, gaunt man, wearing a dark suit and wire-rimmed spectacles, sat alone in a corner in the back room at Bewley's enjoying a full Irish breakfast served by his favorite waitress, Mary Sullivan, a bright ray of sunshine who always seemed so cheerful and happy no matter how gloomy the day outside. Bacon, sausage, fried eggs, tomatoes, toast, marmalade and a scone he was saving to conclude the meal, all accompanied by a pot of Irish breakfast tea. He was more than mildly concerned. He was agitated. He should have heard something before now. He should have heard something at least two, if not three, weeks before. He wasn't certain how next to proceed, but he knew something had to be done. Four million dollars was a serious matter.

"I don't want to spoil your breakfast but I thought you might find this interesting."

Eamon de Valera stopped his fork in midflight, placed the bite of egg back on the nearly empty plate beside the still untouched scone, and looked up into the face of Kurt von Sturm.

"You! What are you doing here?" de Valera asked.

Sturm smiled. "I'm on holiday. I plan to do a spot of fishing. Ireland is such a beautiful country in the fall. Don't you agree?"

"Where is my money?" de Valera asked. "Where is McBride?"

"As to the former question, I don't know. I saw it last in California when I delivered four million dollars in gold bearer bonds to your man McBride. Here," Sturm said, "is the receipt he gave me."

De Valera accepted the sheet of paper and inspected it closely. It was McBride's signature.

"But as to your latter question," Sturm continued smoothly, "I can certainly answer that. It's there in the newspaper clipping I laid beside your plate."

Sturm sat down at the table and looked de Valera in the eye. "Things did not go as well in America as we planned. I'm here to remind you that my colleagues expect you to keep our business dealings confidential. They would be most disturbed if you discussed them with anyone. Don't disappoint them. I'm on holiday now. You wouldn't like me to return here on business."

De Valera watched as Sturm pushed his chair back and rose from the table, gave him a small salute with two fingers, turned and walked away. He turned his attention to the small newspaper clipping Sturm had placed beside his plate. It was from the *Los Angeles Herald Examiner* dated 6 September 1929. The headline caught his attention: SHARK ATTACK NEAR SAN DIEGO. He never made it past the article's second sentence:

> The legless torso of a tourist washed ashore near San Diego today, the apparent victim of a shark attack. Authorities identified the victim as an Irish citizen, Thomas F. McBride....

De Valera felt an uncontrollable reaction as his insides heaved and he threw up on the plate the full Irish breakfast his system had barely begun to digest.

He didn't finish the scone.

77.

Sand Castles

Barstow, California
Saturday, 28 September 1929
2:00 p.m.

Winston Churchill sat on the railway hotel's terrace and squinted out at the early afternoon sun, a glass of champagne beside him.

My darling Clemmie,
We are traveling across the Californian desert in Mr. Schwab's railway car, & we have stopped for 2 hours at this oasis. We have left the train for a bath in the hotel, & I will write you a few of the things it is wiser not to dictate.

Hearst was most interesting to meet, & I got to like him—a grave simple child —with no doubt a nasty temper—playing with the most costly toys. A vast income always overspent: Ceaseless building & collecting not vy discriminatingly works of art: two magnificent establishments, two charming wives; complete indifference to public opinion, a strong liberal & democratic outlook, a 15 million daily circulation, oriental hospitalities, extreme personal courtesies & the appearance of a Quaker elder—or perhaps Mormon elder.

At Los Angeles (hard g) we passed into the domain of Marion Davies; & were all charmed by her. She is not strikingly beautiful nor impressive in any way. But her personality is most attractive; naive, childlike, bon enfant.

She works all day at her films & retires to her palace on the ocean to bathe & entertain in the evenings. She asked us to use her house as if it was our own.

Our little "adventure" of which I have been keeping you posted concluded happily earlier this month. The cargo we were so concerned about met an untimely end in an exceptionally large explosion. And Smythe ended up falling out of an airplane. Imagine that! Otherwise, everything was uneventful. Nice luncheon in Hollywood for those Graf Zeppelin chaps and their passengers. .

I have also made friends with Mr Van Antwerp & his wife. He is a gt friend of England and a reader of all my books—quite an old fashioned figure—He is going to look after some of my money for me. His stockbroking firm have the best information about the American market & I have opened an account with them in wh I have placed £3,000. He will manipulate it with the best possible chances of success. All this looks vy confiding—but I am sure it will prove wise.

Now I have to rush for my train wh is just off.

Goodbye my sweetest Clemmie
With tender love from your devoted
W

£3,000, Churchill thought. A few articles for his new patron, W. R. Hearst. With any luck and if his imagination didn't fail him, he could crank out at least five more articles before he returned to England. At this rate, he would soon be the highest paid journalist in the world. There were worse things, he thought, than being out of office. Out of money was far worse.

The Cedars
Sands Point, Long Island
Sunday, 29 September 1929
4:00 p.m.

It was a perfect early autumn afternoon as Mattie McGary sat in a low-slung canvas chair, nursing a gin and tonic, a copy of the September 6 *Los Angeles Herald Examiner* on the sand beside her, watching Bourke and Paddy Cockran build a sand castle on the beach in front of her.

Up at the house, Cockran's mother-in-law, Mary Morrisey, was setting the table on the patio which looked out over Long Island Sound. Bill Donovan and his wife, Ruth, were coming to dinner and Cockran was going to grill steaks.

"It's the least you can do, you ungrateful bastard," Mattie had heard Donovan say when Cockran had extended the invitation over the phone, his voice easily carrying to where Mattie stood behind Cockran. "Do you know how many favors I had to call in to get that arrest warrant lifted? It was all I could do to keep a straight face when I gave them that bogus affidavit from McBride confessing to Devoy's murder. Not all Irish cops are as dumb as their reputation."

Cockran had laughed. "I know I owe you more than a steak dinner, Bill, but it will have to do for now. Besides, I want Mattie to meet your Ruth. Mattie should see it's possible for a Protestant girl to fall in love with a Catholic boy."

Mattie smiled. She watched as Bourke used a shovel to build up a large pile of sand, three feet wide and three feet high. Paddy then walked a few yards into the surf, filled a pail of water and returned it to his father, who poured it onto the sand pile. The process was repeated until the pile had received four full buckets of water. The two boys—and yes, Mattie thought to herself, Bourke really was a big Irish boy, too, just like his son—proceeded to pat the pile with their hands, firming it up. After that, Bourke used a straight edge to level off the top of the sand pile, leaving a flat surface. He twice made a trip to the surf where he filled a pail with wet sand, tightly packed. He twice brought the pail back to the sand pile and placed the pail upside down on the pile's level surface and carefully removed the pail, each time leaving a thick cylinder of sand behind. Using the straight edge, he converted the two squat cylinders into square towers. He used a bread knife to make indentations for the narrow windows. Using a large funnel which he filled with wet sand, Paddy then placed cupolas on top of each tower.

"You don't actually build sand castles," Bourke had explained to her before they started. "Mostly, you carve them." She watched as Bourke and Paddy set to work on either side of the pile, each using a straight edge and a spatula to carve terraces and stairways leading down from the twin towers. They took their time, clearly enjoying themselves, each pausing occasionally to ask the other to come over to his side of the castle and admire the curving staircase here, an elaborate balcony there.

Mattie smiled again and sighed. She missed her family. Two brothers lost in the war. Then Eric. Her parents soon after. She had kept the family estate near Skye but rarely went there. She had made no home elsewhere, a small one-bedroom apartment in Edinburgh the only place from which her mail was received and forwarded. She knew she could love this man. It wouldn't be that difficult. But to do so, she had to let down the defenses she had so carefully built up, brick by brick, over the years. Could she do that? Could she be content with the same man and stop moving, in one sense at least, from one *aventure* to another? And if she could do that, would Bourke accept a woman whose work took her all over the world, often without much notice? A woman who could scarcely bear not being in control? Who valued deeply her freedom, her independence, her privacy? Who despised boredom and secretly thrilled each time an assignment exposed her to danger? She honestly didn't know. But she would think about it.

"Mattie, come on down and help us finish," she heard Cockran call to her.

"Yes, Mattie, please come," Paddy said, now standing beside her chair, holding out his hand. "We finished two sides of the castle. And we've got two more to go. You can help me do one side while Dad finishes the other. Ours will be a lot better than his."

Mattie smiled as she took the young boy's hand and rose from her chair and followed him down to the sand castle. Cockran's good points were beginning to outweigh his bad. Yes, she would definitely think about it.

Epilogue
Munich, 1930

Hitler offered something to almost every German voter in 1930—the farmer, the worker, the student, the patriot, the racist and the middle-class burgher. The common denominator of his wide appeal was the world depression which had followed the Wall Street crash of 1929 and abruptly ended Germany's remarkable recovery.

John Toland,
Adolf Hitler

In the most remarkable result in German parliamentary history, the NSDAP advanced at one stroke from the twelve seats and mere 2.6 per cent of the vote gained in the 1928 Reichstag election, to 107 seats at 18.3 per cent, making it the second largest party in the Reichstag. Almost 6.5 million Germans now voted for Hitler's party—eight times as many as two years earlier. The Nazi bandwagon was rolling.

Ian Kershaw,
Hitler, 1889–1936: Hubris

K urt von Sturm was the first there. He made his way to the rear of the heavily-timbered old coffee house, the smoke-filled Café Heck, and took his seat at the familiar scarred wooden table. A year had passed since his return from America. Much had happened. More was to come. Now, they would begin to change history. Germany would soon have its revenge..

On the surface, many things remained the same. He was still Fritz von Thyssen's chief assistant at the United Steel Works; he still served as the Executive Director of the Geneva Group; and a special committee appointed by Zurich had absolved him of any personal responsibility for his failure to recover Geneva's $4 million from the IRA.

In other respects, everything was different. The invasion of Poland was dead, consigned to the ash heap of history. The Geneva Group had been of two minds, debating the wisdom of proceeding in the face of the failure of the Free State *coup d'etat*. Then Stalin made the decision for them. An inherently conservative man, Stalin was also a patient one. He would take no risks with Poland. If Marx and Lenin were right, capitalist democracy was doomed anyway and Poland, no longer a democracy herself, would eventually drop into their hands like a ripe fruit.

When the Reichstag was dissolved in mid-July, von Thyssen— Berlin—had given Sturm a fully paid eight-week leave of absence to work in the national election campaign which ended yesterday. Berlin had assured him that both he and Munich had given their blessing and that no one from Geneva would know. So now Sturm waited, eager for the future to begin.

He heard the applause first, from the front of the coffee house, followed by the cries and shouts of encouragement. It was time. Sturm rose to his feet as the noise continued to grow.

Adolf Hitler had arrived.

The usual entourage was with him—Joseph Goebbels, Hermann Goering, Rudolph Hess, Ernst Hanfstaengl—but Sturm ignored them, greeting only Hitler, captured once again by the piercing blue eyes which held his gaze, making him feel as if he were the most important person in the world to this man. And, on this day, perhaps he was.

"Good to see you, Kurt," Hitler said, extending a pasty white hand, his piercing blue eyes focused on Sturm. "Have you recovered from your celebration last night? You should follow my example. No alcohol. You won't be young forever."

Sturm smiled. "Yes, my *Führer*. But it was a special time. We had reason to celebrate."

Hitler chuckled. "I agree. There was much to celebrate. And you deserve more of the credit than most. Before you, nothing seemed possible. After you, everything came our way. You're exactly what Putzi needed. A real German to keep the foreign journalists under control."

"Thank you, my *Führer*," Sturm said.

Hitler went on as if Sturm had not spoken, his voice rising above the din created by the other patrons, his tone euphoric. "Think of it. We held 34,000 meetings all over Germany in the last four weeks. I gave twenty speeches myself. 16,000 in Berlin. 30,000 in Breslau."

Hitler paused, wiped a trickle of spittle from the corner of his mouth, and resumed his monologue. "Money. All we needed was money to get my message to the people. And the people did the rest. An eightfold increase in our vote from 1929. Think of it. 6.5 million Germans voted for me. Only 12 seats before and now we have 107 seats in the Reichstag!"

Hitler looked over at his small Propaganda Chief. "Even Goebbels was surprised, weren't you Joseph? Last April he thought he was an optimist when he predicted 40 seats. Not me. I knew better. I told you so."

Hitler turned to Ernst Hanfstaengl, the tall American-born, Harvard-educated Foreign Press Chief of the National Socialist German Workers' Party, "Isn't that true, Putzi? Didn't I say 100 seats in my speech on 20 August?"

"Yes, *Herr* Hitler," Hanfstaengl responded.

Not really, Sturm thought to himself. With his command of English solidified by his sojourn last year in America, Sturm had been appointed Putzi's assistant during the eight-week campaign. Privately, Hitler had told Hanfstaengl and Sturm he only expected 30 to 40 seats.

Hitler took a sip of mineral water and continued. "We are the second largest party in Germany. Even the foreign press pays attention to us. Here, Kurt", Hitler said, "read to us from this English paper. Putzi says it is favorable but you can't always trust a half-American."

All but Hanfstaengl joined in the laughter as Hitler passed over to Sturm yesterday's edition of London's *Daily Mail* and he began reading the article to the group, translating to German as he read. "The article is by Rothay Reynolds. It says that 'Hitler spoke with great simplicity and with great earnestness. There was not a trace in his manner of those arts which political leaders are apt to employ when they wish to impress. I was conscious that I was talking to a man whose power lies not, as many still think, in his eloquence and in his ability to hold the attention of the mob, but in his conviction.'"

Sturm paused but, before he could resume reading, Hitler interrupted and started to speak again in a rising, compelling voice. All at the table turned their heads away from Sturm and back to Hitler. Others in the coffee house stopped their conversation and strained to hear.

"Yes, conviction," Hitler said. "Conviction. He understands. I am not a politician who makes empty campaign promises to entice people with their own selfish interests. I offer a program, a gigantic new program behind which must stand not a new government but a new German people. No longer a mixture of classes and professions but a community of people who will overcome their differences and rescue the common strength of the nation."

An attractive, blonde-haired waitress approached the table and offered to clear but, with a smile, Hitler gently turned her away. "What we promise," Hitler continued, "is not material improvement for the individual but an increase in the strength of the nation, because only this shows the way to power and with it the liberation of the entire German people."

Hitler paused. He locked eyes with everyone at the table, going from face to face. Goebbels. Goering. Hanfstaengl. Hess. And, finally, Sturm. "It's true," Hitler said. "It's true. We are less than three years away. Three years. Does anyone doubt?"

The entire coffee house was silent. Hitler had been speaking in a conversational tone but his words carried to adjacent tables. A few started to applaud and soon the entire room was on its feet cheering the man of the moment. Hitler acknowledged their applause with a modest wave of his hand. His chair scraped the wooden floor as Hitler rose to leave, motioned the others at the table to stay seated and invited Kurt to join him. He slowly made his way to the front of the restaurant pausing at tables, shaking hands, signing autographs, accepting well wishes.

Outside, the afternoon sun had broken through the dark clouds of an approaching storm. Hitler paused and pulled the brim of his soft felt hat lower on his head. "I was too pessimistic this time," Hitler said in a quiet voice. "I set my sights too low. You know I thought 30 seats were the most we could hope for." Hitler tightened the belt on his trench coat and walked down the tree-lined street, his bodyguards in front of him, Sturm beside him and the rest of his entourage now bringing up the rear.

"For the first time, Kurt, I truly can see success within our grasp," Hitler said. They reached Hitler's Mercedes. His chauffeur held the rear door open as Hitler turned to Sturm and and spoke in a surprisingly quiet voice. "We will achieve our aim with constitutional means. We shall gain decisive majorities in the legislative bodies at all levels so that the moment we succeed, we can give the state the form that corresponds to our ideas."

"That is all I ever wanted, my *Führer*. To atone for the shame of those terrible days after the war," Sturm said.

"You have nothing to atone for, Kurt. You were one of our heroes then. More of a hero than even our Hermann with his Blue Max because you had your own. But now, you are so much more. Once we succeed—and we will succeed—you will be hailed as a savior."

Hitler sat back in the open motorcar's back seat and smiled. "Von Sturm the savior. Or, very soon, von Strasser the savior. The others can't be told now. Your current position is too critical. But the day we take power, all will know. The four million dollars in gold bearer bonds you brought us from America made all the difference. I shall never forget. And that means Germany will never forget."

Hitler reached out, grasped Sturm's hand in his, pulled the younger man close, and whispered in his ear. "It won't take us three years," said Hitler. "Only two. Be prepared, Kurt. In two years' time, Germany will come to me. The people shall once again know your name and we shall do great things together."

"Thank you, my *Führer*," Sturm replied.

"The 1918 revolution will be avenged, my young friend, and heads will roll. Then, all of Germany will have its revenge."

Sturm watched as the Mercedes drove away, outlined against the afternoon sun, until it disappeared in the shadows of the trees. Yes, he thought. Revenge. His father would be proud and Germany at last would have its revenge.

Historical Note

*T*he *De Valera Deception* is a work of fiction but there are historical facts which provide a foundation and framework for the story.

Winston Churchill. It's not the first time nor will it be the last that Churchill will be cast as a key character in an historical thriller. In fact, you might say Winston did so himself in his 1897 romantic adventure novel, *Savrola,* where a hero strongly resembling Churchill overthrows an evil dictator in a mythical European country and steals the love of the dictator's beautiful wife in the bargain.

Churchill's detractors, of which there was no shortage before 1940, called him an "adventurer", a "half-breed American" and a "swashbuckler". He was all these things and more. In addition to fighting Islamic warriors on the Afghan-Indian border and in the Sudan in the late 1890s, bloody no-quarter battles where Churchill killed many men at close range, he also accepted in 1900 the surrender of the Boer prisoner of war camp in South Africa from which he had escaped the previous year. A crack shot, he bagged a rare white rhino in Africa in 1908, drawing the admiration and envy of Theodore Roosevelt who tried to do the same but was not so fortunate. He became a seaplane pilot in the early 1910s after being appointed at age 38 the First Lord of the British Admiralty and survived more than one crash landing in that pioneering era's flimsy aircraft. In the First World War, while stationed in the same Ypres salient where Corporal Adolf Hitler also served, the two future adversaries drew sketches in their spare time of the same bombed-out Belgian church. Contrary to some views, Hitler was a talented artist but Churchill was better, a gifted Impressionist whose works anonymously won awards.

Churchill's 1929 North American Holiday. Churchill took a three month holiday in North America in the summer of 1929 with his brother and their two sons at approximately the same time as portrayed in *The De Valera Deception.* Churchill wrote articles for William Randolph Hearst and was a guest at both his palatial home in San Simeon and Marion Davies' seaside mansion in Santa Monica. He was present in October, 1929 on Wall Street on Black Tuesday and was badly damaged financially by the Crash.

Bourke Cockran (1854-1923). Churchill's real-life Irish-American mentor, both a political and oratorical role model, was the prominent turn-of-the-century New York lawyer, statesman and Congressman William Bourke Cockran whose fictional son's exploits (Cockran was childless) are depicted in *The De Valera Deception* and subsequent Winston Churchill Thrillers. Everything said by Churchill and others about Cockran in the book is accurate. A Democrat and close adviser to President Grover Cleveland, he was acclaimed by members of both parties, including his friend and Long Island neighbor Theodore Roosevelt, as America's greatest orator. He was TR's principal economic adviser in the presidential election of 1912. Churchill was only 20 years old when the two men were brought together in November 1895 by Churchill's mother, the stunningly beautiful American-born heiress Jennie Jerome with whom Cockran had an affair in Paris in the Spring of that year following the deaths of their respective spouses. Sixty years later, Churchill could still recite from memory the speeches of Bourke Cockran he had memorized as a young man. Those wishing to know more about the close relationship between Churchill and Cockran are referred to *Becoming Winston Churchill: The Untold Story of Young Winston and His American Mentor* by Michael McMenamin and Curt Zoller and available from Enigma Books.

The Graf Zeppelin. The record-setting German airship made an historic around-the-world voyage in the summer of 1929 funded by William Randolph Hearst. Hearst held a grand banquet in honor of the zeppelin's crew in Los Angeles but neither Hoover nor Churchill were present.

The Russo-German military alliance in the 1920s. German rearmament after the Great War did not begin with Adolf Hitler. Weimar Germany and the Soviet Union had a clandestine military alliance throughout the 1920s whereby German engineers and industrialists developed in Russia beyond the Urals the most modern weapons sytems in Europe from artillery to aircraft to tanks, all in violation of the Versailles Treaty. The purpose of the alliance was the destruction of Poland. The letter to this effect from General Hans von Seekt, Chief of the German General Staff and mentioned by Trotsky in the Prologue is genuine.

Eamon de Valera and John Devoy. De Valera spent most of the Anglo-Irish war safely in America raising funds in the approximate amount of $5M of which $1M was sent back to Ireland and another $1M was spent by de Valera and his entourage on first class rail travel and luxury hotels where no expense was spared. $3M was left behind in American bank accounts and later used by de Valera to buy an Irish newspaper in 1931. John Devoy's opinions of de Valera are accurately portrayed as is de Valera's sabotage of the heretofore unified position on the Irish self-determination planks at the 1920 Democratic and Republican convention. Devoy died in September 1928 but his fictional counterpart was pleased to live for another year and play a role in de Valera's true nature being exposed and depriving him, if only fictionally, of the $3M he selfishly had kept for himself instead of buying much-needed arms and ammunition for the Irish fighting for their freedom in 1920 and 1921. Dev did famously say that history would record Michael Collins as a great man and that it would be at Dev's expense. We couldn't agree more. Check out Neil Jordan's classic film *Michael Collins* if you want to know why.

Herbert Hoover and William J. "Wild Bill" Donovan. The First World War Medal of Honor hero and later head of the Office of Strategic Services in World War Two—the predecessor to the CIA—was Hoover's campaign manager in the 1928 election. Hoover asked Donovan to be his running mate but Donovan had declined, securing Hoover's promise to make him Attorney General if he managed Hoover's campaign. Hoover later reneged on his promise solely because Donovan was a Roman Catholic. Hoover had reaped the benefit of a vicious anti-Catholic campaign against his Democratic opponent, New York Governor Al Smith. As a result of Hoover's bigotry, his cabinet was exclusively white, male and Protestant. Hoover's intense dislike of Churchill stemming from his time in London during the First World War in charge of food relief for Belgium is accurately portrayed. Churchill didn't personally have Hoover arrested in 1915 but thought he should have been.

Miscellaneous. Jack Manion and his San Francisco Chinatown Squad, LA's police chief "Two Gun" Ed Davis and Woodrow Wilson's secret organization "The Inquiry" are accurately portrayed except that The Inquiry had no "Irish Section" and Irish self-determination was never seriously on the table at Versailles. Woodrow Wilson's famous 14 Points didn't include Ireland.

Michael McMenamin & Patrick McMenamin
March 2010

Acknowledgements

We owe a debt of gratitude to many people who helped bring this book to light. Katie McMenamin Sabo, our daughter and sister and the first writing teacher either of us ever had. With an MFA in Creative Writing from NYU, she really is, as she often reminds us, Rose Wilder Lane to our Laura Ingalls. Kelly McMenamin Wang, our other daughter and sister who, even with her MBA from Dartmouth, is a really good writer herself and is always giving us new and clever marketing and promotion ideas. Check out both Katie and Kelly's writing at their home and life organization website www.pixiesdidit.com whose motto is "Life Should Be Easy." Mystery writer Les Roberts, our close friend and ever-patient writing mentor, from whom Patrick took a college screen writing course when he was a junior in high school and who, like any good mentor, validated our dream while continuing to give us candid and insightful advice. Robert Miller, the editor and publisher of Enigma Books who published the first paperback edition of Michael's book *Becoming Winston Churchill* and who agreed with us that the world really needed a series of historical thrillers set in the 1930s featuring Winston Churchill. The creative folks at Brainchild Studios/NYC who came up with a killer cover design. Alexis Dragony, Michael's former assistant who typed so many iterations of the book and is now living in Long Beach California hiding out from the IRA under the Witness Protection Program using the name "Emma" and kept safe by a horde of stuffed mice. And, finally, to all our good friends and relatives who read our book as well as our second and third Churchill Thrillers, *The Parsifal Pursuit* and *The Gemini Agenda* [to be published in 2011 by Enigma Books] who, along with Les Roberts, told us they thought our stories were a lot better than than many other thrillers they'd read. They were probably just being polite but its praise like that which keeps us writing. Thanks guys.

Bourke Cockran and Mattie McGary's next adventure takes them in 1931 on a quest high into the Austrian Alps and places in peril both their lives and their romance . . .

The Parsifal Pursuit

by

Michael McMenamin
and
Patrick McMenamin

Coming from Enigma Books
In Spring, 2011
Read on for an excerpt . . .

"The Threat To The Spear"

Castle Lanz
The Austrian Alps
March, 1914

M ajor Josef Lanz was no stranger to violence. A shade over six feet, he was taller than the average man under his command in the elite unit of ten Austrian Army mountain troops standing patiently behind him on their wooden skis, semi-automatic carbines slung over their shoulders, awaiting his order. He pushed the hood of his white parka back and his dark hair and sunburned face stood out against the white of the snow, a pale scar running diagonally across his left cheek, a souvenir of more youthful days and happier times.

Lanz turned to the man beside him, his second in command, Captain Hans Weber, "The snow is letting up. Have the men camp here for the night. Tell them we will ski out at first light. You and I will ascend to the castle but only after the men are asleep. The threat to the spear, the *heilege* lance, is real. And it comes from our German friends, not the Black Hand."

After midnight, the two men returned from the castle looming above their camp site and approached the five tents in silence. A few embers in the campfire still glowed amidst the dormant ashes surrounding them. Nearby, stacked neatly against one another in a circle, a group of 7.92 mm Mannlicher M98/40 assault rifles stood ready. Lanz counted them. There were ten. He turned to Weber and unslung his weapon, a Bergmann MP 18/1 submachine gun, and watched while Weber did the same. Lanz crossed himself and turned to Weber, who also made the sign of the cross, then pulled the bolt back on his 9 mm weapon. "Ready." Lanz said.

Weber brought a whistle to his lips and gave three short blasts, the shrill sound echoing in the thin mountain air. One by one, the flaps on the five tents opened and the men mechanically stumbled out and arranged themselves in an orderly line, still wearing the white parkas in which they had slept. Without warning, Lanz opened fire and Weber did the same. The men's bodies danced like marionettes on a string as the 9 mm rounds ripped into their chests and bellies, blowing out their backs with great gouts of blood. In fifteen seconds, all the men had collapsed, their white parkas now stained red. Still, Lanz and Weber kept firing into the prone bodies which continued to jerk and jump as the bullets hammered home.

Ater a full thirty seconds of sustained automatic weapons fire, they stopped, smoke rising from the perforated barrels of their Bergmanns. They slung the weapons back over their shoulders. They each withdrew from their holsters an M 1903 model Mannlicher locked-breach automatic pistol and walked over to the bodies. Going down the row methodically, a *coup de grâce* was delivered to the temple or forehead of each man, whichever was more convenient.

I wish we could give them a proper Christian burial." Weber said
I share your sentiments, Hans, but the ground is frozen. By

spring, the wolves in these mountains will make sure no trace of our men remains." Lanz said as he looked back at the castle, "What we have left here must never be disturbed nor discovered. You and I are the only ones who know. For anyone else who learns or even guesses at the secret, their lives are forfeit."

Hearst's phone call put a spanner in her plans. Before it, Mattie McGary was looking forward to an ocean crossing followed by a fortnight on holiday in Venice with her lover, that big beautiful Irish bastard Bourke Cockran. A few hours later, the voyage was abandoned and she was packing her bags with an adrenalin rush fueled by landing an exclusive interview with a leading European statesman followed by the prospect of an exciting new adventure. The Venice holiday had been relegated to a pleasant interlude sandwiched between two more big steps up the ladder in her rising career. But she would phrase that differently when she gave her man the bad news.

Mattie and her boss, William Randolph Hearst, had been walking in the garden at Hearst's castle-like home on Long Island's Gold Coast when he reached inside his tan Harris tweed sport coat and pulled out a long brown envelope and handed it to Mattie.

"What's this?" she asked.

"A one-way ticket on the *Graf Zeppelin* which leaves tomorrow morning from Lakehurst, New Jersey for its home base in Friedrichschafen. The day after you land, you have an appointment in Berchtesgaden with the leader of Germany's second-largest political party.

"Adolf Hitler?"

"Yes. I understand you interviewed him twice prior to his Beer Hall *putsch* in 1923."

"Not many people know that, Chief. Where did you hear about it?"

"From Hitler himself. Through Ted Hudson, my resident correspondent in Europe who has been negotiating with him, unsuccessfully I am afraid, to sign an exclusive contract to write articles for my newspapers. Mussolini writes for me. So does Churchill. I want Hitler as well."

"But why me?" Mattie asked.

"Hitler refuses to negotiate further with Hudson. He demands twice what we pay Mussolini and Churchill and he says he will only consider a lesser amount if we send you as a representative the one he refers to as 'that beautiful and talented young Englishwoman.'"

"I'm *not* English." Mattie said as if it were an insult. "I'm a Scot."

"A distinction which is lost on Hitler." Hearst put his hand on Mattie's back and gently directed her out of the garden and towards the beach. "Hitler is important to me, Mattie. He may well become Germany's leader just as I am certain Winston will one day lead England. I want him to write for my papers and you're the person he wants. Please do this for me."

"Why must I leave tomorrow?" she asked. "Bourke and I will be sailing on the *Europa* this Sunday. Once we land, I can fly to Germany."

Hearst frowned. "We don't have the luxury of time, my dear. Scripps-Howard—*The New York Telegram*—is sitting on Hitler's doorstep like a vulture waiting to swoop in if we fail. I'll be damned if I'm going to let Roy Howard best me again. It was bad enough when he bought out Pulitzer's New York papers. This is most important to me, Mattie. Please say you'll go."

Mattie sighed. She was licked and Cockran had lost. Hearst was disarmingly direct. He was incapable of dissembling. When he said "please" and asked twice, it really *was* that important to him and she knew she couldn't disappoint him.

"Okay, Chief, I'm your girl," she said and gave him a hug and a kiss.

"Wait a moment," Hearst said as Mattie turned to depart. "There's more."

"More?" Mattie said, turning back, raising her eyebrows at Hearst.

"Yes, my dear. I had a long telephone call from Churchill this morning and he presented an interesting proposition. It may cost £10,000 but, if you agree, I'm inclined to accept."

"Winston?" Mattie said, frowning, looking at her watch. "Will this take long, Chief? I've got to leave for court. I promised Cockran I'd be there to watch his oral argument in the state court of appeals. It's a big case for him. Those damn eugenics zealouts are trying to sterilize another young girl. What did my dear godfather propose now?"

Mattie listened to Hearst as they walked up from the beach. "Winston told me it involved an expedition to locate something called 'the Spear of Destiny.' He said you would know what he was talking about. Seems it may be missing from a museum in Vienna and Winston is raising capital to mount an expedition to retrieve it. He said you would understand."

The Spear of Destiny? Mattie understood all right, her pulse quickening. It meant everything to her late grail scholar father, Winston's closest political friend in Parliament back in 1904 after Churchill bolted the Tories and joined her father's Liberals. The Spear of Destiny missing? This was going to take awhile. Mattie knew she wasn't going to make it to court now. But it was her father, after all. What could a girl do? "Tell me more," Mattie said.

"Not much more to tell. Some professor-type has Winston convinced that the Spear in the museum is a fake and the real one is hidden somewhere in the Alps," Hearst said.

"The Alps? Where?"

"In Austria. That's where the expedition comes in. They aren't sure exactly where so it may take some time to locate it. They figure a proper expedition may cost upwards of £20,000. Winston says he's persuaded an industrialist friend of his, Sir Archibald Hampton, to put up half the money. For the other half, we would have exclusive worldwide rights on the photos and the story." Hearst smiled and looked down at her. "Do you think we should? Is it that big a story?"

"If it's true, Chief, it really is," Mattie answered and gave him the short course on the history of the Spear she had learned from her father. Constantine, Charlemagne, Frederick the Great. Bloodthirsty believers who held the Spear before them as they waged war without quarter.

"So, this means you would be interested in covering the story yourself?"

Mattie hesitated. Of course she was interested. How could she not be? She looked at her watch. Cockran was only minutes away from his oral argument she was going to miss. Later today, she would have to tell him they wouldn't be sailing together for Europe as planned.

But Venice? No, she couldn't blow it off too, especially not after their fight last night. They both had been so looking forward to Venice. Still, things like this were her father's lifelong obsession and now his daughter was being offered the real-life equivalent of a grail quest. Could she really pass it up? She sighed. Yes, she could. She loved her father and missed him still. But she had chosen Cockran. He was the man in her life now and she loved him. He came first. She had compromised on Hitler to please Hearst. She would not compromise on Venice.

"How soon would the expedition have to begin? After Hitler, I've got some interviews in Berlin with international arms dealers. Then it's two weeks in Venice with Bourke."

"Fine with me my dear. Just bring me back a good story with plenty of photographs."

Well, that was easy, Mattie thought as Hearst escorted her to Cockran's big Packard towncar and bade her farewell. As Mattie sank back in the tufted leather upholstery, she realized she was one happy girl. Her father had once told her that happiness was a simple and uncomplicated matter requiring only three things. Someone to love. Something interesting to do. And something to look forward to. Mattie smiled. She had all three. The someone she loved would be disappointed but she knew exactly how to make it up to Cockran later tonight.

"A Problem With The Kaiser"

New York City
Spring, 1931
Monday

urt von Sturm liked the Oak Bar at the Plaza. The dark wood,
the smoky atmosphere. In fact, Sturm liked America. It was
only his second visit and it was a different America than the one
which had captivated him during the summer of 1929. This America
was still prosperous, of course, but there were unemployed men
living in shacks in Central Park who had not been there previously. It
was such a large country, however, that he found it difficult to
believe that the economic bad times would last as long here as they
had in Germany.

Sturm's eyes carefully roamed the room after he had been taken
a corner table, looking for enemies where there should have been
none. And there weren't. But old habits were hard to break and
Sturm had no intention of starting now. Assassins lived longer that
way.

Sturm also liked the American custom of cocktails before dinner.
Prohibition was on its last legs but a drink in New York had never
been hard to come by. He raised his glass of Bell's 12 year old scotch
in a silent toast before he spoke in German to his companion, "I
return to Germany tomorrow on the *Graf.* How did you fare on your
recent visit to Holland?"

Anton Dressler, a Swiss banker who was Chairman of the
Geneva Group for Scientific and Industrial Progress which Sturm
served as Executive Director, frowned and drained the last of his
cognac. "Not so well, my young friend. But I do not wish to discuss
so sensitive a subject here. Walk with me back to my apartment.
We'll discuss it along the way." Dressler leaned in close and

whispered to Sturm. "We have a problem with the Kaiser."

The white-haired Dressler spoke softly as the two men walked out of the Plaza, declined the offer of a taxi and began to walk north on Fifth Avenue. "I had not mentioned this to our directors because I thought I had a ready solution," Dressler began, "but it seems I was mistaken. The Kaiser, it appears, is a superstitious man. He has persuaded the Crown Prince not to accept our proposition to place him on the German throne upon our assassination of President Hindenburg without an ancient artifact he calls the Spear of Destiny, the spear which the Roman centurion Longinus reportedly used to pierce the side of Christ on the cross and mercifully bring an end to his suffering. It seems the Spear has been possessed at one time or another by all of the great German emperors, including Barbarossa and Frederick the Great. I had not thought it a problem to deliver the so-called sacred talisman to the Kaiser because I had already arranged with the director of the Hofburg Museum in Vienna, where this Spear is on display, to loan it to a Berlin Museum as part of a special exhibition of historic Germanic artifacts."

"You arranged for an exhibition? Aren't the Austrians especially prickly about their German neighbors on matters like this?"

Dressler linked his arm with the taller man's and patted him with a kid-skinned gloved hand. "It is the way of the world, Kurt. A generous contribution to the museum's acquisition fund and an equally generous deposit in the museum director's account in my bank in Zurich."

"So what is the problem?"

"The Kaiser no longer believes the Spear at the Hofburg is the true Spear once possessed by his illustrious ancestors. He thinks it's a fake."

"The old man believes the Spear is a fake? Does he want us to produce the true Spear?"

"In a manner of speaking, yes," Dressler replied, handing Sturm a manila envelope. "This is a translation of a monograph by an English archeology professor claiming that the Hofburg Spear is a fake and that the real Spear was hidden in the Austrian Alps before the war."

"I'll read the monograph later. So, my former monarch and his eldest son now want us to go off on a wild goose chase in the Alps based on an obscure article by an English archeologist?

"Yes, but it's more than that. The Kaiser and his son firmly believe that with the Spear by their side, Germany would have prevailed in the Great War. German intelligence apparently reported to the Kaiser before the war that the Emperor Franz Josef personally vetoed an exhibit of the Spear and other artifacts in Berlin. He feared the Kaiser would never return them, a fear which the Kaiser indicates was correct. That is why he believes the Englishman's story. Hiding the Spear, he says, is something Franz Josef would think to do. More importantly, the Englishman has been to Doorn at the Kaiser's request and they were quite taken with his story."

The two men reached the apartment building on Fifth Avenue where Dressler's bank maintained a residence for visiting bank officers. The uniformed doorman held the door open for Dressler as he shook hands with Sturm. "I am sorry you could not join us for dinner tonight."

Sturm smiled. "I regret it also, *Herr* Dressler. But I am dining with a quite beautiful young woman I met the other evening at a reception given by the Swedish Consul General. And tonight, most conveniently, her husband is out of the city on a business trip."

Now it was Dressler's turn to smile. "Enjoy yourself, my friend. I will see you soon in Geneva. Godspeed. Find the Kaiser his Spear."

Bourke Cockran, Jr. noticed Mattie was still stiff when they arrived at the airfield in Lakehurst. Neither had spoken to the other since their fight in the taxi the night before except to discuss their respective travel details which would reunite them in Venice. Two arguments in two days was *not* how he wanted to part with the woman he loved. But it was not their first fight nor would it be the last. It was probably how most Celts—Scots or Irish—procreated, he thought. Fights followed by fierce lovemaking. But that hadn't happened last night. He wished it had.

Cockran escorted Mattie out onto the tarmac to the wooden steps leading up to the passenger cabin of the *Graf Zeppelin*, its size and beauty still a wonder to him nearly two years after he had first seen the globe-trotting airship in Los Angeles. They briefly kissed and told each other, "I love you," but he knew they both were still upset. "See you in Venice," Mattie said, with a weak smile. Someone who didn't know them would not think they were lovers.

"It's a date," he said but he was worried. How had they so quickly gone in two days from his planning to buy her an engagement ring in Venice to her saying perhaps they were not right for each other? Maybe two weeks apart would give her time to think. Maybe what he said would start to sink in. He hoped so. He loved her dearly but she had covered far too many wars and taken far too many risks in her work for Hearst. She was wrong to claim he was trying to control her life. He was just trying to keep her safe. And alive. Why couldn't she see that?

Cockran walked back through the departure lounge. He glanced over to a coffee and tea stand, where two uniformed members of the *Graf Zeppelin*'s crew stood beside the armrests of a couple of chairs. They were talking with a striking figure in a well-tailored three-piece suit. A face from the past. Cockran recognized him though he couldn't place where. He was tall, his blond hair neatly combed, and he had a scar on his right temple. A handsome guy but not the kind of face you'd mistake for somebody else.

* * *

The breeze ruffled Kurt von Sturm's blond hair as he once more thrilled at the sight of the giant silver airship, the largest in the world, floating patiently at its mooring mast, gleaming in the bright morning sunlight. These giant airships had once been his life and the two members of the *Graf Zeppelin*'s crew to whom he talked had flown under his command during the war.

"It is an honor, *Käpitanleutenant*, to have you flying with us again."

Sturm gave a short bow. "No, Fritz, it is you who honor me. I am merely a passenger."

"Your time will come again, *Käpitanleutenant*. The *Graf* is only the beginning of a new era in travel. We are building more airships and one of them should be yours."

"You are very kind. Have you seen to the passenger arrangements I've requested?"

A broad smile crossed Fritz Esser's face. "Indeed, I have, *Käpitanleutenant*. The passenger manifest is full but I have arranged a single cabin for her side by side with yours."

"And the dining salon?"

"Yes. A table for two by a window. Only you and the *fräulein*. She is very beautiful."

Now it was Sturm's turn to smile. "Yes, she is, isn't she?"

"Have a pleasant voyage, sir."

"Thank you, Fritz. Thanks to you, I believe I will."

Sturm marveled at his good fortune as he walked through the double doors of the passenger reception area out toward the great dirigible. First, a successful mission in America. Then last night and this morning spent seducing yet another man's beautiful wife. Now, a glorious airship voyage. And, most extraordinarily, three days and two nights alone in the sky with another beautiful woman as his companion, someone he had coveted from afar more than once. He wondered if she would remember him. He didn't think so. Other men had been monopolizing her attention on those occasions. Munich in 1923 on the eve of the Beer Hall *putsch* and then again in California two years ago. He had envied her companion on the latter occasion because of her obvious tenderness toward him. But now the field was all his, his prey unsuspecting. Perfect.

Sturm had a highly developed sense on matters like this and he had not failed to notice the tension between the woman and her escort. A tension that was not there two years ago. A vulnerability to exploit. And more than enough time in which to exploit it. Due to the nature of his profession, married women were his preferred prey but he was more than prepared to make an exception if the reward would be bedding someone so brave and so beautiful. It had been nearly two years since last he saw her but he had never forgotten her. While she was with the same companion then as now, she was not wearing a wedding or even an engagement ring. He wondered why. Details. A predator like Kurt von Sturm always noticed details. He lived for the chase and the rewards to be claimed at the end of the hunt. He had *never* lost. And the hunt was about to begin.